THE HOUSE ON SEAVIEW ROAD

Alison Walsh has worked in publishing and literary journalism for a number of years. She wrote a popular and humorous column on family life for the *Irish Independent* for some years, and this was followed by a memoir on motherhood, *In My Mother's Shoes*, which became a number-one Irish bestseller in 2010. She is a regular contributor to the *Sunday Independent* books pages. Alison lives in Dublin with her husband and three children.

Follow her on Twitter at @authoralison or visit her website at www.alisonwalsh.net

Also by Alison Walsh
All that I Leave Behind

THE HOUSE ON SEAVIEW ROAD

Alison Walsh

First published in Ireland in 2016 by
HACHETTE BOOKS IRELAND

1

'Sailing to Byzantium' by W.B. Yeats used with permission of United Agents on
behalf of Catríona Yeats.

Cataloguing in Publication Data is available from the British Library

ISBN 9781473612853

Typeset in Adobe Caslon Pro by Bookends Publishing Services, Dublin
Printed and bound in Great Britain by Clays Ltd, St Ives plc

Hachette Books Ireland policy is to use papers that are natural, renewable and
recyclable products and made from wood grown in sustainable forests. The logging
and manufacturing processes are expected to conform to the environmental
regulations of the country of origin.

Hachette Books Ireland
8 Castlecourt Centre
Castleknock
Dublin 15, Ireland

A division of Hachette UK Ltd
Carmelite House
50 Victoria Embankment
EC4Y 0DZ

www.hachettebooksireland.ie

To my sister, Caitriona

'You know full well as I do the value of sisters' affections. There is nothing like it in this world.'

CHARLOTTE BRONTË

La Grande Résidence pour la Royaux Famille
12 Juillet 1975

Chère Marie

Don't worry — I'm not going to write the rest of this letter in French — I know how much you hate French! But I thought a little joke at the beginning might make it easier to write what I'm going to write.

I am sitting up on the bed in the bedroom and I can hear you and Grainne in the garden. You're not fighting, the two of you: instead, you are patiently explaining the rules of German Jumps to her. I can hear you telling her where to put her feet and how to hop over the elastic when it's around your knees — you're so kind to her, Marie, and it breaks my heart. Before all of this nonsense — I refuse to call it 'illness' or to use that horrible word, 'cancer', because that would be to dignify something so baffling and downright silly — all the two of you did was fight! Do you remember

1

those lovely fur-lined gilets that Mick and Biddy bought you in Dunnes Stores? Grainne took yours because she thought the colour was much nicer. And then there was the Communion money that Aunty Peggy sent all the way over from Chicago, a wad of dollar bills stuffed into a brown envelope. I can still see you both, sitting on either side of the coffee table in the drawing room, Grainne watching you as you dealt them out – 'one for you, one for me' – in case you cheated. I know that you gave her an extra two dollars. I saw you put them to one side.

That's our Grainne. She always wants what she hasn't got and it's hard to resist her. You'll need to be strong, Marie, but I know that you will be. Just remember what I taught you.

Very soon, you'll only have each other, my two lovely girls. Of course, you'll have Dada too, but it's not the same for him as it is for the two of you. You have a bond that not even Dada or I share with you. Remember that. And you need each other so much … Dada is a grown-up and even though it will be very hard for him, he will know what it all means. You will need to help your sister with that, because she won't be able to understand it. Some things are just too big for her to comprehend.

Marie, I want you to remember me as Mum – lover of music, cake and all things French – not as this shrivelled old walnut on the bed. It is so hard to say goodbye to you, to say goodbye to life, but I know that I must, because it is all saying goodbye to me. It's not fair and I was very angry about it before, but I've made my peace with that. I've been so lucky in my life, to have you two eejits and Dada and

Mick and Biddy, even Granny Stephenson, the old bat. I have loved, Marie, and that's all I could have asked of life, even if I'd lived to be a hundred.

I need to ask you something now, love. Look after your sister. I know that you already do and I also know that it hasn't always been fair – 'just' as Dada would put it – but she needs you, love, more than you know. So, promise me, will you? I can go off happy then.

And now, I can hear that Grainne has just yelled at you that you've cheated and you've yelled back that she should just follow the bloody rules, and she has told you that 'bloody' is a rude word. I can lean back on my pillow and laugh, because order has been restored. Be good, Marie, be clever, as you are, be funny and be strong.

All my love,

Mum

PART 1

AUGUST 1982

Chapter 1

A sudden breeze wafted in through the window, carrying on it the tang of salt and suncream. The sun was obscured by a sheen of thin cloud, but it was sticky and warm, as it had been all summer, and the crowds had already gathered at the beach across the road down the steep hill to the sea. Marie could hear them through the open window as she lay on her bed, feeling sorry for herself.

She could still see the stupid make-up palette on the dressing table, beside Mum's old hairbrush and comb set, and as it caught her eye, it seemed to rebuke her. Look at how silly you are, it seemed to say. Do you think you'll ever become a foreign correspondent and travel the world if you spend all your time learning to apply make-up?

Buying that set had been her summer project, to do

something about being a complete hick. She'd had enough of being the butt of that Queen Bitch Imelda's jokes, so she'd saved up a whole six weeks' pocket money for it, when she could have bought that second edition of *The Female Eunuch* that she'd spotted in Greene's bookshop instead. Mrs Brogan, in the chemist's, had had to order the set in 'from London, so that'll take three weeks', she'd said as she'd written the order into her ledger, shuffling the carbon paper in between the sheets and handing Marie a copy.

Six weeks and ten whole quid, to look just like herself, with her long face, straight nose and narrow forehead, dark brown eyes set just a little bit too closely together for her liking – herself, only with make-up. What would Queen Bitch Imelda have to say? Well, she'd never find out now anyway, because of Grainne, Marie thought angrily.

She'd planned to begin with the make-up, moving to clothes and then thinking about how to behave. She had to try to look bored and superior, like Imelda. She flicked her hair and tapped ash from her cigarette expertly onto the ground – and everyone would think she was amazing, even though she didn't have a single sensible thought in her head. Marie didn't really want to be amazing – she wanted to be *substantial* – but she also wanted to fit in. 'Be yourself, love,' Mum had said once. 'There's nothing more important in life.' But Mum wasn't here any more and Marie had found that there *were* more important things in life – like not being a complete social outcast.

She closed her eyes as she thought of the ruined palette, which Grainne had dug big lumps out of, seemingly with a pickaxe, because she wanted to 'test out the blue and purple together'. Grainne always ruined everything, but still, Marie supposed that she hadn't needed to yank out a big clump of her sister's hair, sneaking up behind her on the landing and grabbing a big fistful in her hand. She didn't know where the rage had come from. Maybe it was because, at the same time as ruining her make-up, Grainne had also been wearing Marie's one and only fashionable item – a ra-ra skirt in blue that Aunty Sheila had brought her back from Miss Selfridge in London – which Grainne had stretched out of shape, her big tummy straining against the elastic waistband. Grainne ruined everything she got her hands on and nobody ever told her off, because she was Grainne and therefore allowed to do anything she liked. Marie wasn't clear why – she knew it had something to do with Grainne having spent six months in hospital when she was a baby – something about meningitis – but she wasn't sick now, was she?

The look on Dada's face when he'd had to pull them both apart on the landing, Marie with a lump of Grainne's red hair in her hand. She felt a hot wave of shame wash over her now. He hadn't said a word, but she knew how it would go. His study door would remain closed for the rest of the afternoon, but every time Marie would pass it, she'd be able to feel his presence seeping through the door, underneath the gap where it met the carpet. If she could have seen it, it would have been like a kind of green smoke, she thought, something that crept into every crevice, that snuck into every little corner, filling the house with a thick atmosphere. The green smoke had always been part of Dada, but when Mum was there, she could change it with a laugh or a joke, and then the whole house would fill with light again. But now that she wasn't there anymore, that she hadn't been there for nearly seven years, it just hung around the place, never really lifting.

Sighing, Marie reached into her bedside locker and pulled out a locked wooden writing box, pulling it onto the bed and fumbling under the locker for the key, which she kept taped there. She opened it and sat back, pulling out the travel books and the map of Australia, the names of the places she'd visit highlighted in yellow – Ayers Rock, Darwin, Warrimoo, Binalong – names that she'd roll around on her tongue, imagining harsh desert and hot sun, inhaling the dust and the heat as she read. And then she was there, walking the roads, the shimmering heat rising around her, the baking earth under her feet …

She was on a remote sheep farm in the desert when Grainne crashed into the bedroom. 'Mar?' She had her floral toilet bag in her hand and her hairdryer, with its hundred attachments, in its little case. 'Time for the make-over.'

'Jesus, Gra, do you ever knock?' Marie shoved the books hastily under the bedspread. She'd forgotten that, as part of the truce brokered over egg salad in the kitchen at lunchtime, she'd agreed to let Grainne do her make-up. She had to admit that her sister was better at these things: God knows, she spent enough time in front of her bedroom mirror, admiring herself, puckering up her lips and scrunching up her freckled face under its halo of frizzy red hair. But it was also because Marie wanted Grainne to forgive her – she couldn't bear another one of her baby-seal looks, all big, sad eyes and downturned mouth. Miss Meningitis.

'You can't take the Lord's name in vain. It's a sin,' Grainne said now, her blue eyes flicking over the box. Marie could see her lips part, one of her stupid questions about to come out, but Marie silenced her with a look. 'Can you come back later? I'm reading.'

'Oh, but I'm dying to make you look nice, Mar,' Grainne said, putting the case down on the bed. 'And it's so boring around here at the moment. There's nobody at the beach either. I've been down three times already. Please?'

'Oh, all right,' Marie grumbled. 'What do I have to do?'

Grainne gave a little squeal of delight and sat on the bed beside her. 'Turn around and I'll start with your hair,' she instructed.

An hour later, Marie had a crick in her neck. 'Are you finished yet, Gra?' she said hopefully. Who knew that making yourself look nice could be such a production?

'Give me one more minute,' Grainne said, her tongue poking out of her mouth as she worked. 'I have to make your eyes more widely spaced. You're very pretty but they're too close together.'

'Thanks for the compliment,' Marie said dryly, but she let her sister continue, dabbing at her face with a damp cosmetic sponge. She closed her eyes, but she could hear Grainne's breathing; she always had a blocked nose and she sounded like a pig. Marie was forever telling her to breathe through her mouth so she wouldn't make that awful racket, but Grainne usually forgot.

'You know, I've forgiven you now, Mar,' Grainne said suddenly.

'That's good,' Marie said quietly. 'Thanks, Grainne.'

'I'm not sure about Dada though,' Grainne added. 'I'd say he'll need to pass judgement.'

'I know.' That was the way Dada did it. He was a judge, so he was used to sitting up on the bench, banging his gavel, and he did the same at home, summoning whichever of them had done something wrong into his study for sentencing. All he was missing was the big black cloak and the horsehair wig. 'Can I remind you, Marie, that you are responsible for your sister?' he'd said earlier. As if I need reminding, Marie had thought bleakly.

'I'm sure it won't be that bad, Mar. I told him that you didn't really mean to pull out a lump of my hair, it was just …'

Just what? Marie thought bleakly. Just that Dada likes you more than me? Marie might have Dada's dark brown eyes, the same thick, black hair, but Dada loved Grainne more. Marie could have got six As in the Leaving Cert or undertaken a solo flight of the Atlantic, but none of it would matter. Dada might struggle to talk to Grainne, wrinkling his forehead at some of her sillier sayings, but he would always love her more. Marie knew that.

'So, what's the story at the beach these days?' Marie said, changing the subject to avoid having to think about her fate.

At this, Grainne brightened. 'Oh, it's great. They're all there, Marie. Imelda O'Brien and John and David Crowley. You should come.' She looked a bit guilty then, because she knew what Marie thought about Imelda.

'Hmm,' Marie said. She had gone a few times, but the ordeal of being watched as she walked all the way along to join them, her beach-bag banging clumsily off her hip, had put her off, and anyway, if Queen Bitch Imelda was there – no way. She wasn't ready for the humiliation.

'I don't think so, Gra. You know I don't like the water.' And I don't like Imelda, she added to herself, or David Crowley. She'd only ended up with him that time in the canoe club because he'd pretended he'd liked the book she was reading. She might have known that *The Well of Loneliness* wasn't his kind of book. But she'd been so stupid, when he said he really admired Radclyffe Hall she'd actually believed him, when all he'd wanted was a shift.

'But you could just sit there and talk and listen to the radio. We all make requests for Radio Dublin. Imelda gives them to me and I run up to the house and phone the station. And then by the time I've run back down to the beach, I can hear the request on the radio. It's magic.' She laughed.

'I'll think about it,' Marie said.

'You could meet my new boyfriend that way,' Grainne said, as she swept a brush over Marie's cheekbones.

Marie's eyes had been closed, but they flicked open now. 'What new boyfriend?'

'His name is Con O'Sullivan and he's a friend of Maccer's … I think. Anyway, he's in college. Can you imagine, Mar? I'm going out with a student!'

What on earth was she talking about? Marie thought, sitting up on the bed. Grainne had never had a boyfriend in her life. Marie knew, because she'd watched her like a hawk to make sure that none of the local lads came sniffing around. Grainne was sixteen, a year younger than Marie, but she behaved like a thirteen-year-old. She wouldn't be able for a boyfriend and everything that went with it. She was far too naïve, and far too eager to please.

'I've never been so happy, Marie. I think I might be in love with him.' Grainne clasped her hands together and blushed.

Uh-oh. 'Maybe I will come to the beach with you after all, Gra.'

'Great – I'm going in a few minutes.' Grainne beamed, getting up and putting all of her stuff into her toilet bag, winding the flex of the hairdryer round and round the handle, even though Marie had told her not to a hundred times. 'You can meet him yourself!' And then she turned to Marie. 'You won't embarrass me by being all bossy, will you, Mar?'

'Wouldn't dream of it,' Marie said. How on earth would she manage this, she thought to herself, suddenly filled with a sense of dread. 'I'll just go and get my swimming togs.'

'Get your nice navy blue ones, will you? Not Mum's old black ones – they hang off you.'

'Thanks for the fashion advice,' Marie snapped.

'You're welcome!' Grainne grinned. 'See you at the beach!'

Not so fast, Marie thought. 'Wait a sec and I'll come with you. I just need to change into my shorts.' Marie hated shorts and there was no way she was going to reveal her horrible legs to half of Seaview, but she thought it would give her a second to pull herself together. She got up off the bed, catching a glimpse of herself in her dresser mirror. I'll have to wash that stuff off first, she thought.

Grainne made a face. 'I can go by myself, Mar. I'm perfectly well able.' She was quoting Mrs Delaney, their housekeeper, who always said that Grainne was 'perfectly well able' to clean up after herself and tidy her bedroom, which was always a complete mess.

'I know but—'

'You can follow me down – I'll save you a place on my towel.' And then Grainne was gone. Five minutes later, Marie heard the front door open, and she watched her sister walk down towards the pedestrian crossing on Seaview Road, hoping that she'd wait for the cars to stop, sighing with relief when she did. She knew that Grainne wasn't a baby any more, but she couldn't help it – keeping an eye on her had become a habit at this stage. She watched her sister's broad back in her favourite Snoopy T-shirt, disappear down the steep hill to the beach, her beach bag bumping off her hip. She wasn't wearing sun-cream – Marie could tell, because her pale skin had already begun to burn above the collar of her T-shirt – and she was wearing a pair of blue Levi's that were two sizes too small for her. They're bloody mine, Marie thought. Wait till I get hold of her.

She selected *Pride and Prejudice* from her bookshelf and stuffed her swimming togs and a towel into her rucksack, just in case, then she went over to kiss the picture of Mum that sat on her dressing table, as she always did before she left the house. Mum was sitting on a bench at the tennis court, in a pair of blue shorts and a sweatshirt, her arm around a black cocker spaniel. She was squinting into the sun and smiling and the dog, Frank, was looking dignified. Mum had used to joke that she loved Frank more than any of the rest of them. Marie ran her finger over the picture. 'I'm looking after her, Mum – don't worry.' She kissed the picture, then put it back on the table, before running into the bathroom for the suncream.

She was closing the front door when she heard Mrs Delaney's voice behind her. 'Marie, is that you? Will you come back and eat your—' The rest of her words were swallowed up by the banging of the door. Marie threw, 'I'll be back in an hour,' over her shoulder, then raced down the path, out the gate and onto Seaview Road.

She looked back at the house then, towering over Mrs O'Keeffe's and Mr Byrne's seaside bungalows, Mrs O'Keeffe's with a riot of garden gnomes and bird tables in it; Mr Byrne's with carefully pruned rose bushes and gravel. Claire said that it looked like a giant Hansel and Gretel house, and it did look a bit like that, with its pointed gable with maroon trim, a huge, red chimney pot that leaned to one side and an expanse of shingled roof, the shingles now bleached a pale grey from the sea air. It was completely unlike all of the other pretty seaside cottages, with its ugly pale-pink pebbledash and rash of tiny windows, and Marie remembered how much Mum had hated it: the size of the garden, with its fraying palm trees and dusty tennis court, the warren of badly partitioned rooms inside, the drafts that snaked under every doorway: in the winter, they usually had to retreat to the back of the house, where it was warmer – but Marie thought that it was probably because she'd been raised in a small farmhouse on the Aran Islands – ''Twas far from Victorian splendour I was reared,' she'd often joke.

Marie could hear the squeals of children as she came towards the traffic lights that marked the pedestrian crossing on Seaview Road and felt the thin chill of the sea breeze. She hated Seaview beach. That horrible green water, that sludge at the bottom. Dada took a morning dip there every single day before work, winter and summer. He'd tried to teach her to swim one hot sunny Sunday, that last summer when Mum was still alive. Marie could still see Mum in her black bathing suit, sitting on a rock, her hand shielding her eyes, watching, as Dada had guided Marie through the water. It was cold and the waves kept slapping against her, and she'd stood there on her tippy-toes, teeth chattering.

'Right,' Dada had said, standing in front of her, hands on his hips. His skin was darkly tanned and glistened with drops of water and his black hair was slicked back off his face. 'At the count of three, you put your arms out in front of you like this –' he'd lifted his arms then joined his hands to form an inverted 'v' '– then push up on your toes and glide towards me. Don't worry, I'll be here to catch you.'

Marie had looked at him doubtfully. 'You *have* to catch me, Dada.'

'I'll catch you, don't worry.' And then he'd tutted, 'C'mon, Marie, the sun's gone in and we'll freeze.'

Marie hadn't wanted to glide, or swim, she'd just wanted to get out and sit beside Mum on the beach towel and eat an ice pop from the kiosk. 'I don't want to,' she'd begun to moan.

'For God's sake, Marie, just get on with it, will you?' Dada had made a movement, as if he were coming to get her. With a yelp, Marie had pitched herself forward, forgetting to point her arms anywhere. She'd sunk like a stone, the brown silt of the seabed rising up to meet her as the freezing water had covered her. Her body had felt heavy, her limbs unable to move, a dead silence filling her ears as she dropped to the bottom. It was like she imagined a grave would be, dark and cold and silent, and then she'd felt a sharp tug on the back of her swimming costume and she was being lifted into the air, the sounds of the beach, the bright shrieks, the ding-ding of the ice-cream van seeming suddenly loud after the muffled silence below. Marie had taken in a huge breath, and then coughed and spluttered so much she'd retched, vomiting up a wave of horrible sea water.

Dada hadn't said another word to her, just half-pulled her back to the safety of the rocks. She didn't dare look up at him in case she'd see the expression on his face.

Mum had been waiting, her arms open. 'You poor thing,' she'd murmured. 'You know, you looked just like a little mermaid, dipping down beneath the waves. How amazing is that?' She'd smoothed Marie's hair and wrapped her in a towel and sat her on her knee to warm up, Marie's teeth chattering. Mum's body had been warm beneath hers, and as she'd sat there, the sun had come back out and she'd begun to warm up, the heat of it making her limbs unfurl, relax.

'Cormac, why don't you take Grainne for a swim?' Mum had nodded at her sister, who was building a huge sandcastle, her face fixed in concentration. Dada had stood there for a few moments, saying nothing, before turning and walking over to Grainne. 'Grainne, fancy a swim?'

Grainne had jumped up and reached out for Dada's hand, and the two of them had walked down to the water, Grainne dragging him along, her red hair flying. When they reached the edge, she'd hopped up and down in the waves for a few moments, before throwing herself in, head first. She was like a seal, Marie had thought, gliding through the water.

'Do you know what I think?' Mum had said. 'I think that

you will be a fantastic poet or painter. I can just get a sense of it. You're so creative. And creative people need ice-cream.' She'd smiled, pressing her lips to Marie's salty cheek. 'C'mon, let's treat ourselves to a Choc Ice.'

*

Marie shivered at the memory and at the cold. She wished she'd worn a jumper over her CND T-shirt. She looked down at it and it suddenly seemed so embarrassing – a big, black sack that drooped over her from neck to backside. But then, that was the idea, to conceal, to shroud. Maybe she'd go back and change, she thought. She went to turn around, but then turned back again. For God's sake, Marie, who are you trying to impress, she chided herself. Go and find your sister, before she does something silly.

Crossing at the traffic lights, Marie shuffled down the steep hill to the beach, which was jammed with people. It was called a 'beach' but really it was a large cobbled pier that jutted out into the sea on which people perched on towels and the odd deckchair. A few people had brought transistor radios and there was a clashing blare of pop music from a radio that had been placed on top of the wall surrounding the steps by a group of boys, who were all standing around now in their swimming togs, towels slung around their necks, and another, blasting out traditional Irish music, at the bottom.

Christy Dolan was there, in his wheelchair, wolf-whistling at any girls he fancied as they passed and commenting on their swimwear. 'Nice bikini, love,' he'd yell, from his perch. 'Great pair of tits!' Everyone tried to ignore him. His dad pushed him down to the beach every day during the summer and there he'd stay, embarrassing half the population of the town and turning a shade of tomato red in the process, until his dad came back for him at five o'clock. Sometimes, if the tide came in very fast, a group of lads would pull his chair further back, but no women would ever help him. Served him right.

The whole beach seemed to be filled with strangers, a sea of faces, pale and tanned skin, bottles of sun lotion, towels, noise. Marie scanned the shoreline for any sign of Grainne's red hair, but she couldn't spot her. A tight knot of anxiety began to form in her stomach. Where *was* she?

And then Marie saw the gang of boys and girls, a big crowd over by the rocks at the far end of the beach. She swallowed and clambered down the steps. She walked the hundred yards or so to the group, feeling her skin flush as she trudged along. She wanted to fold her arms across her breasts: even though they could hardly be called that, so minute were they, she still felt the impulse to cover them as she walked in that stupid T-shirt of hers, as her feet slapped along in her flip-flops.

As she got closer, she caught sight of David Crowley and her heart sank. Could it get any worse? He spotted her and nudged his friend, who whispered something in his ear – they both laughed. Marie wanted to turn and run, but instead, she kept on walking, feeling ten pairs of eyes fixed on her as she stumbled along.

Imelda was right in the middle of the group of twelve or so, Queen Bee that she was, wearing a neon green mesh vest and black leotard, her hair piled on top of her head, a pair of very expensive Ray-Bans perched on her nose. She looked like a popstar. John was sitting behind her, smoking. Like his on/off girlfriend, he looked like a pop singer or a movie star, Marie thought, in his faded blue Levis and white T-shirt, a pair of navy espadrilles on his feet. Marie didn't know any other boy who wore espadrilles. There was something rakish about them, like those posh 1930s English writers, all loose white shirts and linen trousers. She bet Christopher Isherwood would have worn espadrilles. She wondered if John was wearing them for effect. He liked to flirt with that kind of thing, to give off false signals and then feign ignorance of what he was doing. That was why she didn't like him, Marie decided. Because he was manipulative and because he was lying to everyone – and to himself – about who he really was. But she supposed they all were. Oh, how she longed to have her best friend Claire by her side, to laugh at them all and to take the likes of Imelda on. She'd make some clever remark that would put Imelda in her place – something that Marie never had the nerve to do. But Claire wouldn't be back until the first of September, so she'd have to manage.

'Didn't expect to see you here,' Imelda said, as Marie approached. 'Aren't you afraid of the water?' She didn't get up or make room for Marie to sit down, and so Marie stood there, like a lump, wishing that the ground would open up and swallow her.

'The word is "hydrophobic",' John snickered.

Marie blushed and tried to think of something witty to say in response, but then a voice said, 'Marie, over here.'

Marie nearly cried with relief. Maccer was sitting at the edge of the little crowd, along with a boy she didn't recognise, with very dark hair and a gloomy look on his face. They weren't close, but she liked Maccer – he had red hair and freckles and a sunny personality to match. And he was nice. Just plain old nice, interested and polite, not arrogant like so many of the St Philip's boys, and with 'lovely manners' as Mrs D said.

Marie also liked Maccer because he'd called around the day after Mum died, on his bike, leaning off the saddle to press the bell, and, when Marie had answered, he'd blurted, 'I'm sorry your mum's dead.' He'd said it in a big rush and bolted off then, but Marie had stood on the doorstep, feeling that there was no longer a big, deep chasm between her and the rest of the world. They'd never spoken about it since, but they'd had that ease that came with understanding each other. Marie was grateful for that.

'How's your summer been?' he asked now, moving over on his towel to let Marie sit down beside him.

'Oh, God, endless,' she said, sitting down beside him. 'Interminable, insufferable and countless other -ables. I haven't done one single interesting thing for the past two months.'

'That good? Maybe you should have come down here sooner and hung around with the gang.' He grinned. 'You could have had some excitement, living on the edge, posing and talking about how bored you are.' He laughed. 'Still, beats school. Can't believe it's nearly over and that we'll be in sixth year in two weeks' time. Scary.'

'I know,' Marie said bleakly.

'I'm not ready to be a grown-up,' Maccer added. 'Imagine, this time next year, I'll be in AIB on O'Connell Street, asking old biddies if they want me to stamp their pension book.' He shook his head at the unfairness of it all. Maccer's dad worked in the bank and he'd already found his son a place on the trainee scheme. All Maccer had to do was get two honours in his Leaving Cert and the rest of his life was mapped out for him. There was something scary about that, Marie thought; about knowing exactly where you were headed. For her, the future was a vast expanse stretching on into the horizon, filled with – what? She tried to picture it, but she couldn't. She tried to imagine herself in various scenarios, as if she'd been dropped into a photo, in a wedding dress, with children, in front of the Eiffel Tower or the Pyramids, but somehow she couldn't quite fit herself into the frame. Adults always said, 'You've got your whole life ahead of you.' As if that were a good thing, somehow.

'At least you know what you want to do,' Marie said, 'and that's good. It doesn't seem quite so scary then.'

He gave her a friendly nudge with his elbow. 'I know what I *have* to do, Mar – there's a big difference.'

'You know, you don't have to do anything,' a voice said behind them. 'There's no rule book any more. You can create your own future. Doing what Mummy and Daddy want is outdated.' It was the gloomy boy with the intense stare and thick, black curly hair. He was wearing a faded black jacket, in spite of the heat, and a collarless shirt and Doc Martens. He must be roasting, Marie thought.

Maccer looked at the guy as if he had six heads. 'Not when they've paid for your education, mate. You owe them, big time.'

'Because they've spent money on developing you into a fine example of south-Dublin bourgeois society, or because they want you to fulfil your potential in life?' The guy was smiling, but Marie knew he wasn't making a joke.

Maccer, normally impossible to rile, was looking affronted.

'Because if I don't follow my dad into the bank it would be like shoving everything he's done for me right back in his face, seeing as you ask.'

'Oh, well, if you put it like that.' The guy smiled, as if at some private joke, and then he offered Maccer his hand. 'Con O'Sullivan.' So, this was Grainne's so-called boyfriend. Marie couldn't see it. For a start, he looked a bit too old for the crowd – he must be at least twenty, Marie thought. And he clearly wasn't one of Maccer's friends. She'd have to ask one of the lads where he'd come from.

'Maccer,' Maccer said brusquely, accepting the handshake, but ending it as swiftly as he could.

'Maccer? Have you got a first name?'

'Not for you, I don't. This is Marie Stephenson.' Maccer nodded in Marie's direction. The laser beam was directed at her now, and Marie felt like squirming. He extended a hand. Marie didn't take it. She knew she was being rude, but she wanted to make a point: he'd insulted Maccer, who just didn't deserve it. Some of us don't get to choose our destinies, she felt like saying to him. Some of us have to make do with what we're given.

He pulled his hand away, giving her a smug-looking grin. 'Nice to meet you, Marie.'

Marie was about to retort that it wasn't a bit nice to meet him, but instead she blurted, 'Whose friend are you anyway?'

The grin faded slightly. 'I came with John.'

But …' Marie began, then she felt a shower of icy drops on her arms. 'Ow!' She looked up to see Grainne looming over her, her breasts and thighs bulging from the pink material of her swimming togs. Marie made a mental note to ask Mrs

D for money to buy her a new one, before she embarrassed herself completely. 'Gra, you're like a wet dog!'

'I went for a swim,' Grainne said unnecessarily, proceeding to pull at the top of her swimming costume, hoiking the arm up and pulling her elbow through until it hung off her left breast. 'Did you think I was good, Con?' She beamed, offering them all a flash of boob.

'Gra – put your towel on,' Marie whispered, throwing her a towel with an elasticated top.

'All right,' Grainne said sulkily, pulling the brightly coloured towel over her head so that it made a tent around her. She rummaged around in her bag, throwing knickers, skirt and T-shirt onto the ground. Even though she had a bit of a tummy, her arms and legs were muscular and athletic and, in her costume, she looked as if she should be in the 50-metre sprint in the Olympics. She'd tried out for the school swimming team and even though she'd swum faster than anyone else, she'd got upset at the swimming instructor's commands yelled from the poolside, and she'd insisted on giving up, refusing to try again.

'I thought you were amazing,' Con said. 'You should swim in a team, you know.'

'She did,' Marie said. 'She didn't enjoy it.'

'"She"?' he repeated, with the faintest edge of sarcasm in his voice. 'Well, maybe she just needs a bit of encouragement, isn't that right, Grainne?'

Grainne turned around and gave him a huge smile.

Oh, God, Marie thought, giving her a significant look, hoping that she'd get the message.

'Oh, no, Con, Marie's right. I didn't like it. But I like

25

swimming in the sea. I can go all the way to the orange buoy,' and she waved at the pointed orange marker that bobbed a couple of hundred yards away on the water. Marie felt her stomach churn at the thought of it.

'Good for you,' Con O'Sullivan said, as if he were the first person alive to give her sister any praise or encouragement. Marie wanted to tell him to eff off, but at the same time, it needled her when he'd said "she", like that, because he was right – she shouldn't have assumed that she knew what Grainne wanted. Maybe she'd done so because she was so used to it, used to assuming.

Maccer gave Marie a 'can you believe this guy?' look. 'I'm off for a smoke,' he grumbled, and got up and rambled off down the pier. Marie shrugged and, not looking at the stupid boy, turned and rummaged in her bag until she found her copy of *Pride and Prejudice* and pulled it out, opening it on the marked page. She'd read the book so often that almost all the pages had dog-ears. She began to read, her eyes scanning the text for the familiar words, but she found that she couldn't settle into her usual rhythm. The words seemed to come in and out of focus, and the child screaming further down the beach was distracting her.

She lifted her head to see where Grainne was, and she was still in her towel, but she was sitting beside Con O'Sullivan now, too close to him, chattering away. Where on earth had he come from, and how was he Grainne's boyfriend? She wasn't sure she liked this at all, and yet, he didn't act like her boyfriend – he just seemed friendly, interested in a normal kind of way. Marie wondered if this boyfriend thing was simply something that Grainne had imagined. She felt that familiar flicker of anxiety that always accompanied anything to do with Grainne.

Then Imelda got up and, smoothing down her endless brown legs, said, 'I'm going for a swim.' She had a habit of announcing things like that, as statements that would interest absolutely everyone, and because she was Imelda and gorgeous, they generally did.

'Oh, wait for me, Imelda!' said Grainne, and Marie just had time to throw her damp togs to her. 'Oh, yes,' she said happily, pulling them back on, not seeming to mind that they were clammy and wet. Imelda gave her a bored look, but waited, adjusting the straps of her tiny polka-dot bikini, pulling the bottoms down a little bit to give the tiniest flash of white skin below her tan line, while Grainne squeezed herself into her costume, her freckled flesh spilling out. Marie looked at her sister and wished she could be like that. Wished she could just not give a damn.

'Con, you'll be here when I get back?' Grainne said anxiously. 'You won't go away?'

Marie heard a loud 'tsk' from Imelda and a muttered, 'How could he get away when you practically sit on top of him?'

Marie felt her ears burn. She should say something, but Grainne was oblivious, chattering away as Imelda walked gingerly down the steps and stood briefly at the water's edge, before gliding in. She didn't squeal or yell like everyone else getting into the chilly water; she didn't jump up and down, teeth chattering, but instead just serenely bobbed across to the little slipway further along the beach.

'Oh, man,' one of the lads could be heard to say. There was

silent agreement in the group, as they watched Imelda walk up the slipway after her dip, droplets of water falling off her tanned limbs. Grainne, meanwhile, was slicing through the water as she headed towards the buoy. Marie breathed a sigh of relief and returned to *Pride and Prejudice*.

'Do you not think that Jane Austen is basically just posh Mills & Boon?' Con O'Sullivan's voice cut through the blessed peace.

For God's sake. Marie didn't lift her head from her book. She just kept reading.

'Prissy, simpering women in frilly dresses trying to marry themselves off to anyone who'll have them. And it's boring.'

'And I suppose you've read it?' She looked at him sharply, her cheeks aflame. She thought she could detect a flicker of triumph in his green eyes.

'I have, as it happens. And I've concluded that wittering on incessantly about looking for a man and what the neighbours are doing isn't all that interesting. I find Mailer and Hemingway more to my taste.'

Marie rolled her eyes to heaven. 'How completely predictable. All that macho nonsense. I suppose you think bullfighting is symbolic of masculinity or some such rubbish, instead of just overblown self-indulgence.'

'Well, have you read *The Executioner's Song*? You should do, because it's about how one man salvages his humanity, even though he's facing the death penalty.'

'You sound as if you're quoting from the reviews.'

It was his turn to get annoyed now. 'Look, it's about real things, about life and death and what makes us human, not about women in frocks who have nothing better to do than wait around playing the piano and giggling until some rich man carries them away and marries them.'

'That's because they had no choice, they—'

'Marie, why are you shouting at Con?' Grainne had reappeared, a chilly shadow looming over them both, dripping on Marie.

'Ah, Gra, not again.' Marie jumped up and brushed the drops off, relieved to have the opportunity to pull herself together. Her heart was thumping in her chest, and her skin was tingling, as if she'd been stung. Maybe there's something wrong with me, she thought. Maybe I'm coming down with something.

'Con, I just need to tell you that Marie can be very cross sometimes,' Grainne was saying. 'She's very bossy, actually.'

'I can see that,' Con replied, an edge of amusement in his voice. 'Grainne, why don't we go and get an ice-cream and we'll leave Marie to cool down a bit.'

Grainne squealed in delight and threw her arms around Con. 'Oh, Connie, that would be great.' And then she turned to Marie. 'Mar, you are to stay here till we get back.'

'Fine.' Marie scowled, not wanting to look at either of them. 'Gra, put a bit of suncream on, will you? Do you remember the time you got sunburned in Tramore? You were sore for days.'

'I'm not a baby,' Grainne mumbled.

'Marie's right, Grainne,' Con said gently. 'You're fair-skinned, so you'll get burned, no matter what age you are.'

Not that it's any of your business, Marie thought. 'Here, Gra, let me put some cream on the back of your neck,' and Marie stood up to smooth cream onto her sister's tender skin.

As she spread it over Grainne's shoulders, she looked up at Con, and as she did, she noticed that he was looking at her very intently. She blushed and continued her work in silence, before saying, 'There, all done.'

Marie watched the two of them walk away, Grainne's strong legs moving under her towelling tent, Con having to pick up speed to keep up with her. He wasn't very tall, but he had broad shoulders, strong arms and legs, and he walked solidly, as if he were used to being outside, throwing bales of hay onto a tractor. Maybe that's why she had the sense that the way he looked wasn't quite right. His clothes looked as if they were both too short and too wide. His trousers flapped around the top of his Doc Martens and his wrists poked out of the sleeves of his jacket. He looked like someone trying to be a student: as if he'd put on a uniform of sorts, but that it wasn't the real him. She didn't know why she thought this: it was just a sense that she had.

'Love's young dream,' came a voice beside her.

Marie turned to see Imelda. 'I know. God help him.' She bit her lip. She'd never seen Grainne like this before. She was always going on about how much she loved Richard Gere, and had dragged Marie to see *An Officer and a Gentleman* three times to prove it. Marie had had to explain carefully that he wasn't real – at least, not in that sense. He was just an actor. On the plus side, nothing could happen to Gra if she had a crush on a film star, but the way she was hanging off Con, it all seemed a bit … much. She'd have to talk to her later.

'Oh, I didn't mean Grainne.' Imelda grinned slyly. 'I don't think that Con is that interested in your little sis, do you?'

'He isn't?' said Marie. She didn't understand, but she had an unfamiliar feeling in her stomach, a kind of fluttering. She certainly didn't feel any fluttering in the presence of David Crowley.

'He isn't.' Imelda smiled to herself again, adjusting her bikini and pulling her Ray Bans down onto her nose. 'Believe me, I know these things.'

'Oh.' Marie didn't know what to say; to defend her sister, the way she always did, or to tell Imelda to piss off, the way Claire would. Of course, in the end, she said nothing, hugging her knees as she sat there, picking up a bit of broken shell and putting it back down again. She wished that she were anywhere else but here, right now, with Imelda staring at her.

'Where exactly did he come from?' Marie asked.

Imelda shrugged. 'I think he's a friend of David's.' She nodded in David Crowley's direction. He was sitting with Maccer, the two of them smoking and jabbing each other in the ribs with their elbows, guffawing with laughter. 'Listen, I think I need chips,' Maccer said then, getting up and rummaging in his pockets. 'I'm off to the chipper, lads, any orders?'

There was a chorus of yesses and 'I'll come with you', and a minute later, Marie was alone on the beach. Even Imelda had sauntered off with Maccer, probably to display her pert backside to anyone in Seaview who'd missed it. The tide was in now and the wind had dropped. The sun was low in the sky, a sudden burst of heat that warmed her bones. Marie leaned back on the towel and closed her eyes. It must be around five, she thought, and she knew that she should gather Grainne up and head home for tea, but she suddenly felt sleepy and it felt good to rest after the day. She could hear the waves crashing off the edge of the pier and the piercing shriek of a seagull. She let herself drift away.

When she woke up, her mouth felt dry and her eyes itchy. She sat up, the book falling off her lap. Con O'Sullivan was sitting beside her.

'You were snoring.'

'Hmm ... what? Where's Grainne?'

'She went home with Imelda. She was getting a bit chilly, so I packed her off. I said I'd wait until you woke up.'

'Oh. Thanks.' Marie shoved her book in her beach bag and stood up, her head dizzy. The sun seemed suddenly too bright and her head was cloudy. She wanted to get home, and badly, and she couldn't shake the feeling that there was something with this boy – this man – that she couldn't quite grasp. Something that made her feel excited and unsettled at the same time

'I'd better go,' she said. 'I have to make sure ... I have to check that Grainne has a shower.'

When he didn't reply, she pulled the beach bag over her shoulder and said, 'Well, see you,' turning on her heel and beginning to walk up the beach. She turned around then and waited, just for a moment, to see if he would say anything, but he was scuffling around in the shingle with the edge of a razor clam, his eyes fixed on making a figure of eight among the shells. He looked unhappy, and Marie wanted to ask him why, but at the same time she thought he was a complete idiot. She turned back and continued her walk.

'I've been a prick.' His voice was louder than it should have been, and an elderly lady further down the beach tutted loudly.

She turned around. 'You have.'

'Sorry.' He looked up at her, his eyes pale in the low sun. 'I have a lot of opinions and I tend to spout … it's a failing of mine.' He had the grace to blush now, his eyes sliding away from her, resuming his task of digging around in the shingle. 'Ehm, maybe we could try again.'

'Okay …' Marie said cautiously.

'There's a debate on in the Kavanagh Theatre on Wednesday,' he said, still addressing the shingle. 'I thought maybe you'd come, you know.'

'What's the Kavanagh Theatre?'

He looked surprised. 'Aren't you in Trinity?'

Marie blushed. 'I'm in St Rachel's,' she blurted, and when she saw the look of surprise on his face added, 'But I'm going into my final year,' a bit too eagerly, and then felt stupid. Trying to pretend that she wasn't a child.

'Oh. Well. Come along anyway. It'll be an education too.' He grinned slyly and she had to resist the urge to tell him to feck off with his debating. He was just so bloody patronising, she fumed.

'I think I'm doing something else,' she found herself saying, even though she was dying to see inside Trinity. They'd been there on a fifth-year trip to see the Book of Kells, and she'd decided she wanted to go the moment she'd stood in the front entrance and saw the beautiful cobbled courtyard, the green lawns and the grand granite buildings; she'd kept it quiet, of course, because Dada had gone to UCD and wanted her to follow in his footsteps, but this time next year, she'd told herself, she'd be there.

He looked as if that wasn't the answer he'd been expecting

and Marie felt a flash of triumph, in spite of her disappointment. She didn't have to say no, she knew that. She just didn't want to give him the bloody satisfaction.

'Oh,' he said sarcastically. 'Washing your hair?'

'Something like that,' she shot back, unable to believe her cheek, turning on her heel and marching back up the beach, up the steps and up the hill to the traffic lights. Only when she was at the front gate did she dare let out the bark of excitement that had bubbled up inside of her. Somebody had asked her out, even if her sister had a crush on him, and Marie wasn't at all sure she liked him – and she'd said no. She was really very pleased with herself that she hadn't been all pathetic and agreed to go along. Maybe she wasn't such a hick after all.

Then a thought occurred to her. Why hadn't he asked Grainne? He was supposed to be her boyfriend after all. She rummaged around in her bag for her keys, stuck them in the front door and ignored Grainne's shrieked 'You're back!' from the kitchen as she opened it. She also ignored the voice in her own head that asked, 'Why didn't you ask him about Grainne?' And the answer: 'Because, for once in my life, I want something that's hers.'

Chapter 2

Marie didn't get the chance to ask Con about Grainne, because he didn't come back to the beach after that. He vanished as suddenly as he'd appeared, and Marie found that she was oddly disappointed. Grainne went to the beach every day for the last week before school began in the hope that he might be there, and every day, she came back and threw herself on the bed, even if Marie was busy reading, declaring that she'd be 'single forever', because she was being denied her chance to hang about with her self-declared boyfriend.

Marie didn't feel terribly sympathetic, because she was too annoyed that her trick had misfired. Grainne's silly *Jackie* magazine said that you had to play hard to get with boys to keep them interested, but it hadn't worked for her. She'd said no and look what had happened. It had completely backfired.

She'd even gone to the beach again herself, suffering

Imelda's bored sarcasm for another four hours, but there was no sign of him. Marie felt stupid and gauche, her face flushing whenever she thought of her pontificating that day about Jane Austen and Norman Mailer. What a silly girl she was. A silly, silly girl.

And now it was the first day of her last year in St Rachel's and she was sitting at the breakfast table munching on Weetabix, listening to an ad for Nilzan liver fluke drench on the radio. Mrs D had gone to Mass – again – leaving them to fend for themselves, and Grainne was late, because she found it hard to get herself organised in the morning and because she insisted on saying her morning prayers before getting up, instead of getting a move on. Marie knew that she'd have to go upstairs to get her, but she just wanted to sit for a moment and look out the window at Creggs, the grumpy gardener who kept the wilderness of plants and trees under control, now that Mum was no longer there to do it, and wonder what the next school year would be like. On the last day of summer term, Sister Aloysius had lined them all up in the yard, under the hot summer sun, and had given them a long lecture about having their whole lives in front of them and about their schooldays being the best days of their lives – Claire had given her a look then and crossed her eyes, making Marie snort with laughter.

Marie couldn't help thinking that if this was supposed to be the best time of her life, she didn't have an awful lot to look forward to. Still, at least she'd see Claire today for the first time in three months. She was always inviting Marie down to Wexford for the summer to their mobile home on Carnsore beach, but Marie always said no, because she didn't like to leave Grainne for too long. Even though Claire had said, 'Bring Grainne too, it'll be great!' Marie knew that she didn't mean it. Bringing Grainne would be great for about five minutes and then she'd bore them all half to death with her questions and stories, or do something stupid and embarrassing and neither of them would ever be invited again. No, Marie thought, she wanted to remain friends with Claire without Grainne ruining it. Maybe she'd ask Claire what to do about Con, Marie thought now. Claire was good at that kind of thing. Unlike Marie, she'd had lots of practice.

Claire and Marie were like chalk and cheese. Marie liked reading and watching old movies and Claire liked smoking and boys. They shouldn't have got on, but they did. Maybe it was because neither of them had a mum – well, they both did, but not alive. Claire's dad was brilliant though – he'd taken over the whole house when Claire's mum had died, and he always opened the door to them both after school in an apron and a pair of Marigold rubber gloves, a big smile on his face. Marie wished Dada could be a bit more like Declan. A bit happier.

The newsreader was droning on about the PLO withdrawing from the Lebanon when there was a shuffling at the back door and Dada appeared, with a towel under his arm. He looked surprised to see her, but then he always looked surprised, as if it only just occurred to him that he had children when he saw them.

'You should come for a swim, you know,' he said, putting his damp towel down on the chair, which Marie knew would annoy Mrs D. 'It sets you up for the day.'

'Mmm hmm,' Marie mumbled through her Weetabix.

Dada knew that she hated swimming, but she knew better than to say so and endure a lecture on the benefits of immersing yourself in freezing water.

'Where's Mrs Delaney?'

'She's gone to Mass, I think.'

'That woman does nothing except pray, for all the good it does her,' he said, putting the kettle onto the hotplate and placing a slice of Mrs D's leathery brown bread into the toaster. Marie gave a small smile. It was easy to find fault with their housekeeper, or to laugh at her endless praying and scapulars and Miraculous Medals, or the cryptic remarks she'd make about the past she never spoke about, apart from to warn them never, ever, to remove any items of clothing near a boy. If it wasn't for Mrs D, she knew she'd have ended up with Granny in Rathgar when Mum got really ill. Dada had wanted her to go, said he wasn't able to manage the girls by himself, but it had been Aunty Biddy, Mum's old friend, who had suggested a housekeeper, and Marie had been grateful to her ever since Mrs D had turned up on the doorstep one day, a tweed-patterned suitcase in one hand and a large Thermos in the other. She was the glue that stuck them all together, Mrs D, as much as they could be stuck together.

Dada pulled out one of the mahogany dining chairs that he'd moved into the kitchen from the dining room, because they weren't being used – they hadn't used the dining room since Mum died – and sat down. There was a silence while Marie ate. She could sense him looking at her, wondering what he might say to her. She wondered if she should stop chewing, if she was making too much noise as she lifted her spoon to her mouth, or was dripping milk down her front.

Dada hated poor table manners, thanks to Granny, who had a bit of a thing about cutlery being in the right place and elbows not being on the table. Marie could remember Mum joking about it when they'd come home from one of Granny's awful dinners, encouraging them to pick their food up in their fingers and to jab at peas with their forks and laughing uproariously about it. Even Dada had managed to see the funny side of it then, which he certainly didn't now.

'Marie?'

She looked at him warily from under her fringe. She was hoping he'd forgotten about passing judgement for the make-up incident, but Dada had a memory like an elephant.

'You know, it's a very important year for you.'

Uh-oh, Marie thought. Here we go. She pretended to look interested. 'Yes.'

He cleared his throat and shifted awkwardly in his seat. The mahogany dining chairs were stiff-backed and uncomfortable and, with their red plush seats and elaborate carving, looked completely wrong in the scuffed, tatty kitchen. 'You'll have some significant decisions to make, Marie, on the future course of your life.'

'Yes, Dada.'

He lifted the salt cellar and absentmindedly tipped a bit of salt onto the table, before tutting and putting the cellar back. 'What you do now, your choices that is, can affect you for the rest of your life, so it's important to consider them carefully, Marie, do you understand?'

'Yes, Dada.' Marie found it was best just to agree with Dada when he was in lecture mode, because to do anything else would just make it go on for longer. Anyway, she couldn't really see what he meant by 'choices'. She couldn't see what choices she had, really, apart from to follow Dada into 'the law', which made her feel vaguely ill even at the prospect, and to look after Grainne. She couldn't imagine Grainne ever being able to look after herself. Then she thought of Con O'Sullivan and that afternoon by the sea and she blushed and looked down at the table.

'What I'm saying, Marie, is that you need to work steadily to achieve your goals.'

'I know.'

He had an uncertain look on his face and then he said, 'It's what your mother would have wanted.'

Oh, no.

'I've been asking her for guidance quite often lately,' Dada said suddenly. 'I find that it helps. And she gives good advice.' He gave a short smile. 'She always did.'

Marie wondered if she should say something, but she couldn't work out what the right response might be. She wasn't like Mum – she couldn't give Dada the right advice. She couldn't give him any advice at all.

There was a clearing of the throat again. 'What I'm saying is that I know your mother would want ... ' He hesitated. 'Look, you know, you can come to me with any ... issues,' he said finally. 'I'll try to help.'

'Oh. Thanks, Dada,' Marie said, wondering what it was Mum would want, but being too afraid to ask him. And being too afraid to say that she often asked Mum for advice too, and she'd found that once she'd asked Mum, Mum would find a way of answering. Something would happen, and even if it wasn't what Marie wanted, it was always the right thing, and she understood that it was Mum at work. She could have asked Dada if he felt the same way, but she'd rather have died, she thought now, eyeing her watery breakfast. She couldn't begin to imagine what it might be like to really talk to Dada – mortifying, probably.

'Yes, well.' He lifted the newspaper from its resting place on top of the toast rack. 'I'm sure you have your schoolbag to prepare.'

'Oh. Yes. I'd better check on Grainne.' Marie jumped up from the table, grateful that the ordeal was finally over. She was relieved that he had only begun to talk about Mum, but had stopped himself in time, because if he talked about her, Marie knew that she just wouldn't be able for it – she wouldn't be able to handle his feelings on top of her own. It was too much.

'Good luck.'

'Thanks, Dada.'

*

Five hours later, Marie was sitting in the airless language lab at St Rachel's, just as she had been every Monday for the previous five years. She was declining the *passé composé* of *avoir*, as she had also done more or less every day since the start of secondary school. Sister Dominic had a thing about it. 'If you know the *passé composé* of *avoir*, the whole of the French language will open up to you,' she would say. Marie found that it simply meant she was very good at declining the verb *avoir* in the past tense. The rest was still a baffling mystery to her. A mystery and a living hell, she thought miserably as she doodled in the margin of her French textbook.

Sister Dominic was walking up and down between the rows of chairs, stopping every now and then to peer into a girl's copybook, her fingers perched on the edge of the desk, the silver ring on the fourth finger of her left hand glinting in the sunshine … *J'ai eu deux bonbons …*' when Gillian Byrne nudged Marie on the arm and nodded in Imelda's direction. At first, Marie didn't react, because she couldn't imagine what Imelda would want from her. She ignored Marie, and when she wasn't ignoring her, she was calling her an absolute tit. Marie preferred being ignored.

'Psst,' Gillian persisted, and when Marie looked up at her, she shoved a note under her elbow. Marie quickly pressed her elbow down, in case Sister Dominic saw, then furtively shoved her other hand in and pulled the note out.

Does Marie have a boyfriend?

Beside the words was a sketch of a stick man kissing a stick woman, a little circle of love hearts around their heads. Marie stared at the note for a long time, then she looked up and shook her head slightly, shoving the note down into her skirt pocket.

'Liar,' Imelda mouthed. Marie just looked straight ahead at Sister Dominic, who had moved to the board and was writing *'j'ai eu'* in her looping handwriting, as if she found conjugating French verbs suddenly fascinating. Her mind was spinning. Did Imelda O'Brien know about Con asking her out? She'd gone by the time he'd said anything … that bitch had some kind of sixth sense, Marie knew it. She had a sudden thought about what it might be like to kiss him. Please God, it wouldn't be a tongue down the mouth like that eejit David Crowley who'd cornered her in the canoe club one evening. But then she chastised herself – what was she, a total bimbo? Future foreign correspondents didn't spend their time thinking about being kissed, she was sure of it. She blushed at the thought and looked up to make sure Imelda O'Brien wasn't watching, but she clearly had Marie in her sights. She made a kissing motion with her lips and Marie looked down at the pages of her copybook, as if she hadn't seen.

French class was interminable, as usual, and the dusty morning dragged, the way it always did in school, the stuffy, airless room making Marie's eyes droop. The only time she woke up was when Mr Hanrahan, the English teacher, picked the texts for the exam; she was looking forward to reading *The Great Gatsby*, but she hated Dickens and his heavy-handed preaching – the idea of re-reading *Hard Times* made her grit her teeth. She tuned out again during biology and the life cycle of the newt, looking out the window at the cars whizzing along the road, imagining what it might be like to be a different person, not to have to do anything that she didn't want to do. To be free.

At last, the hands of the clock above the blackboard, which hung beside a statue of Holy Mary, seemed to grind towards lunchtime and ancient Sister Patricia appeared in the yard, bell under her arm. She proceeded to ring it and, with a scraping of chairs, the girls got up and filed out of the classroom. Thank God, Marie thought, I can finally find Claire. They'd been too late that morning, thanks to Grainne losing her maths set, and Claire had already gone in by the time she'd raced in the front door, ten minutes late for assembly.

As she trudged down the stairs to the yard, Marie looked around for her sister, but there was no sign of her and she felt an unfamiliar light-headedness at the thought of lunch without Grainne. Reaching into her bag for her lunchbox, she looked around the yard for any sign of Claire. She hoped that Grainne had remembered to bring hers – she was always forgetting and Marie would have to share with her. And Mrs D wasn't exactly generous with the sandwiches: two small cheese ones and a Digestive biscuit was generally all that was on offer and any protests were met with a long lecture on how she'd gone to school with no shoes and had eaten half a potato for lunch.

She spotted Grainne sitting in her usual spot in the small shelter the nuns had built beside the bicycle shed, her lunchbox on her knees. She looked so lonely, Marie thought. Grainne wasn't *unpopular* exactly – she was too smiley and friendly for that – but somehow she never quite seemed to be able to keep up with the girls in her class; she wasn't smart or pretty like Dympna O'Rourke, who played the harp and hockey for Leinster, and she wasn't one of the cynical ones, like Anne-Marie Dempsey, who sat at the back of the class, chewing gum and making remarks about the teacher. So, Grainne drifted from group to group, laughing along with the jokes that she didn't quite get, and Marie felt bad for her, she really did, but sometimes she wondered what it would be like to have a whole lunch break to gossip with Claire, without Grainne for company.

'Aw, is little sis all alone?' As Imelda came up behind Marie, a sickly waft of Poison drifted over Marie's shoulder. When Marie turned to look at her, she saw that Imelda was wearing bright blue eyeliner – how she'd escaped the attention of Sister Patricia, Marie didn't know.

'Looks that way.' Marie didn't want to say anything else, in case she offered Imelda an opening. She had a habit of seizing on innocent remarks and twisting them, so that you couldn't say that she was being downright nasty, but you certainly got the message.

'Hmm, we'll have to see about that,' and Imelda sauntered across the yard, her legs long beneath her skirt, which had been rolled up as high as she could get away with. She had a yellow woven bag, which had been covered in graffiti, the lightning sign for Led Zeppelin a flash across the back. Her hair was pulled tight on top of her head in a kind of pineapple. Claire said that that was a sure sign she was a psychopath. 'Beware the hair,' she'd say in a spooky voice, whenever Imelda would pass. She'd give her two fingers and pass on.

'Hi, Grainne,' Imelda cooed. 'Mind if I sit here?'

Grainne looked up from her sandwich, and a smile split her face. 'Oh, yes, Imelda,' she said, blushing bright red, lifting her sandwich wrapper off the bench and letting the other girl sit down.

'I love your hair,' Imelda said. 'Will I tidy it up a bit for you? I think I have a scrunchie in my bag.'

'Thanks, Imelda. Mrs Delaney says it's like straw.' Grainne giggled.

'Mrs Delaney must be blind if she can't see how gorgeous it is. Now turn your back to me and I'll brush it out,' Imelda said, reaching into her bag and pulling out an afro comb. 'So, any goss?' she began.

'What's she up to?' Claire's voice made Marie jump.

'Claire!' Marie turned and gave her friend as fierce a hug as she could manage under the beady eye of Sister Patricia, who didn't like exuberance of any kind in the yard. 'Boy, am I glad to see you.'

Claire returned the hug, planting a lip-glossed kiss on Marie's cheek. 'That bad, eh?'

'You have no idea,' Marie said. 'It was the longest and most boring summer on record, I believe.'

'Well, it must be better than eight weeks in a mobile home with two smelly brothers, a Labrador and aunty Maeve from Boston, who kept breaking into decades of the Rosary. And it rained most of the time. And the boys were all acne-ridden weaklings that I wouldn't be seen dead with. I didn't have one decent shift all summer.' She sighed dramatically.

'Oh, poor you.' Marie giggled, a sudden image of Con O'Sullivan popping into her head. Don't go red, she told herself. She noticed that Claire didn't ask her if she'd met anyone – she'd probably given up at this stage, so barren was Marie's love life.

'Anyway, what does Queen Bitch want with your sister?'

'Dunno,' Marie said glumly. What *did* Imelda want? She had always treated Grainne with disdain, calling her 'little sis', a sneer on her face. Now, she was all over Grainne. Marie should be going over there and asking, she knew, but something was stopping her: a sense of relief that Grainne was otherwise occupied.

'She's just trying to annoy you,' Claire decided. 'She's always had a thing about you.'

'She has?' Marie said doubtfully. 'Why would she have a thing about me?'

'Because even though she looks good, she has the intellect of a snail, unlike you, my dear Marie. She feels intimidated.'

'Oh,' Marie said.

Claire rolled her eyes to heaven. 'For a clever clogs, you can be a bit slow on the uptake sometimes.' Then she grinned. 'C'mon, we'll leave the poisoned witch to weave her spell – joking,' she added, seeing the look of anxiety on Marie's face. 'Grainne will be fine just this once. I am dying for a ciggie and I've got five minutes before religion class – I want to know every detail about your utterly boring summer.'

'Well, you'll have four minutes and thirty seconds left to smoke your cigarette then,' Marie said, thinking, as she did, that she was only half telling the truth.

The two of them moved off past the bike sheds and across the hockey field to the old changing rooms at the bottom, behind which lurked a number of girls, a cloud of smoke rising into the chilly air.

'Hi, Claire,' they chorused.

'Hi, Marie,' Amy Fitzpatrick said, taking a drag on her cigarette and stamping it out under her foot. 'Don't tell me you're taking up smoking.'

'Nope,' Marie said. 'Just coming along for the ride.' There was a snigger from spotty Eleanor Bradley, with her curtain of dark brown hair. 'Won't get any rides here, Marie. Sorry – unless you're a lezzer, that is,' and she guffawed at her own joke.

'Do you know, you are a complete spa, Eleanor,' Claire said coolly, lighting her John Player Blue and taking a big drag on it.

'Actually, I will have a cigarette,' Marie said suddenly.

'Are you sure?' Claire looked at her closely.

'Yes.' Marie's mouth was dry as she accepted the box of cigarettes from her friend. She pulled one out and put it in her mouth. The filter felt warm, but the smell of tobacco made her feel sick.

'Light?'

Marie nodded and accepted the light from Eleanor, puffing on the cigarette, so that a cloud of smoke blew up in her face, making her eyes water.

'Take it easy, Mar,' Claire said. 'Inhale just a tiny bit and then blow the smoke out,' and she demonstrated by taking a small pull and then exhaling with a hiss. She looked sophisticated and Marie wondered if she'd ever be able to master it. She took a short pull and the smoke filled her throat. She began to cough and her eyes burned. 'Oh, God,' she spluttered, unable to hold the massive coughing fit in. She thought she'd throw her lungs up.

'Here,' Claire said, taking the cigarette from her and tapping it carefully out on the ground so that she wouldn't waste it. 'Don't say I didn't tell you.'

Marie felt like such an eejit – how gauche did she look, coughing and spluttering? Next time, she wouldn't make such a fool of herself. She'd have to practise a bit first though, she thought. She'd need to re-read *Bonjour Tristesse* first, to get some hints – they were always taking big drags on cigarettes in that novel, because they were French and terribly sophisticated. Marie had read it at the start of the summer and hadn't been able to believe that French people could be so interesting. She hated French grammar so much, and learning those dreary lists of masculine and feminine objects, that her love for the literature had surprised her. She couldn't believe how Cécile, who was only seventeen, could be so jealous of her father's relationship with a real, grown-up woman; she'd wondered if she would be as hostile if Dada had another girlfriend; if she'd scheme, like Cécile had, to separate them. But then, the thought of Dada actually having another girlfriend was laughable.

'Marie, your skin looks fantastic,' Amy Fitzpatrick said. 'What are you using?'

'Ehm, nothing ...' Marie said. 'I think it's the sun. I don't really burn.'

'Hmm.' Amy eyed her appraisingly. 'Your skin *is* a bit swarthy. Do you find that you have problems with facial hair?'

'No.' Marie blushed. 'At least, I don't think so. My skin's a bit sallow, that's all.'

'Oh.' Amy gave Marie a look, as if remembering exactly why she found her so boring, then turned away and said to no one in particular, 'So, what's the ska?'

'Did you hear that the SPUC-ies are coming in for a lecture on the unborn child?' Gillian Byrne said.

'Jesus H. Christ.' Claire rolled her eyes to heaven. 'I wonder will it be as bad as the one on Padre Pio – I've never been so bored in my entire life.'

'Hang on a minute,' Eleanor broke in, her face red. 'You can't compare the two. I mean, have you any idea what they do during an abortion?' she said. 'They attach this vacuum cleaner hose to you and suck out the baby and throw it in a bucket ... it's murder, nothing less.'

'Fine. We get the message,' Claire said sulkily, rolling her eyes at Marie. 'All I know is that women should be allowed to control their own bodies. It shouldn't be dictated to them by anyone, least of all the Catholic Church.'

'Oh, well, that would be about right from a heathen. You haven't darkened the door of St Malachy's in about a year. Do you know what your problem is, Claire?'

'I've a feeling you're going to tell me,' Claire said dryly.

'You don't know the difference between right and wrong. You're one of those quasi-liberals, who believes that the world is composed of shades of grey, but do you know, it isn't. It's black or white, right or wrong, and abortion is just wrong.' Eleanor was warming to her theme now, jabbing the air with her cigarette. Marie wondered where she'd got her ideas from, because they didn't sound as if they came from her – it was as if she was parroting someone else's words – and 'quasi-liberals'? As Mrs D would have said, 'What's a quasi-liberal when it's at home?'

Eleanor stabbed her cigarette out on the ground. 'See you,' she said brusquely, disappearing off in the direction of the school. 'Spoken like a true SPUC-ie,' Claire muttered. 'Her mother's always handing out leaflets down the town. She makes sure she has the goriest pictures on them and she's always on the radio, going on about inalienable rights and all that shite.'

Marie didn't know what to say, so she just nodded her head and agreed with her friend. She didn't really know how she felt about abortion. The way Eleanor put it, it did sound like murder, but what would she do if she became pregnant? A picture of Dada in his gown and wig came into her head, the gavel banging down on the bench in front of her. And then she thought, I don't know what I'm worrying about –

you have to have sex to become pregnant. Fat chance of that. And then she thought of Con O'Sullivan, and prayed that she wouldn't go bright red and give herself away.

'For God's sake, let's change the record,' Amy Fitzpatrick said, as they all watched Eleanor stomp off back to school. 'I've invited Simon Hayes to the debs,' and she gave a little squeal, stamping her tiny feet into the grass with excitement.

'Now, that's news,' Claire said, with only a trace of sarcasm.

Amy smiled, showing a great big set of train tracks on her teeth. 'You're just jealous.'

'I can assure you, I'm not.' Claire pursed her lips and blew a series of smoke rings into the air. There was a long silence, then Amy said, 'How about you, Marie? Going to ask David?' There was a general snigger and Marie wished the ground would open up and swallow her.

'No, she is not,' Claire shot back. 'Because Marie prefers men to boys, especially if they are rugger maniacs and squares, like Mr Crowley.' And with that, she ground her cigarette butt into the grass and threw a wave over her shoulder. She linked arms with Marie and off they strode, the two of them trying to keep the giggles in until they'd reached the bike sheds, when they felt safe to let out the pent-up laughter.

'God, Amy Fitzpatrick is a moron.' Claire giggled.

'Ah, she's not that bad,' Marie said, because she felt sorry for Amy, getting the benefit of Claire's acid tongue. And besides, the rumour was that Amy had been 'around the block' with Mark O'Hanlon, who was a nasty piece of work. Funny how they always referred to girls as 'the class bike', and never boys, Marie thought.

'If someone asks you out and you say no, is that the end?'

Marie blurted. 'I mean, can you change your mind, or …' her voice trailed off as she caught the smile on her friend's face.

'Oh … so your summer wasn't that boring after all.'

'No … at least …' Marie found herself suddenly tongue-tied. 'It's hardly worth talking about, really.'

'Spill. Tell me everything,' Claire demanded, just as Sister Patricia re-emerged, bell in hand.

'There's nothing to tell,' Marie insisted as they shuffled in through the door, but her face went beetroot red. Because even as she said the words, she got that gnawing feeling in her stomach again, the one she'd had ever since she'd gone to the beach that afternoon. She wasn't sure what it was – she didn't know what to call it, but it felt like a longing.

Marie wanted to go straight home after school, because Sister Dominic had given her a big pile of irregular verbs to learn, but Grainne usually insisted on going down to Fusco's on the seafront for chips, where big gangs of schoolboys and -girls hung around outside, hitting each other with schoolbags and smoking. It was full of silly idiots who had nothing whatsoever to say to each other – at least, nothing that made any sense. She'd much prefer to be at home reading, she thought, scanning the crowds coming out of St Rachel's for any sign of her sister.

She spotted David Crowley coming down the drive of St Philip's, just down the hill, and she tried to look the other way, to pretend she hadn't seen him, but it was too late. He was a head taller than all the other boys and his jumper was too small for him and as he came towards her, pushing his bike, his cheeks went bright red. God, Marie thought, he must be as embarrassed as me. They'd known each other for ever, and they'd even had that awful kiss, but she never had a clue what to say to him.

'Hi, Marie.'

'Hi, David,' Marie had replied, hoping to God he wouldn't say anything else, but he stopped, pulling the strap of his bag up onto his shoulder. 'So … how's it going?'

'Oh, grand. You know …'

'Yeah.' There was a long silence while he looked at his feet. He didn't have much in the way of talk, Marie thought, but then maybe that was the point. He was always throwing a rugby ball around.

'Did you have a good summer?' he asked.

Jesus. 'Oh, yeah. Didn't get up to much. What about you?'

'Was in the folks' place in Connemara. Rained the whole time.'

'Right.'

'Well,' he said eventually, 'better go. The Old Dear will be waiting. She gets worried if I'm five minutes late.' He smiled briefly, flashing a set of teeth that weren't too bad, Marie thought. In fact, he wouldn't be that bad looking if he didn't have that stupid mullet.

'How is your mum?' It was a source of mutual embarrassment that they'd played together as children when David's mum, Patricia, and Marie's mum had been in the same mother-and-toddler playgroup.

'Yeah,' he said, scratching his head, a muscle working in his jaw. 'She's OK. On my back all the time about study.'

There was a silence then, as they'd both thought the same

thing: that Marie didn't have a mum to be on her back all the time. David opened his mouth as if he was going to say something, but then thought better of it.

'I'm just waiting for Grainne,' Marie said.

'Oh, I saw her leave about ten minutes ago. I think she was with Imelda.'

'Oh.' Marie tried not to look as disappointed as she felt.

'Anyway, see you around,' he said, swinging a leg over the crossbar of his racer and slouching off down the road, schoolbag balanced on his back.

'Yeah, see you,' Marie muttered as she pulled her own bag onto her back. She walked down the hill towards the village to find Grainne standing outside the chipper with Imelda and a group of girls from sixth year. She was laughing too loudly at something. When she saw Marie, she looked guilty for a minute, then went to wave at Marie, but Imelda put a hand on hers and whispered something in her ear. They both laughed. Marie knew that Imelda was just being a wagon, but she still felt hurt and a bit silly.

'Hi, Marie,' Imelda said in that sing-song, bitchy tone that she always used. 'I thought you'd be off with the boyfriend.' And she gave a little snigger.

'What boyfriend?' Grainne said. 'I didn't know you had a boyfriend, Mar.'

'I don't. Imelda's wrong,' Marie barked.

'I do,' Grainne said dreamily, but then she looked doubtful. 'Or I did anyway. I'm not sure now. Anyway,' she brightened, 'do you think I could ask him to the debs?'

'You're too young,' Marie began, 'it's for sixth years only—' but Imelda interrupted, 'I think that would be brilliant,

Grainne. I'm sure you could tag along with me. Now, who would we ask for you? Anthony Daly's not going out with Alma Ryan any more. We'll try him!' Anthony Daly was a big, rough boy from St John's, and there was no way on earth Marie would let him anywhere near Grainne, but before she could think of a smart remark, Grainne said, 'Oh, it's OK, thanks, Imelda, I think I'm going to invite Con to the debs. I'm asking him out on a date and by the time the debs comes around, we'll have been going out for ages, so …' Her voice trailed off when the group fell into silence.

'Well, well,' Imelda said slyly. 'Looks as if you'll have a battle on your hands, won't she, Marie?'

There was a long silence, while Marie glared at Imelda and Grainne looked from one to the other, a puzzled expression on her face. She dipped her hand into her bag of chips then and took one out, blowing on it then putting it into her mouth. Marie felt embarrassed for her when Imelda's crony, Mary, tutted and rolled her eyes to heaven.

'Listen, are you heading to the canoe club later?' Mary asked Imelda, as if neither of the other two girls was there. 'There's a thing on.'

'Oh, can I come?' Grainne said. 'Is there another party?'

'No,' Mary said blankly. 'It's members only tonight.'

'Oh.' Grainne looked at Marie. 'Am I a member, Mar?'

Marie shook her head.

'Does that mean I can't go?'

Marie was about to nod, when Mary interrupted, 'Yes, that means you can't go.'

'Ah, well, maybe if you come along after eleven,' Imelda said. 'They let anyone in then.'

ALISON WALSH

Bitch, Marie thought, grabbing Grainne's sleeve and pulling her gently towards her. 'C'mon, Gra, we're going out later,' she improvised. 'We'd better go home and get ready.'

'Oh, Marie's going "out",' Mary said. 'Maybe there's some foreign play on or something, or one of those rude French movies,' she cackled. 'All lesbians and God knows what else.' She nudged Imelda. 'They're supposed to like it … up the bum!' she mouthed, her eyes round.

Grainne looked mystified and opened her mouth, clearly to ask what Mary meant, but Marie cut her off at the pass. 'Come on, Gra, let's go,' she said. She turned her back on the Queen Bitches and walked off, Grainne turning and looking regretfully behind her.

'Bye, Marie. Give Con my love,' Imelda called out behind her. Thankfully, Grainne didn't notice, because she was too absorbed in eating her chips. She'd managed to get a clump of potato in her hair and Marie's stomach turned as she tried to pull it out. 'Hold still, Gra, will you?' she snapped. 'Honestly, do you have to eat like a complete pig?'

She knew that she was being mean, but Grainne seemed to take no notice, a small smile on her face. 'You know, Imelda says that I'm going to look like Princess Caroline of Monaco by the time she's finished with me.'

'I'm sure you'll look gorgeous, Gra,' Marie said. She wanted to get off the subject of the debs, in case Grainne started probing her about who she was inviting. The answer was no one, but she didn't want to get into it now. There was no way on earth she'd invite David Crowley. And, she thought quietly to herself, she couldn't invite Con, because it would only upset her sister, and anyway, she'd only met

56

him once. She had a sudden vision of herself walking in the door of the hotel in some fantastic dress, with Con on her arm, and everyone turning around, Imelda gasping in surprise. How she'd love to show them all that she wasn't the boring old swot they thought she was.

'How do you ask someone on a date?' Grainne suddenly asked.

'Why, are you planning on taking someone out?' Marie said, putting her hand in the bag of chips to take one, to be rewarded by Grainne squeezing her fingers so tightly Marie gave a little scream.

'Jesus, Gra, you've broken my fingers,' Marie protested.

'They're *my* chips,' Grainne said happily, popping another one into her mouth. 'Anyway, I told you – I am asking Con on a date, because then I can pluck up the courage to ask him to the debs … once he's my boyfriend properly,' she added helpfully.

But you can't, Marie thought, because he likes *me*. She found herself gripping the handle of her schoolbag in a tight squeeze. Why did Grainne have to ruin everything?

'Tell you what,' Grainne said suddenly, waving her chip bag in the air, 'let's practise. I'll be me and you be Con O'Sullivan and I'll ask you out.' And she clapped her hands with glee.

'Oh, go on then,' Marie sighed, stopping in the middle of the pavement, folding her arms across her chest and watching as Grainne put her schoolbag down and stood in front of her, simpering and batting her eyelashes. 'Con, would you like to go and see *An Officer and a Gentleman* with me?'

'No, no, Gra. That's awful,' Marie found herself saying. 'You don't have to be Marilyn Monroe. Just relax and act normally.'

'OK, OK,' Grainne said, dropping her shoulders and putting her hands on her hips. Then she adopted a big scowl. 'Look, Con, do you want to go out with me or don't you?'

In spite of herself, Marie was seized with a fit of the giggles. 'Is that normal? I'd hate to see you when you're angry.' She laughed.

'Mar, be serious. I need a boyfriend.' Grainne sulked. 'I'm not pretty like you and I'm not intelligent, but Con likes me, and I think if I asked him, he'd say yes.'

And you'll probably get your way, Marie thought, because you are you. Because you are special, whatever that is. And because you're special, you always get what you want.

'Mar. Please?'

I don't believe this, Marie thought to herself. 'OK, sorry.' Marie arranged her features to look more serious. 'Why don't you just go up to him and say, "Con, I got these free tickets for *Tootsie* and I was just wondering …"'

'Oh, *Tootsie*, great. I really want to see that,' Grainne said. 'It's got Dustin Hoffman in it and he's a man, but he dresses up as a woman to get that lovely Jessica Lange—'

'Get on with it, Gra,' Marie barked. 'You have the free tickets …'

'But they wouldn't be free,' Grainne interrupted, 'because I'd have to buy them with my pocket money.'

'For God's sake, Gra, you're just making it up, to sound more casual. Now, will you just listen?'

'OK,' Grainne said quietly. 'Show me, Mar. Please?'

'Fine.' Marie sighed and rummaged in her schoolbag, producing a copy of their *Soundings* poetry book. 'This is the ticket, right?'

'Right.' Grainne's eyes were glued to her.

'So, I'm bumping into him at Seaview, OK?' Marie mimicked sauntering along the seafront. '"Hi Con, how are you?"' Marie said brightly, adding, 'See? You want it to look casual, as if you aren't trying too hard.' And then she continued, '"How's college? Oh? Exams … poor you. Listen, I happened to be passing the Ormonde the other day and they were giving out free tickets to *Tootsie* and—"'

'Do I have to tell him the whole story?' Grainne broke in. 'I'll never remember.'

'Jesus, Gra, will you stop interrupting?' Marie hissed.

'Fine.' Grainne sulked. 'But you're not to take the Lord's name in vain.'

I'll ignore that, Marie thought. '"Anyway, the man gave me two tickets and I wanted Marie to come, because she's my sister and I love her more than anyone … "' at this, Grainne giggled '" … but she's got exams, so would you like to come instead?" So, you don't beat around the bush at the end – you make it clear what you want, but you lead up to it, so that you're not too obvious about it.'

Grainne squealed and rushed over to Marie, giving her a big, wet kiss on the cheek. 'Thanks, Marie, you are my favourite sister!' It was her running joke and she thought it was hilarious.

'OK, now, home,' Marie declared. 'I have an essay on Bismarck to write and a ton of maths problems to solve.'

Grainne picked up her schoolbag and tucked her arm into

Marie's, giving it a squeeze. 'Thanks, Mar. I'll say a prayer for you later.'

'Gee, thanks,' Marie said, smiling.

'I'll say one for Con, too. I'll ask God to make him say yes.'

'He will say yes,' Marie replied. She added to herself, and if he says yes, I will kill you. I really will.

Chapter 3

'Mrs D, thanks for dinner, I'm going to do my homework,' Marie said later that night, as she shuffled down the hall, thinking that she'd at least have five Grainne-free minutes to herself, when she noticed something on the hall table. It was a note, in Mrs Delaney's neat script, the result, as she often said, of 'five years' beating' in some convent in Letterkenny. 'Mr Con O'Sullivan.' And after, a number. Marie looked around as if Grainne might be lurking behind her and pocketed the note. Then she pulled the phone into the cupboard under the stairs and rang the number. Her heart was thumping so loudly in her chest, she barely heard the ringing. It rang for ages and she was about to put the phone down, when a voice answered, a girl's. 'Hello,' she bellowed into the mouthpiece, so loudly Marie had to pull the phone away from her ear.

'Ehm, can I speak to Con, please?'

The girl didn't answer, just roared, 'Con, phone call!' and then the phone made a loud 'clunk'.

There was a long silence. Marie wondered who the girl was. Maybe he shared a flat. She wondered what his life was like and she realised that she knew absolutely nothing about it. She had no idea what age he was, not exactly, or where he came from or how many brothers and sisters he had. She didn't really know who he was.

I can just hang up now, Marie thought. I can just hang up now and everything will be the same as it always was. And she felt it suddenly, a sense that there were two ways her life could go – the way it always had gone and this path that led somewhere else. She sucked in a deep breath and felt her hand move down towards the phone, the receiver about to rest in the cradle, when she heard a voice, 'Hello?'

His voice sounded deeper on the phone, more resonant than she remembered. Her hand hovered over the phone, and she swallowed the great big lump in her throat.

'Hello?' The voice said, 'who is this?'

'Hi, ehm, it's Marie.' She found that she'd lifted the receiver to her ear again and was talking quietly into it.

'You're whispering.' He sounded amused.

'I know. I'm under the stairs.'

'Oh. Is that usually where you make your phone calls?'

'It is when I don't want to be overheard.'

'Oh. Is this top secret or something?'

He was laughing at her. She'd done the wrong thing not putting down the phone. 'It's not funny,' she barked. 'Where did you get my number anyway?'

There was a long pause. 'In the phone book. I told your housekeeper that I was a maths tutor you'd contacted about needing grinds. She sounded a bit suspicious.' He still sounded amused.

'She's always suspicious,' Marie said. She didn't know what to say next. 'So, are you looking for Grainne?' she ventured. 'I'll just get her—'

He interrupted her, 'Actually, I was looking for you. I thought that you might have forgotten what a total prick I was the last time.'

'I haven't,' Marie said. 'I remember very well what a prick you were, as you put it.'

'Good. Well then, this time you'll want to go out with me, with the memory fresh in your mind.'

'What makes you think that?'

'Well, because *you* rang *me*.'

'Ah.' Marie felt her cheeks redden and she was glad he couldn't see her.

'Ah, indeed. So, a few of us are going up the mountains. There's a party on. Some posh girl who has a big pile in Stepaside. You'll feel right at home. You on for it?'

Marie bit her lip. How on earth did he think she was going to be able to go up the mountains on a school night? Thoughts began to flit through her head, plans and excuses. It was ridiculous, she knew, but she suddenly wanted to go to Stepaside more than anything else in the whole world.

'I promise I'll have you there and back before midnight, if that's what you're worried about.'

'I'm not a child,' she said hurriedly. 'I *am* allowed out, you know.'

'Right.' He sounded amused again and she wanted to scream.

'Wait a bit up the sea road from the house. I'll meet you there at ten.'

'Why? Do you have to sneak out without Daddy seeing?'

'Yes, actually,' she said. 'I'll see you then.' And she slammed the phone down so hard into the cradle, she thought it would break. Stupid, bloody Con O'Sullivan, she thought, her stomach flipping with excitement.

As Marie tiptoed across the landing, she could hear the sounds of Duran Duran coming out from under Grainne's bedroom door. She stood in front of it for a few moments, running over the various excuses she was about to make to her sister in her head for her disappearance at ten o'clock at night. Then she tapped quietly and stuck her head around the door.

Grainne was sitting on the bed, surrounded by Mrs D's *Woman's Way* magazines. She'd arranged them in a circle around her and she was pulling a comb through her tight curls, a grimace on her face.

'What are you up to, Gra?'

'Oh, I'm just trying to copy some of the hairstyles,' Grainne said, nodding at the magazine in front of her. 'I like this one and Imelda says I have lovely hair, but it won't go like the photo,' and she winced as she pulled the comb through.

'Oh, let me have a look,' Marie said and she sat down beside Grainne on the bed. The girl in the photo had a perm, but unlike Grainne's wild, frizzy curls, hers were tidy waves that framed her pretty face. 'Hmm,' Marie said. 'I wonder if a chignon or something like that might suit you better.'

'What's that?' Grainne looked doubtful.

'Here, let me try something,' and Marie sat behind her sister on the bed and smoothed her hair into as tidy a ponytail as she could manage, teasing out the knots until she could get an afro comb through it. Then she twisted the ponytail around until it formed a neat bun at the nape of Grainne's neck, and secured it with a few of the hairclips Grainne had strewn around the bed, pulling each clip apart so that it formed an inverted 'v', which she jabbed into the knot until it stayed in place.

'There.' Marie sat back to admire her handiwork. Her sister looked totally different with her hair pulled back – her neck looked more slender and her face, which was normally obscured by her frizzy mat, looked fresh, her blue eyes sparkling. 'Very nice, Gra – you look lovely!'

'I do?' Grainne got up off her bed and went to look in her dressing table mirror. She stared at herself for a long time. 'Do you think Con will like it?' She whirled around and beamed at Marie.

Oh God. 'I'm sure he'd love it,' Marie managed.

'Maybe when I'm going to the debs, I can ask Imelda to do my hair like this.'

'Maybe.'

'Do you think Con will go with me, Mar?'

Marie couldn't help herself. 'Well, didn't we practise asking him earlier? You'll just have to give it a try.' She knew that she sounded sharp, a bit mean, but she wished Grainne would just stop talking about him, because if she didn't, the expression on Marie's face would give something away.

'Well, I'm afraid he'll say no,' Grainne said sadly. 'Everyone thinks I'm fat and plain – what boy would want to go with stupid old me?'

Even though Marie wanted to kill her sister, she found herself sitting down beside her, shoving aside one of the magazines and putting an arm around her shoulders. 'That's nonsense, Gra. You're so bright and bouncy, do you know that? And fun. You always make people happy to be around you. Boys are just mad if they can't see that.'

'Boys don't want bright and bouncy, Mar. They want pretty and thin. And cool and clever and witty. Like Imelda.'

Imelda was very far from cool and clever and witty, but Marie had to concede that Grainne was right about the rest. 'Is that why you're hanging around with her?'

Grainne shrugged. 'She likes me, Marie, and I don't have any other friends, not proper ones anyway.'

'That's not true,' Marie began, but she was silenced by Grainne's look. It *was* kind of true – when everyone else was busy concentrating on being cool, Grainne was just so eager to please, so bouncy, like a silly puppy. Marie wondered when Grainne would ever grow up, or if she'd remain a child for ever. She suddenly felt a rush of emotion for her sister.

'You have me,' Marie said. 'You'll always have me, you silly eejit,' and she gave her sister a squeeze.

Grainne rewarded her with a smile, putting her head on Marie's shoulder and giving a sigh. 'I wish I could be more like you, Mar,' Grainne said.

'Why on earth do you say that?' Marie laughed.

'Because you're very clever and you think very hard about everything,' Grainne said.

'But I don't have a queue of boys around the block waiting to ask me to the debs,' Marie said ruefully. 'I don't think they like clever either, Gra, if that's any consolation.'

'What do boys like, do you think?' Grainne looked at Marie earnestly and Marie wondered what Mum would say if she were sitting there with them both. She thought for a while and then said, 'Just be yourself, Gra, and the right boy will come along. That's what I think.'

'Hmm.' Grainne had to think about this for a while. 'Thanks, Mar.' And then she looked as if she'd just thought of something. 'Like David Crowley!'

'Well, you could ask him, I suppose …' Marie said doubtfully, wondering if Grainne had listened to a single word she'd said. David Crowley? She must be mad.

'Not me, Mar. You!'

'Me, what?'

'He likes you, Marie, and I'm sure he'd ask you. I think he's just a bit afraid, because you're so clever.'

'Well, that's an interesting theory, Gra,' Marie said. 'But I'd rather pluck both my eyebrows to nothing rather than ask David Crowley. Or maybe pull all my toenails out, what do you think?'

'He's not that bad.' Grainne giggled.

'Well, *you* have him then,' Marie teased, getting up. She took a furtive look at her watch. Nine o'clock already. Shit.

'Gra, look … I have to sit down and study. I have the Leaving Cert this year and I won't get good marks if I don't knuckle down now, before it's too late. So don't disturb me tonight, will you? No knocking on my door asking for the hairdryer or anything.' She couldn't believe herself, she really couldn't.

Grainne nodded. 'OK, I'll go and watch *That's Life* with Mrs D. I want to see what funny animals they have on this week.'

'Good idea. And I'll just go and study the Austro-Hungarian empire,' Marie said, rolling her eyes to heaven as if she could imagine nothing more boring. And then she turned to leave, trying not to hurry out of the room, then speeding into her bedroom, running around like a headless chicken trying to find any item of clothing that didn't look idiotic. She settled on her favourite pair of blue Levi's that she'd managed to extract from the bottom of Grainne's wardrobe and a blue batwing top that she loved. She hastily applied electric blue mascara and a pair of giant hoop earrings that Mrs D had given her for Christmas last year. She looked at herself in the mirror and wished she had a perm instead of looking like a relic from decades past, but Dada thought perms were 'cheap'. Her cheeks were flushed and her eyes bright, and she didn't look guilty, considering what she was doing. She didn't really *feel* guilty either, she thought to herself. Con had rung her and asked her out – it wasn't as if she'd tracked him down and forced him to invite her to a party. There was nothing for her to feel guilty about, was there? Her sister thought that he was her boyfriend, but he wasn't, and besides, Marie had no intention of letting anything happen. The two of them were just going to be friends. 'So that's okay, then,' she said to herself in the mirror.

She found her handbag and shoved lip balm and two pounds in it and opened her bedroom door as gently as she could. She didn't have to sneak down the stairs, because Mrs D and Grainne would hear nothing in Mrs D's flat at the back of the house, and Dada wasn't in his study. He was working late, and Marie knew he wouldn't look in on her when he came home if she turned her bedroom light off, which she had. Dada had a mortal fear of girls' bedrooms.

Biting her lip, she pulled open the front door, and then she was out on the step, the autumn wind threatening to snatch the door out of her hand. She managed to pull it gently closed, and then she walked quickly down the front path.

She was at the gate when a voice said, 'Where are you going?'

Shit. Marie debated for a second whether or not to pretend she hadn't heard, but then the game would be up. She turned around and said, 'Gra, be quiet,' putting a finger to her lips.

Grainne stood for a second on the front doorstep, then tiptoed down the path to the gate.

'I'm going to meet Claire for half an hour – OK?'

'Can I come?' She was standing in front of Marie, teeth chattering, her hair already coming loose from the bun. 'Please? I never get to do anything exciting like this.'

'What about Mrs D?'

'She's asleep on the sofa.'

Marie thought for a second. If she didn't go now, Con would think she wasn't coming and he'd go on without her. If she went without Grainne, her sister would have alerted half of Dublin to her disappearance and she'd get it in the neck from Dada. 'All right – but if you breathe a single word about this to another living soul, I will kill you, do you hear?' Marie hissed. 'Go and put some shoes on and a coat, and I'll meet you at the end of the road,' and before she could change her mind, Marie opened the gate and then closed it behind her, turning left towards the sea. As she did, the knot in her stomach grew tighter. She hadn't factored Grainne into things and she was sure to blab to someone, sooner or later, and then Marie would really be in trouble. Maybe she should just turn around and head for home. But she'd rather die than miss this party, she realised, Grainne or no Grainne. She'd rather die than miss seeing Con.

There was nobody about at this time of night, and the sea was an inky black, broken by a line of twinkling lights on the Howth Road, the other side of the bay. Marie stood by the side of the road, waiting. Her teeth chattered and she wished she'd brought a coat. Where on earth was Con?

'I found you.' Grainne appeared out of the gloom, in her old tennis shoes and a tiny cardigan.

'Gra, what on earth are you wearing? I told you to put a coat on,' Marie said.

'*You* haven't got one. And why are we standing here? Claire lives that way.' Grainne nodded in the other direction.

'We're getting a lift.'

A car came down the road towards her, slowing as it approached. She didn't think it was Con, because the car looked too posh: Marie thought it was a Mercedes. It drove slowly past, and she could see the driver peer out at her through the window. It was a middle-aged man. Then the car speeded up and headed towards Dalkey. Marie suddenly felt frightened. She didn't like being here. She looked at Grainne. Maybe this wasn't a good idea, she thought to herself. Maybe they should just go home.

She was about to turn around when a loud honking broke the silence, and a tiny Mini came hurtling down the hill, screeching to a halt beside her. There was a blast of laughter as the driver wound the window down. 'Taxi, love?' the guy inside it said, grinning, a head of light brown curls bobbing as he nodded his head in time to the music. He turned the radio down and hopped out of the car, pulling the seat forward to allow them in. 'Your carriage awaits,' he said with a flourish.

Marie hesitated for a moment, casting a glance at Grainne, who looked anxious, shifting from side to side, pulling the cardigan around her shoulders. 'Dada said we should never get into a car with strangers, Marie.'

'They're not strangers,' Marie said, trying to peer into the car to see if Con was actually in it, then seeing him sitting in the passenger seat, looking straight ahead, as if she wasn't there.

'Indeed we are not strangers, ladies. Seamus O'Loughlin, third-year student of the subject of Economic and Social Studies. Pleased to meet you both.' And Seamus beamed his most charming smile, extending a hand to Grainne and then Marie in turn.

Grainne hesitated before taking it and giving it a half-hearted shake.

'Get in, for God's sake,' Marie said to her eventually, pushing her into the dark interior of the tiny car and, when Grainne sat down by the window, bending down to climb in beside her. She stepped over a pair of slender, jeans-clad legs that belonged to a girl, before squeezing herself into the space made for her.

'Well, this is cosy,' the girl said dryly. Marie turned to see a girl with a chalk-white face and eyes rimmed in black, her hair a black quiff sticking up from her head. Grainne craned her neck to look at the girl and then sat back, as if she'd encountered an alien.

'Hi,' Marie said, trying to make up for her.

'Hi.' The girl said, smiling shyly. 'I'm Dee.'

'Marie. And this is Grainne.' Grainne was still trying to work out how she'd ended up in a car with complete strangers when a voice said, 'Hi, Gra – glad you could come along.' Con O'Sullivan turned around and looked into the back, where the three girls sat, squashed together. He'd had a haircut since she'd last seen him, and his dark curls were now tight around his head, and he was wearing the faded jacket and the PLO scarf. He still looked wrong-but-right and his eyes flicked briefly over Marie, almost as if he didn't see her, before smiling at Grainne.

'Con!' Grainne leaned forward in her seat and put her hand on his shoulder, giving it a squeeze. 'Marie told me we were going to Claire's, but this is much more exciting.'

'Good,' Con replied. 'That's the general idea.' And then, he turned around, and Seamus said, 'Hang onto your hats, girls!' With a screech of tyres, they were off, zooming along the coast road, and then inland to the mountains. Grainne chattered away at Con but Marie found that she couldn't speak. The streetlights whizzed past the window, the sky growing darker and the trees thicker as they wound their way up through Dundrum towards the mountains. Her stomach was in a tight knot. Why hadn't Con looked at her, even acknowledged that she was there? Why go to all the trouble of asking her out and then ignore her, chatting away to her sister instead. Maybe he'd have preferred if Grainne had just gone by herself, she reflected bitterly, before she reminded herself that he'd asked her first. Maybe he was annoyed that she'd turned him down the first time they'd met. Men didn't like that, she remembered Claire saying once – it was a blow to their egos. And worse, this was supposed to be her escape, her adventure and she'd dragged Grainne into it. She'd have to watch her sister like a hawk all night. She didn't understand things like alcohol – Marie still had nightmares about Granny's Christmas party, when Grainne had got hold of the Advocaat and swigged half the bottle, before throwing up on Granny's rubber plant. Marie had had to invent a stomach bug for her and bustle her home before Dada found out.

Marie turned to her left and caught Dee looking at Grainne and Con, smiling to herself as Grainne leaned forward to talk to him, her breasts almost spilling out of the too-small cardigan, her hand reaching out to touch him on the arm every now and again. It was mortifying, the way she launched herself at Con, but he didn't seem to mind. In fact, he talked much more easily to Grainne than he did to Marie, laughing at her silly chatter and talking to her as if she were a really good friend, telling her all about his final year in Trinity and how boring economics and politics was. How come the most he could manage with Marie was a grumpy comment every now and again? Marie could see now why Grainne had this thing about Con – maybe it wasn't so stupid after all, she thought miserably as she sat there, trapped in the little car. Mum, please don't let anything happen, please, she found herself thinking. I need you now, because I don't know what to do.

And then, in a brief gap in Grainne's chatter, Con looked

at her and said, 'You OK?' and she realised that he didn't look at Grainne like that at all.

'I'm fine,' Marie said, unable to return his gaze, looking out the window instead.

'So, tell me, ladies, where did you have the great misfortune to meet my good friend here?' Seamus said, his eyes amused as he looked into the rear-view mirror.

'Oh, didn't you hear, Seamus? I hung out with the cream of Dublin society over the summer,' Con said in a mock high-pitched voice, 'and I met Marie and Grainne at Seaview.'

Seamus looked astonished, leaning back in the driver's seat. 'Seaview, you say? How very *Brideshead*. Tell me, Con, were there servants, crustless sandwiches, ice in the G and T?'

'And a brace of pheasant before lunch,' Con responded, before the two of them dissolved in laughter.

'Why are you laughing at us?' Grainne sounded a bit hurt. 'I've only ever eaten pheasant once,' she added. 'And it tasted horrible.'

There was a snort of laughter again from the front seat, before Seamus said, 'Ah, we're only teasing, girls. We're just not used to mingling with high society, that's all. They don't have too many pheasant where I'm from, in the glorious city of Limerick.'

'What about all those posh girls in Trinity?' Marie piped up, unable to help herself. 'The place is coming down with them.' So why us? was the unspoken question.

There was a brief silence, before Seamus said, 'Ah, but none with your undoubted charm and sophistication, ladies, eh, Con?' His eyes crinkled as he looked in the rear-view.

Con said nothing, just shifted in his seat and glared out the window. What's your problem? Marie thought.

'Yes, we are charming, aren't we, Mar?' Grainne giggled flirtatiously, nudging her sister. 'No one's ever called me sophisticated though,' she said dreamily.

'Well, consider it done,' Con said suddenly, turning around and flashing her a smile. 'Because you are charming and witty and fun.'

Jesus Christ, Marie thought, as her sister simpered beside her.

After what seemed like hours, the little car wheezed its way around a bend and shot in through two large, stone pillars into a huge driveway filled with sleek cars. Seamus squeezed the Mini in between a Mercedes and a Rolls Royce. 'Who did you say owned this place?' he said.

'Katie Fitzgerald – her dad's something in aeroplanes,' Dee replied.

They all sat in silence and watched people drifting in through the front door, before Grainne said, 'This place is like a palace. Do you think somebody royal lives here, like in Buckingham Palace?'

'No, Grainne,' Con said patiently. 'They're just very wealthy, that's all.'

'Oh,' Grainne said, looking disappointed.

'But it sure looks like a palace inside,' Seamus said, opening the door and clambering out. 'A twentieth-century one.'

They all stood in the huge hall, with its double-height ceiling, a massive bronze chandelier hanging from the centre.

Marie looked down at her jeans, at her batwing top, and suddenly felt stupid. How on earth could she have thought she was sophisticated? She looked like a total hick, she thought miserably, looking at a group of thin girls drinking wine and smoking Balkan Sobranie Black Russian cigarettes – Dada would kill her if she drank wine, Marie thought, eyeing one girl in a bright green jumpsuit, her hair framing her perfect face, never mind smoking cigarettes.

'Jesus Christ, what kind of a party is this?' Seamus was saying, eyeing a large silver tray of canapés being borne along by a snooty-looking waiter.

'Katie said it was just something casual,' Con said faintly, as a gaggle of girls in ruched satin passed, looking like birds of paradise in glowing colours, each with an identical French plait, pinned at the end with a huge bow.

'What's her idea of formal?' Seamus laughed. 'C'mon, Grainne, let's go and eat all of their free food. I need to stock up for the next week until I get my grant money. We don't get much to eat in Limerick, you know.' He winked at Con and took Grainne by the elbow. Marie saw the wink and looked down at her feet in their black suede loafers. She didn't want to catch Con's eye.

'But, I want to talk to Con,' Grainne protested.

'Ah, you do not, he's an awful old bore.' Seamus laughed, half-dragging her towards the kitchen, leaving Con and Marie alone at the edge of the room, looking at the partygoers laughing and drinking. They didn't say anything for a few moments, then Con caught her eye. 'Want to get out of here?' he said.

Marie hesitated, looking in the direction of the kitchen.

'She'll be OK. Seamus will keep an eye on her.'

'Well …' Marie nodded slowly.

'Great.' He smiled at her for the first time that entire night, and he led her through the crowds. 'Sorry, excuse us,' he said, as he weaved his way through, reaching a hand out behind him, which she grabbed hold of. The air in the room was stuffy and the overwhelming smell of Opium made Marie's stomach heave. Claire loved Opium – she'd saved up for six months to buy a bottle and she arrived every day drenched in a cloud of the stuff. Marie didn't wear any perfume, apart from the odd squirt of Mum's L'air du Temps. Her perfume bottles were still on the dressing table in Dada's bedroom, which he'd left untouched since Mum died. Her dressing gown was still on the back of the bedroom door and her jewellery box, with its strands of pearls and her diamond and sapphire engagement ring, on the top shelf of the wardrobe, beside Dada's Vick's inhaler and supply of collars. Marie would go in every now and again, when Dada was safely at work, and open the jewellery box and take out the pearls, feeling them chilly and heavy around her neck. She didn't like them, and neither had Mum, she remembered. Mum had complained about how fusty they were, but as they'd been a present from Granny, she'd had to wear them. 'Your father loves his mother more than he loves me,' she'd said once to Marie, then made her swear not to repeat it.

'You OK?' Con mouthed above the music. Marie nodded, but she was beginning to panic in the press of bodies, and the heat was suffocating. Finally, she broke through the crowd and she could feel the chilly September air through the open French windows as they went out into the garden.

The patio was in darkness and Marie took in great gulps of cold air. She leaned against something solid, and when she looked up, a Grecian lady with a naked torso, clutching the folds of her robe around her hips, was staring back at her.

'It's Aphrodite, the goddess of love.' He was standing half in the shadow of an elaborate pergola, a cloud of yellow roses twisted around the frame.

'Oh.'

'Yes, I know Greek mythology. Maybe you find that surprising, in a culchie like myself.'

'So, you're a culchie. At least now I know something about you.'

He shrugged. 'There's nothing much to know. I'm really not very interesting. I come from the middle of nowhere, a one-horse town.'

'And you have an attachment to that chip on your shoulder as a result,' Marie said smartly. 'I don't care where you were brought up or what you know about ancient history or any of that stuff.' She sounded convincing, she knew, but even as she said the words, she wondered if they were true. All she'd ever known was Seaview Road, her big house, the tennis courts, the beach. What would she know about the world beyond it?

'Oh, really? I suppose that's easy enough when you come from the privileged classes of south County Dublin. Bet it was all concerts and galleries and lunches in the golf club for you. Or – don't tell me – sailing. I can see you going about the westward buoy.'

'Actually, I hate sailing, but yes, my mother brought me to art galleries – so what? I'm not going to apologise for it,'

Marie said hotly. 'It's not all about class and money, you know,' she said, thinking of Mum, and the little house she'd grown up in on Inisheer, and the stories she used to tell them about cutting turf all summer long. 'You don't know anything at all about me, so you have no right to judge. And please, don't start quoting Aristotle at me, because I won't be impressed. I really won't. The only person who will be impressed is you.'

'What do you mean?'

'I mean, I think that you're just trying too hard.'

'I am?'

'Yes, you are. Remember all that stuff about Norman Mailer?' Marie didn't usually talk to anyone like this, but there was something in Con O'Sullivan that made her want to: something unbelievably irritating that just made her lose reason, that made the words spill out.

He looked enraged for a moment, but then brightened, once he thought of a response. 'Remember when I asked you out and you said no?'

It was Marie's turn to look sheepish now. 'Yes, well that's because I find you very annoying.'

He smiled. 'Fair enough. I find you annoying too.' There was a silence then and the two of them looked at each other and grinned. 'Truce?' Con said.

'Truce,' Marie agreed.

When he saw Marie shivering, he came over and unwrapped the PLO scarf from around his neck, and put it around her shoulders. He'd stopped looking angry now and instead there was another expression on his face. He looked a bit embarrassed. 'There. Very fashionable.'

'I've always wanted a PLO scarf,' Marie said.

'It suits you.' And then he sighed and rummaged in his jacket, pulling out a bent-looking rollup and a Zippo lighter. He put the flame to the cigarette and inhaled, then exhaled into the night air, before offering her the cigarette.

She took a deep pull and handed it back to him, her head already dizzy.

'So,' he said.

'So,' Marie replied. 'Let's start again.'

'OK,' he said warily.

There was a long silence and then they both burst out laughing. Marie took the cigarette again and took another pull. 'Careful, you'll get addicted.' He smiled.

She shrugged and there was another long silence while she racked her brain, trying to think of something interesting to say to him. She felt the need to impress Con, the need to make an impact, so that his face would brighten and he'd nod and laugh, the way he did with her sister. 'I know. I'll tell you something about myself. Something I haven't told anybody, and then you tell me something.'

'Why?'

'Because then we can find out more about each other, the way normal people do. And we can stop the bickering.'

'What's wrong with the bickering? I quite enjoy it.'

'It's stupid and trivial and … and …' Marie hesitated.

'And what?'

'And I think we have more interesting things to say to each other.'

He took a long pull on his cigarette and gave an enigmatic smile. 'Fine. Shoot.'

'Right.' Marie thought for a bit. 'I hate water.'

'What, you hate drinking it? That's hardly a personal revelation,' he snorted.

'No, I meant swimming in it,' Marie said. 'I actually have a bit of a phobia. And before you say it, that's a big admission for me.'

'I'm honoured,' he said, taking another drag on the cigarette and handing it to her. She shook her head.

'I did a sailing course a couple of years ago. I nearly drowned.'

'Oh. Really?'

'Yes. We had to do a test to see if we could swim in the water fully clothed. I remember that Claire, my friend, wore a T-shirt and shorts and, like an eejit, I wore jeans and a jumper and these really clumpy blue basketball boots. The minute I got into the water, I just sank. It was like I had lead weights attached to my arms. I just remember flailing around, and I thought I'd go under. The instructor had to pull me out.'

There was a silence while Con digested this. 'Thanks, I guess,' he said finally.

'Your turn,' Marie said.

He gave a grimace of distaste. 'I don't like playing games,' he muttered, but when Marie didn't reply, he gave a long sigh. 'OK, then.' There was another long pause. 'I've actually never been to an art gallery.'

'You haven't? Well, maybe there weren't any near you.'

'Eh, no. I spent my youth in the pub.' He shrugged. 'My brother and me used to spend Saturday afternoons filling skips with mineral bottles for a penny a go.'

'Did your parents own a pub?'

'Not exactly.' He gave a thin smile. 'My mother was fond of the drink, shall we say.'

'Oh.' Marie was at a loss for words. 'That must have been hard,' was all she could manage. 'What about your dad?'

'That's another story.'

'And what about your brother? Is he a student too?'

He shook his head. 'Look, can we leave it? That's enough truth-telling for me for one night.' He looked down the garden, towards the glittering lights of Dublin at the foot of the mountain, a muscle working in his jaw.

What did he mean, 'that's enough'? Was there more? What wasn't he telling her? Was he really telling the truth? He certainly looked upset now, and Marie went over to him and tucked her arm into his. He resisted at first, then relaxed, letting her tuck her hand into the crook of his elbow, resting her head on his shoulder.

'I suppose you think it's a bit exciting,' he said. 'A bit dangerous.'

Marie sighed. 'Actually, no. It doesn't sound like that at all.' She waited and then said, 'Was it that bad?'

He nodded, and she squeezed his arm again and then he kissed the top of her head just as she lifted her face to look at him, so the kiss landed on the tip of her nose. And then he was pulling her towards him, wrapping his arms around her, so that she had to rest her head against his chest. She could hear his heart, inside his T-shirt, a steady thump.

'Will you just look at those stars?' he said suddenly, head tilting upwards. Marie looked up and the sky was filled with them, great washes of silver across the sky, a puff of cotton wool for the Milky Way.

'Con?'

'Yeah?' He looked down at her and then he kissed her, gently on the lips. She had never been kissed like that before, softly. She'd only been subjected to David Crowley's kissing, where he prised her mouth open and attempted to stick his tongue as far down her throat as it would go. This didn't even compare, she thought, as Con kissed her again and again, very gently. And then he pushed her hair away from her face and looked at her for a long time, and she felt that he could see right inside her. And then the kissing started again and, after a while, she felt a hand just under her top, a cold finger stroking the flesh at the top of her jeans, then pulling at the waistband, gently, his fingers now stroking downwards towards the top of her knickers. She sucked in a deep breath.

'Do you want me to stop?' Con's breath was hot in her ear.

'No, it's just cold,' she replied, because she didn't want him to stop what he was doing, not at all.

Suddenly, there was a noise from behind them that made them both jump apart. Marie turned around in time to see one of the French doors swinging open, then banging softly shut again, the faint flicker of a shadow disappearing into the darkness.

The spell was broken then. 'C'mon, it's freezing,' Con said, putting an arm around her and leading her gently back to the party. Dazed, Marie followed him meekly into the house.

It was bedlam in the living room. A girl was standing on a table, a bottle of rum in her hand, singing along to 'Jack and Diane', and a boy was lying on top of another girl on the sofa, and he seemed to be taking her clothes off. Marie had never been anywhere like this, but she couldn't admit it to Con: that the only parties she'd ever been to had been those awful ones at the canoe club and Granny's horrible Christmas drinks with the neighbours in their golfing sweaters and a rash of priests. She felt light-headed. She'd never known that such a world existed, and it was as if a door had opened in her mind, and through that door, she could glimpse a future that looked so much larger than anything she might have imagined. Her bedroom, her house with all its nooks and crannies, the path between home and school, the little laneways around the town, suddenly seemed very far away. There was an alternative to her lonely life lying on her bed, reading Jane Austen. The idea was suddenly extraordinary to her, but she also found that she wanted to run for the safety of home. She wasn't sure that she did want to live this other life, when she could simply imagine it instead, the way she always had done, with her maps of Australia and her novels, too afraid to think about any other kind of future. A future without responsibility for Grainne.

So, even though Con O'Sullivan was rude, he was also the most exciting person she'd ever met.

She was a bit confused about what had happened on the patio though. He'd kissed her, and then he'd stopped. Didn't he like it? Maybe she'd put him off by playing that stupid truth-telling game. He certainly hadn't wanted to tell her about his mother and father, or his brother, that was for sure – it was the first time he'd even mentioned that he had one. She wondered if he was different to Con. Maybe they were a bit like Grainne and herself – driving each other mad, but somehow stuck to each other, like limpets.

And then she remembered Grainne and her heart fluttered

in her chest. She'd better find her. Without stopping to see where Con was, Marie went quickly into the kitchen, where Seamus was holding court, pint glass in one hand, chicken drumstick in the other. There was no sign of Grainne and she was worried. Grainne always loved the food at parties, especially if it was like this, she thought, taking in the trays of canapés. Where *was* she?

'Ah, the young lovers,' Seamus intoned. 'Here have a drumstick.' And then he put an arm around Marie. 'Marie, this man is too old for you, and totally disreputable, but Uncle Seamus will take it upon himself to look after you, to cast the odd fatherly glance in your direction.' He was drunk, Marie could tell, because he was slurring his speech and grinning stupidly. She began to wonder how exactly they'd make it home in his car.

'You're her uncle, you can't cast fatherly glances,' a voice said. Marie turned to see Dee standing there, a large glass of red wine in her hand. She had a slight smile on her face. It wasn't a friendly smile, but nor was it unfriendly exactly, it was just … hard to read.

'Well, the odd, uncle-like glance in your direction then,' Seamus corrected himself. 'Marie, do you partake in the demon alcohol?'

'Ehm, no,' Marie said. 'Is there any 7-Up?'

'Ah, out of the mouths of babes.' Seamus smiled, turning to rummage among the bottles piled next to the sink, lifting a half-empty bottle of champagne up and examining it for a few moments before taking a big swig.

'How old are you?' Dee said.

Marie blushed to the roots of her hair. 'Seventeen.'

'Jeez, Con, find someone your own age,' Dee said, the tip of her quiff tilting back as she took a sip of her wine. 'Wouldn't you think you'd have learned?'

There was a deafening silence in the kitchen. Marie looked at the lovely terracotta floor tiles and wished a big hole would open in them to swallow her up. Eventually, she muttered, 'I need to go and find my sister.'

At this, Seamus said, 'Oh, yeah, Grainne. She went out to see you a few moments ago, but then she went back upstairs. Something about needing money for poker.'

'She what? She doesn't play poker.'

'Sorry, I didn't know …' Seamus began, but Marie was gone, clumping up the stairs, hopping over bodies, saying 'excuse me, excuse me,' over and over again, and wondering where on earth Grainne could be. And Seamus – she should never have allowed him to keep an eye on her – he hadn't a clue. He probably thought she was a bit ditzy, not … but what did she expect him to know anyway? She was the only person who could look after Grainne properly.

She found Grainne in one of the bedrooms, in her bra and knickers. There were a dozen others with her sitting on the bed and on two armchairs, in various states of undress, an empty bottle on the ground at their feet. When the door opened, Grainne turned around. She didn't have her usual big smile on her face, and her eyes were red, as if she'd been crying. 'I'm playing strip poker, Mar,' she said.

'Gra, put your clothes on, it's time to go home,' Marie said gently.

'No, thank you, Marie,' Grainne said. 'You're not the only one who can have fun, you know.'

'What does that mean?'

Grainne looked at the ground, her cheeks flushed.

'It means leave her alone and stop being a spoilsport,' a voice came from half-behind the bed, and a young guy with red cheeks and a shock of blond hair sat up. He was wearing only a pair of boxer shorts. 'We're just getting to the fun bit.'

'It might be your idea of fun,' Marie said, a needle of anger rising in her. 'But it's not mine or my sister's.'

'Steady on, pet, no need to get your knickers in a twist.' There was a snicker from one of the half-dressed girls.

'You haven't a clue, any of you,' Marie muttered, stepping into the room. She walked briskly over to Grainne and took her by the arm. 'Gra, let's go. Now.'

'But I don't want to,' Grainne said. 'I like it here and it's fun and you can't make me.'

It sure doesn't look like you're having fun, Marie thought.

'Yeah, you can't make her,' the red-cheeked guy said again. 'What's the deal anyway, are you her mother?'

'Oh, my mother's gone to heaven,' Grainne said, and then, when they all laughed, she burst into tears. 'Why are they being so mean, Mar?'

'Because they're idiots, Grainne. Now, where are your clothes?' Marie leaned over the bed to see Grainne's cardigan on the other side. She picked it up and scouted around for her T-shirt, which she found under a pile of clothes, and then her jeans, scrunched up in a ball under a girl's feet. Marie tugged them out, hard, and didn't bother apologising when the girl protested. 'Ow.'

'Let's go to the bathroom, Grainne, and get dressed,' she

said, thanking God, as she led Grainne out of the room, that she didn't protest. 'What a complete prude,' she heard as she pulled the door closed behind them.

'I am not a prude,' Grainne protested as Marie pushed her along the corridor. 'At least, I don't think so …'

'Into the bathroom, Grainne. Hurry up,' she ordered her sister, when she located the right door, pushing her into the room with her clothes and banging the door shut.

Grainne meekly complied and, within five minutes, reappeared at the door, clothed, cheeks flushed. 'I'm ready.'

'Gra, have you any idea how silly it is to take off your clothes like that? I mean, anything could happen,' Marie began crossly.

Grainne hung her head. 'I wanted to join in, Mar. I didn't want to be the only one left out, the way I always am. Everyone else was doing it. And look,' she said, putting her hand in her pocket and pulling out two crumpled pound notes. 'I won two hands of poker.'

'Oh, Gra, you silly girl.' Marie sighed.

'Should I give back the money?'

'God no! Keep it. Just … put it away. Now, let's go or we'll be in big trouble.'

Marie turned to go down the stairs, and she only half-heard what Grainne said next. 'He said if I took my knickers off, he'd give me more, but I said no. I'm not that stupid.'

Seamus was standing miserably at the bottom of the stairs when Marie appeared with Grainne. 'I'm sorry, Marie, I had no idea.' He shifted anxiously from foot to foot.

'It's fine. I shouldn't have left her,' Marie said. 'Look, I think it's time we went home.'

'Sure, I'll go and put the heater on in the car for a sec, to warm it up,' he said, getting up. Marie didn't like to ask if he should be driving in his condition, because she had no choice. She had to get Grainne home and into bed before anyone spotted them. Why, oh, why had she let her sister come? She always ruined everything.

Marie looked around to see if there was any sign of Con.

'He's gone outside for a smoke,' Seamus said, as if reading her mind.

'Oh,' Marie said quietly. She wanted to go and say goodbye, but she didn't dare leave Grainne again. She thought it was a bit strange that he hadn't come with her to look for her sister, and she tried not to think about what had happened in the garden, because now it felt a bit like a dream.

'Why don't you take a seat right there,' Seamus nodded at the huge leather sofa just inside the hall door, 'and I'll go and warm the car up for you.' He pulled on his jacket then, only swaying slightly as he put his arms into the sleeves. 'Whoops. Night air will wake me up,' he said, winking at Grainne.

Oh, Jesus. Seamus was nice, though, Marie thought. There was something very decent about him, and she wondered if she could be interested in him, but when she thought about Seamus, she didn't feel as if her insides would melt, or that her thoughts were flying about all over the place, like butterflies.

Marie and Grainne sat down together on the sofa, side by side. Grainne looked miserable, her face pinched. It wasn't just the poker, Marie knew – Grainne had never exactly been self-conscious. There was something else.

Then Grainne turned to her. 'Mar?'

'Yes, Grainne,' Marie said hopefully.

'You don't have to mind me all the time. I wanted to play that game, and you came in and stopped me. I can mind myself, you know.'

'Do you know what you were doing, Gra?'

'I was only doing what you were doing,' Grainne said suddenly, her face contorted with anger.

'What—' Marie began, but they were interrupted by an icy blast from the front door, and Seamus reappeared, rubbing his hands together, a woolly hat now on his head. He looked a bit more together. 'Ladies, your carriage awaits.'

Grainne got up and followed Seamus, without even glancing back at Marie. She climbed into the back seat of the Mini, which was now belching out fumes into the driveway. Marie stood on the doorstep for a few moments, taking in deep breaths of the chilly autumn air.

And then Con was beside her. 'I was looking for you. Were you leaving without saying goodbye?'

'I—' Marie began, but he interrupted her. 'So you believe what Dee said, then?'

'Oh, Con, I can't, not now. Grainne needs to go home and so do I.' She stepped onto the gravel of the driveway, which crunched underfoot, and then felt his hand on her arm. His grip was tight – too tight – and she wanted to tell him that it was hurting, but she felt herself being pulled backwards, until she was just in front of him, his breath warm on her hair. 'Don't believe everything you hear, Marie.'

'I have to go,' Marie said, pulling her arm out of his grip. She walked towards the Mini, not looking back, and got into the passenger seat beside Seamus. She didn't turn to Grainne, but looked straight ahead.

'Right,' Seamus said cheerfully. 'I can tell it's going to be a laugh a minute on the way home,' and with that, he accelerated, sending a spray of gravel up behind him as they shot off down the drive. He was silent, thankfully, as the car wound its way down the hill towards the crossroads, the lights of the city twinkling in front of them. There wasn't another car on the road and the night was inky black around them as they drove along. Marie's mind was a jumble of thoughts, all racing through her head. That kiss out in the garden, Grainne sitting there in that bedroom, in her bra and knickers, cheeks flushed with excitement, the noise and colour of the party, the sophistication of the champagne and Balkan Sobranie – she felt light-headed, as if she'd been drinking champagne herself. She could still feel the slight ache in her arm where Con had gripped it, and as she thought about it, her stomach flipped.

'She's asleep.' Seamus's voice seemed suddenly loud and Marie turned around to see Grainne, eyes closed, mouth open, emitting a little snore. Her head was rolling back and then tilting forward with the movement of the car and Marie wanted to put a cushion under her sister's chin so she wouldn't have a sore neck when she woke up, but she figured that she couldn't ask Seamus to stop.

'Marie, I think you're a really nice girl,' Seamus said, peering out through the windscreen, which had misted up in the night air.

'Thanks. I think,' Marie said. 'How well can you see out that windscreen?'

He grinned. 'Well enough.' And then there was a pause. 'Can I give you some fatherly advice?'

'I thought you were my uncle,' Marie attempted a joke.

'Well, uncle-ly advice, then.' He sucked in a deep breath and glanced at her quickly before turning his attention back to the road. 'Dee was fucking rude back there, but she has a point.'

'What do you mean?"

'Con has this thing going on. This kind of tortured soul routine and … look, all I'll say is that I've seen it before. That's not to say that he doesn't like you – he does. Who wouldn't?' Seamus smiled. 'But he kind of adopts people, and then, well …'

People like me, you mean, Marie thought bleakly. People who don't know any better.

'And when they get too close, he doesn't like it. And then he drops people. And you're too nice a girl to be dropped.'

'Oh.' Marie looked at Seamus who was hunched over the steering wheel now, a look of concentration on his face. He didn't look at her as he continued, 'I just want to help, because … '

'Because I'm a nice girl and you like me. Thanks,' Marie said, 'but I can manage fine, Seamus.'

Seamus pulled in now as he spotted the Martello Tower at Seaview.

'Marie—' he began, but she interrupted him.

'Thanks for the lift, Seamus.' And then, before he could say anything more, she turned around in her seat and gave Grainne a nudge with her hand. 'Gra? We're home.'

Grainne's eyes flicked open and, for a second, she was her

usual self, that happy expression on her face. And then she looked at Marie and her eyes clouded over. 'Thanks, Seamus, I had a great time,' she said getting out of the car.

'Great to meet you, Grainne.'

She didn't even manage a smile.

Marie didn't catch Seamus's eye when she closed the door gently behind them. She didn't want to talk to him, because she couldn't decide if she liked him any more. If she could trust him.

'Have you got your key?' Grainne turned to her.

'Shush,' Marie hissed. 'You'll wake Dada and then we'll be for it.' Marie twiddled her key in the lock, the way she always did, because there was a knack to it, and slipped inside.

She pulled Grainne in and leaned against the hall door for a moment, taking in the silence, the darkness that fell around them both. They were safe.

And then the light flicked on and Dada was standing at the bottom of the stairs. He was wearing his red stripy dressing gown, but it might as well have been his judge's cloak.

Marie stopped dead, blood pumping in her ears. She reached out a hand, as if to protect her sister.

'Where have you both been?'

'Ehm, we went for a walk, didn't we, Grainne?'

'A walk. At …' he looked at his watch, 'half-past midnight.'

'Yes,' Marie whispered.

'You and your sister were supposed to be in your beds at ten o'clock, but instead you disappeared for three hours. Where did you go, Marie? Don't lie to me.' His voice was low, but she knew that tone.

'I went to a party.'

'Where?'

'In Stepaside.'

'And you thought it wise to take your sister to this party in Stepaside?'

No, Marie thought. It was very unwise indeed, as it turned out.

'She didn't make me, Dada, I asked her to go,' Grainne broke in, but was silenced with a gesture.

There was a pause, and then he started firing questions at her. With whom? For how long? In whose car? She answered as briefly as she could, sensing him growing frustrated, hands tightening around the tie of his dressing gown.

And then there was a flurry of movement beside him and Mrs D appeared, in her dressing gown. They'd never seen her like that, without her housecoat on and her hair tightly wound into a bun. Now, it hung down her back, a long plait of silver hair. 'The Lord have mercy, the two of you are home. I thought you'd both be lying in a ditch somewhere—'

'Thank you, Mrs Delaney,' Dada interrupted. 'Girls, I'm sure you'll want to thank Mrs Delaney for staying up until this hour to make sure you came home safely.'

'Thanks, Mrs Delaney,' the two girls muttered.

'Maybe they'd have a cup of tea and a scone, I have some in the kitchen,' Mrs D began, fingering the collar of her dressing gown nervously.

'There'll be no need, Mrs Delaney, the girls are heading up directly to bed. Thank you.'

Muttering under her breath, Mrs D disappeared in the direction of her flat. Dada gave Marie a look of such bitter disappointment, she felt like a naughty five-year-old. 'Now, off to bed the two of you. I will deal with you both in the morning.'

The two of them sloped off up the stairs, Grainne first. At the top of the stairs, Dada called, 'Marie?'

The two girls turned around and Dada said, 'Grainne, off you go.'

Grainne shot Marie a look and then shuffled off to her bedroom, closing the door firmly behind her.

Dada stood in silence for a while, before saying, 'Marie, I don't know what possessed you, but if you do anything like that again with your sister, I will hold you personally responsible for whatever happens, do you understand?'

'No.' The words were out of her mouth before Marie could prevent them.

At first, Dada didn't react, as if she'd actually said 'yes'. There was a deafening silence, while Marie waited for the volcano to erupt, but instead, he said quietly, 'What did you say?'

'I said no.'

'What, exactly, have I not made clear to you Marie?'

'Grainne is my sister, but she's *your* daughter. Why do I have to be responsible for her?' Marie's hands were balled into tight fists. 'Why don't you try taking some responsibility yourself, instead of hiding away? If you weren't buried in that study of yours, you'd know what it's like to have to look out for her all the time.'

Dada looked perplexed for a moment. 'Your mother …'

'Yes, I know, Mum said I was to look after her and I always have, but I seem to be the only one, Dada. And I can't do it any more.' The tears came now, rolling down her cheeks. She knew that she wasn't just crying about Grainne, but there was no way on earth she would ever tell Dada what the matter was. Not really.

'You're stronger than your sister, Marie,' Dada said, this time a bit more softly. 'I know that it's a burden sometimes, but she needs you. I need you.'

Marie looked up at Dada, who was fiddling with the belt of his dressing gown. 'Well, maybe I don't want to be needed any more,' she said bitterly. 'Maybe it's time you managed on your own.'

And, without stopping to see his reaction, Marie stomped up the stairs, her footsteps muffled by the thick carpet, feeling his eyes bore into her from behind. She didn't go to the bathroom to brush her teeth; instead, she went straight into her bedroom and threw herself down on the bed. And she thought that she hated Dada right then. She just hated him. Not just for acting like some old Victorian, or even for making her look after her sister, but just for disappearing like that, for all of those years. I'm lonely, she thought, as she looked out into the night sky. I'm lonely and I don't want to be any more.

And then she heard the sobs from Grainne's room, and her heart sank. Of course, she'd heard everything.

Chapter 4

October was a very long month. Marie spent it walking to school by herself, then wandering back by herself, before eating a lonely supper, then telling Mrs D that she was going up to her room to study. There, she would lie on her bed and stare at the ceiling, or doodle in her diary, or look at the photo of Mum and Frank the dog and ask it what to do. It didn't answer – and she wasn't expecting it to – but she found herself wanting her mother more than ever before. Mum would know what to do, she thought. She'd know whether Con was too old or whether there was something wrong with him; maybe she'd disapprove, tell her that he wasn't right for her, but that'd be fine, because at least it'd be something. Not like Dada, who had simply told her the morning after the party that she was grounded for a whole month and that there was to be 'no discussion on the matter'. Gavel hammered. Trial over.

And Grainne had refused to speak to her. Every time Marie appeared in the kitchen, Grainne would get up and take whatever she was doing elsewhere; she didn't set foot in Marie's room, to dig around under her bed or to try to destroy her make-up, and Marie found herself wishing that she would. She'd told Dada that she didn't want to be responsible for her any more, but she hadn't meant it, she told herself. She really hadn't.

She'd tried to reason with Grainne, but her sister wouldn't listen, and then she'd gone in one day and found that Grainne had defaced all the animal photos she loved to cut out of magazines. All the cute Labradors and spaniels, slashed with the sharp end of the scissors or scribbled all over with a blue biro, the point digging holes in the paper. Then Grainne had started to hang around with Imelda all the time, sitting with her and her idiotic friends every lunchtime, laughing as if she got their jokes, and then looking puzzled when she thought they weren't looking. Marie knew that it wouldn't end well with Imelda, but what she didn't know was how or when. And, because Grainne wouldn't talk to her, she'd just have to wait, that feeling of doom in her head every time she saw them together.

Once, she'd knocked on her sister's bedroom door and tried to speak to her. 'Go away,' Grainne had said from the other side.

'Gra, I'm sorry, I didn't mean to say what I said, it's just—'

'I don't want to hear from you. I'm not talking to you, because you told me a big lie. I thought you liked me, Mar. I thought you were my friend.'

'I am your friend, it's just—'

'You took Con, and he was my boyfriend.'

'Grainne, it wasn't like that,' she said through the closed door. She didn't want to spell it out, that Con wasn't Grainne's boyfriend. He'd asked her, Marie, to the party, not Grainne. He'd kissed *her*, not Grainne and … Anyway, she didn't want to forget it, even though he'd done a disappearing act after the party and she didn't know whether this was because he'd found her disappointing. Maybe she was an awful kisser, like David, all rubber lips and snakey tongue. Or maybe she was too dull, with all her chat about the Brontës. Too earnest. Or maybe Claire was right, and she was just being a drip, sitting around, waiting to be called. The fact that it made her feel sick all the time was neither here nor there. She felt fluey: hot one minute and cold the next, and her stomach kept churning. She kept sighing, too, as if her heart would come out through her mouth. She had no idea what was wrong with her, but she wasn't sure she liked feeling like this. 'Lovesick' was how she'd describe it, like Emma Bovary, or Thérèse Raquin – not that she'd been able to read her books lately. She just hadn't felt like it.

One day, she'd decided that she couldn't wait any longer. She'd waited until Mrs D went into town in the afternoon to the shops and to meet her friends for a cup of tea, then sneaked down to the hall and opened the door to the cupboard under the stairs. She'd got as far as dialling his number, but then she'd heard the front door open and slammed the phone down, holding her breath until Mrs D's footsteps retreated into the kitchen.

Maybe it was for the best, she concluded miserably, trudging up the stairs to her bedroom. She hadn't really recognised the Marie who went to parties with strangers. She was reading about the Paris riots of 1968 in history at the moment and she thought that she wouldn't have made a particularly good revolutionary, because she'd have been afraid of being on the Champs-Élysées after nine o'clock at night. She'd used to feel a bit ashamed of herself, that she couldn't be a bit more adventurous. She'd thought that there was no point in being a revolutionary, because she'd only have to return after storming the barricades to make Grainne her nightly hot chocolate. But when she'd been in the garden with Con at the party, when she'd kissed him under the statue of Aphrodite, she'd had a brief glimpse of someone else, another Marie, someone bolder, braver, ready to take chances, to take on the world.

The Marie she was now was altogether more familiar, and her world fitted like an old coat. She'd never see herself in a Crombie or a Harrington jacket – her world was the equivalent of the gabardine coat they had to wear to school in the winter: hers was worn, heavy and dull in colour, but she'd take it out of the wardrobe every year because she was used to it. She didn't really mind, she told herself; it was the same when Claire went on about moving to New York 'far away from this dump' – she knew she wouldn't be going, so it seemed easier to ignore it, and to keep on wearing the coat.

*

And then, after that long, dreary month when not one single thing happened, everything happened all at once.

It was almost Hallowe'en and the entire school was

squashed into the too-small assembly hall. Marie's thoughts drifted along as she watched Fidelma O'Reilly read the morning's reading, her tidy plait and immaculate uniform a rebuke to the rest of them in their tatty jumpers with torn sleeves. Marie had a big iron mark on her skirt from the one and only time she'd tried to iron it, a big black stain in the shape of an iron. Mrs D had nearly killed her. Why was it the nuns always liked girls like Fidelma? Maybe because she was a nun in waiting, she mused as Sister Aloysius took to the lectern, staring at them forbiddingly over the rims of her spectacles. Claire nudged her in the ribs. 'Here comes the lecture.'

Sure enough, Sister Aloysius adjusted the front of her veil, pushed her glasses up on her nose and began. 'Ladies, as we all know, some of you will be leaving St Rachel's for the last time in a few short months, going out into the world and making your own way. The world can seem dangerous sometimes, and you will be faced with a large number of choices.' Here she stopped, for dramatic effect, before continuing. 'The choices you make at this time will be very important, particularly on the moral plane. It's a Godless world, and you must go into it and hold your faith intact.' There was a titter of laughter from the back row and Sister Aloysius, without looking up from her speech, said, 'Imelda O'Brien, I know it's you.'

There was a small murmur and another squeak of repressed laughter. Marie turned around, hoping to God it wasn't Grainne. That squeak sounded remarkably like one of hers. '"Satan himself masquerades as an angel of light. It is not surprising, then, if his servants also masquerade as servants of righteousness. Their end will be what their actions deserve."'

And here, Sister Aloysius raised a bony finger and pointed towards the back of the room. 'Do I make myself clear?'

There was a general murmur of 'Yes, Sister.' Sister Aloysius looked pleased with herself, adjusted her veil again and returned to her script. 'Temptation is always close at hand, girls, and you must be ready to fight it at all times,' she continued. Marie craned her neck to try to locate her sister in the crowd, and to make it clear to her that she was to shut up.

'Marie Stephenson, is there something of interest behind you?' Sister Aloysius bellowed.

Face ablaze, Marie said, 'No, Sister. Sorry, Sister.'

'Well, pay attention then,' Sister Aloysius barked. 'His Holiness has made his position on the Right to Life of the unborn child very clear. We recite his prayer against the abomination of abortion every day.' Here, she glared at the front row of girls, before returning to her script. 'And in the spirit of our faith, we will welcome three speakers from SPUC to our school this afternoon.' She pronounced the words 'Ess Pee U Cee' and there was a ripple of laughter from the back of the hall. Sister Aloysius glared again and the laughter subsided. 'I hope you will accord these ladies your attention and respect.'

There was a long silence, a silence which Sister Aloysius encouraged, holding the script in her hand and staring fixedly at the statue of Holy Mary at the back of the hall. The silence was deafening. Eventually, she said, 'Very well. Off you go girls and *go n-éirí an maidin libh*,' she said. Marie turned her head to see if she could spot Grainne. She'd need to talk to her before those women came in, because if she didn't, God only knows what Grainne would make of it all. She'd be terrified, Marie knew. How she wished she was there to protect her sister, the way she always had been, but it seemed that Grainne didn't want her protection any more.

The ladies came in after lunch, as promised, three women in denim skirts and sensible raincoats. Marie knew one of them, Mrs O'Connell; she lived near the church and had endless amounts of children. They filed into the meeting room, now smelling of crisps and stale air after lunch, and unfurled a row of unpleasant-looking posters to gasps from the girls. Mary Devane, that eejit, made a gagging noise and had to leave the room.

Marie knew what the images would be like, because Dada had received an anonymous postcard at the beginning of September with a weeping girl on it in front of a series of crosses: 'Where have all the children gone?' it demanded. 'Abortion Kills.' And then another, every day for a week, each with a picture of a cute baby on it and a slogan: 'Another reason not to allow abortion'. Dada had been tutting and muttering about it all month, talking about 'hysterics' and 'dark forces' and 'turning back the tide'. But these three women, in their knitted cardigans, didn't look hysterical at all. They looked like the mums who waited at the school gate in cars at the end of the day, or who made sandwiches for sports day – normal, nice mums with glasses and half-brushed hair. As she listened to the talk, and looked at slides of little feet and foetuses in a bucket, Marie felt her stomach knot. This was just propaganda, she could see that, but it still made her feel ill. And then she thought of Grainne and her heart thumped in her chest. She stole a look across the assembly hall and saw her, sitting beside Imelda, eyes round. Imelda, the witch, put a consoling arm around her shoulder and whispered into her ear.

At the end of the talk, there was a long silence, punctuated by weeping. The women looked satisfied, as if they'd done their work. There was a queue then, for the little badges, two gold feet on a pin – apparently, this was the size of the feet of the average ten-week-old foetus. Marie queued like everyone else, holding the two little feet in her hand, the little toes, the wrinkles at the heel. She felt her cheeks grow hot. 'I'm never going to take this off,' Mary O'Sullivan announced, pinning it to her jumper beside her class captain's badge. Marie shoved her badge in her pocket. She didn't feel she could pin it to her jumper – she was too confused. Killing babies was wrong; it must be, and yet, she knew that these smiling ladies weren't telling her the full story.

She managed to catch Grainne on the way out – she had a bundle of anti-amendment leaflets in her hand and the badge was pinned to her jumper. Her eyes were huge in her face and Marie could tell that she was terrified, poor thing. 'Gra ...' She put a hand on her sister's arm.

'I'm going to make sure that everyone reads this leaflet,' Grainne said grimly, brandishing the bundled of coloured paper. 'And that way, no one can be in any doubt that it's against God's will. It's murder, plain and simple.'

Uh-oh, Marie thought. Worse than I'd imagined.

★

'My God, that was gruesome,' Claire said, when they met at the chipper after school, shuffling onto the bench and opening her bag of chips, a cloud of steam and the smell of hot chips reaching Marie's nostrils. 'Want one?'

Marie shook her head. 'I'm not hungry.'

'Don't blame you,' Claire said, shovelling chips into her mouth. 'Pity it's such a pile of crap.'

'What do you mean?'

'It doesn't happen like that at all; they just pick those photos to shock us all into not having sex. And anyway, have you noticed the way they tell us all about that kind of thing but not a single word about the deed itself?'

'We had a class about it – Sister Evangelina gave it, do you not remember?' Marie smiled, in spite of herself.

'Oh, God, how could I forget?' Claire spluttered, sitting bolt upright on her seat, assuming Sister Evangelina's scowl. '"The sexual act occurs when a man and a woman hold each other so close as to allow for the transfer of his seed."' And the two girls collapsed in giggles.

'Anyway,' Claire said smartly, 'I learned all about it years ago, courtesy of *Last Tango in Paris*. I caught my parents watching it once. It's pure porn, you know. He puts butter on his thing, can you imagine it? Kerrygold, I'm sure,' and she giggled.

'Right,' Marie said vaguely. She hadn't seen *Last Tango in Paris* – she didn't think Mrs Delaney would be into it, seeing as her nightly viewing consisted of the news followed by *Today Tonight*. She was very exercised at the moment about the lack of the Rosary in schools. 'I got my education from *Lady Chatterley's Lover*,' Marie admitted ruefully, pinching a chip from Claire's bag.

Claire guffawed. 'You didn't pay Anne-Marie O'Keeffe for

it, I hope. She was passing copies around the changing rooms before the summer and charging 20p for a look. Nice work if you can get it.'

'I have my own copy,' Marie said primly.

'Of course you do,' Claire said cheerfully. 'All in the interests of literature, of course,' and the two of them broke into a fit of the giggles again.

It *was* kind of in the interests of literature, Marie had told herself, when she'd come across the well-worn copies of the works of D. H. Lawrence in a box in the attic before the summer. She'd devoted all of June to reading *The Rainbow*, *Women in Love* and *Lady Chatterley's Lover*, in a kind of fever, wondering when, if ever, she would experience what the people in those novels were experiencing: nothing in her life had prepared her for it, for the idea that a relationship between a man and a woman could be like *that*. She wondered if the books had been Mum's – she supposed they must have been. Maybe that's why Dada had hidden them in the attic. The thought of him ever having been interested in them made Marie feel a bit queasy.

Mrs D had come across them when she was hoovering under the bed and had pointedly left them on top of Marie's eiderdown, for her to find when she got home from school. 'Your mother thought that you should know that kind of thing,' and she wrinkled her nose. 'Apparently it's "literature", but my only advice to you would be to keep your legs crossed until you're fifty. Unless you want to end up like me.'

Marie had an idea that she was alluding to the mystery love affair that she'd once had. Grainne and Marie used to ask her when they were children why there was no Mr D, and she'd make dark comments about her heart having been broken *fadó fadó'*. Grainne used to imitate her, Marie remembered, scrunching up her face and mimicking her Donegal accent, 'Oh, *fadó fadó*, when I was a wee girleen,' she'd say and the two of them would dissolve into fits of laughter. Poor Mrs D. Marie made sure she found a better hiding place for the books.

She didn't really understand it, she thought now, looking out the window of the chipper onto the busy sea road – there seemed to be a very big gap between what she'd read and understood about sex on the one hand and 'Abortion kills' on the other.

'Do you know, Imelda's sister is supposed to have had one.'

'One what?'

Claire gave her a pitying look. 'An abortion.'

'Oh.' Marie thought of Imelda's sister, a blonde called Tara who wore a fur coat and who had always smiled at her and said hello when she'd pass her on the way to school. She was an awful lot nicer than her sister, that was for sure. Poor Tara, to be faced with a decision like that.

'Total knacker, mind you,' Claire continued happily.

'How do you know it's true?' Claire could be silly sometimes – passing judgement without even being sure of the facts.

'Well, because one minute she was pregnant and the next, poof.' Claire mimed something disappearing up in smoke.

'Anything could have happened,' Marie said.

'Maybe,' Claire said smartly, 'but I know what I heard. Listen, speaking of *Last Tango*, what's happening with that boy of yours? The one you met at the beach?' Marie had sworn to herself that she wouldn't, but in a fit of weakness, she'd told Claire about Con, and now Claire kept bringing it up all the time, going on about Marie's 'mystery man', as if she couldn't quite believe Marie had one.

'Oh, nothing,' she said miserably. 'We went to that bloody party, but I haven't heard from him since. I'd say he's forgotten all about me by now.'

'Marie, you silly eejit, there's no way he'd forget about you,' Claire said. 'You're not the kind of girl any man could forget in a hurry.'

'What do you mean?' Marie felt herself blush. What was wrong with her anyway?

'You're gorgeous, do you not know that? OK, you're a bit of a bookworm and a know-it-all, but you're bright and funny and you look memorable.'

'I look memorable. Is that a compliment?' Marie muttered.

'Yes it is, love. None of the rest of us look even slightly interesting, but you ... you have the kind of looks that people don't forget.'

'Thanks. I think.'

'You're welcome. And he's mad for not ringing you,' Claire added. 'A total idiot, but that's men for you. They think, Oh, I like her. We had a great time, so what will I do? I'll lose her number or get distracted and forget to call. He'll be in touch, don't worry.'

'I don't know,' Marie said sadly.

'Look, if you like him that much, why not just ask him out? Go in to Trinners and track him down. Take the initiative, unlike every other simpering woman. Times have changed, you know. We don't have to wait around to be asked.'

'You're in Feminist Lecture mode,' Marie joked. Claire was an ardent feminist, insisting that Marie watch *Women Today* on RTÉ every Tuesday. She did make sure to watch it every week, bewildered and excited by the earnest discussions. It all felt foreign to her – the world of real, grown-up women seemed so different, so distant and full of difficulty, with so many things to worry about. It was all confusing and dangerous at the same time.

Claire's eyes flashed. 'Well, maybe we should all be, or else the likes of the Ess Pee U Cee will win the day.'

'I'll think about it,' Marie said. 'I'd better go.' She looked hastily at her watch. 'Mrs D will be after me if I don't turn up at half-past on the dot.'

Claire waved as Marie opened the chipper door, a cloud of steam following her out into the street. She hunched her shoulders against the bitter wind that was sweeping in from the sea, which was an iron grey, low clouds scudding overhead, and scuttled home.

★

When she woke up on the following Saturday morning, she could hear Claire's voice wafting out from the kitchen. 'Oh, yes, Mrs Delaney, you're right … yes, we'll be careful.' What was Claire doing in the kitchen? she thought sleepily to herself. She clambered out of bed, wondering what time it was, and stumbled down the stairs, pulling her dressing gown on as she went. She opened the kitchen door to find Claire sitting at the kitchen table, a mug of tea and a half-eaten scone in front of her.

'I was just telling Brenda here about the demonstration in town. You'd want to keep well away from it,' Mrs D said.

'It's Claire, Mrs D,' Claire said politely.

'Oh, sorry, pet, I thought you were Brenda. Oh, but she's the big girl, isn't she? The one with all the chins. I'd forgotten.'

Mrs D shoved her hands into her apron, her silvery hair catching the sunlight, her watery blue eyes fixed on Claire. Then she turned to the stove and began to clatter pots and pans and Marie made a thumbing sign in the direction of the kitchen door, mouthing 'upstairs' to Claire.

'So, are you all set for study group, Marie?' Claire said loudly.

'Study group? Oh, yes. Just let me put some clothes on and pull a comb through my hair.' Marie played along. Maybe they'd get the bus into town and have a look in Golden Discs, or a rummage in Books Upstairs.

'I'll come up with you,' Claire said, getting up from her chair. 'Thanks for the scone, Mrs D. It was delicious,' she lied. Mrs D's scones were like ready-mixed concrete.

'Ah, you're welcome, Brenda, love. We'll see you again. I love having Marie's friends over … and Grainne's,' and here, Mrs Delaney looked stricken. 'Anyway, off you go girls and remember what I said about that demonstration. Those feminists will have the country ruined altogether, so they will.'

'I'll remember that, Mrs Delaney.' Claire smiled. 'See you again.'

'Study group?' Marie said when the kitchen door was closed safely behind them.

'Yeah, well.' Claire grinned. 'It's always a sure-fire winner with the grown-ups.'

'So, where are we going?'

'You'll see,' Claire said. 'Hurry up and get dressed, will you? And wear a warm coat.'

'Okay. Wait there,' Marie said and she bounded off up the stairs to her bedroom, where she had a quick wash and dragged a brush through her hair, wondering if she should put on a bit of mascara or lip gloss, then deciding against it. Who would she be meeting anyway? She grabbed her coat and scarf and closed the bedroom door behind her, unable to suppress a surge of excitement that she'd be getting out of the house at long last. She looked at Grainne's bedroom door, which was closed, as it always was these days. She could hear Spandau Ballet wafting out from under it. Marie hesitated. It seemed strange to go somewhere and not ask Grainne along, but after the party, there was just no way. And besides, what would they say to each other? Let her stay at home by herself, she thought. Just let her.

Marie and Claire walked to the bus stop on the main road, the wind whipping in off the sea making their eyes water. 'Sorry she called you Brenda.' Marie giggled. 'You know, the big girl, whoever she is. The one with all the chins.'

'Ah, Mrs D's not so bad.' Claire smiled.

Marie felt a bit mean then, because it wasn't fair to take the mick out of Mrs D.

'As long as we stay away from the feminists, we'll be grand.' Claire laughed. 'Which is ironic, really.'

'Why?' Marie said as the 7A trundled along Seaview Road towards them, black smoke belching from behind. She stuck her hand out and waved it around for a bit, because sometimes the driver ignored you and zoomed past, but now, it slowed to a halt with an asthmatic wheeze and rattle. It was one of the old buses, cream on top and navy on the bottom, with an open back and a low platform, and Marie and Claire hopped on, the bus pulling away with a shudder.

'Because we're joining them,' Claire said blithely as she led them up the stairs to the upper deck. 'We are going on an anti-amendment march.'

'We are?'

'We are, and we are going to show Miss Holy Joe Eleanor how quasi-liberals do it.' Claire snorted with laughter. 'Here, read this.' She handed Marie a booklet: 'NO MORE CHAINS' it announced in block capitals, with a sketch of two hands bound together. Marie opened it and scanned the lines, telling her why she should oppose the amendment to the constitution, which would outlaw even the very mention of the word abortion, denouncing the 'hysteria' of the Pro-Lifers. There was a cartoon, with a huddled mass of SPUC protestors gathered around a sign: 'For sale, 50 new condominiums on this site!' Very funny, she thought. And then she flicked to the middle of the pamphlet, and a sketch of a man and a woman's genitals leapt out at her. She blushed and tried not to close the booklet too quickly. Claire nudged her and the two of them found themselves convulsed with laughter.

'Stop!' Claire eventually said, clutching her stomach. 'We're supposed to be taking this seriously.' And then she peered at the genitals. 'Is that penis on the wrong way around?'

At this, there was a loud tutting from behind and Marie turned to see an elderly lady glaring at them.

The lady got off at Munster Parade, the huge ice-cream houses with their peeling facades looming above them. She turned and pointed a bony finger at them. 'You two ladies should be ashamed of yourselves. Brazen hussies.' And with that, she lugged her string shopping bag, with its wrapped packages of sausages and bacon, down the stairs behind her.

The two of them dissolved in laughter again. 'Brazen hussies,' Claire gasped. 'If only she knew.'

The thought made them lapse into silence for a few moments, as the bus climbed the hill towards the next village, the grey sea sliding past the window, and then trundled on into town, the sea replaced by red-brick and grimy doorways, cars whizzing past, streaming down toward St Stephen's Green. The bus chugged along for a bit and then ground to a halt outside the vivid green awning of Greene's bookshop. There was a silence and then the driver roared up the stairs. 'Bus terminates here. All off.'

'C'mon, let's go and get our stuff,' Claire said, tugging at Marie's sleeve when she attempted to have a browse in the window of the bookshop, peering past the tottering heaps of books into the gloomy interior. She loved Greene's, and she'd found some of her best books there. 'Not today,' Claire said briskly. 'Today we are going to do something rather than just dream about it.'

'That's a bit harsh,' Marie said.

'Harsh, but true,' Claire replied, pulling her down Clare Street, along Nassau Street with all the really boring shops, which sold hand-knitted sweaters and heraldic shields to the tourists, then around the corner past the stern grey front of Trinity College. Standing in front of the statue of Oliver Goldsmith, Claire punched the air. '*Viva la revolución!*'

Two nuns scurried past them, worried looks on their faces,

and Marie and Claire exploded in fits of giggles, shuffling through the crowds on the bridge across the grey ribbon of the Liffey, the two of them sucking in deep breaths as the bitter wind whipped their hair around their heads, then trudging all the way up O'Connell Street and past the grimy red-brick buildings of Parnell Square until they reached the Garden of Remembrance at the top, where a small crowd had gathered. Marie could feel a lump in her throat as they approached them. Then one of them, a man with thick glasses and a beard and a shock of wild, red, woolly hair, caught sight of Claire. 'Oh, here she is, the demonstration can begin.'

'Very funny, Liam,' Claire said, as she walked up to him, before planting a kiss on his lips. Marie pretended not to notice that he was nearly twice Claire's age.

'This is my friend Marie. I've brought her along for the ride.'

'Hi, Marie,' Liam extended a hand to her. His handshake was warm and firm and she decided immediately that she liked him. 'So, you've joined our band of delinquents.'

'Are you a band of delinquents?'

'Wait and see.' He grinned, pulling Claire towards him and squeezing her shoulder, before kissing her tenderly on the forehead. Marie blushed. She couldn't help it – there was something so grown-up about Claire; that she was with a man – an actual *man*, not a boy – suddenly her … whatever it was with Con seemed silly.

'See this girl?' Liam was saying. 'Without her, we'd just be sitting in the pub, knocking back pints. Instead, here we are, changing the world.' And he threw his head back and roared, and the crowd around him clapped and cheered.

'Shut up, will you?' Claire said, but Marie could tell she was pleased. And Liam was right. Claire was a doer, and without her, the world would just be full of people like Marie, dreaming rather than making things happen. She thought of her sister in her little bubble, in her bedroom, with her bunny posters and her clock radio and her signed photo of Duran Duran and she felt lonely for her. Lonely and, at the same time, she felt a thrill that Grainne wasn't there, making her feel that she couldn't fully be herself. Maybe this could be her life, she thought, without her sister, before she immediately felt guilty and dismissed the thought.

When Claire gave her a placard with 'Vote No to the Amendment' scrawled on it in thick black marker, Marie waved it in the air and marched down the street with the rest of them, chanting slogans until she was hoarse. She felt light, euphoric, as she walked around Trinity and down Nassau Street, linking arms with Claire on one side and a tall girl with braces on the other. Then they got to the corner of Molesworth Street, the gates of Leinster House in front of them, and they came to an abrupt halt. There was shouting, some of it in Irish, and Marie got a glimpse of a placard: '*The abortion mills of England grind Irish babies into blood that cries out to heaven for veangeance.*' It was the other side. She wondered what would happen now.

'See? They can't even spell.'

Marie didn't have time to respond, because a woman was standing in front of her, in a raincoat, her hair shoved into a cream knitted cap. 'You filthy girls should be ashamed of yourselves,' she roared, her face contorted with rage. And then Marie felt it, the warm trickle of saliva that spattered her cheeks.

'Ugh, she spat on me, the bitch,' Claire was saying. The woman was gone, and then another was in her place, yelling in Irish. She had a big sticker pinned to her ample bosom with a mangled foetus on it. That, and the saliva, made Marie suddenly feel queasy. And then the crowd surged forward again, the voice from a loudhailer urging them on towards the gates of Leinster House, where a cordon of gardaí awaited. There was silence and then Marie heard Liam's voice, high over the crowd. 'We believe in choice. We believe in democracy. Vote no to the amendment.' The cheers and roars swelled through the crowd, as they tried to drown out the shouts of the opposition. Marie continued to shout louder than anyone else until her voice was almost completely gone and all that came out was a squeak. She waved her arms and urged everyone to vote for democracy and tolerance and tried not to hear those yelling that they were just a bunch of baby killers and murderers. She wasn't sure if she was shouting because of what she believed or because it felt good to shout, to yell into the chilly air, to forget herself for an hour and be part of something bigger, something that moved and swelled and rippled around her. It was so exciting and fun, she realised – she supposed she should feel guilty about finding an anti-amendment demonstration 'fun', but it was just that: liberating and exhilarating.

After, they tucked their placards behind a big bin down a laneway and walked to Bewley's, the fug of frying food and coffee greeting them as they opened the doors into the café. They found seats under the stained glass windows, and Marie and Claire were left to mind them while Liam went to queue for breakfast. The girls were silent, exhausted from their efforts, and then Marie plucked up the courage to ask the question that had been on her mind all afternoon. 'Where did you meet Liam?'

'At an anti-amendment meeting. He was leading the Dublin South campaign.'

'Oh.'

'You can ask, you know.' Claire grinned. 'Everyone else does.'

'Ask what?'

'The question that I know you want to ask. How old he is.'

'OK, how old is he?'

'He's twenty-seven.'

'That's old,' Marie said quietly, and they both collapsed in giggles.

'Is he ... I mean, has he ever been ...?'

'Married? Yes, but he's separated. Well, sort of. Himself and his wife are only living together for the sake of the kids.'

The *kids*? Marie was about to open her mouth and ask Claire if she was totally mad, when a voice said, 'Here we are, ladies, a big feed.' And Liam plonked a tray down on the table, crammed with three plates of fried food, a big pot of tea and a mountain of toast. He sat down beside Claire and nuzzled her neck. Marie felt as if she shouldn't be looking.

'So, tell me all about yourself, Marie,' Liam said, cutting into a sausage, lifting it to his lips and chewing it, hot steam coming out through his mouth.

'Liam, no interrogations, you promised,' Claire said softly, stroking his curls tenderly.

'Maybe I just want to make sure that your friends aren't

like you,' he teased, 'paid-up members of the southside bourgeoisie.'

'Oh, Marie's definitely one of those,' Claire said cheerfully, pulling a corner off her white toast and stuffing it into her mouth. 'Her daddy's a judge.'

Liam turned to look at her, his eyes alive with mockery and amusement. 'A judge? Well, you can't get more establishment than that. Vested interests all over the shop.'

Marie didn't know what he meant by 'vested interests' when it came to Dada. 'The only interests he has are in preserving justice,' she said, regretting immediately her prissy tone.

Sure enough, Liam jumped right in. '"Preserving justice", is that it? How about preserving the status quo, making sure his banker friends get off their driving offences while the man on the street does time for crimes he didn't commit?'

Marie had no idea what he was talking about and she looked down miserably at her greasy fry. Why wasn't Claire defending her? Maybe he thought Dada was just one of the faceless bourgeoisie, concerned only with his own life and that of his friends, but she knew that wasn't true. She knew that Dada really cared. 'At least he makes a difference,' she said, looking up from her dinner. 'At least he does something, rather than just shout about it.' And, she thought, go out with girls half his age.

There was a pause and then Liam guffawed with laughter. 'Well, that told me,' and he gave her a playful punch on the shoulder. She wanted to tell him to fuck off, but for Claire's sake, she just smiled blandly, shrugged and tucked into her breakfast.

Liam spent the next half an hour pontificating, Claire

looking on adoringly, while Marie's mind wandered. God, this afternoon had been brilliant, just brilliant – she felt like a different person – like one of the women on *Women Today*, bold and opinionated and strong. And it felt good, she realised. Maybe this is who I really am, she thought, not the other Marie, with all of her books, hiding away in her bedroom. Maybe I've shed that coat after all.

Liam was going on about the capitalist dynamic when Marie had an idea. She stood up and pulled her bag onto her shoulder. 'I've had a brilliant time, but I have to be somewhere.'

'Oh? Where?' Claire began, and then, when the penny dropped, she gave a cheeky grin. 'Be careful.'

'At the dentist's?' Marie replied. 'I can't think what you mean.' And with a wave, she was gone, pushing the heavy mahogany doors of the café open and then closed again behind her.

She stood on busy Grafton Street for a few moments, stepping back from the crush of pedestrians on the narrow pavement as a bus trundled by. She walked past the shop and onto the corner of Andrew Street, waiting for the lights to change, telling herself that she could still change her mind. No one would know, least of all Con, but then she remembered the person she'd been this afternoon, and she kept going, letting herself be carried along past the shop at the bottom of the street that sold fur coats and those awful stoat things that old ladies hung around their necks, with its huddle of protestors outside, past the pipe shop with its portrait of Sherlock Holmes in the window, pipe in his mouth, and then to the crossing in front of the filthy grey stone of Trinity. She took a deep breath and crossed, walking in through the arch, leaving the noise of the city behind.

And then she stopped, when she realised that she had no idea where she'd find him. He probably wasn't even in college today, she thought to herself, as she wandered along, feeling suddenly a bit foolish. And then, out of the gloom, she saw Seamus, his mop of curls visible as he came out of the library and crossed the front square.

'Seamus!' she yelled, running after him. He didn't recognise her at first, but then smiled broadly. 'I thought you'd deserted us after the party – not that I'd blame you.' He grinned. 'Bit of a disaster.'

'Oh, it wasn't that bad,' Marie lied.

'So, how have you been?' He looked at her kindly, and she wanted to give him a big hug.

'Great. I was at an anti-amendment march with a friend and thought I'd see if Con was in.' She hoped it sounded as casual as she'd intended.

'Ooh, get you with your anti-amendment march,' Seamus teased her, poking her gently in the ribs. Marie giggled – she couldn't take offence, because Seamus was far too nice. 'He's on his way anyway,' he said kindly. 'He's just getting some tobacco from the newsagent's.'

'Great,' Marie said, and, as Seamus sauntered off, 'Are you not waiting?'

'And interrupt the course of true love?' He turned and waved. 'Not likely,' and, less distinctly, 'but don't say I didn't warn you.'

Then he was gone and Marie was standing there, alone, in the middle of the square. It was dark now and the wind had picked up, lifting leaves and wrappers in little eddies, swirling them around before they scattered along the ground. It was chilly, too, and Marie pulled her collar up, her teeth beginning to chatter. Where was he? she wondered, deciding that she'd wait another few minutes for him and then she'd go.

The hands that covered her eyes were chilly and smelled faintly of smoke. 'Guess who?' The voice was a warm, deep rumble and Marie gave a little scream.

She turned to face him.

'You've got new clothes!'

He looked down at the new Levi 501s and black polo shirt. 'So I have. What do you think?'

'They look nice. They suit you,' she said. And they did suit him, even though they looked too shiny, too new, and she had that sense again that he was dressing up in some way; he was being Con the Trinity Student, as if it was a role in a play. But then, she reasoned, isn't that what we all do – what had she been doing marching with Claire up Kildare Street, if not playing a role?

'I was at the march.' She said it in a way that she hoped made it sound like an afterthought – a diversion on a gloomy autumn evening instead of a high point in her unbearably boring life, which was going precisely nowhere. Which *had* been going precisely nowhere until she'd met Con. Anything that had happened to her since that summer had happened because of him. She found herself grinning stupidly at the idea.

'So, Marie's growing up,' he said softly.

She didn't know how to answer that. She felt uneasy and irritated, the way she always did with Con.

'You are probably the most patronising person I know,' she said bitterly.

'Thanks for the compliment,' he replied.

'I'm going home,' Marie said sniffily, pulling her bag onto her shoulder, her earlier happiness now replaced with a feeling of complete deflation.

His hand, when he took hers, was warmer now, and he stroked his thumb across her wrist. 'Ah, come on, Marie, don't be like that. You're here now.'

'I'm grounded and I'll never be allowed out again if I'm any later home. I'm in study group at the moment.' She smiled ruefully.

'Was that after the party?'

Marie nodded.

'Sorry,' he said quietly.

'Why are you sorry?' He kept doing that thing with his thumb, stroking her wrist, and she was beginning to feel a bit faint.

He shrugged. 'C'mon, let's find somewhere quiet.' He pulled her by the hand, through a narrow archway into a small courtyard with a few red-painted tables in it. Apart from a guy in a dark woollen overcoat, smoking a cigarette, it was deserted. Con sat down on one chair and she sat down on another. He pulled a packet of rolling tobacco out of his pocket and proceeded to roll a cigarette.

'Can I have one?'

He didn't reply, just continued rolling, then handed her his cigarette. 'Thanks,' she replied, accepting the light he offered her and taking a pull, trying not to cough. God, this was strong.

'So, any truths for me today?'

'Hmm.' Marie pretended to think. 'I might well ask you the same question.'

'You might,' he conceded. 'But I like your truths better.'

'But it's one-sided.' She smiled. 'So, if I tell you mine, you have to tell me yours. Deal?'

'Deal.' She thought she saw a flicker of anxiety cross his face.

'Right …' She thought for a moment. 'I know! I stole my mother's gold charm bracelet.'

'You did? Little Miss Goody-two-shoes Marie?'

'I know.' She giggled.

'Did she notice?'

'Yes. She got really upset about it. It had been her mother's and she'd left it to her. I remember, it had all kinds of charms … there was a thatched cottage and a wolfhound and a Claddagh ring with a big ruby in it.'

'Why did you steal it?'

'I don't know. I always used to take it out of her jewellery box and try it on when I was small. I loved it because it felt so heavy, and I used to imagine I was the queen, with my expensive jewellery. And then one day I went into her bedroom and … well, she was quite sick then, and she was asleep and I just took it out of the box.'

She could still remember it, the smell of Mum's room when she was sick. It had a cloying, sweet smell that clung to Marie's nostrils. It used to cling to her clothes, too, if she spent any time in Mum's room, reading the *Irish Times* to her – 'the black bits' as she used to call them, which were the crime stories, helpfully picked out by the paper in bold. Mum used to love the crime stories; she loved a good drugs bust or a big bank robbery, demanding that the details be read out several times, a satisfied look on her face. It was funny, because when she was well, Mum had hated violence of any sort – she'd liked gardening and classical music. Maybe she was angry, Marie thought now, and that's why she'd wanted to know all about a cannabis haul in Rathmines.

'What do you mean "quite sick"? Is she better now?'

'No. She died.'

'Oh.' His cheeks reddened. 'Sorry.'

'It's OK,' Marie found herself saying. 'It was a long time ago.' It wasn't OK, of course, but what could Marie really say?

'So?'

'So, what?'

'So … continue the story,' he said, taking a drag on his cigarette.

'Oh. OK.' Marie was flustered. 'Anyway, I think it was more that I was angry with her. I wanted her to stop being sick and get better and I thought that if I stole the bracelet … oh, I don't know,' she finished, shrugging her shoulders. 'Maybe I just wanted it because it was pretty.'

'You must miss your mum,' Con said quietly.

'I don't know. I mean, of course I miss her, but not the way you think I might. It's just … we seem normal, you know. We walk and talk and eat dinner, like normal people, but we're not normal at all. We're all just … lost.' As soon as she said the words, Marie felt stupid, blurting out the truth to Con like that. She'd never told anyone how she really felt about missing Mum, not even Claire.

'I'm sorry,' Marie said. 'It's just … missing her, it's funny.

124

It's not like I thought it would be, a pain or an ache. It's that life just seems … wrong, you know?'

'Yeah.' He patted her on the knee, looking absently into space, and Marie couldn't help feeling the tiniest bit disappointed. She wasn't sure what she'd been hoping for, but it wasn't this.

'Right. Your turn.'

Con made a face. 'Crap. I thought you'd forget.'

Marie managed a smile. 'Nope.'

'Right, well …' He thought for a while, before brightening. 'You know the way you hate water?'

'Yes.'

'Well, I can't swim.'

'You mean that's it?' Marie said indignantly.

'Well, it's the truth. I can't.'

'You're cheating, you know.' Marie managed a smile.

'I can't ride a bike.'

'Everyone can ride a bike,' Marie said.

Con shook his head. 'I can't. Well, I can get up on the bike and try to pedal, but the minute I get started, I just fall over.'

'Did nobody teach you?'

'Nope.'

'Why not?'

'Because my dad wasn't there and my mum just sat on the couch all day, watching telly. She just left me to my own devices.'

'So, where was your dad?'

'Oh, he left.' He said it as if it were the most normal thing in the world. 'Last thing I heard, he was in England somewhere.'

'How old were you?'

He cleared his throat. 'I was five.'

'A long time ago.'

He nodded.

'But it still feels like yesterday,' Marie added quietly.

'Yeah.' He was silent for a long time before he said, 'There was one of those CIÉ bus stops across the road from our house – you know, for the bus that comes once a day, that kind of thing. I used to spend hours looking out my bedroom window at that bus stop, waiting for Dad to come back. I watched every bus that pulled up and I'd wait for it to pull away again, and imagine I'd see him just standing there, hands in his pockets, as if he'd just been up to town for a few messages. But he never was. And it changes you, you know. You just can't trust people. You don't have that belief that the world will somehow turn out OK, do you know? I'm not really sure it will.'

'Hmm,' Marie said doubtfully. She wasn't sure if she agreed with him, because fundamentally, she believed that things *would* be OK – probably because Mum had instilled that belief in her. She'd left Marie and Grainne and Dada, but it hadn't been of her own free will – if she'd been able to stay, she absolutely would. Marie had never had to look out her bedroom window, hoping that she'd return and she couldn't imagine what that might be like. How it would make you look at the world.

'Would you look at the two of us,' Con said softly. 'Two lost souls.'

She thought he might kiss her then, but he didn't. It was strange, she thought, because he didn't seem like the same person he'd been at the party. He didn't seem as interested in her, at least, not in that way, and she found that she was terribly disappointed.

'C'mon, I've got a lecture in fifteen minutes. I'll walk you to the bus.'

They hurried back up Grafton Street and into St Stephen's Green, which was deserted at this time of the evening, a low mist hanging just above the trees. Marie could hear the muted quacking of ducks and the clucking of the hens that lived in the bushes near the bandstand. She hoped that Con might take her hand or try to kiss her, but instead, he just started walking a bit faster, because the park attendant was ringing the bell to say that the park was closing. She didn't know what she was doing wrong. Maybe she wasn't pretty enough, or maybe her breath smelled – something really obvious that no one had thought to tell her. She wanted to ask Con, but she didn't dare.

Then, as they walked out the back gate, past the huge, lumpen statue of Wolfe Tone with the greeny-bronze twig-like figures behind him, he suddenly reached out and tucked her hair down behind her shoulders. 'There, that's better.'

'I have a hairbrush.' She laughed.

'I have a thing about hair.' He smiled. 'I like it long and straight and tidy.' And he pulled her towards him. 'Like this.' He smoothed her hair down from the top of her head, tucking it behind her ears.

'I feel like I'm about nine,' Marie said. 'Can I cover my ears, please? The breeze makes them cold.'

'I'll warm them up,' he said, placing a hand over each ear. The sounds of the Green and the traffic were muffled as they stood there, his hands on her ears, his face inches from hers. She wondered if it was time for her to close her eyes and wait for the kiss, but instead, he just gave that enigmatic smile and took his hands away, sticking them in his pockets. 'I'd better run.'

'Would you come to the debs with me?' Marie blurted. She'd never even thought she wanted to go to the debs – it was such a silly thing, to dress up in a bit of ruched satin, a boy with a bow tie and an ill-fitting suit beside her. She probably didn't want to go to the debs, she realised, but she wanted to ask Con, to test him out and see what he really felt about her, because she didn't know. He seemed to be fighting with himself about her, liking her and not liking her at the same time.

But she'd never expected him to say no. He didn't say anything for a few moments, and Marie wondered if he'd heard her, if she should repeat the question, but, as the number 7A trundled into view, he blurted, 'There's nothing I'd like more, but I'm afraid I'm already taken.'

'Oh.' Marie began to fumble in her bag for her purse, pulling it out and digging around in it for her bus fare, her cheeks flaming with embarrassment and humiliation.

She turned to get on the bus, which had pulled up at the stop, a long queue shuffling toward the door. 'It's not what you think,' he said suddenly. A lady in a red woolly hat turned, as if he'd spoken to her.

'It's all right,' Marie said sulkily, jingling the coins in her hand. 'You don't need to explain.'

'I do,' he said, so abruptly that a few people in the queue turned to see what the commotion was. 'Look.' He pulled her towards him, so that she was facing him, and he tucked a stray lock of hair behind her ear. 'Your sister asked me at the party and I promised her I'd take her.'

She might have known. How on earth had Grainne managed it – and right under her nose. She wasn't even in bloody sixth year. Imelda must have put her up to it. 'And of course, there's no way you could say no to her, is there?' Marie said. She was aware that she sounded mean, spiteful, but it was true. Nobody ever said no to Grainne.

Con was shaking his head. 'Look, it wasn't like that. That was before … before …'

'Before what? It's not as if there was an after, was there?' Marie hissed, pulling herself away from him and, with a loud 'Excuse me,' pushing her way through the queue to the bus door. She couldn't get on the bus fast enough. She just wanted to be far away from here as quickly as possible.

'Hey,' a young man in a denim jacket and jeans shouted as she brushed past him, 'there's a queue here, love.'

'Ah, leave her,' red woolly hat said. 'She's just had a row with the fellah.'

'Go on so, love,' denim jacket said, grinning.

Marie thought she'd just die of humiliation. 'Thanks,' she muttered, jumping on and clambering up the stairs, where she took a seat by the window on the opposite side to where she'd left Con on the pavement. She thought she'd never hated her sister quite so much in her whole life.

Chapter 5

It was just after Hallowe'en, and all the talk in school was about the debs – who was going from St Rachel's and who was going from St Philip's, who wasn't, who was wearing what. Marie tried to ignore it, to hang out with Claire, who wasn't going because she thought it was completely ridiculous to go with some pimply, spotty boy when she had a real man already. Eleanor talked about not going either, which was hardly surprising, because all she talked about was the abortion issue, which was hardly going to endear her to any of the boys.

Grainne and Imelda sat together every day at break, heads bent over magazines with dresses in them, nodding and pointing and giggling. When Marie would pass them, Grainne would look guilty. 'Hi, Mar. Want to take a look?'

'Oh, Marie's far too busy to do that, aren't you, Marie?' Imelda would say sarcastically. 'Listen, how's that boyfriend of yours, Con, isn't it? Oh, sorry, he's Grainne's.'

'Yes, that's right.' Grainne nodded enthusiastically. 'Con's my boyfriend now.' She didn't intend to be mean, but the words made Marie want to choke.

Which is why, when David Crowley nabbed her at the gate after school and asked her to go, she said yes. She knew he probably didn't want to ask her, and she definitely didn't want to go with him, but when he came wobbling up to her on his racer at 3.45, red hands clutching the handlebars, grey eyes twitching beneath his thatch of dark-brown hair, and mumbled, 'Ehm, do you want to go to the debs with me?' looking at the ground as if it were far more interesting than her, she found herself saying, 'Yes, thanks.'

He didn't even look pleased. 'Right, see you.'

'See you.'

And off he went, back down the hill on his racer.

'Yes, thanks.' How pathetic did she sound? she later thought, standing in front of her wardrobe, wondering what she could pick out of it and do up in the space of two days. Everyone knew that only desperate people asked someone this close to the event, and David Crowley must be desperate. But then, so must she, she thought as she pulled a navy-blue jumpsuit out and flapped it a bit to get the creases out of it. She couldn't wear a jumpsuit, for God's sake. She'd need something properly formal and she had no idea how she'd get hold of that. And she only had fifteen quid in her post office book – that wouldn't get her a dress. She sighed and sat down on the bed. She knew why she'd said yes to David Crowley

… because she wanted to show up at the debs and let Con know that she could do without him. That she didn't need him and she didn't need Grainne. But she didn't want to go. The thought of it made her feel sick.

Mum, I need you, she thought. I don't know what to do. Everything's a mess.

She listened for a while, as if her mother would answer her back. As if she'd hear a voice in the silence, which of course, she wouldn't. Then, it suddenly struck her. Mrs Delaney. She'd go and see her and see what she might be able to do. Thanks, Mum, she thought.

Mrs Delaney was in her sitting room, the hum of the radio in the background. 'A request now for Mary in Carrick-on-Shannon …' She was lying on the sofa, her feet up on a pouffe in front of her, eyes closed. Her lips were moving – she was probably saying the Rosary.

'Mrs D?'

The eyes shot open and, for a moment, Mrs D just stared at her before saying, 'Yes, pet, what is it?'

'Ehm, I've been invited to the debs at St Philip's and I've nothing to wear.'

A smile split her face. 'Ah, well, we can't have that. Let Mrs Delaney see what's in her box of tricks.' And she got up and went into her bedroom, her voice calling after her. 'Come on in here, pet, and we'll see.'

In all the years Mrs D had been with them, Marie had never once set foot in her bedroom and she hesitated before following her.

The room was surprisingly bright and cheery, a flowered bedspread on the bed, a vase of leaves with bright autumn berries from the garden on the dressing table. There was a collection of holy statues on the windowsill – the child of Prague, Holy Mary, St Francis of Assisi – but there was also a bright red embroidered cushion and a pretty flowery vase. A pile of Mills & Boon stood on the bedside table – Marie could just catch the names of a couple of them. *Nurse Miller* and *Doctor on Call*. Draped across them was a set of shiny white rosary beads, which seemed a bit of a contradiction, but still. 'Now,' Mrs D was saying, sticking her head into a large walnut wardrobe, so that her voice was muffled, 'I have a few things … they're a bit ancient, but sure, we can do them up, can't we?'

When she turned around, she had a number of tufts of shiny material draped over her arms. 'Now, let's see,' she murmured, placing each on the bed, then standing back to have a look. 'Hmm, the green one won't do, unless you want to look like someone dressed up for St Patrick's Day.'

Thank God, Marie thought, as Mrs D hung the dress back in the wardrobe. It was the colour of a Quality Street wrapper and had a yellow plastic belt – she'd look like a leprechaun in it.

'Now, this one,' Mrs D was saying, fingering a length of scarlet satin. 'It's a bit lady of the night, I think, don't you?'

Marie nodded mutely. This wasn't looking good, not at all. Where on earth had Mrs D got this stuff anyway? She'd be the laughing stock of the debs. She wanted Con to look at her and think about what he'd missed, not breathe a sigh of relief that he'd dodged a sartorial bullet.

The two of them stood there, eyeing the awful dresses, before Mrs D brightened. 'Oh, I have one other one,' she said, turning and disappearing back into the depths of the wardrobe, emerging with a pale turquoise dress that didn't look too bad. 'Now, this is lovely. You'll be the belle of the ball in this one, I can tell you.'

She hung the dress on the wardrobe door and they both stood back to look at it. It was mid-length, a soft shiny fabric that had none of the stiffness of satin. It had a dropped waist and a flowing hem, along which winked tiny sequins. 'It's nice,' Marie exclaimed.

'I know. Who'd have thought it?' Mrs D chuckled and, when Marie made to apologise, 'Will you go away out of that. I've never been known for my fashion sense, so no offence taken, pet. This dress was my sister's – she lent it to me for the garda dance in Ballyshannon and I never gave it back to her.' She began to look dreamy, but then pulled herself together. 'Try it on.'

Marie looked around to see if there might be somewhere private, and Mrs D said, 'I'll go and put the kettle on. Come out to me when you're ready.'

The dress was a little long, but it seemed to fit. Not that Marie could tell, because there wasn't a mirror in the bedroom. Strange, not to have a mirror in a bedroom, she thought, smoothing down the fabric. It felt unfamiliar, and it smelled a bit musty, but it also made her feel light, flowy. She walked into the living room, where Mrs D was pouring a cup of tea into one of two floral cups.

'What do you think?'

She couldn't understand why Mrs D suddenly began to well up, flapping her hands as she sniffed. Maybe she was thinking about her sister, or the garda in Ballyshannon.

'I think you look just like your mother,' Mrs D blurted.

'Oh, it takes me back, it really does.'

There was a moment's silence. Marie could feel Mrs D's eyes on her and she felt self-conscious, as if she was pretending to be someone she wasn't, a girl in grown-up's clothing.

'Your mother loved dancing, so she did, and your father did, too. I know, you'd never know it to look at him, but he did. He told me once. They used to love formals in the Capital ballroom, he said – the dressier, the better. What was your mother's song now …' she thought for a second, before brightening, 'Oh, I know. "Fly me to the Moon", that's it. Lovely. Oh, the fun your mum and dad must have had when you were both little girls. Do you not remember anything?'

'I don't think so …' Marie said, but she did, kind of. It wasn't a memory, more of an impression: a rustle of something and a cloud of perfume, a stiff fabric being rubbed up against Marie's cheek. She took in a deep breath. Mum was here, Marie knew she was. What do you think, Mum? she thought, doing a little twirl. Do I look good?

'Your mother would have just loved to be here to see you and your sister on your big day. Mind you, that sister of yours …' Mrs D was all business now as she brought her wicker sewing basket over and began to take pins out of it, lifting the hem of the dress up and pinning it gently in a pleat, to avoid losing the sequinned hem. 'That Imelda O'Brien is a bad influence, mark my words.'

Marie looked at her sharply.

'Oh, yes, you think an aul' one like myself would know nothing about the ways of the world. But I know a brazen hussy when I see one, I can tell you.'

Marie giggled. Brazen hussy was Imelda all over.

Mrs D continued to pin and tuck, humming under her breath until she leaned back on her hunkers and said, 'Now, all ready.'

She led Marie to the door, pulling back a bundle of coats to reveal a full-length mirror. 'I don't have one in the bedroom. I can't sleep if I have to look at myself. It makes me think of all the years that have passed,' she said sadly.

So that explained it, Marie thought, even if it was a bit … strange. And what did she mean by 'all the years that have passed'? She wasn't *that* old. It wasn't as if she was going to die any time soon.

Marie stood there for a long time. She'd never worn anything like this before, something that wasn't a big baggy jumper or a sweatshirt, or a shirt with a belt at the waist, and she didn't know what to make of herself in a dress that fitted her. That went in in some places and out in others. She thought she looked a bit like Tracy Lord in *The Philadelphia Story*. It was her absolute favourite movie of all time and she felt a thrill as she examined herself, that she looked as sophisticated as Katherine Hepburn – maybe she'd start talking like her, wisecracking and putting men in their places.

'That fellow will be sorry you passed him by, that's for sure,' Mrs D said softly, her eyes filling with tears.

'What fellow?'

'Do not patronise Mrs Delaney. It doesn't look well on you. Whatever young man it is you are "seeing".' She rolled her eyes to heaven at the phrase.

'I'm not seeing anyone, Mrs D.' It was the truth, because Con didn't count, Marie knew that. Not anymore anyway, and David Crowley definitely didn't count.

The two exchanged a glance, and Mrs D dabbed at her eyes, blowing her nose with a big honk. 'Well, he's a fool is all I can say. You are a wonderful young woman, full of intelligence and wit, and whatever young man has been lucky enough to take you to the debs, he should be counting his lucky stars.'

'Thanks, Mrs D.'

'And your mother …' Mrs D began. 'What she asked you to do … looking after your sister, well, you're doing it well, love, and we all know that. It wasn't easy for her to ask you, no easier than it was for you be asked and to take on that responsibility, but you did. And you have no idea how proud she'd have been of you. Or your father. Oh, he doesn't say it,' she continued, seeing the look on Marie's face, 'but I know that it's true. Your father was left, you see, with two little girls to raise and he just didn't have a clue, but you … you knew just what to do. And he knows that, even if he doesn't say it.'

'I don't think he does, Mrs D,' Marie said quietly.

'Oh, he does. But men like him,' she said, brushing down her skirt, 'they feel that they always have to save the world and that makes them forget the people closest to them. They can see the big picture but not the small one.'

'Hmm,' Marie said. Mrs D was probably right. Dada was always lecturing them about people 'less fortunate than ourselves', and making sure that they never forgot their social duties. As Marie would trudge up the road to the old folks' home to serve dinner on Christmas morning, she would hear his voice in her head, hoping that she appreciated how lucky she was to be helping others in this way. 'You are one of the lucky ones,' was one of his favourite sayings. How exactly,

Dada, she'd often wanted to say. How am I one of the lucky ones?

Mrs D clasped her hands together. 'But that's enough of that. I want you to do something for me.'

'What?'

'I want you to go to that debs and have the time of your life, will you do that?'

Marie looked down at the ground. She couldn't see how she would have the time of her life with David Crowley, or watching her sister dance around the place with Con.

'You just need to forget yourself, just for a little bit.'

'Forget yourself.' Marie nodded. She knew what Mrs D meant. 'I'll try.' She thought instantly of Grainne and realised that 'forgetting' herself would be nigh-on impossible.

'I'll talk to your sister and make sure she behaves herself. You don't need to be worrying about her. I know you always do, but give yourself a break from it just for one night.'

Marie nodded, really just to please Mrs D, because asking her to forget Grainne was like asking her to forget her left leg.

'Good girl. And now, *Today Tonight* is on, and I want to have a good give out about the state of the world, so off you go with yourself. I'll have the dress taken up for you on Friday.'

Marie found herself pressing herself against Mrs D. The older woman felt like a warm cushion, with lots of soft padding. 'Ah, will you go away out of that. You'll ruin my make-up.'

Marie giggled, looking at Mrs D's freshly scrubbed cheeks.

*

Mrs D's encouragement lasted until the second dance at the St Philip's debs. Marie had been doing so well: she'd managed to put curlers in her hair, somehow even getting to the hair on the back of her head, which she normally needed help with. She'd had to manage, because Grainne wasn't there to do it, the way she usually did. She'd gone to Imelda's to get ready, so Marie had to do it all herself. But, when she looked at herself in the bedroom mirror before David called, she thought she didn't look too bad. She'd found a nice shade of green eyeshadow to match her dress and had coated her lashes in a navy mascara that she'd found in one of Grainne's drawers, with a dab of shiny lip gloss on her lips. The gloop on her lips made her feel a bit sick, but they looked better with a bit of shine. Plumper. She'd found a pair of Mum's old high heels in her wardrobe. She knew that Dada wouldn't notice, for once, because he was always out these days, 'at work', as he called it, returning at all hours of the day and night, smelling of whiskey and cigarettes. He must have taken them up again. Mum had made him stop when she'd got sick, but Marie always suspected that he smoked on the quiet. Dada would never have admitted to a weakness like smoking. Not after Mum anyway.

The doorbell rang when she was putting on a string of beads Mum had given her for her tenth birthday. She'd forgotten all about them, but then had found them at the bottom of an old handbag. They were only cheap, made of shiny glass, but they were a vivid green and they went with the dress. She swallowed and took one last look at herself in the mirror. Her cheeks were flushed and her eyes sparkled, and her hair didn't look bad at all, she thought. She'd managed to get a bit of a wave in it, for once. I look OK, she thought. I wonder if Con will think I look good in this?

She felt guilty when she saw David waiting at the bottom of the stairs. He was shifting nervously from one foot to another and fiddling with the knot on his red bow tie. He actually looked quite handsome, with his freshly cut hair and smart suit, and Marie suddenly felt a bit sorry for him. She knew that she hadn't exactly been his first choice, but then he certainly wasn't hers, and she'd kind of made it obvious, refusing to take most of his calls about the 'arrangements' and keeping her distance after school. It wasn't fair to take it out on him. She'd try to behave nicely tonight, she promised herself.

'Hi, David,' she called from the top of the stairs. He looked up and his eyes widened. She blushed as she trotted down the stairs, her heels digging into the carpet. She hoped she wouldn't fall flat on her face. When she got down to the hall, Mrs D appeared from the kitchen, wiping her hands on a tea towel, just in time to see David clasp her in an awkward embrace, his breath minty on her cheek. 'You look nice.'

'Thanks. So do you,' Marie managed, accepting the bouquet of flowers he handed to her.

'Well, would you look at herself,' Mrs D said. 'And your young man. You make a handsome couple,' she said, standing back to admire them. 'Wait a minute,' she said suddenly, and dashed off into the kitchen.

'She's probably left something on the range,' Marie ventured.

David shifted from foot to foot. 'Yeah.'

Oh, God. It was going to be a long night.

'I've found it,' Mrs D was saying as she swept back through the kitchen door. In her hand she was carrying a black-and-grey box, which, on closer inspection, Marie realised was a camera. It looked ancient, with its chunky glass panel in the top and two round eyes in front.

'My old faithful,' Mrs D said, holding it in front of her and squinting down into the glass. 'Say cheese!'

'Cheese,' Marie and David murmured in unison. With a click, the photo was taken. Mrs D beamed up at them. 'I'll get it developed during the week. And now,' she reached into her apron pocket and produced a ten-pound note, 'enjoy yourselves, the two of you.'

'Thanks, Mrs D,' Marie said, taking the note and stuffing it into her little evening bag.

'Right, well, we'd better head,' David muttered, as if he were being led to the gallows, not to a night out with dinner and dancing.

He didn't say anything until they were on the bus, the two of them hopping on in all their finery and sitting on the top deck, taking a seat behind a middle-aged couple who smiled at them and told them that they looked only gorgeous, the two of them.

She was looking out the window at the inky black night, when he said, 'Thanks for coming, Marie.'

She turned to him and managed her first real smile of the evening. 'I'm happy to be here.' And she was happy – kind of. She felt glamorous and grown up, like she imagined one of the women on *Women Today* might be, off on a night with her boyfriend. The fact that it wasn't Con made her feel odd, as if she was just pretending, but even if she was, she decided she'd give it her best try. It wasn't fair on David to do anything else. And besides, she wanted Con to see her looking her best and understand what he'd missed, just like Mrs D had said.

'Yeah, well.' He looked down at his knees and his cheeks reddened.

'Look, I know I wasn't your first choice, but—'

At this, his head shot up. 'You were.'

'I *was*? I mean …'

'I know, it looked a bit last-minute, but I've wanted to ask you for ages. It was just … I didn't have the balls.' He gave a quick smile, flashing his not-bad teeth at her. 'So I left it until the last minute. It's not exactly the gentlemanly thing to do, but …'

'But you asked in the end.'

He grinned sheepishly. 'Yeah, I did. And you said yes. That was a surprise.'

It sure was, Marie thought bleakly.

He shifted slightly in the seat and Marie felt sure he wanted to put his arm around her shoulder, so she settled down a bit to let him. She couldn't help it though; she tensed a bit as he snaked his arm along the back of the seat. He looked awkward and made to remove his arm, but she said, 'It's fine.'

'Oh, OK.' But she'd clearly given him the wrong message, because he sat upright then, like a guard dog, his knee jigging nervously up and down. She tried to make up for it by leaning into him a bit more, a waft of aftershave reaching her as she settled against him. It didn't feel that bad, actually. He was big and kind of solid, unlike Con, and she found that she fitted into the space under his shoulder quite neatly.

The rest of the journey was spent staring out of the window, Marie wishing the miles past so that she could get on with it. Could go into the function room of the hotel and see Con and Grainne and get it over with. She didn't want to go near them, or even to say hello. She just wanted to lay eyes on them and then have her dinner and dance with David, for all the world as if she hadn't seen them at all. She wanted to be dignified, like Lizzie Bennett when she saw Mr Darcy at Pemberley. It was what Mum had taught her, all those years ago, when she'd come home and complained about someone being mean to her at school. 'Don't show them that you're upset, love,' Mum had counselled. 'That's a sign of weakness. Rise above it and then they'll know who's boss.' Marie vowed, now, not to be weak by showing Con how she felt.

David held his arm out as she tottered off the bus at the last stop, just before the beach, and she took it, tucking her arm into his to steady herself, as she clattered up the steep driveway to the hotel, mouth dry and palms sweaty.

She wasn't ready for Con at all.

He was standing at the front door with a boy she didn't know, smoking, one hand in the pocket of his dress suit trousers. He was smiling and laughing with the other guy, clearly sharing a joke, and then he saw her.

She wanted to run, to bolt down the drive and onto the bus and home to the safety of her bedroom, but she knew that she couldn't. She just had to keep walking up the drive to the front door. She tried to sweep past, as if she hadn't seen him, but he ruined it by putting out a hand and touching her lightly on the arm. 'I was waiting to see you come in.'

'Why?'

At her tone, he flinched. 'Oh, just …'

Marie turned to David, who was looking a bit bewildered. 'David, will we go in?' He nodded, and she tucked her hand into the crook of his arm and walked past. She didn't ask Con where Grainne was. She didn't want to know. She closed her eyes for a second when she made it safely into the foyer, trying to steady her breathing.

'Will I take your, ehm … thing?' David pointed to the light woollen shawl she'd draped around her shoulders. Mrs D had tried to persuade her to wear her fox-fur stole, but Marie had been firm. No dead animals around her shoulders, thank you.

'It's OK,' Marie said quietly. She was shivering. David pulled it more tightly around her shoulders. 'Better?'

'Thanks.'

'C'mon then,' he said, offering her his arm again. 'Let's make our entrance.' He didn't ask her what Con was doing there or why she'd bitten his head off and she was grateful to him for that. He barely knew Con, but Marie wondered if he'd heard about him from bitchy Imelda or one of her cronies – Marie wouldn't put it past her.

The music was blaring in the half-empty ballroom, a steady thump-thump that made Marie's ears ring. She looked around for a sign of anyone she knew, but no one seemed to be familiar. She felt as if she'd walked into a room full of strangers all dressed to the nines. When her eyes had adjusted to the gloom, she spotted a few people she knew. Anne-Marie O'Keeffe looked like a human Christmas cracker in a bright green ruched satin number, complete with white court shoes, and Eleanor was dressed prissily in big puffy sleeves and a square neck, with a hemline that practically reached her ankles – the quasi-liberals would have loved it, Marie thought to herself.

And then she saw Grainne. She was standing in a huddle with Imelda and her cronies, giggling like an idiot. What on earth is she wearing, Marie thought, as she caught sight of her sister's large bosom straining against the fabric of her too-tight black satin bodice. Worse, the huge sleeves and full, flared skirt were in red tartan, and Grainne looked awful in it, like a big overweight Snow White. That bitch, Imelda, Marie thought – she'd done it on purpose. She almost felt sorry for Grainne, but then, Grainne had chosen Imelda, so maybe she deserved what she'd got.

As if she sensed that her sister was there, Grainne turned around and her face lit up. 'Marie!' she shrieked and made to come towards her, but Imelda shot out an arm to stop her. Grainne seemed to protest for a minute and then just hung her head. She's upset, Marie thought. I'd better see what I can do, but then Imelda leaned towards her and whispered something in her ear and Grainne burst out laughing, like a child. Marie felt her cheeks redden. She decided that she wouldn't go near Grainne for the whole night. She would have to look after herself for once in her life.

David and she made halting conversation through the main course – roast fillet of beef, which was grey and dry, served with two scoops of mashed potato and a slick of gravy over the top that made Marie feel a bit sick. She tried not to look across the function room to see where her sister was. She must be sitting with Con now, in her tartan ball gown, laughing away and telling her silly jokes. Marie wondered if he thought Grainne was funny; if he liked her as much as everyone else did. Maybe that's why he'd said yes – because he liked her sister better than he liked her, she thought as she chewed a bit of fatty meat. God, when would the night end?

'What are you going to do in college?' David eventually asked her, a weary tone in his voice that made it clear that he was just being polite.

'Ehm, I'd like to be a journalist,' Marie said.

He looked suddenly impressed, leaning back on his chair, resting one arm on the back of hers, proprietorially. 'That sounds interesting. I thought you were going to say languages or something boring like that. But I can see you as a journalist.'

'You can?'

'Yep.' David smiled, helping himself to another mouthful of grey beef. 'You have that spark about you. As if you're not afraid to ask awkward questions. And you always have your head in a book.'

Marie was stunned. She didn't think she had any spark at all. 'I suppose I do,' she said. 'I like books, because I think the world inside them is so much more interesting than our own, you know? I open a book and I can be anywhere at all, just for a while. I like the escape, I suppose.' She put her hand over her mouth then. What was she like, wittering on like this to David Crowley. He'd think she was such a hick.

'I don't blame you. But I don't agree about the world in books being more interesting. My dad's a GP, and I helped him in the surgery over the summer, because I want to be a doctor, believe it or not. The things people came in with ... and you'd be surprised how many of them didn't even need a prescription. They just needed someone to talk to, they were lonely, you know? But the stories they had to tell ... I can tell you, I didn't see anything half as interesting in bloody Shakespeare.'

'What about Dickens?' Marie said, putting her fork down on her plate. 'He was commenting about the lives of real people, but through these amazing stories, and ... I'm being a pretentious bore, amn't I?' she said, seeing the amused look on his face. She'd been surprised that he'd even been able to hold a conversation, not to mention throw in a few literary references, or that he wanted to be a doctor. She'd thought that he was just a lad, into throwing a rugby ball around all the time, but she had to admit that she was quite impressed with this side of him.

'You know, that guy would be lucky to have you.' David interrupted her through a mouthful of food.

'What guy?'

He looked at her and smiled. 'I'm thick, Marie, like most guys, but I'm not *that* thick.'

'What do you mean?'

'Thick – you know, stupid, idiotic ...'

'No ... what guy?'

'That Con O'Sullivan. You're the only girl he's interested in.'

'I don't think so,' Marie said quietly.

'Trust me. I'm a guy. I know when a guy is interested in a girl, and he's interested in you. And you're interested in him.'

'No, I'm not,' Marie said hotly. 'Anyway, he's here with my sister.'

'I know,' David said kindly, and reached out and squeezed her hand. 'But we're stuck with each other for the night, so let's have a dance and pretend for a bit, will we?'

Marie found that she didn't really have to pretend, because she was actually having fun after all. They danced to 'Fame' and 'Do You Really Want to Hurt Me?', even though Marie thought it was a bit moany, and then the whole class got on the floor for 'Come on Eileen', arms waving and jigging up and down to the beat. David was a really good dancer, which Marie found surprising, and he was quite funny, in his own way, and she didn't have to dodge any French-kissing even once, not even during the slow set, when the DJ played 'Just the Way You Are'. David sang along with Billy Joel in an out-of-tune baritone that made Marie laugh, in spite of herself. He did pull her a bit too close, so that she could feel his legs pressing into her, and she had to pull herself back to avoid feeling even more, but he was fun, and she found herself loosening up and forgetting everything for a while – Con, Grainne, that witch Imelda – she just danced and laughed and drank Coke, refusing to let David tip a bit of his hip flask of vodka into it. If she knew anything, it was that she would enjoy this night without needing any help.

She was dancing to 'Eye of the Tiger' when she felt a tap on her shoulder. It was Mary Devane from her year. 'Fancy a fag?' she mouthed.

Marie shook her head. She'd had a few cigarettes, but wouldn't have called herself a smoker, and anyway, she hardly knew Mary Devane.

'I insist,' Mary said, pulling her firmly by the arm. David was dancing with a big group, so she just waved at him and made for the exit. Mary's hand was clamped around her upper arm and it hurt, and Marie tried to shake her off, but Mary was determined, marching forward towards the door.

It was chilly outside and in her light dress, Marie's teeth began to chatter. 'Mary, I don't really want a cigarette, thanks,' she began, but Mary interrupted her.

'See that boy over there,' Mary pointed towards the trees that bordered the car park. 'He asked me to get you out here. And I have, so toodle-ooo,' and she waved an arm over her shoulder as she retreated.

Marie couldn't see anyone, and it was freezing, so she turned to go back inside. She was hovering in the doorway when she heard the half-shout: 'Marie.'

She turned around, to see Con standing at the bottom of the steps. He was swaying slightly and his tie was askew. He had a half-empty bottle of wine in his hand. 'Marie, I have to speak to you.'

'No,' Marie said quietly. 'You're drunk.'

'Not drunk enough,' he said bitterly.

Really? Marie thought, she could slap him right now. It was his choice to come with Grainne. Nobody made him. Maybe he was just being nice to her, but that made it hurt even more. Everyone was nice to Grainne. What about being nice to me for once, Marie thought. Don't I deserve it?

'Where's Grainne?'

He had the grace to look sheepish. 'She's inside with the girls, dancing.'

Marie felt a wave of relief wash over her. 'Right, I'll go inside then.'

Within a few seconds, he was standing beside her, his grip on her arm warm and firm.

'Don't go. I had to pay that Mary girl a tenner to go and get you. Please.' There was something in his tone that made her hesitate, just for a second. And while she hesitated, he leaned in and pressed his lips to hers. They were warm and his breath smelled of wine, and he pulled her to him, kissing her with such force, her mouth felt as if it were getting crushed. She managed to pull herself away. 'For God's sake,' she snapped.

His breath was coming in short puffs. 'I'm sorry. But I had to do that. You see, I love you and I just want you. I don't want anyone else. And I don't want you to think that I do. And anyway, you know that, because you love me too. I know you do.'

There was a long silence, while Marie digested this. She wasn't able to process what Con was saying. One minute she'd been dancing and laughing with David Crowley, the next … and what did it all mean – what was 'love' anyway? She had no idea. She thought of Mum and Dada on a summer morning in the kitchen, laughing over a shared joke; or Mick and Biddy sitting together on the sofa, watching some really boring Irish-language programme, even though he couldn't understand a single word of it. What about Liam and Claire, was that love? She didn't think so – at least, not the kind that would have a happy ending. But herself and Con? She couldn't see how that might be. She liked him, she knew – really liked him – but how could she say she loved him? She hardly knew him. And he was the first person who had ever said anything like this to her, so she didn't exactly have much practice.

'Why now?' she asked.

He came towards her and pulled her into his chest, where she rested her head, listening to his heartbeat, and then he lifted her chin and kissed her. The kiss was better this time. He still smelled of wine, but his lips were soft and his tongue flickered on hers. He ran his fingers through her hair and she felt herself relax, and a feeling like dizziness swept through her. She thought she might be lifted from the ground. All of a sudden, the noises around her seemed sharper; the rustle of the wind in the trees, the roar of the waves on the beach at the end of the car park, the laughter in the function room of the hotel. She reached her arms around him and she hugged him tightly, and he was warm and solid. 'I love you,' he said.

The words were frightening and exciting and she didn't really know what to make of them. She didn't know if she loved him, or what love was, but she found herself saying the words back: 'I love you too.'

'Let's go for a walk on the beach,' he said, taking off his dinner jacket and putting it around her shoulders. It was warm and it smelled of him and she let herself be enveloped by it, let it hug her and hold her up. It felt good, she realised, to be held like this. When he took her hand in his, she squeezed it and she felt her heart squeeze too.

They walked down the main drive, through the gate and

out onto the coast road. The wind was chilly and Marie tucked herself in against Con. 'Your teeth are chattering.' She laughed.

'That's because I'm a gentleman and I've given you my jacket.'

'Here, you can have it back,' and Marie made to take it off, but he reached out and tucked it more tightly around her shoulders. 'You'll freeze.' And he brushed his lips against her cheek.

The beach was deserted and they crunched over the stony bit at the top, until they reached the sand. Marie took off Mum's strappy shoes and let her bare feet sink into the sand, which was chilly and damp. But it felt good: her feet had been so hot in the heels. Mum had loved heels, Marie remembered. She had no idea how Mum had been able to wear them. Had she and Dada gone for a walk along the beach like this? Maybe they had, on some little sandy beach on Inisheer; maybe they'd stopped when they'd seen a shoal of dolphins or porpoises, maybe Dada had told Mum he loved her, like Con was telling Marie.

She trotted across the sand to the foam, which was sliding up the beach from the breaking waves, booming and hissing. The water was icy around her toes, but she stayed where she was, watching the water swish around her feet. It was funny, normally she'd be scared, but she wasn't now; the fluttering inside was excitement and something else, a feeling she didn't recognise – she couldn't put a name to it. She was still holding Con's hand, and he tugged at it as he took off his socks and shoes. 'Christ it's freezing,' he said, as the water covered his feet. 'Hang on,' he said, bending down to roll up his trousers. 'That's better. I look like one of those men on deckchairs on Blackpool beach. All I need is a knotted hankie on my head.' He slipped his hand back into hers.

They stood at the edge of the water for a few moments, the waves rolling in, foam covering their feet. The sea looked vast and inky black, and Marie felt that unfamiliar feeling again. She didn't like it, she decided, and so she turned to walk back up the beach. 'C'mon, let's go up to the tearooms.'

'They won't be open at eleven o'clock at night.'

'I know that, you eejit,' she said. 'I want to show you something.'

Marie pulled Con towards the balustrade that surrounded the warren of rooms set into the cliff. 'C'mon,' and she walked over to the two stone pillars that marked the entrance to the tearooms. 'Tea Emporium' read the letters on the pillar. 'I think it's here,' Marie said, bending down to examine the bottom of the pillar. 'Yes, look,' and she pulled his hand until he was bending down beside her. 'See?'

He shook his head. 'Sorry.'

She pulled his hand towards the pillar and lifted his fingers to trace the outline of the letters. 'MS/MS'. 'Mum and I did that, when I was nine,' she explained. 'We used to come here on Fridays in the summer and I remember they'd just finished plastering the pillar. We had to wait until the owner had cleared away the tables and then we got a stone and carved our initials. Just Mum and me.'

Con didn't say anything, so Marie blabbered on, feeling a

bit foolish now; a bit exposed. 'I hear my mother sometimes, you know. Well, I don't hear her exactly. I'm not delusional. But I feel her presence.'

Con made a face. 'I don't feel a thing about my dad. He's just gone. And my mum … well, it's a relief not to have her around, to be honest. I feel free without her.'

'You don't mean that,' Marie said quietly. She had no idea how anyone could see this as liberating. She knew that when Mum died, she'd felt the opposite. She'd felt as if there was something pressing down on her, tightening its hold on her, and that feeling had grown as the years had passed.

'I do,' Con was saying. 'I don't have to feel guilty any more, that I can't help her, or my family. That I can't do anything for them. I'm on my own and, quite honestly, it feels right. It feels that I can reinvent myself; I can begin again to be the person I've always wanted to be. I can be anyone. Anyone at all.'

It was a big speech for Con, but he didn't sound as if he believed himself. Marie couldn't see how you could just cut off your past, like it was a limb that needed amputating. You could pretend to be just about anyone, she knew that, but deep down, *you'd* know who you really were. You could run all you liked, but you'd always be yourself.

'I don't see how you can just shed yourself, like a snake shedding its skin,' she said carefully. 'It's just not possible.'

'Watch me,' he said with a grin. 'Just watch me.' And he ran down the beach towards the sea. 'Watch meee,' he yelled, the wind whipping his hair away from his face. Marie ran down the beach towards him, wincing as the stones dug into her feet. 'Con, wait,' she yelled, but the wind whipped her words out of her mouth. And then he was running towards her again, kissing her, and his lips were cold and wet. 'Ooh,' she said, 'you're like a fish. Stop.'

He laughed and kissed her again, this time harder, and his hands were on her back, cold and wet. She shivered. 'C'mon, let's go back before you catch your death.' He took her hand and they both walked slowly up the beach. Marie felt suddenly very tired, and she leaned her head against Con's shoulder. He put an arm around her and drew her close, kissing the top of her head.

'Can I tell you a truth?' she said suddenly.

'You can.'

'Thank you. I really want to get out of here.'

'Ah, it's not that bad,' Con said. 'I thought you liked me.'

'Not here, *here*,' Marie said, punching him on the arm. 'I meant here, this place, home, everything. I dream about it all the time, that one day, I'll wake up and find myself not looking out my bedroom window. That I'll be far away from here.'

She could see a muscle twitching in his jaw. 'Where would you go?'

'Oh, God, anywhere. London, Paris … I have this book about Australia … I keep it under my bed, and every so often I take it out and I look at Ayers Rock and Darwin and places that look nothing whatsoever like here and I think, "That's where I want to go. That's me." Except, of course, I never will. And that's the truth,' she said sadly. 'I'm stuck here.'

'No you're not,' Con said. 'It doesn't have to be like that. Besides,' he said, 'you're not the only one who dreams of escape.'

'I'm not?'

He shook his head and smiled. 'No. You're not.' He let that settle for a few moments, and then said, 'Do you love me, Marie?'

She couldn't help it, she hesitated, just for a second, until she saw the look on his face, like a dog that'd been kicked. 'Yes. Yes, of course I do.' And as she said the words, she believed them.

'Then promise me something.' He took her hand gently in his and squeezed it, putting it to his lips and kissing it softly.

'What?'

'I'll be at the canoe club on the first of January.'

'Why?' Marie interrupted, but he put a finger to her lips. 'I'll be there, and so will you. And if you stand under the noticeboard, and wait for me, we'll do it together.'

'Do *what* together? I don't understand.'

'Escape.' The beaten-dog look had gone now, to be replaced by the expression of an eager little boy, telling his friend that they were going to run away forever.

'Con, that's stupid. I have to finish school and I can't possibly leave home. And you have to finish college. I can't leave Grainne anyway. She'll never manage without me.' And besides, Marie thought to herself, I can't really run away. I can only dream about it. I'm too scared to really do it.

'If that's what you want, I'll make it happen,' he said. 'Promise me you'll come.'

Marie shook her head. 'No.'

'OK. Promise me you'll think about it.'

Marie sighed. 'OK'.

He pulled her hand towards him, and wound his little

finger around hers. They were both freezing at this stage, teeth chattering. 'First of January.'

Marie nodded. 'First of January.'

'No matter what,' Con added.

'No matter what.'

They were nearly at the top of the beach when they caught sight of Imelda, her blonde hair whipping around her face. She was hugging herself, her strapless blue satin dress no protection against the bitter winter wind. She was scanning the beach, and when she caught sight of them both, she ran towards them, a look of terror on her face. When she caught up with them, she was gasping for breath. 'Have you seen Grainne?' Her face was chalk white.

'No … I thought you were looking after her.' Marie couldn't keep the sarcasm out of her voice.

'I was, but … oh, I'm really sorry, Marie!' she wailed.

Marie felt herself go cold. 'Sorry about what?'

'I bumped into David outside the toilets and, well …' She looked down at her feet. 'I know you came with him, but he said you didn't really want to and he said I looked really nice in this dress and …'

'Oh, for God's sake, Imelda, I couldn't care less about David bloody Crowley. Where is Grainne?'

'Ehm, Mary said she went off with a boy from St Philip's.'

'What boy?' Con added, and Imelda looked at him, as if it was the first time she'd seen him.

'I dunno. One of the sixth years. Anthony Daly, I think his name is.'

Marie felt her scalp prickle with fear. 'Right, well, we'd better start looking for her.' Marie grabbed Imelda by the arm and pulled her up the beach towards the road. 'We'll start in the woods.' She didn't want to think too much about it, but she knew that the woods were full of boys and girls shifting. Maybe Grainne had gone there with this Anthony Daly. Grainne was desperate for love, for a boyfriend and probably for sex, but she had no clue. Marie suddenly felt her stomach clench, her scalp prickle with anxiety. She needed to find Grainne, quickly.

'I don't think she went for a walk, Marie,' Imelda said, as Marie dragged her along. She didn't look behind to see where Con was. She suddenly didn't care.

'Well, have you any better suggestion?' Marie snapped, turning to Imelda, who was now almost as blue as her dress, her teeth chattering, arms wrapped tightly around herself. When Imelda shook her head, Marie said, 'If anything happens to her, I will hold you personally responsible.' Marie knew that she was being mean to Imelda, but it was really because she was angry with herself. Why had she left Grainne to her own devices. Why? If anything happened, Marie would hold herself responsible, not Imelda.

'I'm sorry, Marie,' Imelda groaned. 'I didn't know that she was that …'

'What?'

'That innocent,' Imelda said quietly. 'I really am sorry, Marie.'

'You used my sister for your own entertainment, and now you're sorry,' Marie said flatly. 'You can tell her sorry yourself when we find her.' Marie took off down the hotel car park at a trot. She didn't look to see if Imelda or Con were following her; she just kept jogging until she reached the line of trees at the boundary of the hotel. She stood there for a moment, trying to get her bearings in the gloom. She could make out the shapes of various couples, all clinging together like limpets. 'Grainne?' she yelled. 'Are you there?'

'Hey, take it easy,' a voice said from behind one of the trees. But there was no Grainne. Marie ran another hundred yards or so until she reached the wall that ran around the hotel and then stopped. Where had Grainne gone? She turned right and walked along by the wall until she came to a small gateway that led down some steps back to the beach. It wasn't the nice end of the beach – there were slippery dark rocks and the water was full of jellyfish in summer, but maybe she was there, Marie thought, peering over the steps into the darkness. The sea was churning below, white flecks of foam covering the bottom two steps. Marie felt her stomach tighten. 'Grainne!' she yelled, but there was no reply.

'Have you found her?' Imelda was suddenly beside her, cheeks flushed, eyes bright with anxiety.

'No,' Marie said dully. 'I have no idea where she's gone.'

'I'm sorry, Marie.' Imelda began to wail. Her cheeks were streaked with tears, and she was hopping from foot to foot with anxiety.

'For Christ's sake,' Marie said. 'Will you shut up?'

And then Con was beside them both. 'Any sign?'

Marie shook her head.

Con took her arm. 'We'll find her, Marie.'

Marie looked at him. 'What if we don't?'

'We will,' he said grimly. 'Go and get your coat and I'll wait here.'

Marie walked back to the hotel, shoulders slumped. She looked down at her feet and realised that they were still bare, that her big toe was bleeding and that somewhere along the way, she'd lost her shoes. She looked up at the sky. Mum, she thought. I need you. Tell me where Grainne is. But as she put one foot in front of the other and climbed the steps to the hotel, there was complete silence. Mum just wasn't there. What did it mean? Marie thought, as she grabbed her coat from the cloakroom. Had Mum deserted her when she needed her most? She felt the tears come then, but she dashed them away with the back of her hand, willing herself to stop. Crying wouldn't help Grainne.

As she walked back down the driveway, the only thing she could think was that she wished she'd never set eyes on Con O'Sullivan. If he hadn't appeared in their lives, none of this would have happened.

They looked everywhere – in the hotel, in the car park, even in the canoe club on their way home, but there was no sign of Grainne. Marie's stomach was now a tight, hot ball of anxiety and she thought she might need to be sick. Her blood was pounding in her ears, as she trudged along the coast road, back towards home, and her eyes watered from the stinging wind. But she didn't care. She had to find Grainne.

'Your feet must be sore,' Con said to Marie.

'Hmm? No, they're fine,' Marie said, looking down at her feet, which were now black with dirt, a large streak of blood visible at the heel. She wanted Con to go away and leave her in peace to look for her sister. 'C'mon,' she said to Imelda, hoping that he'd take the hint. 'We'll have to go home and tell Mrs D. She might need to ring the guards.' She was saying this to frighten Imelda – she hoped that Grainne was safe at home, tucked up in bed, but she wanted to punish the silly girl for leaving her on her own.

Imelda put her hands to her face. 'Oh, no, no, Marie, you can't do that!'

'What's your solution, Imelda? That we just keep wandering around the town all night until she turns up? Anything at all could have happened to her. Anything.'

'I know,' Imelda whispered.

'I'm going home,' Marie said firmly.

'I'll come with you,' Con said, tucking his arm into hers.

Marie pulled her arm gently away, trying to ignore the hurt look that flashed across his face. 'It'll just make matters worse. I'll ring you later on.'

'No.' He shook his head.

'*Yes*,' Marie insisted. 'I'll call you later.' And she grabbed Imelda and marched off up the seafront, leaving Con on the footpath, and turned left into her road, walking briskly until she got to the front gate. She hesitated for a second, but then marched to the front door, rummaging in her little evening bag until she found her keys. 'C'mon Imelda,' she said grimly.

She was about to put the key in the lock, when the door opened, and Mrs D stood in front of her. She had two spots of red on her cheeks and her arms were folded across her chest. 'Get inside.'

'Mrs D …' Marie began, then shrank back as Mrs D's eyes bore into her. 'Do not start with me, Missy.'

'Where's Grainne?' Marie whispered.

Mrs D didn't reply, just opened the door and closed it behind them both, motioning Marie to be quiet and pointing upstairs.

'Thank God,' Marie began. 'She ran off and I had no idea where she'd gone. I looked everywhere …'

Mrs D silenced her with a look. She turned and walked upstairs, and Marie followed, her heart thumping in her chest. When Imelda shuffled along behind them, Mrs D just turned and pointed to the telephone seat in the hall. 'Wait there, Missy,' she barked.

Imelda scuttled back down the stairs and sat on the hard little chair, face pinched, rocking gently back and forth. Marie almost felt sorry for her, but then remembered what she'd done. What they both had done. She could blame Imelda – that would be really easy – but really, it was all her fault. She'd left her sister to fend for herself, knowing what Imelda was like, and all because she was jealous. Right at that moment, she wanted to just die.

Grainne was lying on the bed, her back turned towards them both. She had a big stain down the back of her dress, which was ripped at the shoulder. She was quiet, but Marie could hear the little sobs that shook her whole body, her shoulders heaving as she cried.

'Gra? Gra … what happened?' Marie said from the doorway. It was as if Grainne was an injured animal, and she was afraid to disturb it.

There was a long silence. 'I don't want to speak to you.'

Grainne's voice was muffled, as she turned and pressed her face into the pillow, giving another soft moan.

Marie looked at Mrs D. 'She's been like that since she came in,' Mrs D said grimly. 'I can't get a word out of her.'

Marie went over and sat gently down on Grainne's bed. She leaned across and put her hand out to touch her sister's arm, but Grainne flinched and pulled it away.

'Gra. Tell me what happened. You know you can tell me anything.'

There was a ragged sob. 'I don't want to talk about it. I want to forget everything, so please don't ask me.'

'OK,' Marie said softly. 'Would you like me to make you a hot chocolate?' She felt stupid, but she had to think of something, and hot chocolate usually did the trick with Grainne.

There was a long silence, followed by a polite, 'No, thank you.' Marie heard a sob, then, 'Mrs D?'

'Yes, *a stór*?'

'Will you tell Marie to go away, please?'

Stunned, Marie looked at Mrs D, who whispered, 'Leave her be for a bit, Marie.' Then, to Grainne, 'I'll be back in a moment, pet.'

Outside, on the landing, Mrs D stood, impassive, in front of Grainne's bedroom door. 'Tell me what happened.'

'I don't know,' Marie said quietly. 'I went for a walk on the beach and when I came back, Imelda said she'd gone.'

'You went for a walk. On the beach.'

'Yes.'

'With your boyfriend?'

'Yes,' Marie lied. Mrs D was talking about David. She didn't need to know about Con.

'And …?'

'And Grainne was dancing with Imelda and—'

'That article? Surely you know better than to leave her with that piece of trash. If she's anything like her sister …' Mrs D spat. 'Mother of God. I'm going to call Dr McDonnell and then I'm going to call the guards. Anything at all could have happened to that poor child.'

She turned on her heel to go downstairs to the phone, but Grainne's bedroom door opened and she was standing there, hair on end, make-up smeared all over her face. 'Don't tell anyone, Mrs D. I don't want them to know,' she wailed. '*Please.*'

'Shush, child, it's all right,' Mrs D said, shooting Marie a look. Marie knew what that look meant. Mrs D didn't need to say a single word.

She ushered Grainne back through the bedroom door and closed it in Marie's face.

Marie stood alone on the landing and burst into tears.

Chapter 6

In the end, they said nothing to Dr McDonnell or the guards or to Dada. They sat around the breakfast table the next day, in silence, broken only by the odd sniff from Grainne. Mrs D didn't even put on the radio and she always had it on, Gay Byrne burbling away in the background while they munched on toast and slurped tea. But now, there was nothing. Thankfully, Dada didn't notice. He'd gone to Seaview for a swim and when he came back, he came into the kitchen and asked the girls if they'd had a nice evening, failing to notice Grainne's big, watery eyes, as she said, 'Yes, Dada, thanks.' He nodded then, as if hearing what he'd expected to hear, tucked the *Irish Times* under his arm and locked himself in his study, the occasional phone call punctuating the deafening silence.

And, once they'd started with silence, it seemed that they had to continue, right the way through the end of that long, miserable month and into December, when the nights grew short and the sea was a bleak line of inky grey. Marie tried to break it more than once, when she'd come across Grainne sitting by herself at the kitchen table, her dinner untouched in front of her, staring out the window, or sitting on the sofa in Mrs D's, where she seemed to spend all of her time now, getting up and leaving as soon as Marie came in. She even tried to broach the subject of whatever had happened that evening once, but Grainne put a hand up and said, 'I am not talking to you, Marie.' And then she turned and went upstairs to her bedroom, leaving Marie to sit miserably in the kitchen. She looked at Mrs D for answers, but she'd simply shrugged and continued cleaning the range or doing the washing up. From the set of her shoulders, from the way she plonked Marie's dinner down in front of her with a thump on the table, it was clear that she blamed Marie for whatever had happened to Grainne. And she was right, Marie reflected bitterly. If she hadn't gone for that walk, none of this would have happened. If Con O'Sullivan hadn't come into their lives, none of this would have happened. Why on earth had he left Grainne at the dance anyway – he was supposed to be her date for the night?

Because of me, was her next, glum thought.

When he'd rung, the day after the debs, and Mrs D had told him crisply that neither Marie nor Grainne could come to the phone right then, she hadn't contradicted her. She'd simply listened through her half-open bedroom door, holding in her breath until she heard the receiver clunk back down, then breathing out again. Con seemed to come from another time, far away, and it was better like that, Marie thought. It was the least Grainne deserved.

She'd cornered Imelda in the corridor outside the prayer room when they'd got back to school on the Monday after the debs. 'Imelda, you need to tell me what happened to Grainne.'

Imelda's face was grey and when she looked at Marie, her eyes were huge and filled with tears. 'I don't know,' she whispered. 'Honestly, Marie. One minute she was there, dancing away with us all. I could see her talking to Anthony Daly and she seemed to be really enjoying herself, just having fun, like any normal girl—' and as if realising what she'd said, she'd looked down at the ground. 'I know, Marie, you think it's all my fault, and it is, but I just felt sorry for her. You have everything and she doesn't have anything at all.'

Marie gave her a long, hard stare. 'I don't know what you mean, Imelda.'

★

Marie knew that there was something very wrong when Grainne showed none of her usual enthusiasm for Christmas. Normally, she was all about the twinkly lights and the holly and the tinsel, driving Marie mad with constant requests to put the crib up in the hall and to go with Mrs D into the town to select a Christmas tree, but now, nothing could persuade her to show any interest at all. Marie had even tried asking her what she'd like as a present, but instead of making one of her usual lists of fifty things that she'd like from 'Santa', Grainne had simply shaken her head and said that she wasn't really that bothered. 'How about some fluffy bed socks?' Marie found herself saying, in desperation. Grainne loved fluffy bed socks and had a huge collection, but her sister didn't say a single word, just wandered off, as if Marie had said nothing at all.

Then it was ten days before Christmas, and Marie was lying in bed, staring out at the grey sky, waiting for it to get light, when there was a knock on the door. 'Come in,' Marie said, hopefully, heaving herself up. Maybe Grainne had changed her mind at last and had come to sit at the end of her bed, the way she used to, and chatter on. Marie was unable to conceal her disappointment when Mrs D stuck her head around the door. She closed the door behind her, but not before looking anxiously over her shoulder. 'I need to check that the Master isn't around,' she said, coming in and sitting on the edge of Marie's bed. She shifted around, as if looking for a comfortable spot, and then blurted, 'It's worse than I thought.'

'What's worse?'

'Grainne keeps being sick in the mornings.'

Marie sat up straight, pulling the blankets over her knees, patting the sheet down over them. She was playing for time, while her mind spun and whirred, trying to take it in. 'Maybe she has a tummy upset.'

Mrs D gave her that look. 'I don't think so,' she said. 'I'm going to take her to the doctor and if she confirms what I think it is, the Lord alone knows what we'll do.' She looked around the room, as if she expected Dada to jump out from behind the bookshelves. 'Do you understand me, Marie? This is very serious.'

Marie swallowed the lump forming in her throat. She thought she did understand, but the idea made her feel ill. Grainne? It couldn't be true. Marie thought of that awful SPUC lecture, and Grainne's pinched, scared face. There was no way, she thought. No way.

'We'll have to ask her.'

Mrs D looked at her as if she had six heads. 'How on earth can we ask the child that? Sure, she doesn't know the first thing about that kind of thing.'

Marie let the idea hang in the silence, that Grainne must have known something about 'that kind of thing' after all.

'Yes, well.' Mrs D's hands twisted on her lap. 'May God strike me down if I'm wrong about this. I'm going to make a phone call, Marie, and you are not to breathe a word about this, to Grainne or to anyone, do you hear me?'

'Grainne probably knows, Mrs D.'

'Don't you be smart with me, do you hear, you cheeky little miss,' Mrs D hissed. 'I hold you entirely responsible. If you hadn't gone gallivanting along the beach and, as Grainne has since told me, with your sister's date for the night into the bargain, like a brazen madam, Grainne would be sitting up in bed reading her magazines and cutting out pictures of fluffy animals, instead of … instead of … ' Mrs D couldn't say the words, so instead she pointed a finger at Marie, her eyes black with anger. 'This is all your fault.'

Marie just wanted to die. She'd let her sister down, but worse, she'd broken her promise to Mum. That was all that Mum had asked, 'look after your sister', and she hadn't even been able to do that. She was ashamed. So ashamed that she couldn't even look at Grainne, couldn't even think of the words to say to help her sister and to ask the question that was clearly at the back of everyone's mind. What had really happened with Anthony Daly, a boy she'd barely heard of just a few weeks before?

The next morning, Mrs D appeared again at Marie's bedroom door. 'Put on your coat,' she barked. 'We're going out for the day.' The bedroom door was closed behind Mrs D and Marie knew that she had no choice but to get ready.

When Marie came down to the hall, Grainne was already sitting there, in her grey winter coat, her face ashen.

'You OK?' Marie said quietly.

Grainne nodded. 'I feel a bit sick and everything smells awful.'

Marie tried to rub her sister's back, but Grainne shuffled out of her way. The two of them sat there in silence until Mrs D appeared, clutching her 'going out' handbag, wearing a hat and warm woollen scarf. 'Let's go,' she said, and the two of them got up and followed her, like sheep. Marie didn't even want to ask where they were going – she didn't dare.

They walked along the promenade in silence, a bitter wind whipping their hair around their faces. Grainne's teeth were chattering and Mrs D put a protective arm around her. They turned left down a narrow, dark little alleyway full of semi-derelict houses. It was where all the junkies lived – Marie knew this because Dada had told her once – and they passed a man with sunken cheeks and a yellow face, sitting on an old chair, broken bottles and rubbish around him.

'A'right, girls – having the tubes tied then?' and he cackled with laughter.

'What are tubes?' Grainne asked loudly, but Mrs D hurried them both past, until they reached the last house on the left. It was only in slightly better shape than the others, a discreet grey-painted door with 'Women's Health Services' on a newly polished brass plaque. Mrs D looked around, as if they were being followed, and pressed the bell. When the door was opened by a smiling older lady in a brightly patterned scarf and a thick knitted cardigan, Mrs D ushered them both in.

'Grainne, is it?' the lady said kindly. 'And this must be your mam,' she said, as she led them down a darkened hallway and through a battered door into a large reception room.

'Oh no, this is Mrs … ' Grainne began, but Mrs D gave her a sharp dig in the ribs with her elbow.

'Take a seat and Dr Stapleton will be with you in just a second.' The lady smiled, as the three of them sat down on a cheap-looking black plastic sofa. Marie looked around at the yellow-painted woodchip wallpaper, at the tired-looking Christmas decorations hanging from the ceiling and the plastic pot plants, at the row of leaflets neatly lined up on the counter, leaflets with names like 'Syphilis – the Silent Killer' and 'Contraception and You'. Her eye was caught by one of the leaflets in particular, with a worried-looking young woman on the front, called 'Unplanned Pregnancy – Your Options'. She wondered if she could stand up, walk across the room and take one, but one look at Grainne, worrying a hole in her old corduroys with her finger, told her otherwise.

The three of them sat there in silence, until the nice lady got up from behind the reception desk and came over to them, a clipboard in her hand. 'Now, Grainne, is it?' She looked at Marie.

'This is Grainne,' Marie said, pointing to her sister.

The woman hesitated for just a fraction of a second, but it was enough. 'Of course.' She smiled sympathetically. 'Can you fill this out for me while you're waiting for the doctor? It's just a quick medical history.'

Grainne looked at Marie and took the clipboard, looking blankly at the pages that had been neatly attached to the front. She removed the pen from its plastic holder at the side and stuck it in her mouth, before writing her name in block capitals, followed by her address. Marie watched her silently – she looked like a child, filling in a homework sheet.

Grainne stopped then, and looked up at her. 'What's next of kin?'

'It's your family,' Marie began, before Mrs D interrupted. 'Put my name down.'

'But it's not the same as mine,' Grainne began, as Mrs D jabbed at the page. 'Just do as I say. I'll explain to the doctor.' Her lips were pursed and Grainne meekly obeyed, chewing her pen again, before asking about childhood vaccinations.

And then the nice lady reappeared and took the clipboard, pronouncing it all 'lovely' and retreated to her eyrie, from which they could hear the clatter of a typewriter and then the long ring of a telephone. 'I'll send her in,' the nice lady said, getting up from her seat.

Grainne began to panic then, refusing to get off the sofa,

shaking her head and saying, 'No, no, no,' over and over again. Mrs D tried shushing her at first, but then resorted to the tone she used when she was trying to get Grainne to do her homework. 'Grainne, the doctor is here to help you and we need to talk to her, so get up off that sofa right now.'

Marie looked up to see what the nice lady made of this exchange, but she was clearly used to it, because she just kept on smiling and, when Grainne reluctantly got up, led her gently away.

'Wait here,' Mrs D threw over her shoulder as they left the room. Marie sat back down on the sofa and waited, heart thumping in her chest.

'What year are you in?' Nice Lady's voice broke into the silence. Marie, who had been eyeing a leaflet on gonorrhea, said, 'Sixth year.'

'Oh, my goodness, a big year.' The voice was soft and warm, and hearing it made Marie want to cry, but she swallowed her tears. Yes, she agreed, even though the whole thing seemed laughable now; the whole idea of studying and points and the life that she was going to have with Con was a big joke. And then the lady said softly, 'Your sister will be in good hands. Dr Stapleton is excellent. And it's wonderful that she has her mother's support.'

Marie didn't know what the woman was talking about for a second, but then she realised. She wondered what Mum would have done. Would she have thrown a fit or would she have rolled up her sleeves, like Mrs D, and got on with it? Would she have told Dada? She probably would, Marie thought, because, if Mum were still alive, Dada wouldn't be the way he is now. He'd be able, somehow, to understand.

'I bet you look after your sister really well,' Nice Lady was saying now. 'I can see that you have a great bond.'

Marie didn't even bother to respond, just nodded silently and picked up one of the magazines on the scuffed coffee table, pretending to read, even though the words were blurred through her tears.

When Mrs D and Grainne emerged from the doctor's office, they walked straight past the reception area, down the corridor and out the front door. Marie hesitated for a few moments, wondering if they were coming back, but then Nice Lady got up and said, softly, 'I'll show you out.'

'Oh. It's OK, I know the way,' Marie said, picking up her bag and bolting out the front door, as fast as her legs could carry her. When she got to the door, there was no sign of Grainne and Mrs D. Marie walked to the end of the street and looked right and left, towards the seafront, but again, there was no sign. Marie began to panic until she remembered there was a chipper here that Grainne loved – maybe they'd gone there. Her stomach felt as if it had lead weights in it and she trudged off in the direction of Lombardi's.

The window was full of steam, so she couldn't see inside. She had to open the door and stick her head into the gloomy interior, the wind nearly snatching the door out of her hand. She didn't see Grainne or Mrs D immediately, and she was about to turn around and leave when a voice said, 'Shut the door, love. There's a bloody draught like nothing on earth.'

'Sorry,' she said meekly. Flustered, she stepped inside, shutting the door behind her.

Grainne and Mrs D were sitting in a booth near the back – Marie could see both their heads over the top of the wooden partition. She walked towards them and hovered for a few moments. Neither of them had seen her. Mrs D was saying, 'I'll buy the ticket later and you can go a couple of days before New Year, that way he's less likely to suspect. We'll say we're going on a little holiday,' and here Mrs D's voice trembled. 'I'll have to face the consequences, I suppose, but there's nothing else to be done.' And then she cleared her throat. 'Grainne, do you understand that after the procedure the baby will be gone?'

'Gone where?' Grainne looked up at Mrs D and her eyes held a mixture of hope and despair.

Mrs D cleared her throat. 'Gone to heaven.'

'Will I come home then?' Grainne asked.

Mrs D hesitated. 'Well—'

Grainne interrupted, 'Because I don't want to. I don't want to come back here ever again. Not after …' She lowered her voice then. 'I don't want to bump into him. I keep seeing him, everywhere I go, Mrs D.'

Mrs D reached out and squeezed Grainne's hand. '*A stór*, don't upset yourself. Leave it to me. I'll make sure that you never have to see that … criminal ever again. But you'll have to stay in London for a while, pet, till it blows over.'

There was a long silence, and Marie debated whether to announce her presence, but then Mrs D said, 'Your father …' She didn't finish the sentence.

'Dada would kill me, Mrs D,' Grainne said.

Mrs D didn't reply, just nodded her head.

'You don't have the right,' Marie heard herself saying. Her voice sounded too loud and there was a sudden hush in the café as the other customers turned to watch.

Mrs D spun around in the booth. 'Sit down here, Missy, this minute.'

Marie slunk over to the booth and sat down beside her sister, who was hunched over a cup of tea, weeping.

'Do not make a holy show of me, do you hear me,' Mrs D hissed.

Marie spoke more quietly now. 'You don't have the right, Mrs D. It's not up to you to play God and decide for Grainne whether she has a baby or not. Don't you understand what you're doing? You are deciding who lives and who dies.'

Mrs D sat back in her seat, a smile that wasn't a smile on her face. 'Oh, well, aren't we quite the moralist, Miss Stephenson. Well, let me tell you something, young lady: moral principles aren't worth tuppence ha'penny when you are faced with a decision like this.'

'It's not a moral thing, Mrs D. It's the right thing to do. To give Grainne the choice – it's her baby and her life.'

'Have you any idea …' Mrs D could hardly get the words out. 'Have you even the slightest notion … Grainne isn't capable of making that kind of decision.'

'Have you asked her?' Marie said sharply, looking at her sister. 'Instead of talking over her?'

Grainne was silent for a long time. And then she looked up at Mrs D. 'I don't think I'd like to have a baby, Mrs D.'

'Why, Gra?' Marie interrupted. 'We'd help you, we'd—'

'I don't like babies screaming,' Grainne said. 'They make too much noise.'

'What did I tell you?' Mrs D said with grim satisfaction.

There was a long, shocked silence, while Marie digested

this. The chatter had started up again in the café, the sound of knives scraping on plates, the hissing of the tea urn. And then the waitress, a young, pretty girl in an apron, her dark hair secured by a hair net, appeared with a big plate of chips, which she slid across the table to them. 'On the house,' she said, smiling briefly before returning to her frying behind the high counter. The chips tasted hot, salty and greasy and Marie found herself suddenly hungry. She wanted to gobble them up, but instead, she shoved the plate over to Grainne, who shook her head. 'My tummy's too sore.'

'It'll be all right, love, very soon,' Mrs D soothed, smoothing Grainne's hair and tucking her into her shoulder. 'In a couple of weeks, all this will just have gone away.'

Marie found that she didn't want to eat the chips any more. They felt all wrong, as if they might choke her. She went to stand up, 'I need a bit of air,' but Mrs D shoved her back down in the seat with surprising force. 'Listen to me, Madam. After Christmas, you won't be seeing your sister for a long while. So, you sit down there and say whatever it is you have to say, the two of you. Oh, if your father only knew, he'd skin me alive. And as for your mother …' And she pointed a bony finger at Marie. 'You had a duty, Madam, to look after your sister. And you chose to go for a moonlit flit, leaving your sister at the hands of …' She became aware that her voice was getting louder, that people in the café were turning their heads to look at her. 'No girl should have to go through what your sister has endured, especially with …' and here Mrs D's voice wobbled and she reached over to grab her handbag. 'I'm going out for air, Missy, if you don't mind. Say your goodbyes.'

And with that, she got up, put on her coat and went out the door, banging it so loudly that it clanged shut behind her with a clatter.

Marie wanted to die, right there. 'Grainne,' Marie began. 'I'm sorry.'

Grainne looked at her with those big blue eyes of hers, which now looked weary. 'It's OK, Marie,' she said dully. 'I forgive you.'

'I don't think you do and I don't blame you. I should have stayed with you that night. I shouldn't have left.'

Grainne shook her head sadly. 'You took Con away with you. You made him choose and he chose you. Nobody chooses me, ever,' she said tearfully. 'So I wanted to make somebody else choose me, even if it was Anthony Daly, and his breath smelled really, really bad and ...' She had to stop while she pulled a tissue out of her pocket and honked into it loudly. And then she attempted a whisper. 'I didn't know it would be like that, Marie. That it would be so horrible. It really hurt downstairs. Is sex supposed to be like that?'

'I wouldn't know, Grainne,' Marie said sadly, thinking that 'downstairs' was the most depressing word she'd ever heard.

'Well, I'm never having sex again and I'm never having another baby,' Grainne said, picking up a chip and squashing it into the puddle of ketchup on the side of her plate. 'Mrs D says I can stay with the nuns in London for a while. Maybe I'll become a nun and that way I won't ever have to think about Anthony Daly or what he did ever again.'

There was a long silence. 'You don't mean that, do you?' Marie said.

Grainne nodded. 'Maybe I do. Maybe I'll stay forever.'

'But you can't … You have to come back,' Marie whispered.

'What for?' Grainne said bleakly. 'I never want to see this place again.'

For me, Marie thought, before realising how selfish that would sound if she said it out loud. 'Maybe I can come and visit,' she said hopefully.

'I don't know, Mar. Maybe it'd be better if you didn't.' Grainne didn't look at her as she said this, and Marie felt her heart drop. She had always thought that she was in the driving seat when it came to Grainne. That she could decide whether Grainne would be her friend, whether she could tag along or not. She could invite Grainne into her life or not, as she wanted, because Grainne needed her more than she needed Grainne. But not now. Now, everything had changed.

★

Christmas was spent in Granny's in Rathgar, pushing dry turkey around their plates and pretending to laugh at the terrible jokes Granny and Dada read out of the Christmas crackers. Marie had thought it would never end, looking at her sister's white, pinched face over the dinner table. Worse, Dada seemed to be making more of an effort than usual to be cheerful, insisting that both girls had a nip of sherry before dinner and suggesting a game of charades afterwards. Charade would be just about the right word for it, Marie thought bleakly.

They told Dada that Grainne was going up to Ballyshannon with Mrs D to visit her sister for a few days after Christmas. His enthusiasm made Marie cringe; she knew that the 'few days' would become a week, and then two and then … God only knows what she'd do then. The thought made her feel panicky, but she knew that she couldn't give anything away. 'The fresh air will do her a world of good,' he said at the breakfast table. 'She's been looking a bit peaky. Why don't you join them, Marie? Inhale some country air.'

'Oh, Marie has her studies,' Mrs D said sharply, ending the discussion. Dada just shrugged, because it didn't make any difference to him anyway. If only he knew, Marie thought – but then, if he knew, would he care?

When the time came to say goodbye, Grainne stood on the doorstep, a green duffle bag at her feet. Marie thought she had never looked younger, like a child, with her hair neatly combed, her face washed, as if she were ready for a nice day out, and not … Marie couldn't bear to think of it.

'Bye, Mar,' Grainne said sadly.

Marie said, 'Can I give you a hug?'

Her sister moved towards her, but when Marie put her arms around her, she was stiff, like a shop dummy. 'Bye, Grainne. Safe journey.'

Mrs D didn't say a word, but then she took Marie's hand in hers and squeezed it tightly. 'It's better like this, can you see that, Marie? For Grainne's sake.'

'I don't know,' Marie said bleakly, and she didn't. It was all too confusing, too huge. She thought again of the *Women Today* women, with their complications, their sophistication. Maybe they had to make choices like this – maybe this is what being a woman was all about. If it was, it was far more difficult than Marie could ever have imagined.

'Yes, well it is, and you and I will just have to get used to it,' Mrs D said smartly, putting an arm around Grainne and ushering her along the path towards the front gate. Marie watched her sister's strong back, now stooped against the bitter winter wind, Mrs D guiding her along as if she were an old woman, and she thought of all the things she should say to her, about how much she loved her and wanted her to stay; they'd look after the baby together and Mrs D could help … anything but this. But Marie also knew that it was hopeless. Having a baby would destroy Grainne, Marie knew that, after everything that had happened. No, they'd made the only choice they could. Mrs D was just a lot braver than her, that was all.

By the time Marie had thought all of this, fighting the tears as she stood, shivering on the front doorstep, Mrs D and Grainne were out of sight, on their way along Seaview Road to the ferry.

★

Marie spent New Year's Eve making cups of tea, staring out the kitchen window, looking at the bare branches tapping against the glass. Claire had called around to ask her out for New Year's, to some party at the awful canoe club, but she'd said no. 'Are you OK?' Claire had said, eyeing Marie carefully.

'Just the flu,' Marie had muttered, sticking her head around the front door, but blocking Claire's way. She knew that she was being rude, but she just didn't want to talk to anyone right now – not even her best friend. 'I'll give you a call when I'm over it.'

'Get well soon,' Claire had said doubtfully, wandering off down the front path.

Marie went to bed and didn't wake up until three o'clock on New Year's Day, 1 January 1983. A whole year stretched in front of her, a year, or maybe more, without Grainne. Marie didn't know how she'd get through it. Dada had gone to Granny's to drink sherry and eat gone-off canapés, accepting Marie's excuse that she felt too ill. She got up and got dressed, and sat in front of *The Wizard of Oz*, which was on telly for the hundredth time, and as Dorothy clicked her red shoes and the Tin Man talked about not having a heart, the silence settled around her. Grainne and she had always watched it together, the two of them sitting up on the sofa, a blanket spread over them. Grainne knew every single line of the movie and would generally provide a running commentary that would drive Marie mad, but now, she wanted nothing more than to hear Grainne telling her that the Wicked Witch was on next. She leaned her head back on the sofa and let herself drift away.

Only at six o'clock, when she was toasting bread on the hotplate of the range, did she remember. Con. He'd asked her to meet him in the canoe club and she'd promised she would. Oh, well, she thought. It was too late now. It was all too late.

She settled down at the range to eat her toast, which she'd slathered with butter. She'd wanted the comfort of it, but now the yellow gobs of the stuff made her feel ill. She barely heard the knock on the door, but then it came again, louder. Marie had a sudden fear that it might be Con. What on earth would she do, she thought, pulling the collar of her dressing gown around her and creeping into the hall. What would she say? But the shadow through the glass looked taller than Con's and so she opened it cautiously.

David Crowley was standing there, in jumper and jeans, his only concession to the cold, a St Philip's scarf wound around his neck. 'Can I come in?'

Marie hesitated. She'd completely forgotten about David and she wasn't sure she would have anything at all to say to him. She thought of their conversation at the debs and it seemed like years ago.

'I have a spliff,' he said hopefully, producing a battered looking joint from the back pocket of his jeans.

Marie had only smoked once or twice and it had made her a bit sick, but she wanted it now. Suddenly, the idea of a bit of oblivion seemed appealing. 'We'll go into the conservatory,' Marie said. Nobody ever used it because it was freezing and still full of Mum's old gardening things, but Dada wouldn't smell the smoke from there.

The two of them sat in the conservatory, with all the windows open and the gas fire on and smoked.

'I'm sorry about your sister.'

'What do you mean?'

'Imelda told me, the silly bitch. That fucker, Anthony Daly. Did you call the guards?'

Marie shook her head. 'They'd only say it was her fault anyway.'

'They would not, and guys like Anthony Daly need to be stopped—' David began, before Marie interrupted.

'Yes, they would. And it would be worse for Grainne

then. Dada would know and then the shit would really hit the fan.'

The two of them gave an embarrassed half-smile at that.

'How long do you think you can keep your dad in the dark?' David said.

Marie shrugged. 'Forever hopefully.' There was another half-smile as they both understood how hard this would be.

'Where's she gone?'

'I'd rather not say.'

'Ah, c'mon, I won't blab. I know that I'm not Con O'Sullivan, but I can keep my mouth shut.'

'She's gone to London.'

'What do you mean?' He looked puzzled, taking a big puff of the joint, his eyes crinkling against the smoke.

So, Marie found herself telling him the whole, sorry tale, and when he held his arm out, indicating that she should perch beside him on the garden chair, she let herself be tucked in against his chest, listening to his lungs expand and contract as he inhaled and exhaled. She felt better, his solid mass a comfort to her. Eventually he said, 'It's not your fault, you know.'

'It is,' Marie said bleakly, reaching out for the spliff and taking such a big pull, she coughed and spluttered and David had to bang her on the back.

'You're seventeen. Nobody should have to make a decision like that. That's too much, man,' he said, running a hand through his hair. He didn't look too bad in the dim winter light and she felt safe with him and his straightforward 'guy'ness. He was just a bloke, a boy she'd always known. So when he kissed her on the lips, his breath smelling of sweet hash smoke, she didn't mind. And when he asked her if she fancied going to see *Return of the Jedi* in the Ormonde the following week, she said yes, even though she hated *Star Wars*.

'Cool,' he said, getting up and stretching. 'Better get home. Mum has lasagne for dinner.'

He didn't kiss her again, just waved over his shoulder and got up on his bike, disappearing into the darkness.

PART 2

OCTOBER 1983 — TEN MONTHS LATER

Chapter 7

'Nurse Stephenson, will you kindly wash that bedpan again. I can see that it's not entirely clean.' As Sister Dolores pointed a bony finger at the white porcelain, Marie was forced to look down at it, to follow Sister's finger to the offending mark below the lip of the bedpan, and then to stifle the urge to be violently sick. She would never get used to the bedpans; the smell of wee, and worse, that wafted off them, having to hold them in front of her as she took them to the sluice room, then emptying them, holding her nose with one hand and averting her eyes, trying not to gag.

The bedpans were the worst. No, Marie thought, watching Sister Dolores's lips move as she continued to give out, actually, it was the incontinence pads, or the bedsores, she couldn't decide which. St Anthony's, the geriatric ward at St John's hospital, was full of such delights – elderly bottoms with big, raw patches of red on them that made Marie wince every time she saw them, smoothing Sudacrem over papery white skin as Mrs O'Brien or Ms Dunphy moaned in pain. Once, she'd had to help Sister Dolores insert a catheter, standing beside the nun as she carefully inserted a tube into Mrs O'Brien, while Marie tried not to look at the poor woman 'down there' out of respect, instead catching her eye, and understanding, as she did, how mortified the poor woman was to have a nun handling her genitals, never mind the pain. 'There we are,' Sister Dolores eventually said, standing back to admire the flow of pee, while Marie understood, not for the first time, that it took a special kind of person to work here. And she was most definitely not that kind of person.

She'd used to wonder how nuns, of all people, could handle the intimacies of their patients, their bladders and bowels, the contents of their stomachs; it just didn't seem to go with being a nun, but Sister Dolores had no problem at all getting her hands dirty, quite literally, and Marie half-admired her for that, even if she was an old bat. Marie had turned up late on the second day of her Wards and Sister Dolores had eaten her alive, calling her a 'scourge on the body of Jesus Christ' in front of the whole ward, nurses and all. 'Our patients depend on us, Nurse Stephenson. They can't wait to be sick until you decide to turn up to work, or schedule their death at a time that's convenient for you. This is important work, and you take it seriously by turning up on time. Do I make myself clear? There are no dossers in this ward.'

There had been a deafening silence, and Marie had just stood there, head hanging, wishing that the ground would just open and swallow her whole. But she'd never been late again. And even though she hated Sister Dolores with every fibre of her being, she also sort of respected her, because she did a really good job, and because she seemed to care about this awful work, work that Marie found depressing beyond belief.

At St John's, every day was the same bleak trot through cleaning bottoms, changing beds, holding hands, taking pulses, over and over again, and because no day ever varied, Marie felt that she was stuck in some kind of continuous present, where nothing ever moved forward; it just played in a loop: sleep-breakfast-bus-work-bus-tea-bed – on and on, day after day. But she had to admit that the daily rounds of temperature-taking, bed baths, the administering of medicine and the little chats with the patients helped her to forget. Maybe Dada had been right after all to insist that she do nursing – not that she'd had any choice in the matter – it might be hell on earth, but it was at least a busy hell, and it was easier just to live in the present; to try not to think about the past or the future she might have had, because that was just too painful.

Meanwhile, the only thing that kept her going in this place was the prospect of a mid-morning cigarette, followed by a lunchtime one, then a mid-afternoon one, then another after tea. Her cigarettes became her only comfort, that and the chat with Debs or Margaret, the two other student nurses on the ward, the three of them huddled under the porch beside the bins at the back entrance to the hospital, as far away as they could get from Sister Dolores. When Marie would drag herself up the three flights of stairs to the ward after her breaks, Sister Dolores would wrinkle her nose and roll her eyes to heaven and mutter under her breath about cancer sticks. So what, Marie would think, anything would be better than working here, even death. She knew that it was a dreadful, unspeakable thought, because of the way Mum had died, but she couldn't help it. What was it Nietzsche said about nihilism? Well, she was feeling fairly nihilistic these days, she thought, as she met Sister Dolores's beady eye.

The nun was looking at her expectantly now, holding the bedpan out towards her, as if it were a gift. 'Do you think Mrs O'Brien deserves an infection, to add to the indignities of her existence?' The nun's eyes, a watery blue, glared at her from underneath her white veil, and two spots of red appeared on her cheeks. There was a drip hanging off her nose and Marie knew that the nun was dying to whip her large hankie out of her pocket to wipe it, so she delayed taking the bedpan out of her hand. There was a tiny standoff then, and Sister Dolores locked eyes with Marie and Marie wondered just how defiant she'd dare to be, before reluctantly taking it, her stomach churning as she caught a waft of ammonia. Sister Dolores had won, once more.

But she wasn't done yet. 'Well, Nurse Stephenson, you didn't answer my question.'

'No, Sister, she doesn't,' Marie said meekly, before scuttling off to the sluice room, sloshing a waterfall of water around the bowl of the bedpan, then running to the toilet to be sick. Once she'd emptied her breakfast into the toilet bowl and flushed, she washed her hands in the huge porcelain sink, her nose wrinkling at the smell of the carbolic soap, but knowing that Sister Dolores would demand to see them, to make sure that they were clean and that the 'maximum standards of hygiene' were being observed.

After she'd finished washing, she looked at herself in the mirror above the sink. Her hat was crooked on her head, because, no matter how many times Margaret showed her, she could never manage to pin it straight, and a lock of black hair had escaped the tight ponytail into which she'd scraped it that morning. Marie fumbled for a clip, pulling one from the front of her cap and pinning the hair back to the side of her head. The cap tilted further to one side and Marie swore under her breath. I look like a drunken sailor, she thought. She had big, dark circles under her eyes, which were too large in her face, because she'd lost weight last winter when Grainne had left and she hadn't put it back on, so her elbows stuck out in her navy cardigan and her uniform was four sizes too big, because she needed a size 16 in order for it to be the 'correct' length, and not hover around the top of her thighs. She knew that she looked awful, but she supposed it didn't matter very much. It wasn't as if she was trying to attract anyone – quite the opposite.

She sighed and decided that she'd killed enough time, lifting the watch pinned to the front of her uniform and discovering that it was already half-past three. She could go on a break in half an hour, so she had time to give Mrs O'Brien a cup of tea and listen to her talk about the greyhounds her husband used to breed. And Mrs Semple wanted her to help her peruse the Damart catalogue, so that she could order her thermals – Marie had promised that once everyone had picked their items out of the catalogue, she'd go into town and get everything. Maybe she'd get herself a nice vest while she was at it, or a pair of the big woolly knickers she'd seen on page 22.

The thought cheered her up a bit and she returned to the ward, bedpan in hand, giving Sister Dolores a happy smile. 'Mrs O'Brien, it's tea-time,' she said, ignoring Sister's glare: she only liked tea to be served at the designated time of half-past four, but Marie had managed to persuade the nun to make Mrs O'Brien a special case, because she'd been having her tea at half-past three since 1947. It didn't stop Sister signalling her disapproval and as Mrs O'Brien commenced her long, rambling monologue about Mick the Miller and other greyhounds of note, Marie could feel the nun's eyes boring into her back. 'Mrs O'Brien, what about that cup Bob won at Shelbourne Park in 1966?' she said, knowing that she'd get terribly excited and tell her enough to keep her going until four o'clock. She ignored Sister Dolores's loud tuts of disapproval and the snap of the sheets as the nun made up a bed for a new patient.

*

'Jesus Christ, it's freezing,' Margaret said, jumping up and down, cigarette in hand, to try to keep warm. It was only the beginning of October, but already the days were chilly, grey clouds hovering overhead. The leaves still clung to the trees, but they were yellow now, and, as Marie walked to the bus stop on her way to or from St John's, an occasional leaf would drift down in front of her, dropping gently onto the path. It reminded her of how much she loved the autumn, the quietness and the stillness of it, the smell of must and smoke from the bonfires Creggs always built in the garden to get rid of the leaves. He was gone now, of course, back to Monaghan, to the place that, according to Mrs D, was the source of his gloomy silences, and the garden was now a semi-wilderness. The poor man hadn't had much option. Dada had thrown himself into a rage when he'd dug up a row of ancient dahlias that were long since past their best. He wasn't to know that Mum had planted them.

Creggs and Mrs D and Grainne all gone. It was as if the place had fallen apart after Grainne had left. Marie supposed it had, really, but as she took a long drag on the cigarette, she told herself that she didn't want to think about that right now.

'Freezing,' Debs agreed, pulling her cardigan around her, teeth chattering. 'The heating's on the blink in St Attracta's as well, so I can see my breath in the place. Mind you, Sister Veronica says it's much better for the patients, because it allows for the circulation of air. "We don't want germs to fester, ladies, do we?"' she squeaked, in an imitation of Sister Veronica's high, breathy voice.

'For feck's sake. Do you know what that woman needs? "A good ridin'", as my daddy would say. Seriously,' Margaret said, as Marie broke into loud laughter, 'It's not having sex that makes them so uptight. It's not natural, I swear.' Margaret was a big-bosomed girl from Mallow, Co. Cork, and her daddy owned a large farm, so Marie supposed Margaret knew pretty much all there was to know about reproduction. And she had a glint in her eye and a way of having fun that ensured a steady stream of boyfriends, none of whom she took seriously. Debs, on the other hand, was blushing bright red and looking fixedly at the ground, clearly mortified. She was very genteel, a slight, mousy girl from Co. Wexford who was totally cut out for nursing, and probably cut out to be a nun, too. They were an odd trio, and Marie wasn't sure either Debs or Margaret would have been her friend in another life, but they were all she had at St John's.

'Speaking of a good ridin', are we on for the Garda Club on Friday, girls? The new crowd from Templemore will all be up for the night, and we might find ourselves a catch or two. What do you say, Debs?' Margaret winked.

'Yes, well, I might be going home that weekend, I'll let you know,' Debs murmured, still looking at her feet. Oh, God, Marie thought. She'd gone to the Garda Club once before, having been dragged along by Margaret, and she still hadn't quite got over it. She'd been chatted up all night by a motorcycle garda from Tubbercurry: he was very nice, with his neat hair and his red cheeks, and as Marie had nodded and answered his polite questions, and asked him equally polite questions about his Saturday hurling games, she knew that she was probably being a terrible snob, but she could see how it would end, with herself and himself sitting in front of the *Late, Late* on a Friday night, eating a Chinese takeaway, and the thought made her feel desperate somehow.

'I'm not really a nurse,' she'd told him. 'I'm going to be a journalist, a foreign correspondent, actually.' The poor man had been kind enough not to tell her to get over herself, but had simply nodded and said that he thought she was a fascinating woman. 'God, what he'd look like in leathers,' had been Margaret's loud comment, from two yards away, which had only made the poor man blush even more and stare into his pint. He was just so nice, and that made things even worse, and the awkward exchange made her think of Con, whom she'd managed to banish from her life, and who wasn't a bit nice at all.

'Can I have your number?' he'd asked at the end of the night, and Marie could hardly believe she hadn't put him off – she'd even quoted Nietzsche at him, but it hadn't seemed to deter him. She wasn't the kind of girl to give the wrong number, like Margaret did, if she didn't fancy the guy in question, so she wrote it down on a beermat for him and avoided answering the telephone for the following week, in case it was him. No, she thought now, it might be Margaret's only ambition in life to snare a garda and settle down in Rathfarnham or some suburb like that and have three kids. Frankly, Marie would rather die.

'What about you, Mar?'

Marie had been taking another drag on her cigarette, but at the use of her pet name, she stopped so suddenly that half the smoke went up her nose and she began to cough. No one called her Mar, only Grainne, and she didn't like it at all. 'It's Marie,' she managed, in between racking coughs. 'I prefer Marie.'

Margaret gave her a long, hard stare, before saying, 'Sorry, Mar-ee. So, are you coming?'

'I don't think so. I might have something else on.'

Margaret's face twisted in a sneer. 'Oh, going out with the friends from Trinners, is it?'

'As a matter of fact, yes,' Marie said primly. She wasn't – yet, anyway – but she'd ring Claire later and see what she was doing.

'Well, bully for you. If you're so keen on them, why don't

you go there, instead of hanging around the dustbins with culchies like ourselves?'

Because I got one honour in Home Economics in the Leaving Cert and my dad pulled strings to get me into this hellhole, that's why, Marie thought. Not that she was about to reveal that to Margaret. She was just too ashamed.

'Margaret,' Debs said softly. 'That's enough.' And then she turned her pale face to Marie. 'Don't mind her, Marie. A girl like you doesn't need the Garda Club. Those of us who aren't as pretty as you have to try a bit harder, that's all, because we don't have the choice,' and she smiled faintly and Marie felt even worse.

'Look, I'll come,' she said. 'Maybe if I'm lucky I'll meet that guy from Tubbercurry again,' and she attempted a watery smile.

Margaret scowled. 'No, it's all right, you just hang out with your posh friends. We'll be fine with the bog-trotters on Harrington Street. Off you go!' and she made a flapping motion with her hands.

Marie felt the anger surge through her, but she wasn't going to show Margaret, because she sensed that Margaret would use her weakness against her. Instead, she ground her cigarette into the potted geranium by the door and shoved her hands into her pockets. 'I'm going off-shift. I'll see you both tomorrow.'

She could hear Debs giving out to Margaret as she walked back across the car park into the main building, and Margaret's reply, 'So what? She's just a stuck-up bitch.'

★

'A stuck-up bitch'. The words circled around Marie's head as she trudged down the Rathmines Road to the bus stop. I'm not a stuck-up bitch, Marie thought. I am not. I'm just … but what was she, if she wasn't a stuck-up bitch? Who did she really think she was – that she was somehow better than Debs or Margaret or Dave, the motorcycle garda from Tubbercurry? At least they were living honest lives, not like her with her German philosophers and stories about how she was going to be like Kate Adie on the BBC, reporting from the front lines in her bush jacket, as gunfire crackled in the distance. The closest she'd come to journalism was passing the College of Communications at the bottom of the hill, beside the red-brick town hall. She'd look at the students coming out of the door, scarves wound around their necks, and she'd try not to think that that could have been her.

She walked slowly down the hill, past the teacher's college and the rows of tall houses, broken into lots of tiny little flats. She'd been into one of them once, at a nurse's party, thirty of them squashed into a tiny bedsit with a swirly brown carpet and yellow wallpaper, the loo in a wardrobe in the corner; then she was passing the grand library, with its big wooden door, the name picked out in a strip of yellow stone around the top of the building. Sometimes, if she was coming off an early shift, she'd go in and pick a few books, taking them upstairs to the reading room and sitting in the pool of sunlight that came through the big windows, and she'd read, and she'd think how great it was that this space was only for reading, and thinking. A whole big building, devoted only to what you could do with your mind. It was such a haven, an oasis, after St John's, with all the shuffling and coughing and spluttering, the atmosphere of humans in distress, or dying, their bodies, and very often their minds, diminishing. Still, if she remembered, Marie would sometimes borrow a Jean Plaidy for Mrs Spence, who loved the historical yarns. Sometimes, when Sister Dolores had gone off to the chapel for prayers, Marie would read the books aloud to her for a few moments, watching the woman's lovely, pale hands, with their wrinkles and too-big wedding ring, clasped in joy as she lay back on the bed, eyes closed beneath her tight, white wash-and-set, and listened to stories about ancient royals.

Today, though, Marie was too cross, too out of sorts for the library. Maybe she'd have a cup of tea and a plate of chips at the Wimpy Bar, and she'd look out at the people passing the window: the old ladies with their plastic rain-hoods, the men with their newspapers rolled up under their arms, the homeless man who lived in the porch of the library. Or maybe she'd go into the Stella Cinema, which was showing *Staying Alive*, and she'd sit in the darkness for a couple of hours and she'd forget everything. She could do, she thought. After all, it wasn't as if anyone was really expecting her. She'd left cold meat and salad out for Dada, which he'd take into his study, so he'd hardly notice if she didn't come home, would he? And besides, it wasn't as if they'd have long chats sitting either side of the dinner table, the two of them. No, she decided. She wouldn't go to the cinema either, because she didn't like that kind of film – it was Grainne who loved the popcorn movies, not her.

She sighed and decided that there was nothing for it but to take the bus home and spend another evening reading.

The thought of losing herself in Robyn Davidson's *Tracks* cheered her up and depressed her at the same time: cheered her up, because she was looking forward to it, and depressed her, because she had nothing more exciting to do. She looked at her watch – Dada would have finished his tea by now and would have retired to his study, so it would be safe. She picked up her step as she walked to the number 18 bus stop.

It was only when she'd got to the lovely big houses on Waterloo Road on the bus, looking in through the large Georgian windows to catch a glimpse of grand drawing rooms or poky flats, a copy of the precious book in her hand, that she thought about Con. Maybe it was because Robyn Davidson, with her long trek across the Australian desert with just camels for company, didn't seem to need a man – she could exist quite happily without one, which made Marie wonder if she possibly could. Or maybe it was because Marie wanted to be Davidson – with her wild hair and her sun-baked skin, losing herself in an ancient land – instead of sitting on a bus in Dublin, in her nurse's uniform. I couldn't see a way out of here, because, unlike fearless Robyn Davidson, I'm a coward, she thought.

On that last night on the beach, Con had said that he loved her. That he couldn't live without her. Nobody had ever said that about her before, not even David Crowley – *especially* not David Crowley. David was actually quite nice, but she just couldn't after Grainne had gone, and besides, he wasn't very exciting – he was so straightforward, so … upright, that was the word. So, after a few outings to the cinema and dinner in a Chinese restaurant, she'd said that she was sorry. It wasn't going to work out. 'I understand, it's OK,' he'd said. It wasn't really, but it had been a relief. He'd gone to medical school and was dating a girl called Susan, who was big and sporty and loud – she was perfect for him.

She hadn't told David that she thought about Con every day. She hadn't gone to the canoe club on New Year's Day, because she'd left it too late, and then she was too embarrassed to contact him, to try to make it right, because she felt so guilty. She'd never be able to look at Con again, she'd thought, after what had happened to Grainne. And even though she'd desperately wanted to call him, she never had. And then a month passed, then two, then six, and then it was the following summer and she was sitting in a stuffy exam hall, her attention wandering from the Franco-Prussian War, Trinity College seeming like a million miles away. And now, thanks to that single honour in the Leaving Cert, it was. She sighed and tried to bring her attention back to her book, but the words kept blurring in front of her eyes.

*

The house was dark when Marie let herself in and she swore under her breath. No matter how many times she asked that eejit Mrs O'Farrell to leave the lights on, she always forgot. Probably because she was in so much of a hurry to vamoose, Marie thought. When she'd first come to see Dada, after answering the ad for a housekeeper that Marie had placed in the *Evening Press,* she'd fallen over herself to bow and scrape, doing a kind of curtsey when Dada had arrived in the kitchen. Marie was surprised that the woman didn't tug her forelock but her references were very good and even though Marie had seen a hint of something not very nice in the woman's eyes as she'd taken in the size of the hall, the stained glass windows on the landing, she'd had little choice but to follow Dada's instructions to take her on. Marie couldn't really see why they needed a housekeeper, with only the two of them rattling around the place, but Dada insisted on it: maybe dim Mrs O'Farrell, who seemed to do very little apart from sit at the kitchen table, feet up on a chair, reading *Woman's Way*, was a buffer between the two of them.

Or maybe I don't like Mrs O'Farrell because nobody can really replace Mrs D, Marie thought, going to the range and extracting the plate of watery-looking stew Mrs O'Farrell had left in the warming drawer, wrinkling her nose as the smell of fatty lamb reached her nostrils. Her stomach rebelled at the smell and she put the plate down on the kitchen table, putting the kettle on the hotplate and taking her packet of cigarettes out of her handbag. Mrs D's stews were equally watery, and her cast-iron rice pudding had been the stuff of legend, but she was *Mrs D*.

It was funny, Marie thought, how you didn't really notice a person until they weren't there any more.

She hadn't even had that close a connection with Mrs D; it was with Grainne that Mrs D had the real bond, the two of them on the sofa in front of *That's Life* or Delia Smith's cookery show after school, a plate of scones between them. Marie used to envy their closeness, their companionable silence as they sat together.

No, Marie thought, as she chewed the fatty lamb, her face, contorting as she tried to swallow, it had been Mrs D who had made sure everything would be the same. Now she was gone, and everything was different.

Once, Mrs D had told Marie that she was just too clever for her own good and, seeing the hurt look on her face, had said, 'Look, you'll always get along in life. Your sister will find it a struggle on her own. She's not as independent. She needs to know that she'll always have somebody.' What about me? Marie had wanted to say. Who will I have?

And yet, Grainne didn't have somebody any more. She was all on her own, somewhere in London, and Marie was all on her own here. Mrs D had been the one to take Grainne to that clinic and then to get her on the boat. To spirit her away to the nuns, maybe never to come back. Grainne had said she never wanted to come home. She'd told them as much in Lombardi's on that awful day in December. What must that have been like for Mrs D? She'd come back from the ferry the day after New Year's and, after lying to Dada about Grainne staying longer with her sister in Ballyshannon, without so much as a glance in Marie's direction, she had put on her apron and proceeded to clean out the range, a scourer in her hand and a bowl of ammonia in the other, so that the kitchen smelled of wee. She had a tight look on her face and answered Marie in monosyllables, and Marie hadn't known what to say to change that, except to say to herself, 'It's not my fault,' over and over again, even though it was. She had so many questions for Mrs D. How was Grainne? How had she survived the … ordeal. She couldn't even say the word 'abortion' to herself, because the idea of her sister having to go through that was too painful. How would she cope on her own? But the expression on Mrs D's face had told her that it was better not to ask.

Dada, of course, had been oblivious to the whole thing,

until the Epiphany, which fell the day before they were due to return to school. He'd looked up from his newspaper at the breakfast table and said, 'Mrs Delaney, will someone need to collect Grainne from the bus at Busáras? I assume she'll be returning for school in the morning?'

Mrs Delaney was putting a slice of toast in the toaster and she stiffened, the bread hovering over the slot, before responding, 'I'll ring my sister and check what bus she's on.'

'Splendid. Marie, I'll give you money for the necessaries.' The 'necessaries' were what he called their school copybooks and pens, but also the box of tampons that would find its way into the bathroom cabinet, or the Impulse body spray that Grainne insisted on using, liberally, every morning, a noxious smell of cheap alcohol and sugary scent wafting around the breakfast table. Dada never wanted to know about these things, but would hand Marie a tenner every week to cover it. Marie used to save a pound or two every week, and treat herself and Grainne to a trashy magazine or a big bar of Cadbury's every so often. She liked having the freedom to decide what to spend her ten whole pounds on, all the more because that's all Dada would ever give her. He never seemed to have a clue about how much things actually cost, like school uniforms or clothes. Mrs D had to act as a go-between, letting Dada know what the girls needed, always adding on a fiver or two, which she'd stuff in to Marie's hand as she was going out the door. 'Buy yourself a little something,' she'd mutter.

Marie exchanged a look with Mrs D and Marie blushed. She'd saved sixty pounds from the necessaries money and had offered it to Mrs D before she'd left with Grainne. Mrs D had shoved it back in her pocket, her angry fingers jabbing at Marie. 'I will see to that, thank you, Madam. You've done enough.' Marie had just wanted to throw the money on the fire, but instead, she'd put it in an envelope and had hidden it in Grainne's suitcase.

When Dada left the room for his swim, she opened her mouth to ask. Mrs D silenced her with a glare. 'I will think of something,' she said ominously.

That evening, Marie came home from Claire's, where she'd gone to tell her that she hadn't had the flu after all at New Year. She'd told her the whole sorry story, and had accepted Claire's tight hug and the wad of pink tissues she'd shoved into Marie's hand. 'Poor you,' she'd said, putting her arm around Marie and giving her a squeeze. 'Poor, poor you.'

'Poor *me*?' Marie had wailed. 'What about poor Grainne?'

Claire had shrugged. 'I know, but Grainne had people to look after her. You don't.'

'She needed someone, Claire.'

'So do you,' Claire had said sharply.

Marie hadn't thought about it like that, and had allowed herself to wallow in self-pity for a while, which lasted until she got home to find an envelope on the hall table addressed to her. Mrs D was nowhere to be seen, and when Marie went into her room, she stopped dead. It had been cleaned out. The Mills & Boons had been taken off the bedside table, the statue of the Child of Prague, the set of rosary beads. When Marie opened the wardrobe, a pair of wire hangers clanged gently in the empty space. Mrs D had packed her bags and gone.

Marie stood there, in the little pink room, her heart thumping in her chest. She felt the tears prick her eyes, and she sat down on the little, hard chair that Mrs D used to sit on, to say her prayers. Please, please, please, she thought, don't let it be true. Please let Mrs D come in the front door, muttering under her breath, hanging her coat and scarf up on the coat stand inside the hall door; please let her be in the kitchen, clattering pans around. Marie wasn't sure quite whom she was talking to – God? – but she hoped someone was listening. Because she didn't know what to do by herself. She spotted the Miraculous Medal draped over the lampshade on the bedside table. Marie didn't believe in Miraculous Medals, but she took it and put it around her neck, and as she did, she wondered if God had been listening to her. She was still wearing it now.

Mrs D's note had been short. 'Dear Marie. Even though it is not my wish, I have to leave. Please understand that it is for the best. I was protecting your sister – you understand that. You will be fine.' She'd signed it 'Isabel Delaney'.

'You will be fine.' Why on earth would you think that, Mrs D, Marie thought, putting the letter down on the hall table. Mrs D had always thought that Marie was the strong one, the capable one, but she wasn't, she thought as she sat there, letter in hand. She really wasn't, and at that moment, she desperately wanted Mrs D to appear, to squash her into her cushiony bosom and tell her to get a hold of herself. She scanned the lines of the letter, hoping that if she read it a few more times, something might jump out at her, some hidden subtext, some hint that Mrs D wasn't punishing her for failing her sister. Hadn't left her to face Dada alone. But there was nothing else but the bald words on the sheet of blue Basildon Bond.

Marie wanted to pack a bag herself, to run, before Dada came home. She swallowed the big lump in her throat and, clutching the Miraculous Medal, went out. She had no idea where she was going, wandering aimlessly down to Seaview to stare out at the water, at the lights of Howth twinkling across the bay, then turning and heading towards the town, past the chipper, the smells of vinegar and frying reaching her nostrils. She rummaged in her pocket to see if she had the money for chips, but all she found was a ten-pence piece, and she continued miserably, wishing that she'd brought a coat. All she had on was a jumper and jeans, and the wind whipped through them, making her feel chilled to the bone. Her teeth began to chatter and she shoved her hands in her pockets, hunching her shoulders against the cold. She thought of David Crowley then, and she knew she could tell him – he'd help. But it didn't seem fair to involve him in this – to suck him into the big mess any more than she had. She didn't want him to think any more badly of her than he already did. No, as she trudged back up the main street, past McSwiney's, where Mrs D had loved to 'kill time', before and after Mass, the charity shop where she'd haggled over the price of some knick-knack she'd set her eye on, Marie knew that she was truly on her own. And that, unless she wanted to freeze to death, she'd have to face Dada sooner or later.

When she got in, opening the door and closing it as softly as she could behind her, she wondered if she was brave enough to head for the kitchen, before concluding that she wasn't, and she began to tiptoe up the stairs. But then a voice said, 'Marie?'

Fuck. She stopped, mid-stairs, and turned around. Dada was standing beside the open study door. She could see his desk behind him, his papers illuminated in a pool of light. The study was his refuge, his hiding place, and it was disconcerting to catch a glimpse of the inner sanctum, like getting a glimpse into the inside of Dada's head. Marie couldn't understand why Dada wanted her to see it now – maybe he was trying to tell her something.

'Where exactly is your sister?' His arms were folded, and he was looking at her, his dark eyes glittering underneath his wrinkled forehead. But there was something else in his expression, something she'd never seen before. Something uncertain. Marie hesitated for a moment, wondering if she could trust it and tell him the truth about Grainne. She desperately wanted to, to confide in someone, even if it was Dada. Was that what he wanted, she wondered. Was that what the open study door was all about?

'Dada, it's … she's …' she began.

Dada's expression changed then, to a look Marie found familiar. Thank God I didn't tell him, she thought, as she blurted, 'She's in Ballyshannon, with Mrs D's sister. She'll be back.'

Dada was quick. He walked briskly along the hall and took the stairs two at a time, reaching out to grab Marie's arm, before she had time to escape. 'Kindly tell me where she is. And no lies.' Marie shrank back against the wall, and, seeing the look on her face, he sighed heavily, letting go of her arm.

The silence that descended then was deafening and Marie knew that Dada was waiting, but there was no way in a million years that she would tell him anything.

'I have telephoned Mrs D's home in Ballyshannon, and her sister tells me that Grainne has not been staying there and that Mrs Delaney is "unavailable".'

Marie swallowed. 'Yes, Dada.'

Dada got that look on his face again, and his mouth was a thin line. 'Where the hell is she, Marie? And where the hell is Mrs Delaney?'

'I don't know,' Marie said quietly.

'I'll give you one more chance.'

'I don't know,' Marie insisted, not daring to look Dada in the eye. He turned then and walked slowly back down the stairs and into his study. He was about to close the door behind him, when he turned in the doorway and said, 'Marie, why is it so hard for you to tell me the truth?'

Because I'm scared of you, Marie thought. I'm scared of what you'll do if I tell you and I need to protect Grainne and Mrs D, even if she ran away and left it all to me to do. 'It is the truth,' she muttered.

Dada looked very sad then, as if she'd let him down terribly. And she supposed she had. She'd let them all down. 'Tell me one thing. Is she safe?' And his expression was different then – it was as if he were pleading with her.

'Yes.'

Without saying anything further, he nodded and gone into his study, closing the door softly behind him. Marie stood motionless on the stairs, listening to the 'clunk' as he picked up the ancient telephone on his desk, the 'whirr' as he turned the dial and the silence before he said, 'Hello, Mick?' Marie scuttled off to her bedroom, lying there in the dark, looking out at the moon now appearing from behind the raggy clouds. She wondered what Dada was saying to Mick. He was a detective after all. Did that mean that he'd track Grainne down? She wondered exactly where Grainne was and what she was doing right now. Was she thinking of her, of Marie? Or was she trying to forget her, and everything she'd left behind here? Marie remembered that the day before Grainne had left, Marie had asked her that question, 'Will you remember me, Gra?' Grainne had looked at her sadly and said, 'If you don't mind, Marie, I'll try to forget.' Marie knew what her sister meant, but she'd felt it like a blow to the stomach.

Later that evening, Mick turned up and they went into Dada's study and when Mick came out again, the smell of his cigarette smoke wafting down the hall, he didn't come to say hello to her, the way he always did. To tell her how Mum's old friend Biddy was, or to ask her how her studies were going and to congratulate her on being such a brainbox, or to rummage in his pocket for his money clip and pull out a few pound notes, pressing them into her hand.

She was still lying on her bed when she heard the faint knock on her door. When she didn't respond, it opened, and Dada was standing there, the light from the landing behind him making him look like a giant in the doorway. 'Marie. I need to talk to you.'

Marie sat up, fully clothed. Dada sat down gingerly on the side of the bed and he said, 'Mick is going to make enquiries. Do you have anything to say that might help him?' He looked carefully at Marie, inviting her to tell him the truth.

Marie twisted the bedspread in her right hand, looking Dada directly in the eye. 'No, Dada.' She didn't know what

Mick would be able to do, but it seemed more important not to talk, to keep Grainne's secret safe for as long as she could. It seemed the least that she could do.

He looked very disappointed in her, as if he'd given her a chance and she'd failed to take it. 'Fine,' he said, getting up and walking towards the door, turning then. 'I'm worried, Marie.'

'I know, Dada. She's fine. I promise.' Marie knew that this was her last chance, but she wouldn't weaken. She wouldn't do Mrs D's work for her.

He nodded sadly. 'Goodnight.'

Marie knew that it wouldn't take Mick long to find out – he was a detective, after all, and the next day, a squad car pulled up in front of the house. Dada opened the door and there was a lot of muttering and mumbling. Her heart thumping in her chest, she remained rooted to the spot, in the pool of faint sunlight beside her wardrobe, where she'd been looking for her school jumper: with Mrs D no longer there, Marie had no idea where anything was.

She held her breath for what seemed like ages, but then the front door opened and, when she peered out of the bedroom window, Mick was walking down the front path, with a garda in uniform. When he got to the gate, he turned and looked up at her window, giving a little wave. She waved back, and wondered if she could just run downstairs after him, to the safety of the car; if she could ask him to drive her to the ferry and off to England, like Grainne. Somewhere far, far away from here and whatever it was Dada would have to say to her.

Dada didn't look up from his newspaper when Marie came

into the kitchen, school uniform on. She hesitated, wondering whether or not to help herself to a slice of bread and put it in the toaster. She hovered by the range for a moment, Dada's silence bearing down on her, pouring water from the kettle onto a teabag in her mug with 'No. 1 Daughter' on it, and waiting until the toast popped, before carrying them over to the table. She sat down as quietly as she dared and sipped her tea. There was a long silence, punctuated by the 'pip-pip' of the radio reaching eight o'clock, and the news headlines, and then Dada put down his newspaper and proceeded to talk over the radio, his voice blurred by the precise tones of the newsreader, so that Marie had to strain to listen.

'Marie, I am going away for the day and may have to stay overnight. You are to go to school today, and afterwards you are to go to Granny in Rathgar – I've told her you're coming – and then you are to return here after school tomorrow.'

Marie stopped, the mug half-way to her mouth. 'Dada, I—'

He looked at her sharply. 'Please don't tell me that you are capable of looking after yourself, when that is clearly not the case.'

Marie looked down at the black swirly pattern on the china plate in front of her, which seemed to swim as her eyes filled.

He sighed. 'Look, just do as you're told. It's better this way.'

Marie eyed him warily, and then said quietly. 'Where are you going?'

'I have business down the country.'

They both knew that he was lying, but Marie knew better than to say anything further. 'I'll pack a few things,' she said dully.

'Do, so.' And Dada lifted the paper and began to examine it again.

★

The following day, when Marie let herself in after a night spent listening to Granny talking about her herbaceous borders and the scourge of drugs in inner-city Dublin, then a full day watching the clock on the wall in school, willing the hands to turn, Dada appeared at the door to his study, as if he'd been waiting for her. Without a word, he ushered her into the room. Marie put her schoolbag down and shuffled in to the gloom. It was months since she'd set foot in the place, and she was surprised to see that it was tidy and clean. The piles of papers on his desk were neatly stacked and the thick law books arranged in a circle at the foot of his chair. The desk looked as if it was regularly dusted and it must have been by him, as he'd never let Mrs D in. It was strange to think of Dada dusting.

She stood there for a few moments, waiting, while Dada moved some papers on his desk, as if he was looking for something. Eventually, he looked up at her.

'I've let you down, Marie. You and Grainne. I haven't been firm enough with either of you and that's why we are in this … situation.'

Marie waited to see if he'd say anything more about 'this situation'. She wasn't sure what he knew or what he'd learned 'down the country', wherever that was. Her mind spun, but she tried to just focus on keeping her mouth shut and letting Dada do the talking. She'd long since learned that it was better that way. 'I should have been more vigilant. God knows what your mother—' he began. 'Yes, well.' He cleared his throat. 'Here's the thing.'

He began to talk, and Marie watched his lips move as he told her that for the next year, she'd be a virtual prisoner in the house. She was to go to school every day and come home at 4.30, she wasn't allowed out except on a Saturday afternoon until after the Leaving Certificate, and when she got her results, she was going to study nursing. He had no intention of paying for her to 'waste her time' in Trinity College. 'All those stupid novels you fill your head with, Marie, and all those dreams about being a journalist; they are just that, dreams, and dreams will get you nowhere in life. The sooner you learn that, the better.' He softened momentarily then. 'You need to be tough, Marie, to survive in this world. You must know that, and you need real skills to survive, not pipe dreams.' He shook his head. 'I'm only sorry I didn't teach you that lesson sooner. I didn't manage to save your sister, but I will save you.'

'It's not fair,' Marie muttered, looking down at the laces on her sensible black school shoes.

He tutted. 'Life isn't fair, Marie, as you will no doubt have noticed. My job as your father is to keep you safe. This way, at least I can keep an eye on you.'

'Like you kept an eye on Grainne?' The words were out before she could stop them, and when he reached over his desk suddenly she didn't step back quickly enough to avoid the hard slap across her cheek. It made a cracking sound and the two of them stood there then, in silence. Marie lifted a hand to her cheek, and it was smarting, but as Dada came around the table, saying, 'I'm sorry, Marie, I'm sorry,' over and over again, she stepped back. 'Don't touch me.' And she walked out and up the stairs to her bedroom, where she took out her notes on Machiavelli and proceeded to study them, her cheek stinging.

He never said another word about Grainne, but many months later, as they sat in silence at the breakfast table, he said, 'I'm not the monster you think I am, Marie. With your sister … Look, I tried, but I lost her …'

Marie was completely still, before lifting her eyes to Dada's face. He was still chewing his toast, but his eyes had filled with tears.

★

Marie wondered now, as she opened a can of tuna and turned it out onto a saucer with a fork, whether it was possible to hate anyone more than she hated Dada, before realising that she probably knew the answer to that.

She opened the back door. 'Lucy,' she called, 'Lucy-lou, where are you?'

There was a miaow and then a pair of green eyes peered out from behind the row of ox-eye daisies that Creggs had planted for Mum years before.

'Come on. Dinner,' Marie said, as the little black cat with the fluffy coat slunk around her ankles into the kitchen, where she proceeded to demolish the tuna, her tail swishing as she did so, a furry antenna tuned to the atmosphere in the house. What would Mrs D think, Marie smiled to herself, as Lucy ate. She hated cats, saying that they were disease-carrying vermin spreading their germs around the place. But then, Mrs D wasn't around to see anything, was she? Marie went to the kitchen door and sat down on the step, reaching into her pocket and pulling out a packet of Benson & Hedges, taking one out and lighting it, shoving the packet back in her pocket. She inhaled and exhaled with a sigh of satisfaction.

Lucy came out and slithered around Marie's ankles, purring, before settling down on the step, which was chilly and damp. Marie inhaled and exhaled and rubbed between Lucy's ears. 'Just you and me, Lucy, eh?' Lucy's tail swished as if in agreement. 'Crazy cat lady, that's me,' Marie said.

Lucy had turned up the day after Mrs D had left, just appeared on the doorstep, and when Marie had opened the door to put the milk bottles out, Lucy had dashed in through her legs into the hall, where she'd stood, looking around her as if to say, 'So, this is my new home.' She'd never left and even though she made Marie sneeze, she hadn't the heart to kick her out. Instead, Lucy curled up on her bed every night, making sure to lie on Marie's feet, and Marie let her, because even Lucy was better than no one at all.

After a few pulls on the cigarette and a few rubs of Lucy's furry head, Marie felt ready to think about Grainne. While she was at work, she'd manage not to think of her sister, as she lifted Mrs Doherty gently off her bedpan, or took Mrs Langan to the bathroom and back to make sure she exercised after her operation. She'd pretend that it was just another ordinary day at St John's, with the list of duties that kept her from thinking about anything else, like how much she hated what she was doing, the smells, the awful noises that people made, the misery etched on their faces. But now that everything was quiet, she had no choice but to think about her sister. She couldn't avoid it. In the deathly hush of the evening, there was nothing else to do, except to think about her shame at having let her sister down so badly. And about how much she missed her.

'What can I do, Lucy-lou?' she said now. 'Hmm? Do you think I can say sorry to Grainne? I'm not sure I really know how. I don't even know where to start.'

Lucy looked at her, eyes round, then turned and walked off down the garden. Marie knew that it was silly, but she felt like crying, like shouting, 'Come back, Lucy,' as she watched the cat's backside disappear behind the daisies again, leaving Marie alone.

Chapter 8

Marie had rung Claire and asked her to save her from the Garda Club, having told Dada that she was on nights, but as she wove her way through the crowds in the Buttery, she was beginning to think that bumping into the garda from Tubbercurry might not have been such a bad idea after all. It wasn't just the braying tones of the 'West Brits' as Seamus used to call them – from thousand-acre estates in Co. Carlow, or all the posh people who had ended up in Trinity College because they hadn't quite made it to Oxford or Cambridge – it was that the place reminded her of Con. She wasn't afraid that she'd run into him, or Seamus, because they'd left after their finals that summer, it was that Trinity *was* Con; the statues, the front square, the dusty lecture hall; Con, and the Marie she'd almost been.

A man in an England rugby shirt elbowed her as she

pushed her way forward, yelling 'Sorry!' then continuing with his rude joke about pigs. Marie moved out of earshot as he said the punchline, but a roar of laughter followed her towards the bar. God, she hated this place. And where the bloody hell was Claire?

Eventually, Marie spotted her by the jukebox in the corner, a pint in front of her, surrounded by a small crowd, all of whom were laughing at something she was saying. She was waving her arms and her head was thrown back as she told her story. She was dressed in a brown suede jacket from a charity shop, a pair of faded Levi 501s, Doc Martens and a huge PLO scarf around her neck. She didn't look any different to any other student, but she was – she was queen of first-year Economic and Social Studies, a free spirit and a true feminist. She'd ditched Liam before she'd started, not because he wouldn't leave his wife and kids, but because he would. He'd turned up at her door one night and told her that he'd packed his bags. Claire had been horrified and had told him to go straight back and to beg his wife's forgiveness. Since then, she'd had a string of one-night stands, cutting a swathe through first year, living the life that Marie had thought was hers to have, instead of wasting it all at St John's. She'd have been jealous, if she didn't love Claire so much.

'Mareeee,' Claire yelled, when she caught sight of her, pulling her into a hug and planting a big smack of a kiss on her cheek. 'There you are.' And she turned to the crowd that had gathered around her. 'This is my friend, Marie, who is a genius and totally wasted on the nursing profession. And she's funny and lovely … and—' Claire clasped her hands together and Marie blushed to the roots of her hair. 'Stop, Claire, will you?'

'Well, you are all of these things,' Claire yelled, 'And you are also not drunk, like me, so let me get that underway,' and she waved in the direction of the bar. 'Barman! Barman, Monsieur!'

Oh, Lord, Marie thought, she really *was* drunk, but Claire drunk was only funny. She wasn't embarrassing or silly or unpleasant. She didn't do foolish things – she just talked very loudly and then fell asleep somewhere, before gliding home safely, to emerge the next day with an hilarious anecdote – some romantic encounter with a fellow student that had ended in a cloud of kissing and hash smoke and champagne. Claire was too sophisticated to fall over drunk, or to end the night throwing up in the toilet – or worse. An image of Grainne floated into Marie's mind, as she watched her friend try to catch the barman's attention.

'A pint of your finest ale for my friend here.' Claire waved at Marie.

The barman tried not to roll his eyes to heaven. 'Guinness, love?'

'God, no!' Claire shouted, as if he'd offered her arsenic. 'Let's have … something bracingly German.'

'Heineken then,' the barman said tiredly, pulling a pint, then putting it on the counter. 'One ninety, love.'

Claire mumbled and muttered and began to rummage in her pockets. 'Hang on a sec, I need to secure some funds.'

'It's OK, Claire, I have it,' Marie said, reaching into her handbag for her purse. Then a hand stretched across the two of them and stuffed a fiver into the barman's hand.

'Thanking you,' the barman said crisply, turning to the till and ringing up the amount, before returning the change.

Marie knew that hand. It was large and square and she turned to see David Crowley, pint of Guinness in hand. 'Thanks, David,' she said quietly. She was mortified, because the last time they'd met, they'd been on one of their so-called dates, encounters of such supreme awkwardness that even thinking about them made Marie cringe. The last one had been to see the seals at Bullock harbour on a lovely late-summer's evening. The sea was calm and the sky a lovely pink, and a little crowd had gathered on the slipway to look at the family of seals playing in the water, with their huge brown eyes and lovely silvery whiskers. Who couldn't love a seal? Marie thought as she and David stood behind the gang of kids, who were all jumping up and down, waiting for the man who lived in the cottage on the slipway to arrive with his bucket of fish-heads.

They were standing a foot or so apart, and Marie could feel his presence, his hands in his pockets, waiting awkwardly beside her, unsure where to put himself. She knew that he wanted her to get a bit closer, but she couldn't. She was just frozen to the spot. A little boy zoomed past then, knocking into David, who reached out a hand to steady him. 'Easy, son.'

'I'm sorry,' the little boy said, 'I'm just so excited, because I'm going to feed the seals!'

'I know, so am I.' David crouched down so that he was at the same height as the boy and he smiled at him easily.

'Have you got any fish?' the boy asked.

David looked sad. 'Do I need some?'

'Of course you do, you ninny.' The little boy guffawed,

pointing to the bundle of sprats in the little red bucket he was carrying. 'You can share mine, if you like.'

'That's very kind of you,' David said, and allowed the boy to take his hand and to lead him to the edge of the slipway, the two of them leaning forward slightly to look into the water.

Marie had watched them both and she wondered just how much more perfect David Crowley could be. Good father material, she'd heard Claire call someone once. He was exactly that, and kind and considerate, with excellent manners. Not at all the idiot she'd once thought he was. But that didn't mean that she fancied him. She didn't. She looked at David Crowley and she felt … nothing. No tingling, no fluttering, nothing. After that evening, she'd made her excuses and she hadn't seen him since.

'You're welcome,' he said now, clinking his pint glass against Marie's. He was wearing an Aran sweater with two buttons at the side and he looked like a giant traditional music player, with his rosy cheeks and rude good health. He'd had his hair cut so he wasn't sporting his mullet any more, and he was wearing a nice pair of glasses, so he looked almost handsome. When he noticed her staring, he looked rueful. 'My aunty Maeve knitted it. She said it'd keep me warm when I was doing my rounds. She was there when I was getting ready to go out, so I had to put it on.'

Oh God. Only David Crowley would wear a ridiculous jumper out of sheer niceness. 'Right,' Marie said. 'It's very … traditional.'

'You could say that.' There was an awkward pause then, before Marie said, 'Where's Susan?' She looked around, even though she could hardly have missed David's new girlfriend, as she had a voice like a foghorn and wore really bright colours.

He looked down at his pint. 'We split up.'

'Oh, I'm sorry to hear that.'

David shrugged. 'S'alright. She was a bit … loud.'

Marie giggled, and he smiled back. 'I don't have much luck with women.' And he gave her a careful look. Marie took a swig of her pint and tried not to choke as it got stuck in her throat, giving a short cough instead, her eyes filling with tears.

'Are you alright?'

'Yes,' Marie squeaked, wishing she didn't sound quite so stupid.

'So, how's nursing?'

'God-awful. How's medicine?'

'Would you like me to say god-awful?' He smiled at her kindly.

'No. Tell me the truth.'

'I love it, Marie,' he said. 'It's just so … exciting. All that stuff to learn and the hospital rounds, just putting it all into action. I love the way that you can make patients feel better, even if the news isn't good – you can make them feel that you care, and that you want to help them recover.' He leaned back against the bar now, in his Aran jumper, his eyes bright, and Marie understood what it was like to do something you really loved. How much it could add to your life and how much you could add to other people's. There she was, not helping anyone to feel much better at all, hating every minute of her job, making herself miserable, and probably her patients too. But she was stuck with it. There was no way out. At that moment, Marie had a sudden vision of the years ahead, years spent wiping bottoms and emptying bedpans, and the thought felt so overwhelming, she wondered how on earth she'd get through them.

'Marie?'

'Yes?' she said sadly.

'I'm sorry, I didn't mean to be tactless, I …'

'Oh, don't be silly, David. It's great that you love doing what you do. It's brilliant, and I'm sure you are a great doctor and your patients all love you. But you're good at your job. I'm a bit of a disaster.' She smiled bleakly.

'I'm sure you're not.'

'Oh, believe me, I am. Nobody's died just yet, but that's only because Sister Dolores keeps an eye on me to make sure I don't kill anyone. My God, those bedpans, they just make me heave. And as for the catheters – imagine having to stick one inside of another human being. Ugh.' She shuddered.

David burst out laughing.

'What's so funny?'

'You. You're hilarious even when you're being miserable.'

'Hilarious?'

'Yes.'

Marie shrugged and then she began to relax. If David found her misery funny, well, maybe she could feel slightly less miserable about it. She began to tell him a funny story that Eamon, the porter, had told her, about a patient who'd swallowed his son's pet hamster, which sounded a bit unlikely to Marie, but still. Before too long, they found themselves chatting away about books and music and politics and Marie found herself remembering, as she always did, that David Crowley wasn't that bad. He had quite a lot to say for himself, really, and he had a sense of humour. He would make a really good friend, she thought, as she giggled at one of his jokes.

And then he spoiled it all by asking her out.

'David, no,' Marie said firmly. 'It didn't work out the last time.'

He looked crushed, and Marie felt a bit sorry for him. 'That's because it was too soon after Grainne and your exams.' Or so you said, the unspoken accusation hung in the air. At the mention of Grainne's name, David turned a deep shade of red and looked down at his pint.

For God's sake, Marie thought. We should be able to *talk* about her. 'Besides, you've only just split up with Susan. I'd be your rebound girl.'

'Susan and I split up a month ago, after two months of dating, a trip to Dublin Zoo and a walk or two around Howth Head. She was not the love of my life.'

There was a slightly too-long silence, while Marie digested this, which he broke by saying, 'Just as friends. C'mon. I promise not to take you to *Star Wars*. And you can tell me all your medical miseries and I'll help you to keep your job.'

'I'll think about it,' Marie said. David looked very disappointed.

Being David, he insisted on seeing her home, clambering on the number 7A and sitting beside her, taking up more than half the seat, so that Marie was squashed against the window. 'Sorry,' he mumbled, as he moved to one side.

'It's OK,' Marie said, because she quite liked being squashed up against him. It was like being squashed against a giant tree, solid and warm. A fairly silent tree, one who was happy to let her jabber on whilst he nodded, as if she were deeply fascinating, and Marie found herself relaxing, asking him about his sister, who had gone to America for the summer on a J1 visa and who had come home two stone lighter, with a nose piercing and an American accent. David's mother was still going to Mass every morning to pray for her.

'I wonder if I'd like America,' Marie said wistfully.

David shook his head. 'I don't think so. There's no culture, really, not like Europe. And there's nothing really old in it, or exotic. Not like … India. I can see you there.'

'I've always wanted to go,' Marie said sadly. 'I read *A Passage to India* last year and it was so lovely,' she sighed.

'One day you'll go,' David said reassuringly. 'For real.'

'Hmm.' The words 'for real' stung a bit, but she knew what he meant. The pages of a book weren't real – no amount of reading E.M. Forster would equal actually being in India, in the dust and heat. Marie knew that – she wasn't deluded. And yet, for the moment, the book would have to do. And besides, Marie didn't believe David; she didn't see how she could go anywhere except St John's. Oh, it was all such a mess, she thought gloomily, looking out of the window at the sea as the bus drove along the coast road.

Of course, he insisted on seeing her to her door, which only made her more annoyed with him. He was such a perfect gentleman, and she found herself willing him to be a bit meaner, a bit more like … well, a bit more like Con, she supposed. Mean was interesting. Nice wasn't.

'Do you want to come in?' she said grumpily, shoulders hunched in her grey jacket with the padded shoulders that was now too small for her. It was supposed to be like the one Simon Le Bon from Duran Duran wore, and Marie wondered if the man didn't feel the cold in it, as it didn't have a zip. It didn't suit her anyway.

David looked at her sadly. 'No, I have an early start in the morning, but thanks.'

'OK.' She tried not to sound too pleased, sticking her key in the lock and turning it. 'Thanks for seeing me home.'

'That's OK,' he said, turning and giving her a brief wave, before walking down the road. Marie watched the outline of his silly Aran sweater as he disappeared into the dark. She was about to close the front door, when he turned and called out to her. 'Marie?'

'What?' She felt a flicker of impatience. It was freezing now and she wanted to fill a hot water bottle and settle into bed with Robyn Davidson. At first, she didn't hear him properly, because his words were snatched away by the stiff sea breeze.

'It's your life.'

'What?'

'I said, it's your life. Don't forget it.' And with another wave, he was gone.

Feck off, Marie thought bitterly, as she closed the door firmly on him and stood there in the dark of the hall. How dare he lecture her. How dare he? It wasn't her life at all. That was the whole point. She closed her eyes for a second, then opened them into the silence. The house seemed to settle around her like a heavy cloak.

'It's your life.' What did that mean? For so long, her life had meant Grainne, looking after her, making sure that she could navigate her way through life; that she could do all of the practical things and that she, Marie, would take care of the rest. It wasn't that Grainne wasn't capable – well, clearly she wasn't – it was just that Mum had asked Marie to look after her and that's what she'd done. When Grainne went, well, Marie hadn't really known who she was any more. Con had shown her a different kind of Marie, but that Marie had gone almost before she'd really had a chance. Now, she was drifting, letting Dada tell her what to do, because she didn't have the energy to fight him, hating herself for it.

Damn David Crowley. He didn't have a clue.

★

She didn't see the letter until she was climbing the stairs to bed, having sat in the kitchen for a while with Lucy on her lap, a cup of tea and a plate of Fig Rolls on the range beside her. It was on the hall table, propped up in front of the letter holder. She recognised the writing immediately, and later, she'd wonder why on earth Dada had said nothing about it, unless it was silly Mrs O'Farrell who'd placed it there. If Dada had got hold of it, she'd thought later, hands shaking as she'd opened the blue envelope with the heart sticker on the back, God knows what he'd have done with it.

It was the sticker that gave it away. Grainne had a big collection of them, given to her on birthdays and at Christmas, which she'd stick onto absolutely everything, from her schoolbooks to her hairbrush, to the board at the top of her bed, which still had a collection of wrinkled, ancient stickers of animals on it. She had stuck a glittery gold one on the back of the blue envelope, and Marie snagged her nail on it as she ripped the letter open. She pulled the letter out – one page of a copybook, covered in Grainne's scribble – and she began to read.

23 Violet Street,
London SW1
October 1983

Dear Marie
I hope you are well. Mrs D said that I wasn't to write to you. She said that I was to leave you well alone, but I don't think that's very nice. Besides, it's been ten months and I think I'm not as angry with you any more. I need to write to you, because you're my sister and I miss you. How long do you think I'll need to stay, Mar?

I don't want to come back to Seaview Road, but I don't like it here either. There are nuns and some of them are nice – Sister Bonaventure is – but Sister Englebert is horrible. She's deaf and she's really rude. She calls all the girls hussies and she says that wearing no knickers is what got them to St Mary's. I wore knickers, so I don't know what she's talking about. Why are there nuns here as well as in Ireland, Mar? I thought they only lived there.

I'm doing the cooking for St Mary's. That's nice, because I really like it. And it gives me something to do, because it's very lonely here. London is huge, Marie. It just goes on and on, and it's really hard to find your way around. I have to work out the directions before I get on the Tube, so that I don't end up miles away. I go to Oxford Street every Saturday with the money I get paid for working at St Mary's. I go into Top Shop and I look at all the clothes

— they are so amazing, Marie. I spent £20 the first time I went on a skirt and a cropped top, but it was all my money for the week, so Sister Bonaventure had to sit me down and show me how to budget. Now, I don't spend so much. But there's nothing else to do. I don't know anyone here and I haven't got any friends. At home, I had you, Mar. Now, I have no one. I don't count Yvette in my room, because she's not nice. She's always saying mean things. And she smokes all the time.

Mar, do babies go to heaven, even when they're killed? I need to know that. Maybe you'll know the answer. Do you remember Sister Veronica used to go on about Limbo all the time? Do you think that's where my baby is? Please write back.

Love, Grainne.

It was as if Grainne were in the room, with her silly questions; when Marie closed her eyes, she could see her sister in front of her, wearing the clothes that she'd stolen from her, too long and too small for her at the same time, her blue eyes innocent as she said something dim or asked a perfectly ridiculous question. It had used to drive Marie mad, and yet now, as she scanned the lines of Grainne's childish handwriting, she longed to hear her sister's music wafting out through the door, the snip-snip of her scissors as she cut pictures out of magazines. She wanted her to come in and ask that Marie fix her hair or tell her how she was going to marry Michael Douglas because she loved his movies. Stuff that Marie had used to think was utterly stupid, because she had far more important things on her mind, but which she now realised was *Grainne*. Happy Grainne, who loved life, before all of this had happened.

Marie thought of her sister, all alone, in that convent in London, thinking about her dead baby, wondering if he or she was in heaven. Grainne had been so innocent, such a baby herself, and Marie wondered how what had happened to her had changed her. Maybe she'd be a criminal now, in Ireland. Imagine that. Her sister who had had no other choice. Did she think about Anthony Daly, too? Marie blinked away the picture of him in her mind, a big, dark-haired boy with a scowl on his face. She'd seen him around the town, but to her shame, she'd crossed the road to avoid bumping into him.

Maybe I should go to London, Marie thought. Grainne needs me, obviously, but if I go, Dada will know, and he'll kill me. And besides, she thought, I've done enough damage, haven't I? Grainne was better off without her.

She sighed and made her way wearily up the stairs to bed, climbing in and opening the book she'd been reading, but it was no good. The words swam in front of her eyes. She threw Robyn Davidson down on the bedspread. What the hell use was she now? She thought of David Crowley, in his Aran jumper, telling her that it was her life, whatever that meant, and she felt a twist of anger in her gut. She swore and threw back the bedclothes, climbing out of bed and kneeling down so that she could pull the box out from under the bed, coughing at the cloud of dust she'd dislodged, then turning the key in the little lock.

Her books about Australia were still there, but it was as if they belonged to someone else. And a picture of Mum and

Dada on their wedding day, Mum smiling serenely, Dada looking noble beside her. 'Look after your sister.' But what if she's not there, Mum? she asked the photo. What if she no longer needs me?

The writing pad was still there, too, and Marie thought that Grainne would like it, because it was pink and had pictures of rainbows on it. She picked up the biro and began to write. 'Dear Grainne.' But then she stopped. She had nothing to say to Grainne – nothing that would help her anyway.

★

The following week, Marie was sitting on the end of Mrs Spence's bed, reading *The Time of the Hunter's Moon*, by Victoria Holt. Mrs Spence hadn't been terribly impressed when Marie had turned up with it, because she only liked Jean Plaidy, but she was warming to it, particularly when 'dashing' Jason Verringer turned up, who may or may not have murdered his wife with whom, of course, governess Cordelia fell in love. Honestly, Marie thought, what was it about these brooding anti-heroes? What's wrong with a nice man, Cordelia? she thought as she read. She blushed as she thought about David in his Aran jumper, and Con O'Sullivan in his too-short corduroy jacket – what was she, if not silly Cordelia?

'"Jason," Cordelia breathed, "you are everything I desire …"' she began to read, before being interrupted by Mrs Spence's start of surprise, as her eyes opened and she beamed. 'My goodness, look, Marie, it's Jason!'

Marie turned around, wondering if Mrs Spence's dementia

was causing her to see things, to see David Crowley standing at the end of the bed, in a white doctor's coat, a stethoscope around her neck.

Flustered, Marie jumped up, the book clattering to the floor.

'Sorry,' David muttered. 'I should have told you. I'm on rotation here this month.'

'Oh, right.' Marie smoothed down her uniform, tugging at her hat. She felt such a fool, reading that silly nonsense at the top of her voice. David Crowley must have heard it. He must think I'm such an idiot, she thought.

'You're very handsome,' Mrs Spence cut in. 'Are you married?'

David blushed and smiled. 'No, I'm only nineteen.'

'Oh,' Mrs Spence said, with a gleam in her eye. 'A baby. If only I were a few years younger.' She allowed the words to hang in the air for a few seconds, before adding, 'Still, Marie's on the lookout, aren't you, dear?'

'That's not what I hear,' David said dryly.

'Oh, she is. Look at her, don't you think she's a bit lonely? And she's such a lovely girl, too. So pretty … ' Mrs Spence looked wistful.

'Thanks, Mrs Spence, I'll get you that cup of tea now,' Marie said briskly.

'And I'm here to talk to you about your medication, Mrs Spence,' David said warmly, sitting down at the edge of her bed. Marie could hear Mrs Spence telling him that he could adjust her medication any time, if he caught her drift, as she walked as quickly as she could down the ward to the kitchen. She made Mrs Spence her tea, her hands shaking as she filled the mug with boiling water, stirring and adding sugar and milk very slowly, hoping that by the time she emerged David Crowley would be gone. She'd been getting on perfectly well since she'd last seen him, managing not to think once about what he'd said to her; about it being 'her' life. She didn't want to be reminded of it now.

Of course, he wasn't gone. He was sitting beside Mrs O'Brien's bed, listening to the greyhound chat, nodding and smiling as he examined Mrs O'Brien's file, looking as if he completely belonged in St Anthony's. When Marie bustled past with the tea, he glanced up at her and caught her eye, a brief smile flickering on his lips. In spite of herself, Marie smiled back, because Mrs O'Brien was funny. She was quite fond of her, really and she felt really sorry that she had endless bladder infections and a daughter who never visited. It struck her that most of the people's problems in St Anthony's were down to loneliness and could be solved with a simple visit.

Even so, when David Crowley asked her if she had time for lunch in the canteen, she said she hadn't, because she had the meds trolley to do and then she had to check Mrs Spence's blood pressure. She wanted him to know that she was still cross with him.

'Do you know, my dear, I wouldn't be surprised if it *was* high,' Mrs Spence trilled as Marie sat down on the bed with the monitor. 'After my visit from the dashing doctor!' She clutched the neck of her pink dressing gown and giggled. She was like a schoolgirl, Marie thought, with the faint tinge to her cheeks, the sparkling eyes.

'You've been reading too much Victoria Holt,' Marie said briskly, rolling up the elderly lady's sleeve and wrapping the cuff around her tiny arm, with its papery skin. 'All that romance, it's unrealistic.'

Mrs Spence eyed Marie sharply, her blue eyes pale in her face. 'Oh, it may be unrealistic, my dear, but where would we be without love? The world would be a very bleak place indeed. Just you remember that.'

Marie was pressing the rubber bulb to inflate the cuff, and as she let it go, she thought, you're right, Mrs Spence. It is a bleak place. We all think we can manage just fine by ourselves. That we don't need love, but we do. Victoria Holt has a point. 'I'll try, Mrs Spence.'

Mrs Spence looked at her sharply. 'Good, because you are far too young to be that cynical, my dear.' And with that, she reached into her bedside locker and pulled out a bar of Fry's Peppermint Cream, breaking off a bit and staring blissfully into space. Marie took it to mean that she was dismissed. Just as well, she thought bleakly to herself, because it seems that everyone has something to say to me; a little lecture about who I am and what kind of life I'm leading. Why don't they just leave me alone?

Marie waited until she was sure David Crowley had gone home, because she just couldn't face him, going down to the canteen after her shift. She sat there for a few moments, the noises of the canteen around her, the clattering of the catering trays, the rattle of cups on saucers. She could hear someone talking about the big murder trial that was in all the newspapers at the moment, one that the whole country had been following, and she idly thought that she might delay going home by having another cigarette.

She was about to go outside to huddle beside the bins,

when she changed her mind. She wasn't sure if it was David Crowley's arrival that had put her off, or Grainne's letter, which she'd been carrying around with her all week, or Mrs Spence, but she suddenly wondered to herself if she hadn't anything better to do than to smoke cigarettes. Really and truly. She sighed, then she put on her coat and, instead of going for a cigarette, she walked down the Rathmines Road, past the library, until she got to the building beside it, lurking at the back of a dusty car park.

The silvery letters on the dusty grey exterior said: SWIMMING POOL.

She'd passed the building every single day and had never even once had the urge to go in. After all, she hated swimming. But now, something drew her on. She walked across the car park and her eye was caught by a girl coming out of the pool, a stripy bag over her shoulder, her damp hair falling onto her shoulders. She had a look on her face of contentment, as if all of her features were at rest, not like Marie with the line between her eyebrows, the tense, pursed mouth. I'd like to look like that, Marie thought, stopping for a moment, then crossing the empty car park to the side of the building. A clump of dusty trees sheltered the entrance to the pool, and a few bicycles had been dropped on the ground, probably by the local kids. Marie stepped over them, then hesitated outside the heavy wooden door, with its frosted glass panels, before pulling it open.

Inside, it was dark and gloomy, and the distant sounds of splashing made Marie feel as if she was in a fish tank. Her stomach churned, and she felt her heart flutter. Maybe this was a bad idea. She was about to turn around and go back out when a cheerful looking man with a red T-shirt and blue tracksuit bottoms came up to her and said, 'Howya, love, here for a swim?'

'Eh, well, I just wanted to find out about lessons, actually,' Marie found herself saying, even though until just that moment, she'd had no interest in swimming lessons. She was just saying it to be polite. The idea of learning made her feel queasy.

'Swimming lessons.' The cheerful man beamed at her, as if she'd given him the best news of his life and said, 'Come this way, love.'

'Not now,' Marie protested, 'I don't have my swimming togs.' But Cheerful Man wasn't listening to her, because he was walking ahead of her down a long corridor, towards the pool, with its echoey sounds of children screaming and splashing. He was whistling '(Is This the Way to) Amarillo', stopping and stamping his foot when he got to the 'la-la-la' bit, then turning left. Marie followed, until she was at the edge of a swimming pool, echoey and vast, the only light coming from a row of windows set high into the walls. There was a viewing gallery two-thirds of the way up and an anxious looking mother was peering over the edge, scanning the water. Marie eyed it warily, thinking that the blue water looked far too chilly, wincing as a young boy sped past her and dive-bombed into the pool, sending up a huge splash.

'Ah, Jaysus, Anto, will you cop on,' the man yelled cheerfully at the young boy, who gave him an equally cheerful two fingers.

'Kids these days.' The man smiled. 'Now, where's Maureen?'

Maureen was born to be a swimming instructor. Marie

knew it the minute she set eyes on the woman, standing by the edge of the deep end with a swimming pole in her hand, barking instructions at a little girl in a pink costume with a frill around it. 'Kick, Kick!' she commanded, and the little girl dutifully moved her feet up and down in the water. 'I said kick!' Maureen ordered. 'Harder!' A large woman with an even larger bosom and a thatch of bright red hair, a row of gold chains around her neck, a pair of big, strong legs attached to a pair of huge-looking feet in flip-flops, Maureen clearly was built to inspire fear in her subjects.

'Maureen, love, will you stop terrorising the poor kid,' the man shouted. At this, Maureen looked up and her fierce features relaxed into a smile, which was almost more terrifying than her cross face, and then scowled again. 'Joe, you're interrupting my lesson.'

Joe ignored her. 'This lady wants to have swimming lessons,' he said, indicating Marie, who was hovering behind him as if she were trying to hide.

Maureen looked her up and down, as if assessing a race horse. 'Beginner?' she barked.

'Well, I can swim,' Marie began. 'I just—'

'Refresher classes for nervous swimmers, Tuesdays, 7.30,' Maureen barked, then returned to her work of intimidating the small child, who was clinging to the rail around the pool, teeth chattering. 'Did I say to stop kicking? Did I?'

God almighty, thought Marie. I'm never coming back to this place, ever. Frankly, I'd rather drown, if I have to have her as a teacher.

As if reading her mind, Joe said, 'Ah, her bark's worse than her bite. She's a good teacher. Great at building confidence.'

When Marie looked at him doubtfully, he said, 'I know, she looks like Attila the Hun, but she can get anyone to swim. So, you up for it?'

'Ehm ...' Marie said weakly.

'That's the stuff,' the man said, as if she'd said yes. 'You can pay as you go – 50p a session. Can't say fairer than that.' And he offered her a meaty hand to shake. Marie took it gingerly and felt her fingers crack as he squeezed it tightly. 'Good girl yourself. I'll show you the dressing rooms.'

Chapter 9

Grainne's next letter arrived a month later, on a rainy November morning, and Marie managed to swipe it off the doormat before Dada saw it. If Grainne was planning to go incognito, a sparkly yellow envelope with a unicorn sticker wasn't the way to do it. Still, it made Marie smile as she shoved it into her handbag and yelled, 'Bye Dada,' over her shoulder, thumping the door closed behind her. She stood on the doorstep for a moment, the early winter wind sucking the breath out of her, before running down to the sea road to the 8.15 bus, which she knew would be along any minute.

When it arrived, she climbed up to the top deck, for the view of the sea, and took the letter out of her bag, the unicorn envelope sparkling in the early-morning gloom.

Dear Marie,

Why haven't you written back to me? I'm waiting for your letter. Mrs D has, but it's all silly stuff about the flowers of Donegal and how they'll bloom again, whatever that means. Please write! Anything is better than listening to the nuns bicker and squabble all the time. It's driving me mad! Sister Englebert and Sister Roberta had a big row last week about snooker, and whether Steve Davis was better than Jimmy White, and they are still not talking to each other. I thought nuns were supposed to be too holy to row, but I suppose rowing is normal. Look at us!

I miss our rows, Marie, and I miss stealing your clothes, even if mine are probably nicer now. Yvette took me to Carnaby Street last week to go shopping – it's amazing, Mar; there is so much I want to buy, so I have to look at my budget and only take out as much money as I need. Sister Bonaventure says it's important not to splurge. It's so hard when the clothes are so nice!

I thought Yvette was a bit mean when I first came to St Mary's, but she's OK. She puts on face masks and cucumber over her eyes every night, and she's always painting her nails, but she's funny. And she likes shopping, like me. That's nice, because you always hated shopping. She's shown me all the best places and on Sundays we go for a trip. Last Sunday, I went to Tower Bridge to see the Crown Jewels – they are huge!

Mar, I have some news. I've stopped saying my prayers. Don't tell Mrs D, because it'll make her very cross, but I can't believe in God any more. Not after what happened with Anthony Daly. I have to go to Mass because we all have to in St Mary's, but I just mouth the prayers and think about something else. I used to pray that Anthony Daly would die. I know that's wrong, but I used to imagine him squashed by the number 7A bus, or floating upside down in the sea at Seaview, but that's not very Christian, which is another reason why I've given up.

The nuns like telling the girls that everything that has happened to them is their fault, well, all of them except Sister Bonaventure, because she's far too nice. I suppose it is my fault, Mar, isn't it? But even so, I don't know if I want God to tell me that – that I'm a bad person. So that's why I've stopped talking to him and to Holy Mary. Because I don't believe anything they say any more. Do you remember, Sister Veronica used to say that we should all be like Holy Mary; that our bodies should be temples of the Lord? Well, my body certainly isn't a temple, is it? So, there's no point really.

I think I used to go to Mass sometimes because I was lonely. Everyone liked you, Mar, because you're so pretty and funny. I was just not as clever and I certainly am not as funny as you, so Mass was a bit of company for me. But I have some friends in London, Marie; I have Yvette and I have my friends at swimming club in Tooting Lido, where I go open-air swimming. It's freezing, because they don't heat the pool, but the lido's really long and I can swim fast in it.

One thing I've learned about friends is that they aren't just people who are nice to you. For example, they are very rude in London and people don't say hello to each other the way they do in Dublin. But that doesn't mean they are *not nice. They're just shy. Once you get to know them, they are fine. At home, everyone smiles and says hello, how are you, lovely weather and that kind of thing. But they don't really mean it. Here, they mean every word they say.*

I have to go now, Marie, because it's All Soul's Day tomorrow and they have a big Mass and tea and sandwiches in the hall after. I have to make 500 ham sandwiches! Do you think anyone will notice that I'm not praying or taking Holy Communion? Please tell Dada that I said hello.

Please write back, Grainne xx

Marie looked out of the window for a long time, thinking about Grainne's letter. How it wasn't quite as desperate as her first one. She felt pleased about that, she thought. Pleased that her sister wasn't suffering as much as she had been, pleased that she seemed to be making a life for herself in London. Marie had always thought that she'd be the one in London, living in a little flat in Notting Hill, getting the Tube into work in Fleet Street on one of the famous newspapers, spending all of her time in the pub, drinking pale ale, the way all the journalists seemed to do. Grainne's world seemed to be expanding while hers seemed to be getting smaller and smaller, she thought sadly.

Imagine, Grainne giving up religion. She'd clearly thought about it, too. Grainne, who'd never thought deeply about anything. Happy-go-lucky Grainne. Marie couldn't help it, she felt a flicker of jealousy. Marie was the independent thinker, wasn't she? She was the one who always had something to say about everything, because she'd read an article about it in the

Irish Times, or had watched a documentary on it on BBC2, while Grainne just watched silly nonsense with Mrs D. But maybe it wasn't all about thinking; it was more about doing.

Her thoughts were interrupted by a small cough and she turned to see David Crowley standing there, in a sensible anorak, a bag slung over his shoulder. Oh, God.

'Is this seat taken?' He nodded to the empty seat beside Marie and she felt the urge to say that it was, but instead, she just lifted her bag and made room for him beside her. 'This is nice, getting the bus into work together every day,' he said cheerfully.

'Yes,' Marie said unenthusiastically. He was eyeing the yellow envelope in her hand and she tried to shove it into her handbag, but it looked really obvious, so she blushed and said, 'It's from Grainne.'

'How is she?' He didn't get that look everyone got when they mentioned Grainne's name, word having somehow got around, a kind of constipated look of pity and sympathy that Marie found really annoying. Instead, he just looked ... well, normal, as if he were simply enquiring after her sister's health.

'She's managing, actually.'

He smiled. 'You don't sound very pleased.'

'Of course I'm pleased,' Marie said indignantly. 'Why wouldn't I be pleased?'

'Oh, I don't know ... ' David Crowley said quietly. 'Maybe you're used to being in charge.'

Marie shot him a look, to see if he was passing judgement on her, but he didn't seem to be. 'Well, I am, I suppose. You see, I didn't expect her to cope, to be honest. I've always done everything for her. Me and Mrs D.'

'And now she's managing on her own.'

Marie nodded sadly. 'She's only seventeen, David.'

'Yes, I know, but maybe she's more capable than you give her credit for. She must be, after everything she's been through.'

'Maybe …' Marie said doubtfully. How on earth could David think that Grainne was capable of looking after herself, after everything that had happened? Surely that was the whole point – that she wasn't capable at all. But then, neither am I, Marie thought bleakly. If I was capable, I wouldn't have left her alone that night.

'I suppose it means that you have to think more about yourself, with Grainne gone,' David said quietly then.

'What do you mean?' Marie found that she was always on the alert for some kind of hidden meaning these days and she detected that David was about to give one of his preachy sermons. She was absolutely not in the mood for it. Really and truly.

David looked at her carefully, before saying, 'Oh, nothing.' He looked at the red duffle bag at Marie's feet. 'What's in the bag?'

'Swimming gear,' Marie said, with a small smile.

'But you hate swimming.'

'I know, but I've got a notion, as Mrs D would have said.' Marie smiled. 'I just feel that it's a bit stupid to be so afraid of the water, you know? I need to conquer my fears.' Because, she added silently to herself, if I conquer that fear, maybe I can conquer others. 'Maybe it's not having Grainne around to do it for me,' she said with just the slightest trace of sarcasm. 'I've decided that I'm going to learn if it kills me.'

'Good for you,' he said. 'Maybe if you learn swimming, I can pluck up the courage to ditch rugby practice.'

'What?' Marie feigned surprise. 'I thought you Crowleys were all born with rugby balls in your hands.' David had two brothers, one of whom played for the school A team at St Philip's, the other of whom played for Leinster. They were always wandering around the place passing a rugby ball back and forth to each other, like it was on an invisible cord.

'Nah. I hate it. I just play for the Old Dear and Dad. They love seeing me and I don't want to let them down.' A muscle was twitching in his jaw and Marie reached out and gave his arm a squeeze. 'I can relate to that, not letting people down.'

He smiled. 'Maybe we have more in common than you think.'

'Don't get carried away.' Marie smiled. 'Oh, our stop,' she said suddenly, as the bus turned the corner on Castlewood Avenue. David got up and slung the bag over his shoulder, waiting to let her out of the seat. They climbed down the steps and out onto the busy street, turning left and walking up the Rathmines Road to the hospital. Marie felt her stomach begin to churn as she began the familiar trudge, and her limbs felt heavy. So much for facing her fears. And she had a big hole in the hem of her uniform from where she'd caught it climbing over the garden wall the previous week, when she'd forgotten her door keys. She prayed that Sister Dolores wouldn't spot it, because if she did, she'd dock her wages. She was always doing that, because Marie always had something wrong with her uniform or her hair or her shoes, no matter how hard she tried.

David was walking beside her now, a contented look on his

face, happy doing what he was cut out to do. Marie wondered what that must feel like.

'Listen, why don't you come to my next match? We're playing Wanderers,' he said after a few minutes' silence.

Marie wrinkled her nose. 'Oh, I don't think I like rugby.' She had a sudden thought of Con and something he'd said one night about rugby being the panacea of the South Dublin middle classes. 'It's a drug, Marie, administered to all these young kids in Blackrock to make them feel that they're superior, that they rule the world,' he'd said. Marie, of course, had drunk it all in, agreeing with him that, yes, she was just a product of the bourgeoisie and, yes, it was a terrible thing altogether. She wondered what Con would make of her going to a rugby match. Part of her felt a bit glad to be doing something that would annoy him. The other part felt that it missed him.

'Ah, go on.' David broke into her thoughts and she felt a bit irritated. 'Oh, OK then. Do I have to stand at the sideline and cheer you on?'

'It's the touchline, and no, you can sit down and pretend that you don't know me.' He smiled briefly.

'That shouldn't be too hard.' But when Marie saw the hurt look on his face, she said, 'I'm joking.'

'Oh, OK,' he said. 'Marie?'

'Yes.'

'Can I tell you something?'

They'd reached the gates of St John's now, a steady trickle of people streaming in; nurses in their uniforms, doctors with their white coats flapping, a pair of nuns with their starched headdresses, their bright white shoes. David stopped dead, putting his hands in his pockets and shuffling from foot to foot. He looked nervous, as if he were about to make a pronouncement of some kind. Marie was a bit surprised by that, because he regularly made pronouncements without any bother at all. She looked at him expectantly.

'It's … You see,' he began, but then Marie felt a touch on her elbow. 'Hi, Marie.' It was Debs, hunched against the cold in a navy duffle coat, her mousy hair flat against her head.

'Hi, Debs,' Marie said, grateful for the interruption. 'Do you know David Crowley? Doctor David Crowley, I suppose. He's doing a rotation here.' She waved in David's direction and he extended a hand, taking Deb's tiny paw in his.

She looked up at him and blushed. Oh, Marie thought. She looked at David to see if there was any sign, but he just looked cross. Honestly, she thought. What's wrong with him?

'C'mon, Debs, we'd better get a move on or Sister Dolores will be on the warpath,' Marie said, tucking an arm into Deb's. 'See you later, David.'

'Yes, see you,' he muttered, taking off in the opposite direction, to the ambulance bay and to his day in Casualty. Marie breathed a sigh of relief. God, he could be so earnest sometimes.

'He's single, you know,' she said to Debs, as they crossed the car park and went into the nurses' room, a large, gloomy space that had an ancient coffee machine in it, and rows and rows of lockers that smelled of old shoes and deodorant.

'Really?' Debs said dreamily. 'He *is* handsome, I suppose.'

'But …' Marie said.

'But what?' Debs looked at Marie innocently. Marie felt herself grow irritated. Couldn't Debs just take the hint?

'But nothing,' she said, throwing her swimming bag down on the bench and taking out her white shoes. Debs didn't say another word, just gave a little smile to herself and Marie wondered what on earth she found so funny.

The rest of the morning was spent as it always was, taking temperatures and emptying bedpans, the only excitement being when one of the more senior nurses sent the new student, Angela, up to the maternity ward in search of fallopian tubes. It was as old as the hills, but never failed to work, or to provide entertainment, and Margaret and Debs had spent most of the smoking break snorting with laughter at poor Angela, a girl from Waterford, who clearly hadn't been taught the facts of life.

'Don't you think it's a bit sad,' Marie said, taking a big pull on her cigarette, 'that Angela doesn't actually know what they are?'

Margaret shot her a look. 'Oh, lighten up, Marie. Not everything has to be part of the feminist crusade, you know.'

'I don't think it's a feminist crusade to know what fallopian tubes are,' Marie bit back. 'I think it's just a bit disappointing, that's all, that there are some women who don't know what they are. How on earth can we call ourselves responsible if we don't know the basics of the female anatomy? What kind of a country are we if we don't educate our women, but hide behind a veil of nonsense, then we punish them by sending them off God knows where to sort themselves out, or worse, leave them to die for their mistakes … If you ask me, Margaret, fallopian tubes are the tip of the iceberg. It's no joke, you know, to celebrate that kind of ignorance.'

'Jeez, who got out of bed on the wrong side,' Margaret

said, taking a big pull on her cigarette. 'Or maybe it's that handsome doctor is the cause of your bad temper, is that it?' She looked slyly at Debs, who blushed and looked at the ground.

'What handsome doctor … oh, David?'

'"Oh, David",' Margaret mimicked sarcastically. 'Yes, David. Let me tell you, I wouldn't mind letting him at my fallopian tubes.'

There was a moment's silence, and then they all burst into laughter. Margaret was such a silly bimbo, Marie thought, and a disgrace to feminism, but she was funny. 'You're welcome to him, Margaret,' she said happily, crushing her cigarette out under her foot. 'I'll set up a date for you. He won't know what hit him.'

Margaret rolled her eyes to heaven. 'If only, Marie. He only has eyes for you,' she said, waving her cigarette in the air.

'Well, he's wasting his time,' Marie said firmly. 'Now, I have a meds trolley to wheel around St Anthony's, one enema and a bad case of piles to sort out, so if you'll excuse me,' she said, walking away before Margaret could tease her any further. Her cheeks were burning, and she wasn't sure if this was because of David or because of her rant about the fallopian tubes. She knew that it was just a joke and she also knew that she seemed like such a prissy feminist, but when she thought of Grainne and what she'd been through, it didn't seem like such a funny joke after all. If Mum were alive, she'd have made sure that Grainne knew everything she needed to know, but she wasn't, and it had been left to the nuns, who only dealt in half-truths and general obfuscation, Mrs D, whose only comment on the matter was to warn them to keep their legs crossed at all times, which was hardly helpful, and her, Marie. Who had told her sister hardly anything about sex, because she didn't have the heart for all the silly questions she'd be asked about it, or for the cringe-inducing lecture she'd have to give. Whose fault was it that Grainne had found herself pregnant at sixteen?

Marie blinked the tears out of her eyes. Fallopian tubes, indeed.

★

Marie was still miserable about it six hours later, when she stood, shivering, in the changing room in the swimming pool, pulling on her swimming togs. She hadn't gone near water since that summer on the beach, and she must have lost weight, she thought gloomily, as she eyed the costume, which sagged horribly around her breasts, what there was of them, and her stomach. Her long legs were now like twigs, with her big bony knees sticking out in the middle. God, I look like a praying mantis, she thought.

Even though it was as warm as an oven in the changing rooms, her teeth still chattered – probably with nerves – and she felt a tightening in her chest at even the thought of the cold, dark water. Maybe she'd just get dressed and leave, she thought. No one would notice.

'Are you here for the swimming lessons?' a voice said beside her. Marie turned to see a pretty, middle-aged woman in a black swimming costume, putting a stripy bath towel into her bag. Too late, she thought.

'Yes, I am,' Marie said. 'I'm not looking forward to them, to be honest.'

'Is this your first time in the water?' The woman looked at her sympathetically and Marie wondered if that's what Mum would look like now, if this is how she'd behave: like a nice lady who cared.

'No. Which kind of makes it worse. I just hate swimming,' Marie said sheepishly. 'And I kind of want to overcome it, you know? My sister's a really good swimmer,' she added, wondering as she did why on earth she was telling this woman about Grainne.

'Well, you've come to the right place,' the woman said cheerfully. 'I've done six lessons with Maureen and I can't tell you how much more confident I feel. I can even put my face in the water now. It's just great to have that boost, being at home with the kids all day. Oh, the name's Sheila, by the way,' the woman said, extending a hand, which Marie shook. She decided that she liked Sheila; she wondered if she'd look like her in ten years' time, all wobbly and comfortable, like a sofa; if she'd have a gang of kids to escape or if she'd still be bothering old people at St John's. She'd never thought about that, that she might be a mum herself one day. It had simply never been part of her future. She'd only ever thought about being intrepid and significant. Not about being a Sheila.

'Nervous swimmers into the pool, please,' the intercom boomed into the changing room. Marie thought suddenly that she might be sick. She felt her stomach churn and her throat tighten. Oh, God, please don't let me be sick in the swimming pool. Please.

'All set?' Sheila said cheerfully.

Marie shook her head. 'I don't think I can do it.' She was clutching the rail in the little hallway that led to the pool. She could see a sliver of blue water at the end, and she found it hard to resist the urge to heave.

'It'll be OK,' Sheila said kindly. 'The only thing to do is to face your fears.' And she held out her hand to Marie, who took it, like a child, and let herself meekly be led out to the pool. She wondered if she could just hold Sheila's hand for the whole lesson, but then decided that might look a bit silly, so instead, she just stood at the edge, arms clasped around herself, as Sheila introduced her to the small group of women and one solitary man. They were all at least twenty years older than her and Marie felt even more embarrassed. At least they had an excuse not to be able to swim, unlike her, who'd had swimming lessons in school – not that they'd been remotely successful.

Maureen had her substantial back turned towards the little group, busying herself with assembling buoyancy aids, and when she lumbered to the edge of the pool, her flip-flops slapping on the tiles, she didn't acknowledge the new girl, just barked at them all to get into the pool, which they duly did, all except Marie, who stood at the edge, looking into the chilly water.

'In you go,' Maureen said briskly.

'I can't,' Marie said. Her stomach contracted and she had an ominous feeling that she was about to wet herself. And then she felt a sharp nudge to her lower back and suddenly the water was coming towards her, a big blue wall, which she hit with a loud slap, before sinking under the water. Her eyes opened then, and she could see the bottom of the pool coming towards her, the chilly blue-white tiles, with the bits of sticking plaster and rubber bands wafting over their surface, from where they'd fallen off toes and and hair. Marie knew that she needed to be facing the other direction, and so with a growing sense of panic, she lifted her head until she could see legs and arms floating in the water above her and the shimmering outline of the surface. For a second, she wondered if she might just stay there, underneath the water. It was only a split-second, and as soon as she had the thought, it left her, and she was pushing herself up, breaking the surface with a gasping cough. She had to hang onto the rail and suck in a few deep breaths, her nose and mouth filled with horrible chlorinated water.

Maureen was barking orders at the others and barely gave her a glance. Marie felt a surge of anger inside her. 'You pushed me!' she wanted to say, before realising how silly that might sound, how childish. Maybe it was just her imagination anyway. Maybe she'd just tripped.

'Now that we're all in the water,' Maureen said sarcastically, 'it's time to grab the boards and get to work.'

Marie looked over at Sheila, who nodded at the big pile of polystyrene boards by the side of the pool. Marie clung onto the railing with one hand and reached out for a board with the other, bobbing down beneath the surface of the water again. God, would she ever be able to stay afloat? she thought desperately, as she managed to wrestle a board into her right hand. She looked at the others to see that they had a hand on either side of their boards and were happily kicking away, moving down towards the deep end of the pool. Marie took a deep breath, shoved her board out in front of her and hung on for dear life, her body rocking from side to side as she kicked as hard as she could, wondering why she couldn't just stay steady.

'Drop your head!' she heard Maureen bark behind her. Marie dipped her head down as close to the water as she could bear and, sure enough, she steadied and stopped rolling like a boat taking on water. She kept her mouth firmly closed and tried to blink away the horrible water as she bobbed along.

'Right, back you come,' Maureen yelled from the far end. Where are the brakes? Marie thought as she kept going, her legs kicking, her mouth now filling with water so that she began to choke.

'Stop!' Maureen yelled.

I can't, Marie thought as she kept moving. I don't know how to turn around. By this stage, she was in the deep end, and the water was much colder and darker. She felt her chest contract as the water swirled around her. The board wobbled in her hand and, for some reason, she let it go, her arms thrashing around in the water, her head tilting back as she tried to keep it above the surface. Oh, shit, she thought. I'm going to drown. Then she felt a gentle splash beside her and a hand reached out for her, turning her gently around and leading her back into the safety of the shallow end. Marie was so relieved, she didn't look to see who it was until her feet touched the bottom of the pool in the shallow end and she was able to stand up. Only then did she realise that the person leading her was Maureen.

'Just do what I say in future, will you?' Maureen said. Before Marie could say another word, she darted towards the edge of the pool, cutting through the water with confident strokes, and climbed out, still in her shorts and red T-shirt, now dripping wet. Marie wanted to just die. Her first ever lesson and she'd nearly drowned. She'd had to be rescued by the swimming instructor. She had never been so embarrassed in her whole life. She shot a nervous look in Sheila's direction and not even the older woman's comforting smile could make her feel any better.

*

'It was only your first lesson,' Sheila said, as the two of them stood under the shower, the hot jets of water bringing life to Marie's stiff limbs. 'And it got a lot better at the end. You were able to turn around and come back at that stage, so that's great progress, isn't it?'

'Thanks, Sheila,' Marie said weakly. 'At least Maureen didn't have to rescue me again,' and in spite of herself, she gave a small laugh. She caught Sheila's eye and the two of them giggled. Marie thought of poor Maureen, who had spent the rest of the lesson in soaking wet clothes, but who had behaved as if nothing at all had happened, merely giving Marie a brisk 'well done' when she'd managed to turn around all by herself, kicking hard and veering left without overbalancing and ending up on her back. By the end of the lesson, Marie could see what Sheila meant about Maureen, in spite of her terrifying appearance.

'I don't think Maureen will have me back.'

'Oh, she will,' Sheila said. 'She loves a challenge.' She smiled, rubbing shampoo into her hair and rinsing it out quickly, rubbing her hands over her face, with its rosy cheeks, broken veins marking her cheekbones and chin. She seemed worn out, but happy, Marie thought, her limbs relaxed, her face tired, but serene, as she smoothed conditioner into her hair. Would Mum look like that now? Marie wondered.

Sheila caught Marie looking at her. 'I've been trying to lose weight, but even the swimming doesn't work,' she said ruefully. 'All it does is make me want to eat three Mars bars afterwards!'

'Oh, no, I wasn't looking like that,' Marie said, mortified. 'It's just … well, my mum died a long time ago and I suppose I find mums interesting …' Her voice tailed off and she felt like a complete idiot. Poor Sheila.

To her surprise, Sheila just smiled and reached out to squeeze her hand. 'It's nice to hear you say that, Marie, that mums are important enough to be interesting. I don't feel very interesting sometimes, with three kids, I can tell you!' There was a pause. 'I'm sorry to hear about your mum. That must be very hard for you.'

'Thanks,' Marie said briefly, getting out from under the shower and shivering while she pulled the towel over her shoulders. She felt silly all of a sudden, exposed, as if she were caught in the act of something. She felt the tears prick her eyes, and to distract herself, she started rubbing herself dry with the towel, her back turned to Sheila.

'Marie?' Sheila said softly. 'Is there anything I can help you with?'

Without turning around, Marie shook her head. 'I'm fine, Sheila, thanks.' There was another long silence while Marie tried to pull herself together, swallowing the big lump in her throat, wiping her eyes with the corner of her towel. Once she'd managed to get the tears under control, she turned and gave an over-bright smile. 'I think I'm still in shock after the swimming!' she said, hating the fake tone of her voice.

Thankfully, Sheila didn't persist, she simply gave her lovely comfy smile and said, 'Well, I think you've done brilliantly, Marie. See you next week?'

'Of course!' Marie heard herself exclaim, picking up her towel and heading to the changing room before Sheila could say anything further. 'See you then!' she called out over her shoulder. Only when she was in the privacy of the changing room did she yield to the tears and, once she did, it seemed that they wouldn't stop.

She felt totally and utterly exhausted after her swim, barely having the energy to crawl onto the number 18, resting her forehead against the window as the bus made its way slowly through the streets of the city, watching the steady trickle of cars and people that walked up Waterloo Road, past the grand Georgian houses, and then onto Leeson Street, with its tatty bedsits and flats, and then through Donnybrook with its lovely food shops and expensive cars, and out onto the dual carriageway towards home.

She wasn't sure if it was the lesson or the encounter with Sheila that had exhausted her more; the questions that it opened up inside of her, the memories that rose to the surface, like she'd risen to the surface in the swimming pool, the water sloshing around her ears. Herself and Grainne on a hot summer's day, walking all the way up to the Middle Stores in their swimming togs for an ice-cream. Marie could still feel the burning pavement under her toes, the sharp bits of stone and lumps of tarmacadam that stuck to the soles of her feet. Grainne had had a fit, wanting Marie's ice-cream and wailing in indignation all the way home when Marie refused to give it to her. No one ever said no to Grainne and her howls were of outrage and surprise, as much as anything. But Marie had refused to give in, waddling along in her red swimsuit with the frilly white hem, nibbling as slowly as she possibly could on the Iceberger Mum had given her forty pence to buy. Her Holy Communion, the last outing that Mum had been well enough to attend, her back half-turned as Marie stood on the steps of the Holy Rosary Church beside Claire, Marie in a long broderie anglaise dress, Claire in one of the short ones that were fashionable at the time, both of them grinning into the camera, big gaps in their mouths where their front teeth should have been. Grainne was standing behind them, singing the hymn 'Hail Holy Queen' at the top of her voice, just in case Marie would make the mistake of thinking that the day was about her.

She could remember the ice-cream colour of Mum's coat, a mint green, the shine of her black patent-leather shoes, the shape of her hat, like a squashed green cherry on her head. Mum loved the colour green. She was talking to Claire's mum, and they were laughing about something, Marie couldn't remember what; but she remembered Mum's laugh, as if she was laughing from somewhere deep inside of her, a real, genuine laugh, not a polite trill, as if she wasn't afraid to find something funny, and wasn't bothered about what people thought of her. Grainne had the same laugh, but Marie's was quieter, and she often put her hand over her mouth, because she felt a bit embarrassed.

Mum should have been there for all of the other times, Marie thought, all of the Christmases and birthdays, the exams and the outings to Granny, where she would have charmed her while not letting her go on and on about her pet subjects. 'Do you know, you are absolutely right about those shysters in Leinster House, Margaret, but tell me, where did you get this gorgeous pâté?' Marie had always accepted that Mum was gone, had never questioned it, but now, she began to understand just how unfair it was; how Mum had been cheated of a life; how herself and Grainne had stopped really living when Mum died, and Dada too. They'd just gone on as if nothing had happened, rather than the huge explosion that had wrecked their lives. Why did we never talk about it? she thought, rubbing the condensation off the inside of the glass window to peer out at the sea as the bus chugged along. Why did we never get angry? Why did we push it all down, so that it would leak out into us as the years passed, leaching out, like water onto rocks? Only now did Marie see how wrong it all was, but she had no idea how to fix it. Maybe it was too late.

★

'Oh, you're back,' Dada said, when Marie walked into the kitchen, her bag on her shoulder. 'I'm looking for my quinine.'

'Why? Do you have malaria?'

He gave her a stern look. 'No, I just have … something. I'm not sure,' he said, pressing his hand onto his stomach and then his forehead. 'I just feel a bit off. Quinine generally puts me right.'

'Dada, quinine isn't really suitable for long-term use,' Marie said carefully. 'Have you seen Dr McDonnell?'

Dada gave her a look that told her that he had not seen Dr McDonnell and nor did he have any intention of doing so. He had a phobia about doctors, which Marie supposed was understandable. 'Sit down for a minute,' she said.

Reluctantly, he pulled out a kitchen chair and sat on it,

while Marie put a hand on his forehead. It felt hot and clammy and his face was a bit flushed, but he didn't seem to have a temperature. She took his pulse then, hearing the fluttering and thinking that it sounded a bit fast.

She wished she had a blood pressure monitor. 'Dada, when was the last time you had your blood pressure taken?'

Dada was looking a bit sheepish, as Marie asked him to open his mouth and then close it again. 'Oh, I don't know. Your mother was still alive anyway.'

'Dada!' Marie was shocked. 'For goodness' sake go and get it checked out. You can't afford to be careless with your health.' The unspoken words 'at your age' hung in the air. Marie studied Dada's face and thought that he suddenly looked old, his eyes now watery and red-rimmed, his black hair sprinkled with grey. His hands had great splotches of brown age spots on them. She supposed he *was* old, after all, he was sixty-five, but it was strange to suddenly realise this about him – that he would one day die. The thought made her feel suddenly tender towards him, standing over him, a nurse to his patient, a grown-up to his child. She wanted to hug him, to stroke his hair, to kiss his forehead, but she knew better than to try. He'd only clear his throat and say that, yes, well, he'd better be going into his study or out to the garden – anything to get away.

When was the last time she'd kissed him? she thought now. It must have been before Mum died. A long time ago, anyway. She wondered if she ever would again and the thought made her feel sorry for everything they'd missed.

'I'll go to see Doctor McDonnell tomorrow,' he grumbled. 'If you insist. But I'm perfectly healthy, you know.'

'I know. Just as a precaution. Please?'

He tutted then, and his face took on that look, the steely one that Marie was accustomed to seeing, as he got up from the chair. 'For goodness' sake, Marie, I said yes, didn't I?' And then he shuffled off out the kitchen door, closing it firmly behind him.

Marie rolled her eyes to heaven and went to hang her swimming togs on the line. And then she sat down and wrote a letter to her sister.

11 Seaview Road
Abbotstown
Co. Dublin

Dear Grainne
I'm sorry I haven't written to you before now. I suppose that I felt I had nothing useful to say to you, as you seem to be managing so well.

Did that sound a bit bitter, she wondered, a bit resentful?

Nothing much has happened here since you left. But then, it never does! If you think London is vast, this place just seems to get smaller and more boring every day. Nothing ever changes in Abbotstown – the house is the same, Dada is the same, the sea hasn't changed colour and the sky is still the same grey. Listen to me – I sound like such an old moan!

She hesitated then, wondering whether to just scribble it all out. She was sure Jane Austen never wrote such boring letters

– but then, even staring out at a few sheep in Hampshire would be more interesting than here. But she wasn't about to tell Grainne about St John's, because her sister would just pass out with boredom, and she'd probably wonder what Marie was doing there anyway. No, she didn't want any awkward questions. David Crowley was bad enough.

She chewed her pen for a few moments, before continuing.

One bit of news is that I'm having swimming lessons. I know, would you believe it? I have no idea why, really. They're terrible, by the way. Well, I only had one lesson and I went into the deep end and couldn't turn around. The instructor had to jump in and rescue me! Her name is Maureen and she's like an East German wrestler, and totally terrifying, but there's another nice woman there called Sheila. She's a bit like I imagine Mum would be now, if, well, if she'd lived. She's all warm and cushiony and I like her, even though she must be nearly forty.

She stopped herself then, before she went on about how the lessons had opened something inside of her. Grainne didn't need to know that stuff. In fact, she didn't need to know any of this stuff, Marie thought. Grainne was making a new life for herself in London – she didn't need to hear about her old one.

Anyway, I'm sorry to hear that you've gone off religion. That must be strange, because you always loved praying, but it's understandable. I won't tell anyone, especially as I don't go to Mass any more either. I go to McSwiney's for a scone and tea instead, or I go for a walk down the pier. I suppose now there's no one around to nag me, there's no need. And Dada doesn't notice – you know what he's like.

She wasn't sure if Grainne wanted to hear Dada's name, but she put it down anyway, because otherwise this letter would be very short. She didn't say anything about the quinine, because she didn't want to worry Grainne.

Anyway, I'd better go, because I'm going to a rugby match, believe it or not. I know – me! David Crowley asked me to go – he's playing. I'm dragging Claire along for company, because I just couldn't stand there all afternoon by myself, like some pathetic groupie. Anyway, I'll write more later.

She put down her pen, wondering what on earth 'more' she'd have to write later. Maybe she'd tell her sister about the riveting excitement of the match, she thought, tucking the letter under her pillow in case Dada saw it.

Chapter 10

Claire's eyes filled with tears when Marie told her about her swimming lesson. Tears of laughter, as she held her sides, guffawing.

'It's not funny,' Marie said crossly.

'Oh, it is,' Claire said, clapping wildly as a boy in a black-and-purple striped top sped past, a rugby ball in his hand. 'What I wouldn't have given to be a fly on the wall.'

'I'll never live it down. How on earth will I go back next week?'

'You'll put your togs in your bag and walk in the door, that's how – oh, good play!' Claire yelled as the boy passed the ball to another boy, who was now speeding up the field with it. The day was grey and a thin sleet was falling, and Marie wondered if this wasn't marginally more unpleasant than

266

swimming, but decided that the chances of her drowning were slimmer, so that was a bonus.

'I didn't know you liked rugby,' Marie said. She'd been surprised that when she'd rung Claire to see if she'd come to David's match, she hadn't said an immediate no. Instead, she'd sounded positively enthusiastic about the whole thing, which made Marie feel a bit suspicious. Now, looking at Claire's gaze as it followed a strapping guy in a red and green shirt, she understood why.

'I thought you said that rugby was a game played by rich assholes with over-inflated opinions of themselves?'

Claire smiled serenely. 'I did, but when it is played by handsome assholes with over-inflated opinions of themselves,' she said, nodding at the guy in question, 'I am entitled to change my mind.'

'Because you are completely shallow,' Marie teased.

'No, because, unlike you, dear friend, I can understand when someone is interested in me. In fact, I take it as a signal to reciprocate,' and she looked at Marie slyly.

Marie blushed and pretended to ignore her friend, staring fixedly at the lineout, which had now gathered about five yards away. David was at the back, taller than everyone else, a look of fierce concentration on his face. Marie could see that he didn't like what he was doing, though: his movements were stiff and self-conscious, not like the easy grace of some of the other men. It didn't come naturally to him, and as she watched, Marie felt that she really admired David for playing, in spite of his own feelings about it. He was clearly pretty brave.

'He likes you,' Claire sang into her ear.

'I know,' Marie said sadly.

Claire was about to say something in response, but then a look of surprise flashed across her face, followed by an expression of distaste. 'Will you look what the cat dragged in.'

They turned to see Imelda standing there, in full rugby-fan gear, the logo of the club displayed prominently on the bomber jacket she was wearing, the purple-and-black-striped scarf, also club colours, tied in a neat knot around her neck. She looked utterly fabulous, just as she'd looked utterly fabulous the summer before last, when she'd been in her popstar phase – she'd even looked fabulous the night of the debs. Marie had tried to avoid her, but she'd seen her since, walking the dog down the pier, shoulders hunched against the winter wind. She'd pretended not to see Marie as she'd turned the corner onto Seaview Road, her face flushed as she passed her, head down, as if there was something riveting on the pavement.

Now, however, she was cornered. 'Hi, Claire,' she said sadly. 'Hi, Marie.'

'Hi, Imelda,' Marie muttered.

'Fancy meeting you here, Imelda,' Claire said. 'Nice to see you getting on with your life, after *everything*.'

Her meaning was clear and Imelda flushed and shrugged her shoulders. 'Ehm, I came with Eleanor. Her brother's playing.'

'There was a moment's awkward silence, which Imelda broke with a murmured, 'How's Grainne?'

'How's Grainne?' Claire squeaked, but Marie interrupted her.

'She's very well, Imelda, thanks for asking. She's loving London.' Dada would have been proud of her, she thought, of her restraint. She didn't feel restrained inside, but she also knew that yelling at Imelda wouldn't help. Imelda wasn't really the guilty party. The guilty party was her. Blaming Imelda wouldn't make that fact go away.

'She was a bit lonely at first, but she's really found her feet now, and I think that's great.'

Imelda looked disconcerted, as she'd clearly been ready for Marie to be nasty. 'That's good,' she said quietly.

'I'll tell her you were asking for her, will I?'

Imelda had no choice but to nod. Then she blurted, 'I know that you think that I was only using her, but I liked her, Marie, I really did. She was really funny and lively and, well, she was a good friend.'

'Right,' Claire said. 'The kind of friend that you use for your own entertainment and then leave them high and dry when they most need you. *That* kind of friend.'

Marie put a hand on Claire's arm to silence her and the three of them stood there in awkward silence, pretending to watch the game, as Handsome Rugged Man thundered past, the ball under his armpit. Marie could see the wheels turning in Imelda's brain as she tried to think of an exit, thoughts flitting across her pretty face. Eventually, she said, 'So, have you bumped into Con?' She'd brightened now, and the old Imelda was back. Queen Bitch. Maybe she didn't know how to be any other way.

Marie didn't know what to say – the truth, which would make her look her usual sad self, or a lie. She decided to brazen it out. 'No. Why would I?' she said. 'Our paths don't exactly cross these days.'

'Why? Because he's here, of course.' Imelda looked

suddenly quite pleased with herself, that she'd managed to regain the upper hand.

Marie didn't know what to say for a moment. Her throat tightened and she swallowed, to loosen it. She looked at Claire, waiting for her to launch into Imelda, but instead, she was looking into the distance, a muscle working in her jaw. Marie had always suspected that Claire didn't like Con and the unfairness of her friend's judgement of him had stung. Now, she wanted nothing more than for Claire to let rip with one of her remarks, to save her from this sudden feeling that the world had dropped away.

'Yes, he's out with some of the other devils. Some awful tradition they have, where they have to go to a rugby match and then strangle a swan or something – Masonic, obviously. Barristers are all Masons.' Imelda giggled. 'Are you all right, Marie? You look as if you've seen a ghost.'

'I'm fine, Imelda,' Marie said quietly. 'I just need a coffee. I'm going to the chip van. Claire, do you fancy one?' She deliberately didn't offer anything to Imelda, and without waiting for Claire's answer, she wandered off in the direction of the van, parked outside one of the gates of the ground. 'A leopard never changes its spots, does it, Imelda?' she could hear Claire saying as she walked away. Her feet were numb from the cold and the tip of her nose was icy, the way it always got in winter, refusing to warm up. Marie sometimes wondered if it would just fall off, like a nose-shaped block of ice. But now, the unpleasant sensation of cold seemed to wash over her. She felt light-headed and dizzy and a bit sick.

He's here, she thought, somewhere in this big crowd of

people. She wondered what she'd say to him if they bumped into each other, as she scanned the backs of the heads of the people shuffling ahead of her to the entrance. She wasn't sure if she wanted to find him or not. It all seemed like so long ago, and she'd be too embarrassed to confess to him what had really happened. That there had been no attempt to meet him on New Year's Day, no battling against some element or other, some huge obstacle, to make it to him. She had simply not turned up, because suddenly he'd been the last thing on her mind. And she'd been too numb to regret it. How would she find the words? What would she say to make it sound in any way less hurtful?

She was almost at the gate and could see the red writing on the side of the chip van. The smell of frying burgers made her feel a bit queasy, when she spotted him, in a group of young men, each wearing red and green scarves. They were standing around, hands in their pockets, looking a bit tweedy, with their slacks and jackets and open-necked shirts. Marie supposed that barristers would look a bit tweedy, but not Con. Con was the wrong shape for tweedy.

She knew that he hadn't seen her, so she had a good look at him, at his newly short, tidy hair, his pale-brown-and-blue tweed jacket and the same slacks as the others wore, with a big sharp crease down the front of the leg. He was dressed the same as all the rest, but he stood differently, she noticed, holding himself stiffly, laughing along with them, trying to mould himself to their self-assurance, their dry asides. Con, Marie suddenly realised, had always been trying to fit in, whether on the beach with Imelda and her friends, or at Trinity in his black Levi's and his PLO scarf, and now as a trainee barrister at this rugby match. Marie wondered what it was about him that made him want to do that.

He must have felt her staring at him, because he turned around, and when he saw her, his eyes lit up for a second, then he obviously remembered that he wasn't happy to see her and he got that angry scowl on his face. Oh, God, she thought. What'll I do? Will I go up and say hello, or will I just walk on to the bloody chip van? She stood there, unsure of whether to approach and he stood there, his back now turned to his friends, neither of them willing to move forward.

Eventually, Marie sucked in a deep breath and went over. 'Hi, Con.' She waited, shoulders hunched in her too-thin winter coat, wishing that she'd washed her hair before she'd come out, instead of shoving it into an old woolly hat she'd found at the bottom of her wardrobe.

'Hi,' he said sulkily, before turning his back to her and resuming his conversation with his friends.

Marie felt her cheeks grow hot. She stood there for a moment, frozen to the spot, wondering if she should just disappear, melt back into the crowd as if she'd never existed, but she couldn't, because she found herself standing beside one of Con's tweedy friends, who looked at her and gave her an embarrassed smile.

You're not half as embarrassed as I am, Marie thought glumly, as she decided that there was nothing for it but to slink off, tail between her legs. She deserved it, she thought miserably, as she walked back to the chip van, rummaging in her purse for a few coins to buy a coffee. What on earth else did she expect? That he'd indulge in a little chit-chat? A polite 'so what have you been doing since we last met?'

She took her coffee and was shuffling miserably back to Claire, hoping that Imelda would be gone and her misery reduced a little, when she felt him beside her. She turned and he was standing there, the scowl still on his face. 'Sorry, that was a little rude.'

'Well, it wouldn't be you if you weren't a little rude,' Marie said smartly.

He shrugged. 'With good reason.'

'You're right,' Marie said sadly. 'Listen, Con, I—'

He shook his head. 'You don't need to explain.'

'I do.'

'No, you don't. I expected too much of you, after Grainne and everything. I wasn't even that surprised when you didn't turn up.'

'And you never thought of calling around, or getting in touch?' Marie couldn't help it, she had that indignant tone in her voice already – it was funny how quickly it came back; it was like an instinct with Con, a reflex. She thought of David, with whom she had never once felt indignant, and she wondered what that meant. That she didn't feel anything for David – at least, not what she felt for Con?

'You'd made your choice.'

'Hardly,' Marie spat. 'You know what choice I made.'

His expression softened. 'Yes, I do know.' There was a silence as the crowds milled around them. The match had clearly finished, and various announcements were being made over the tannoy, about the man of the match and the next fixtures. Con reached out and smoothed the tuft of Marie's hair that was sticking out of the woolly hat. The gesture was gentle, and Marie closed her eyes for a second, before opening them again. She wanted to take his hand and kiss it, she wanted to press it against her cheek and then …

He was smiling at her. 'So.'

'So.'

'It was nice seeing you.'

'Yes.'

'I have a dinner after, so I'd better be going.' He stuck his hands in the pockets of his slacks.

Marie felt totally crushed. 'Right. Well, see you around,' she said crossly.

'Marie. Don't go.'

Marie had her back to him, but at the words, she turned around. He didn't want her to go. That must mean that he wasn't as angry with her as she'd thought. That maybe …

'Marie, there you are,' a voice cut in. 'Are you ready for the after-match drinks? They're a pain, but we'd better turn up, because the Old Dear has been asking for you – oh.'

David only saw Con when he was almost on top of him. He must have forgotten his glasses, Marie thought, as he stood in front of the two of them, pulling his bag onto his shoulder. His hair was freshly washed and a smell of apples wafted off him. His face was like thunder.

Marie looked at David, but she didn't really see him. He looked hazy to her, as if she were the one missing the glasses, not him. 'I'm just coming. I bumped into Con.'

'I see that,' David said. 'I'll be in the bar.' And he walked off without another word.

'You'd better go after him.' Con's tone was teasing.

Marie thought for a while, before shaking her head. 'Nope.'

Con blinked, shaking his head, then laughing quietly

to himself. 'Guess that means I'm not going to my dinner either.'

'No, you're not,' Marie said, unable to believe her boldness as she took his hand and led him out of the ground.

★

Once they were outside, Marie's courage almost deserted her. She felt like running back inside to David and to Claire, cup of coffee in hand, to have a chat about the game or to say hello to Mr and Mrs Crowley; to do the things that were expected of her. Well, she was finished being sensible, Marie thought as she held Con's hand, pushing all thoughts of what had happened the last time she'd taken Con's hand out of her mind.

'So, where'll we go?' she said.

'How about my place? It's only around the corner.'

Marie bit her lip. She'd never been to Con's place – she'd had very little idea where he lived or what he did when he wasn't hanging around with them on the beach. It was as if he'd only existed when he was with her, and now, she was about to find out who he was. 'OK,' she said shyly.

He didn't say anything further, just led her across the road then around the corner into a long street lined with pretty single-storey cottages. Humming to himself, he led her to the white-painted one at the end, with a narrow path in red and black tiles that led to a blue door, around which twisted a large rose bush. That must look lovely in summer, Marie thought, as Con opened the door and held it ajar for her to enter first.

The little entrance hall was a gloomy cavern that smelled

a bit of mould, but a set of stairs led to a sweet stained-glass window. 'Straight ahead.' Con nodded towards the window and Marie climbed the stairs, catching a glimpse of an overgrown back garden as she passed, and kept walking up to the landing at the top of the stairs. 'It's this one,' Con said, taking another key out of his jacket pocket. The landing was tiny and they were forced to stand close together. Marie could smell him – he smelled of lemons and something quite expensive that went well with the tweedy uniform.

'Excuse me,' Con said, and she realised that she was in the way.

'Oh, sorry,' she said, as she stood to one side, letting him put the key in and turn it.

'After you,' he said, giving a little bow. Marie walked into a sunny, light-filled room, which was almost entirely empty apart from a table with two chairs, a beanbag and a few huge law books that had been left on the table, opened, along with an A4 pad and an orange highlighter pen. The bookshelves that lined the living room wall were almost empty, apart from two big encyclopaedias, one on literature and one on modern history. Through an open door to the right of the room, she could see an unmade bed, a pile of shirts in a ball on top of the duvet.

She didn't know where all the books were. He must have them, because, God knows, he quoted enough from them, but there was nothing here. No sign that Con actually lived here, none of the framed art posters or record collections that told you who somebody was.

'I've just moved in,' he said, as if reading her mind. 'I haven't had the chance to put anything out.'

'Oh. It's a very nice flat,' Marie said.

He smiled. 'You take the beanbag there, while I put the kettle on.'

Marie sat gingerly down on the beanbag, as if she'd been expecting to find something lurking in it, but when nothing happened, she relaxed a little. It was in a pool of sunshine and she allowed herself to relax into it a bit and to close her eyes, enjoying the tiny bit of warmth from the winter sun. She could hear Con rustling around in the tiny, pink-painted kitchen, the hiss of the kettle, the tinkle of the spoons in the cups, the opening and closing of cupboards.

'You must be tired.' His voice broke into her thoughts.

She opened her eyes for a second, before closing them again. 'I've been on nights, and I never sleep very well during the daytime, so ...'

'On nights?'

'Yes, I'm studying nursing.'

'Oh.'

Marie waited for the questions, for the lecture about her abandoning her ambitions, about allowing herself to bow to capitalist ideals by actually doing a job, but Con said nothing, lifting the lid off an old china teapot and putting a few teaspoons of tea leaves in before adding boiling water. He gave the mixture a little stir before putting the lid back on. The teapot was clearly an antique, a delicate white china with a pattern of cornflowers on it, and it looked incongruous in a room in which there was not one other nice thing – not a painting, or a cushion or anything to soften the monastic look of the place.

'I'd say it's a hard job,' he said carefully.

Marie nodded, but didn't say anything further, because she didn't have the energy to go into it all: St John's and Sister Dolores and Mrs O'Brien's bladder and Mrs Spence, and David, with his white coat and his stethoscope. Here in this little room, it all seemed to be part of another life. She found that she didn't want to think about it or talk about it. She just wanted to sit here, with Con and say nothing at all.

She must have drifted off, because when she woke up, the patch of sunlight had moved, and she felt chilly now, with a big crick in her neck. She turned her head, wincing at the pain, to find Con perched on one of the two chairs looking down at her, a small smile on his face. 'You were fast asleep.'

'Oh, God, I'm sorry, I—'

'It's OK,' he said. He looked at his tea for a few moments, before saying, 'I missed you.'

'I missed you too.'

He looked up, surprised. 'You did?'

'I did. But I thought it was pointless, that you'd be too cross with me to see me again.'

He looked hurt. 'How could you think that?' He examined his tea again. 'I thought about you every day, Marie, and I lost count of the amount of times I went to the phone to call you, but I always stopped, I don't know why. Once, I let it ring and you answered and when I heard your voice, I just couldn't talk to you, so I hung up.'

'I'm sorry,' Marie said in a small voice.

'Don't be. I know why you didn't come; I get it. I just wanted to feel that I meant something to you, that's all.' He looked at her with that intense expression of his.

'Oh, you did,' Marie said, struggling to get up from the

beanbag, tipping forward eventually, like a crab, before pushing herself upright. She went over to him and put a hand on his shoulder, and she felt it tense under her. 'You really did, Con, but I just couldn't, not after Grainne.'

He nodded but he didn't look at her, he just stared out the window into the garden, where a blackbird was digging a little hole in a patch of weeds, yellow beak jabbing at the green, an intent look on its face. Eventually, Con sighed deeply and said, 'Do you think I could ever come first, Marie?'

She bent over and kissed him on the forehead, smoothing the curls that fell forward with her hand. She could hear his breathing, the slight wheeze he always had, like air being pushed from a pair of bellows.

'Yes.' She wasn't sure she meant it, really, but she knew that that's what he wanted to hear. She wanted him to believe it, because she hoped it would make up for the hurt she'd caused him. She wanted to make him feel better. She also knew that she wanted to believe it too, because she had to have Con, even if she felt tight and knotted when she was with him – she also felt alive, as if she were thinking about everything more deeply, as if everything was more brightly coloured and vivid. Anyway, she was fed up with David Crowley and his lecturing about having her own life – she wanted to forget him and St John's and Grainne and everything …

Her face was close to his, and he only had to turn his head to kiss her, and to pull her towards him so that she was sitting on his knee. He breathed into her hair and gave a little groan.

'Christ, I missed you, Marie.'

'I missed you too, Con,' Marie whispered. She stroked his face and kissed him and then he kissed her back, harder now, so that her lips opened to his and she felt his tongue dart towards hers. She recoiled a bit and he said, 'Sorry. I just really, really want you.' He gave her that intense look again, and she found herself getting up off his knee and following him into the bedroom, where he pushed aside the pile of shirts, and hurriedly pulled up the duvet, sitting her gently down on the side of the bed. The bed creaked as he sat down beside her, his hip nudging against hers.

'Sorry it's a bit of a mess,' he said.

'Does anyone live here?' Marie joked as she looked around another bare room. There wasn't even a wardrobe, but instead a metal rail on which hung a single blue suit, and on the bedside table was a glass of water, a blister pack of Paracetemol and a set of rosary beads. Shoved to one side was a photo of two small boys, one of whom was obviously Con and the other a taller, thinner version of him, with blond hair. The two of them were standing on a riverbank, holding a small silver fish up between them, identical grins splitting their faces.

'Is that your brother?' Marie asked, thinking, but not adding, the one that you never talk about.

Con reached across the bed and turned the photo away, so that it faced the window. 'Yes, it is, but I'm sure he doesn't want to be looking at us.' He gave a small smile.

'No,' Marie agreed. She sat there for a few moments, wondering if she was supposed to do something first, but he saved her by turning her towards him and whispering, 'Lovely Marie', tugging gently at her shirt, one of those with a lot of fiddly buttons, opening the first one and then the second, and then the third, until he could slide a hand inside, around her left breast. Marie gasped.

'I'm sorry, is it OK?'

She nodded and he continued opening the buttons, muttering something about how many damned buttons did she have on the shirt. Marie wondered if she was supposed to do the same to him. She'd never been in this situation before; David Crowley's hasty groping didn't count. She tried not to think about him as she followed Con's lead, removing the horrible tweedy jacket and pulling the shirt out from the waistband of his trousers. He was wearing a T-shirt underneath and she wondered if she'd have to open the buttons and then worry about the T-shirt, or if she could somehow get it all over his head, or if his head would get stuck. That would be really embarrassing, she thought, as Con pushed her gently back on the bed and began to kiss her from the waistband of her jeans up to her chest. She closed her eyes and let him kiss her, enjoying the feeling of his lips on her skin, and then she felt him push one of the cups of her bra to one side and take a nipple in his mouth, flicking it with his tongue. Marie felt herself respond suddenly; she gave a little moan and she felt a flickering deep inside of her. He gave a small laugh as she instinctively reached for the belt of his trousers, pulling at the tag to open it, then wondering if she could pull the zip down on his fly without injuring him.

'Hang on,' he said gently, 'we'll get to that.'

Marie wondered if he'd done it before. She assumed he must have, if he was twenty-one. He couldn't possibly still be a virgin, she thought, as he fumbled behind her for the clasp of her bra. She found that she wanted to help him, but she was pinned on her back, so instead, she put a hand up under his T-shirt to feel his chest, gasping as she found her fingers entwined in a lot of hair.

'I know, I'm very hairy,' he said. 'It's embarrassing, if you really want to know.'

'No, it's nice,' Marie said and, emboldened, she sat up on the bed, bra falling off her, and she pulled it off and threw it on the bed, before tugging his shirt and his T-shirt over his head. He *was* actually very hairy, his chest covered with a thick mat of dark hair. Curly dark hair. Marie could dimly recall some childhood legend about the devil having curly hair, but she tried not to focus on that. She didn't feel that she could bring herself to kiss Con's chest, so she just pressed herself against it, feeling the hair tickle her breasts. It wasn't unpleasant, and she got that flickering feeling again, that feeling that she wanted to go further, to push harder against him, her breath coming in short gasps, as her hands wandered downwards until they met the bulge in his awful brown slacks. Now, she felt him move against her hand as she pressed it over the bulge, her mouth drying as she felt the size of it, and then his hands were rapidly unzipping his trousers and pulling at his underpants, guiding her hand down to where his penis had sprung up, like a big, fat snake. Nervously, she began to stroke it, watching it stiffen until it stood upright from the nest of curly hair around it. It was faintly terrifying and Marie swallowed as she tried to grasp the idea of that fitting inside of her.

'Harder,' Con gasped, as she began to stroke, watching the angry red tip stiffen further. Marie obliged by tugging at it, watching the outer layer of skin move up and down. He was moaning now, lying back on the bed, his eyes closed, and she wondered if he was going to do anything further to her. The bedroom was cold and her skin was now covered in goosepimples and she'd stopped feeling excited when she'd seen Con's penis appear. Instead, she just felt a bit self-conscious, a bit silly and a bit scared.

Then he grabbed at the waistband of her jeans, muttering, 'Hurry up,' as she pulled them down, until she was standing there in her knickers, eyeing his still-erect penis. He opened his eyes for a second, and gave a little laugh. 'It's OK. I'll show you. Lie down on the bed.'

Obediently, Marie lay down beside him, as he stroked her arm and then kissed her breasts, sucking first one nipple, then the other, but before she could ask him to keep doing what he was doing, he said, 'Ready?'

She nodded and he gently peeled her knickers off, turning until he was half-lying on top of her. He was quite heavy, and she felt her body grow tense at the thought of his penis, but he just kissed her neck, nuzzling against her, then gently pushing her legs apart with his knee, his penis prodding against her. 'It might hurt a bit, but I'll be gentle, OK?'

I don't know, Marie thought. I'm really not sure. She shivered, but she could see that Con took this as a sign that she was excited, and he began to push inside of her. Marie felt a burning sensation fill her, and she gasped with the pain.

'OK?'

She felt a sudden desire to pee, but she didn't want to tell Con that it hurt a bit, so she just whispered, 'Yes', then turned her head to one side and gripped the edge of the bedsheet as he pushed himself inside of her. The pain was worse now, and the desire to wee greater, but Con was moving faster on top of her and making low, animal noises, shoving his penis in and out, which felt like sandpaper inside of her, until with a shout, he lifted his head, tilting it back and rolling his eyes, as if he were having some kind of a fit. She could feel a throbbing deep inside her, and a trickle of warmth spilling out as he leaned back on one elbow.

'Jesus Christ,' he panted, lying back on the bed, his breath coming in short puffs.

Was that it? Marie wondered. It had been nice early on, and she'd been beginning to enjoy herself, but then, she hadn't felt much, apart from the pain, and now she felt stiff and bruised and as she looked down on the bed, she could see a patch of blood mixing with his semen. She knew all about the blood, but seeing it made her feel a bit strange, as if her head was no longer attached to her body. She couldn't connect the blood with her, that it meant the loss of something that had been with her for ever, even if she'd spent the last couple of years not wanting it, feeling that, because of it, there was a chasm that divided her and women like Claire, real women, not silly girls. And now, she'd crossed it, and it didn't really feel that special; although it didn't feel all that terrible either. Was sex like that, she wondered – not too nice and not too awful? But then she thought of Grainne and she understood that sometimes it could be awful. It must have been. The thought made her feel a sudden rush of guilt.

'I'm sorry. I couldn't control myself, Marie,' he said, pushing himself up on one elbow and stroking her hip. 'I meant to wear a condom, but I didn't get the time. I was too excited.

Don't you see, Marie, you've made me forget myself.' He gave a small laugh, as if it were a bit of a joke.

Marie tried to calculate how long it had been since her last period – she was dim about some things, but one of the benefits of nursing was a fairly thorough knowledge of the process of conception. 'I'll need to take something,' she said.

He gave a short laugh. 'It's probably a bit late for that now. You're not on the pill by any chance, are you?'

'No.'

'Well, you're a nurse. Maybe you could do something … you know?'

'I know,' Marie said shortly, reaching out for her bra, which was underneath him, and pulling it harder than she should have, so that he said, 'ow,' as one of the metal clasps scratched him.

'Aw, Marie don't be like that,' he said, sitting up and pulling her towards him, his skin warm against hers. He tickled her and nuzzled her neck and stroked her breasts and her tummy and told her that she was fabulous, gorgeous and that he wanted to stay in bed with her all night, and he whispered something that made Marie go bright red. Reluctantly, she got up from the bed and pulled on her bra and knickers, then her jeans, T-shirt and the thick sweater she'd worn for the rugby match.

He watched her get dressed, lying naked on the bed, looking at her through narrowed eyes. 'C'mon, back to bed.'

'I have to go.' Marie laughed. 'I'm on shift soon and Sister Dolores will dock my wages.'

'Just tell Sister Dolores that you've been having sex all

afternoon. She'll understand.' He snorted with laughter at his own joke.

'Very funny. I'm going now,' Marie said, thinking, as she buttoned her coat, that she sounded all womanly and sophisticated, no longer the hick. So what if the sex had been a bit sore – she'd changed now. She'd become a woman.

Chapter 11

23 Violet Street
London SW1
5 December 1983

Dear Marie
Can you believe it's nearly Christmas?! I went to Oxford
Street with Liam to see the Two Ronnies switch on the
Christmas lights. They're really old-fashioned, but it
was still fun. Do you remember Mrs D used to love the
Two Ronnies – she used to laugh at that sketch about the
fork handles all the time. I couldn't see what was funny
about it. Anyway, I went with Liam – he's my swimming
instructor at the Lido. Oh, don't worry, we're just friends.
I think he might be interested in being my boyfriend,

but I said no. I don't want any boyfriends, Mar. Ever again.

It's been nice to have someone other than Yvette to go to things with. She only wanted to go shopping and to the cinema in Leicester Square, which costs a fortune. Eleven pounds to see Raiders of the Lost Ark! She's actually quite boring, but Liam's nice. His mum's Irish but he 'tawks loike that'! It's funny that he's such a Cockney and his mum sounds like Mrs D. We've been to St James's Park together, and we've see the changing of the guard, which is actually a bit silly – lots of men in red jackets and fur hats marching up and down – and we've been to Soho. We went to a club where the singer was this woman in a red sequinned dress and a gorgeous blonde hairdo. She was so fabulous, but guess what, she was a man! I only found out at the end. She wasn't like that awful Danny La Rue though – she was much more realistic, like a real woman.

I don't think they have anything like that at home, do they? London is like that – really quite exciting and with so many different kinds of people. One minute, I'm in Soho, and the next, I'm eating curry in Brick Lane, where everyone's from Bangladesh and Pakistan. I'm beginning to enjoy that now, Mar, now that I'm not scared any more and now that I have Liam for company. I'm going to do a secretarial course after the summer, once I've saved up enough money. Sister Bonaventure says I'm a really bright, funny girl and that I can do it. She's a really nice nun. I know, you wouldn't think that such a thing existed, but she is. If she knew what I'd done, maybe she wouldn't be so nice, but I'm trying not to think about that. I find that if

I just don't think about it, it goes away. Every time I think about the baby, I just push it away with my mind.

Don't worry about me losing my religion, Mar. I feel a lot happier without God, actually. I know that he'd probably strike me down for saying it (but I suppose he can't, can he, if I don't believe in him?) but it's easier to just think about what happened with Anthony and to try to get over it, without worrying about what God will think all the time, and whether he'll forgive me.

I have to go now, because it's Christmas dinner for the homeless here and Liam said he'd help me to dish up. Are you having Christmas with Granny this year? Hopefully she won't poison you with her horrible trifle again! I miss you and I miss home, but I don't miss Granny or her nasty food. Maybe you could come and visit me in the summer? You'd love it here!

Lots of love, Grainne

Marie tucked the letter into her bag, ignoring Claire's look of sympathy. She didn't want to talk about Grainne and Claire understood. She was good like that, not asking questions if Marie didn't want to answer them. And she was good about things like coming along to the Family Planning clinic, which is where they were now. Con had been only too happy to let her go. 'I *would* get condoms,' he moaned, 'but you know how hard it is to get hold of them.' Marie suspected he just didn't have the stomach for the mortifying trip to the chemist's, prescription in hand, pretending that he was a married man. So, after a chat with Margaret beside the bins, cigarettes in hand, she'd gone to the women's clinic to get a coil fitted. Margaret said it was painless and would deal with the little problem of having had sex without protection. 'Little problem' – the euphemism seemed too small for the possibility of having a baby, she thought, as she sat in the waiting room with Claire, along with another girl with red hair, who was flicking through a magazine.

She remembered the last time she'd sat in a room like this, a year ago, her sister beside her, school jumper pulled down over her hands, knees jigging up and down with nerves. She wondered what Grainne would make of her and the choices she'd been able to make. How she'd been able to say yes to Con, and Grainne – well, she didn't really know, and the thought made her feel a bit uneasy. She'd always considered that she was cleverer than Grainne, but really, was she any different now? She supposed she didn't feel ashamed; that was it. Instead, she felt worldly, like the women she used to look at on *Women Today* with their grown-up, complicated problems.

'It's not painful, you know,' Claire was saying, showing her a photo in a magazine of Demi Moore looking fabulous at some film premiere. 'It hurts a bit when they put it in, but then, hey presto, a life of worry-free sex awaits. Mind you, not that we should be having to hide the fact down little laneways like this, but there you go. That's Ireland for you in 1983.' The girl with the red hair looked up abruptly, then blushed and looked intently back at her magazine.

Marie knew that Claire was right, but she wished she'd just shut up, because she was making Marie feel uncomfortable. Shouting about things wouldn't make them any better, but then, she supposed, neither would hiding them, or scuttling off to England, like poor Grainne.

'I'm sorry, Marie, that wasn't very tactful,' Claire said quietly.

'It's OK,' Marie said, hoping that Claire would be quiet now.

'I hope it was worth it anyway,' Claire added, with a glint in her eye.

Marie gave a small smile.

'Well?'

'Well what?'

'Was it worth it?'

Marie shrugged. 'I don't know. It was exciting I suppose, but …' She hesitated. 'It was painful.'

Claire looked at her sympathetically, 'Well, it can be at first, but it shouldn't be after. My first time, it was like having a red hot poker up me, but I never looked back, I can tell you.'

'Hmm.' Marie watched the red-haired girl shift uncomfortably in her seat. Sometimes she wished Claire wouldn't be quite so … frank. She thought of the previous night, her third night in a row in Con's flat, and a world which she had never known existed until last Sunday. Con hadn't even let her get her clothes off, pulling at her knickers and lifting up her skirt, licking her ear and tweaking her breast through her uniform cardigan, so that it hurt a bit. He seemed in a desperate hurry and it hadn't really been all that pleasant, but he'd said that was because he'd had to pull out because he didn't have any condoms. 'It was fantastic, Marie. You are just amazing, do you know that?' he'd said after, as she'd sat on the edge of the bed, skirt up around her waist, bra half-off, and he lay on the bed, trousers around his ankles, a big wad of toilet paper wrapped around his penis. When

Marie didn't say anything, he'd pushed himself upright in the bed and stroked her hair, kissing the back of her neck. 'I've never loved anyone the way I love you, Marie.'

She'd felt better then, knowing that at least Con loved her and she loved him. Even if he didn't seem to be the Con she remembered, full of fire and passion. That seemed to have got lost somewhere. Maybe that was the law for you – it made you wear brown slacks and tweed jackets on your day off and pinstripes at work and quote from big dusty law books. Marie thought she knew quite enough about tort at this stage. She kept trying to steer the conversation towards the novels she was reading – she'd just read *The Last September* by Elizabeth Bowen and she'd loved all of that Anglo-Irish big-house stuff, but Con had never heard of it. She'd even mentioned the Maze breakout, to see if he might get het up about the IRA and their great escape, but he'd simply shrugged his shoulders and said it was desperate all right. Where had the old Con gone, Marie had wondered. But she didn't want to tell Claire, because Claire would only tell her to end it and she didn't want to do that. She felt that she was somewhere she'd never been before and she didn't want it to be over. She wanted to enjoy the feeling of being a real woman at last.

'Marie, if it's not what you want, you need to tell him,' Claire said, lowering her voice for once. 'Sex isn't just the man's right, you know. It's a woman's right to enjoy it too.'

'Thanks for the lecture.' Marie smiled.

'You are welcome. Mind you, I thought you were making a go of things with the lovely doctor David. It's like something out of a Jane Austen novel, really,' Claire said, clasping her hands together and looking upwards. 'Without the sex, that is.'

'There isn't any sex in Jane Austen.' Marie giggled.

The girl with the red hair tutted now, but Claire was oblivious. 'I like David Crowley. He's a bit of a rugger bugger, and he's a bit square, but he's nice, and niceness is underrated, you know.'

'Is it?' Marie said. She didn't really want to think about David. He'd been on shift that Sunday night, when she'd left Con's, and he hadn't looked at her when she'd said hello, just shoved the medicine trolley across to her and asked her to double check Mrs O'Brien's catheter if she would. He'd been very polite. *Too* polite and she knew that he was offended. But she also knew that he couldn't offer her what Con was offering.

'Yes, and from what you tell me, Con O'Sullivan isn't nice at all. And one minute he's gone out of your life and the next minute he's back. I mean, what's with that?'

'I met him at the rugby match, Claire. He wasn't exactly hiding. And I lost touch with him, not the other way around,' she said, trying not to remember that bleak New Year's Day, when she'd sat on the sofa, alone, watching *The Wizard of Oz.* How she hadn't even given him a moment's thought, and now, here she was in a little waiting room, looking at a leaflet which told her how they would insert what looked like a bedspring inside of her. She hoped they'd get a move on. She was meeting Con at half-past six.

'The rugby match that you went to with David,' Claire said.

'Isn't that a bit rich, coming from you?' Marie attempted a smile.

'I suppose it is. But then, I've never loved any of them. That's the difference,' Claire said smartly. 'Be careful, Marie, will you?'

Marie said yes, of course she'd be careful, even if it was probably too late for that now.

★

Marie decided to surprise Con by getting a Chinese takeaway, queuing in the Great Wall on Serpentine Avenue, at the high counter with the brightly coloured posters of pandas and laughing girls in red pyjamas on the walls, listening to the hissing and frying coming from the kitchen. She wanted to sit down, because her tummy was cramping and she felt a bit weak. The nurse said she might, but that it would settle down. 'You shouldn't experience any further difficulties, unless, of course, you have an STD,' she said brightly, as if it were something to cheer about.

Marie ordered spring rolls and chicken chow mein, taking the paper bag with the cardboard cartons in it and walking slowly out of the door into the thin winter wind, which stung her eyes as it blew up the busy road. She tucked her scarf around her more tightly and buttoned her coat, holding the bag, with its contents, close to her, like a hot water bottle. She felt exhausted suddenly, as if she'd run a marathon, and her head felt too heavy for the rest of her. A bus passed and, for a moment, she debated getting on it and going home to Dada, but she quickly changed her mind. He wouldn't exactly be chatty and he'd never eat Chinese takeaway, she reasoned.

She wasn't sure why she felt like that, when she was in love. Was it supposed to feel like running a long and exhausting race? She wasn't sure, because she'd never been in love before. David didn't count, she knew, because when she looked at him, her pulse didn't race, her heart didn't flutter – she just felt happy to see him, but surely that wasn't love. He listened when she went on about books and classical music, and he'd taken an interest in her swimming lessons, but that was hardly a *coup de foudre*, as the French called it, like being struck by lightning. She shook her head, because she didn't want to think about David, and she kept going, crossing at the lights and walking down the little street lined with the sweet little cottages, wondering if she could see herself living here with Con, walking up and down this street every morning and evening after work, drinking tea with him in the morning, before kissing him goodbye and heading into … She stopped herself – the dream didn't end with heading into St John's, surely? No, that dream was part of another life altogether.

She hesitated outside the door before ringing the bell, wishing Con would hurry up, because she was so tired she could drop and the cramps were getting worse. She felt a sudden dart of resentment, that he'd left it to her when all he needed to do was find a nice GP and overcome his embarrassment.

'I haven't been able to stop thinking about you,' were Con's opening words as he stood at the door in a T-shirt and a pair of underpants. He grabbed her and pulled her into the hallway, kissing her fervently. 'Mmm, I've missed you, Marie, you have no idea.'

'Hang on,' Marie laughed, 'let me just put the dinner down. And what are you doing in your underpants?'

At the sound of the word 'dinner' he looked a bit disappointed. He looked down at his clothes and then at her. 'I had a study day.'

'And you didn't get out of bed?'

He pulled her towards him again and wrapped his arms around her. 'Why would I need to get out of bed, when all I have to do is wait for you? C'mon, let's go upstairs.'

'Con, I'm exhausted,' Marie protested. 'I went straight to the clinic when I came off shift and it's really wiped me out.'

His mouth turned down and he shrugged. She knew that he wasn't pleased, but she didn't care. She needed to sit down. Now. 'C'mon,' she said, walking past him up the stairs to the flat, 'let's have some chow mein.' He didn't answer and she closed her eyes for a minute, before opening them again and trudging up the stairs, pulling out one of the two kitchen chairs and sitting down gingerly, resting her head on her hands against the cool surface of the table. That feels good, she thought.

Con went into the bedroom without saying a word and came out dressed in jeans and a jumper. He didn't look at her as he went to the kitchen cupboard and took down a single white plate, which he put on the table in front of her. 'We'll have to share.'

Marie lifted her head and watched him dole out the chicken chow mein. She thought that it looked sad, a single white plate, as if he never expected to share with anyone else.

'Chopsticks or fork?'

'Chopsticks, please.'

'Good job, because I can't handle them,' he said. He found

two glasses, rinsed them under the tap and filled them with the contents of a half-empty bottle of white wine, which he pulled from the fridge, then set them down on the table, He pulled out his chair and put it down beside hers. 'Shove up,' he said gently.

Marie moved her chair a bit, so that he was sitting down beside her, his leg pressing against hers, his elbow nudging her elbow. He jabbed at the noodles with his fork, wrapping them around it then spearing a bit of chicken. Then he held it out to her. 'Eat up.'

She laughed. 'I can feed myself.'

'I know, but you're tired. So let me feed you.'

Marie let him lift forkfuls of shiny noodles into her mouth, resting her head in her hand as she chewed, taking small sips of white wine from the glass. She must have been starving, because after a few minutes, the mountain of chow mein had become more of a hillock. 'God, I'm sorry,' she said. 'I didn't leave any for you.'

He shrugged and rubbed her shoulder. 'I'm not hungry.'

'I was starving. I haven't eaten much in the last few days.'

'Lovesick?'

Marie looked down at her dinner. 'I think I was a bit nervous, you know ...'

'The chances would be really small, Marie.'

'I know.'

'Would it be that much of a disaster? I mean, you and me and a little O'Sullivan?' He was joking, sort of, but Marie's stomach lurched. Had he learned nothing after what happened to Grainne? Was he really that oblivious, she wondered. It was all she could do to be polite.

'Con, I'm nineteen, and I haven't a penny to my name, and you're a student.' And, you know full well what happened to my sister, she silently added.

'Yes, but soon I'll be a wealthy barrister and you'll be able to live in a big house in leafy Ranelagh and have everything you want and you won't have to work and ...'

He was warming to this vision of their future and Marie had to stop him. 'Hang on a minute, what about if I want to work?'

'But you hate St John's.'

'Yes, but maybe I'd like to do something else.'

Con seemed to be genuinely puzzled about this. 'Like what?'

'Oh, I don't know. Maybe become a foreign correspondent, like Kate Adie, and go to the Congo or places like that.'

His laugh caught her unawares, and she stopped dead. 'You knew that, Con. I told you often enough.'

He shifted uncomfortably in his seat, but didn't say anything, reaching out and stroking her hand. He looked as if he were disappointed in her, as if she wasn't the woman he'd thought she was, and yet, she didn't know what he expected. The Marie she'd been eighteen months ago and the Marie she was now were two completely different people. Maybe he preferred the original one, she thought. 'Do you remember our truth-telling?'

'Oh, God, is it time for some more?' He was smiling, but the smile didn't reach his eyes.

'Yes,' she said quietly.

He sighed. 'OK. You go first.'

'Well, it's more of a truth asking, really,' Marie said.

'OK,' he said warily.

'Con, what do you want from me?'

'What do you mean?' He was scowling now.

'What do you want me to be? I feel that since we met at the rugby match—'

'Which was all of five days ago,' he interrupted.

'Which was all of five days ago,' Marie agreed, 'that we've basically taken up where we left off, as if nothing ever happened, but everything has happened, everything and we can't be the same. We can't just carry on regardless. We can't just pretend that Grainne isn't gone and that I haven't changed and you—'

'I'm not the one pretending that Grainne hasn't gone, Marie,' Con said gently. 'You haven't mentioned her name once.'

Marie shook her head sadly. 'I've started going to swimming lessons recently.'

His laughter was sudden. 'But you hate swimming.'

Marie remembered David saying exactly the same thing. 'Yes, I do hate swimming, but I'm doing it for Grainne. I want her to be proud of me.' Marie felt the tears spring to her eyes. 'I think I'm trying to make up for letting her down.'

His face was tight. 'You didn't let her down, Marie.'

'Oh, I did.' Marie shook her head sadly. 'I miss her so much, Con.'

He didn't say anything, instead taking hold of a chopstick and twirling it around and around in his fingers. Marie wanted to reach out and grab it off him.

'She really loved you, you know.'

Con shrugged. 'I know. I couldn't help that, Marie.'

'I know you couldn't. I was so jealous of her, you know. I wanted to strangle her with her "Con this" and "Con that". It wasn't fair, because you were the first thing in my life that was actually mine and she—'

'You make me sound like a toy the two of you were fighting over.'

'I'm sorry. It wasn't like that, really.' As Marie said it, she wondered if Con wasn't a bit pleased that the two of them had fought over him. And then it struck her that maybe he'd wanted that.

'If you knew she liked you like that, why did you want me?'

'Oh, Marie, don't you see?'

'No, I don't see,' Marie said sulkily. 'It's like I said, Con. What do you want from me? We just seem to have picked up where we left off. There's a lot I don't know about you. Why your flat is empty, and why you don't have any books, and where you come from, who your friends are. Normal stuff that couples tell each other. We just live in this strange kind of bubble, where there's just the two of us.'

'Yes, but that's the point, Marie. It's you and me against the world,' he said softly. 'Just the two of us. Don't you think it's better like that?'

'I don't know, Con,' Marie said sadly.

'C'mon, I'll cheer you up,' he said, putting an arm around her, pulling her towards him, kissing her softly on the cheek. His breath was warm and smelled of white wine. He dropped his arm to the ticklish bit underneath her ribs and she giggled in spite of herself. 'Hmm, feeling happier?' he said, the other arm snaking its way down to the bottom of her cardigan, which he began to unbutton.

She couldn't help but laugh. 'Yes.'

'Well, good,' he said, pulling her gently up to a standing position, pressing his forehead against hers. 'I love you, Marie. The day you walked back into my life was the best ever. I mean that.'

Marie tried to nod, but she couldn't, because she'd bang his head, so she just said, 'I love you too.'

'Good,' he said, as if she'd said the right thing, and he led her into the bedroom. 'Look, I've even made the bed.'

'I'm honoured,' Marie said, sitting heavily down on it, thanking God for the feeling of the soft mattress under her, as she lifted her feet onto it and lay down.

★

When she awoke, she didn't know where she was for a moment. She had a blanket over her and the room was dark and she could hear the sounds of the city outside. She turned her head to the side and Con was beside her on the bed, fully clothed, snoring gently. She sat up and swung her legs down then, shuffling across to the curtains, peered outside. The sky was a faint pink and she could hear birds tweeting. Oh, God, she thought, what the hell time is it? She ran to her handbag and pulled out her nurse's fob watch, her heart thumping in her chest when she saw that it was seven o'clock in the morning. Dada would kill her. She'd be surprised if he hadn't called Mick at this stage.

She ran around Con's flat in circles for a few moments, trying to find her cardigan, because she didn't have the money to buy a new one, and shoving her cigarettes into her handbag. Would she brush her teeth or would that make her even later?

she wondered, before chastising herself. For God's sake, Dada wouldn't be any easier on her because she'd brushed her teeth. 'Just go, Marie,' she told herself firmly, putting her bag over her shoulder and closing the flat door gently behind her.

She ran down the little road to Serpentine Avenue, looking up and down in the early-morning gloom for any sign of a bus, but there was only the roar of distant traffic. She kept going, even though her stomach cramps had come back, racing down to the next bus stop, at the crossroads, where she thought she might get the number 18. She arrived at the bus stop breathless and feeling sick, bending over to rest her hands on her knees, then lifting her head to see the bus coming down the hill to the traffic lights. Thank you God, she thought, as she dug around in her pocket for the bus fare.

Thankfully the bus went really fast at this time in the morning, and there was practically no one on it, apart from an older lady with a Yorkshire terrier on her lap. The two of them were looking happily out of the window, and as she sat down behind them, Marie wondered where they were going that they were so delighted with themselves, the two of them looking out at the sea as it whizzed by, a blur of blue-grey, past the window. When the dog caught sight of another dog on the soggy grey sand at Sandymount, it gave a little yap, and the lady said, 'Yes, Freddie, that's one of your friends. Woof Woof!' And then she turned to Marie. 'He loves the bus, so we take a little trip every week or so, out to Killiney and back.'

'That's nice,' Marie said faintly.

'Well, you have to make the most of life, don't you, love? Because one thing I can tell you – it's short. It's over before you know it.'

'Aha,' Marie said politely. She wasn't really listening, because she was trying to think what she'd say to Dada. What excuse she'd make. She'd better not say that she was at Claire's, because he'd probably have rung her mother at this stage. Maybe she'd say that she'd gone to a nurse's party after work and missed the last bus, so she'd stayed at Margaret's and she'd fallen asleep without realising that she should have called him. That might do it. There was no way that she'd tell him about Con – Dada wasn't even aware of Con's existence and Marie wanted to keep it that way. She had a feeling that Dada wouldn't understand Con. He understood David, because David was the kind of boy Dada had seen every day of his life – David was the kind of boy Dada had been once – and he even liked him, as much as Dada liked anyone. But Con?

That didn't mean that Con wasn't right for her, though, Marie thought. Their time together in his little house – his cave – felt so intense, almost dreamlike, as if the two of them didn't exist outside of it: they were only truly themselves in those two little rooms. Even though Marie understood that she didn't know Con, and he didn't really know her, she felt that there was something about him that she just understood. Was that a good thing, she wondered now? Was that what love was? A difficult, hidden thing?

The lady was chattering away, and Marie hadn't been listening, so she said, 'Pardon?'

'I was just saying that you have your whole life in front of you, and you are so lucky. What I wouldn't give to live my life again,' the lady said wistfully.

Marie wondered if she'd really like to live this life all over again. She supposed she might, if all she had to do was take a bus up and down the coast all day with her beloved pet. As it was, she wasn't all that sure. She got up and smiled and waved at Freddie, who was looking intently at a pigeon sitting on the sea wall, and she rang the bell, climbing off the bus when it got to the stop at the seafront, looking at the two of them as they disappeared into the distance, happy as Larry. Maybe life really could be that simple, she thought.

When she got off the bus, the wind on the sea road was icy, making her eyes sting, but the swimmers were still out, even in mid-December, a row of hats bobbing in the water. The swimmers were all like Dada – a mixture of leather and steel, hardy, no-nonsense, not given to crises of the spirit. No wonder she hated it, Marie thought, squinting to see if there was any sign of Dada – if he was out swimming, she could sneak in without him seeing her. She couldn't see his green swimming hat, so she sighed and steeled herself for the Inquisition as she walked up to the front door and turned the key in the lock.

The first thing that struck her was the deafening silence. She breathed a sigh of relief – Dada must be out at Seaview then, she thought, hanging her coat up and going into the kitchen, emptying a tin of cat food onto a saucer and opening the back door. 'Lucy-lou, where are you?' she called. There was no movement of the gladioli, no swish of her tail as she appeared from the bottom of the garden. Where was she? Marie thought.

She went back into the kitchen and felt the silence of the house settle around her, putting the kettle on and reaching into her handbag for her cigarettes. She sat down on the old chair beside the range, debating whether or not she had the energy to go to the back door to smoke or how much time she might have before Dada came back. At least now she could pretend she'd been home all night or on shift. She closed her eyes for a moment, breathing in the quiet. It felt nice, the silence. It gave her the space to have a think.

And then she heard it, a faint meowing. She couldn't work out where it was coming from, but it seemed to be from above her head. She hoped Lucy-lou hadn't wandered upstairs, because Dada would kill her – he hated cats. Wearily, Marie got up from the chair and went into the hall, looking up the stairs. 'Lucy?'

The meowing was still faint, but seemed to be coming from the top of the landing. Tutting to herself, Marie climbed the stairs. She'd kill Lucy when she got hold of her, she thought. She hoped the cat hadn't done anything – once, she'd 'decorated' Dada's bed with something she'd sicked up and Marie had had to clean it up, then wash Dada's bedspread and put it back before he noticed.

At the top of the stairs, Marie paused. She couldn't hear anything. 'Lucy?' she called again. This time the meowing was louder, a plaintive cry. She must have got locked into the airing cupboard, Marie thought, opening it and looking around. But Lucy didn't shoot out from beneath the pile of old towels that she liked to use as a bed, so Marie closed the door and stood there for a moment. Where on earth was that bloody cat? she thought.

Then she heard the faint scratching coming from behind the bathroom door. How had she got in there? Marie wondered, pushing the door open. But it wouldn't give, because there seemed to be something in the way. Marie pushed at the door again, but it wouldn't budge. Whatever was behind it was heavy. Lucy's wails were becoming louder now and Marie said, 'Hang on, Lucy, will you?'

She managed to get the door open enough to stick her head around it, dipping her chin so that she could see whatever it was that was on the floor.

Lucy was standing on Dada, her tail swishing as she emitted a series of plaintive meows. He wasn't moving, his arm twisted outwards at a funny angle. He had a big gash on his head from where he must have hit the sink when he'd fallen. The cabinet above the sink was open and the mirrored door reflected Marie's horrified face back to her.

'Hang on,' she said to no one in particular, as she tried to push the door again. For God's sake, she told herself, what was she thinking? Dada wasn't able to move out of the way. She pulled the door closed for a second and stood there, hands to her head, trying to get her thoughts in a straight line. 'Ambulance, I need an ambulance,' she said to herself, running down the stairs to the hall, then running back up again. 'Dada, I'm just calling an ambulance,' she yelled through the door. As if he'd hear her.

She called David Crowley first. She didn't know why she didn't just call 999, but for some weird reason, she thought they wouldn't be able to break down the door. David would know, she reasoned. When he answered, he sounded frosty for a second, until she blurted, 'It's Dada, David. He's lying on the bathroom floor and I can't move him.'

David went straight into medical mode, and Marie felt grateful for that. 'Is he breathing?'

'I don't know,' she whispered. 'I think so.'

'All right,' he said briskly. 'I want you to put the phone down and call 999 and I'll be over straight away.' Without saying anything further, she disconnected and dialled 999, listening to the nice lady at the other end asking her which service she required. 'Ambulance,' she managed, giving the address.

'Is the patient sitting up?'

'What? No, of course he's not sitting up,' Marie snapped. 'He's lying down and he could be dead.'

The nice lady was calm. 'Can you check his breathing?'

'No, because he's blocking the bathroom door and I can't open it,' Marie said. 'And Lucy's in there with him,' she added pointlessly.

'Maybe Lucy might be able to check his breathing?' the lady offered helpfully. Marie didn't even bother explaining that that wouldn't be likely, instead repeating the address and slamming the phone down in its cradle and running to the top of the stairs again. 'Dada, the ambulance is coming,' she yelled through the bathroom door. Maybe he might hear her somehow.

She thought he might need a bag for the hospital, so she ran into his bedroom, taking his old sports bag from the top of the wardrobe, then running around the room filling it with pyjamas, slippers, a cardigan, the book of Yeats' poems that was lying on his bedside table. I didn't know you liked Yeats, Dada, she thought, as she looked at the poet's owlish face. I didn't even know you liked poetry. Then she snapped back to reality. For God's sake, Dada could be dead, and here she was thinking about poetry. She tossed the book into the bag, along with a comb – his shaving gear was in the bathroom, so that would have to wait, she thought, wondering if there was anything she'd forgotten. Then she thought of the photo of Mum and Frank in her bedroom. Maybe he'd like to have that to look at, she thought. She went into her bedroom and took the photo, in its little silver frame, and she kissed Mum's kind face, and she asked her to make Dada OK, and then put the photo into the bag.

She could hear the banging on the front door then and she bolted down the stairs to find David there, panting, leaning on his bicycle. 'I'm here,' he said unnecessarily.

'He's upstairs, but you can't get into the bathroom, because he's fallen against the door.'

'Right,' he said, leaning his bicycle against the hedge. 'Can I climb in the window?'

'What?' Marie found that she couldn't quite hear him, and that she couldn't get her hands to stop shaking, pressing them hard against her thighs to keep them steady.

'I said, can I climb in the bathroom window?' he said quietly, but firmly.

'Yes,' she said finally. 'You can climb up from the shed roof. But only the top window is open and you're too big to fit in it. I'll do it.' He looked at her doubtfully, but she didn't say anything, just went into the shed and took out the old ladder, leaning it up against the side of the house. 'Hold onto the bottom for me,' she said to David.

'Right.' He took hold of the bottom of the ladder as she began to climb upwards, shouting, 'Open the bottom window for me when you get in, will you?'

Marie didn't say anything, just kept climbing until she got to the window, pulling herself up on the windowsill, sucking in a deep breath as she stuck her hand in the top of the little window, hoping that she might be able to reach the handle of the bigger one. She could see the outline of Dada's body on the floor, as she stood on tiptoe and reached out for the handle, which felt cold and nubbly in her hand. She gave it a tug and the window flew open so suddenly that she wobbled on the windowsill, grabbing hold of the frame of the little window and hanging onto it, her heart thumping in her chest.

'Be careful.' She could hear David's voice below, but it sounded as if it were coming from a long way away, as she clambered in through the window, into the bath then onto the floor, manoeuvring her way around Dada and Lucy, whose tail shot into the air and who began purring and wailing at the same time.

'I know, Lucy,' Marie said as she felt Dada's neck for a pulse. It was faint, but it was there. She didn't think she could move him into the recovery position, because he was so heavy and because he'd fallen at an awkward angle, so instead, she just examined the wound on his head, a thick red gash that was now surrounded by a cloud of black bruising, and felt his skin, which was cold and clammy. She didn't know how long he'd been lying there – it could have been half an hour or all night.

David appeared in the window, his large frame filling the space, then hopped gingerly down into the bath.

'I'll take a look,' he said quietly. David calmly bent down to listen to Dada's breathing. As he did, Dada's eyes flickered open for a moment and he looked at David. 'Who are you?'

'It's David Crowley, Mr Stephenson. You fell and hit your head.'

'It was the quinine,' Dada muttered. 'I needed it and then ...' He waved his hand. 'I can't remember anything.'

'Mr Stephenson, try not to talk or to move,' David said firmly, but Dada didn't seem to be listening. 'Toora loora loora,' he began to sing softly under his breath. 'Your mother loved that song, Marie,' he said wistfully, eyes gazing upwards to the window, where the pale winter sun was now streaming in. 'How I long to see her again,' he said sadly, closing his eyes and slumping back onto the floor.

Marie put a hand to her mouth. 'Is he dead?'

David's hand was warm on her arm. 'He's concussed, probably, and confused, but he's not dead, Marie. It'll be OK.' She looked up at him and he'd lost that frosty, tense look. Instead, his eyes were crinkling up at the corners, and his smile was genuine, as if he didn't hate her. Suddenly, hunkered down opposite her in the tiny space, his presence seemed to fill the room.

Oh, Marie thought. Oh. The thought was new and surprising and, for a moment, she held it in front of her, she examined it and she wondered about it, before David spoke.

'We can't move him too much, but we'll need to clear the doorway.'

'Right,' Marie said, but she didn't move.

'Ehm, so can you help?'

'What? Oh. Yes.' Marie helped David to shuffle Dada as gently as possible over towards the bath, so that the door would open. Lucy shot out with an anguished wail and disappeared onto the landing, tail aloft.

'That's the ambulance,' David said, as the faint sound of sirens became louder, and then stopped as the roar of an engine could be heard outside.

'We'd better open the door to them.'

'Right.'

'So?' David was looking at her now as if she had a screw loose.

'I'll get it,' Marie said suddenly, getting to her feet and running down the stairs to the hall door, heart thumping in her chest.

Chapter 12

'Is your father a religious man?' the nurse asked Marie after Dada had been wheeled into Casualty and been examined by a doctor.

'I'm not sure what you mean,' Marie said.

'Well, he seems to be very keen on the Hail Mary,' the nurse replied, trying to hide a smile.

Marie could hear Dada behind the curtain. 'Hail Mary, full of Grace, the Lord is with Thee, Blessed art Thou …' She'd never heard Dada pray even once, let alone a Hail Mary. It wouldn't have been any stranger if he'd been reciting the Koran or the Talmud. 'Maybe it's the head injury,' she said doubtfully.

'It could be,' the nurse said cheerfully. 'I had one patient who got a blow to his head and could recite all of Shakespeare's sonnets backwards,' she said, jotting something down on her clipboard

'Right,' Marie said faintly, unable to work out how that could possibly be helpful. Instead, she answered the nurse's questions about Dada's name, date of birth, which she had to struggle to remember, as Dada had always refused to celebrate it, and religion.

'I'll take it he's a Catholic.' The nurse smirked.

What gives you the right to assume that, Marie thought. 'Of sorts,' she said.

'Well, there isn't a box for "of sorts",' the nurse said, with a trace of sarcasm.

'Put nothing then,' Marie barked. She wasn't sure that Dada was an atheist, exactly, but she knew that he wouldn't want to wake up with a priest standing over him. 'When can I see him?'

'Mr Moriarty's examining him now, he'll be out in a few minutes to talk to you,' the nurse said, getting up smartly and disappearing off up the corridor.

What's her problem? Marie thought crossly. She listened to the doctor, who was trying to interrupt the flow of Hail Marys to ask Dada some questions. 'Tell me … Cormac. What day of the week is it?'

'Blessed be the fruit of thy womb, Jesus,' was the answer.

'And who's the Taoiseach at the moment, do you know that?' Uh-oh, he'd regret asking that, Marie thought, as there was a long pause. Dada hated Garret FitzGerald, calling him a damp, liberal academic, which Marie had always thought a bit harsh. 'Hail Mary, full of Grace, the Lord is with Thee …'

David came into the little waiting room then, holding two

plastic cups of coffee, handing one to her. 'Mum and Dad are outside in the car,' he said.

'Oh, right, do you need to go?' Please don't go, she thought. Marie closed her eyes for a second and she wished that Mrs D would just bustle into the room and start folding blankets and giving out to the nurses – she needed anyone who could just take charge, because Marie wasn't sure she could do it. And yet, she had to, she supposed. There was nobody else. Granny would have to be sedated when Marie told her ... and then there was Grainne, but Marie wasn't ready to tell her sister yet. Grainne would only get agitated and start asking her questions again and Marie had enough on her plate at the moment.

'Not for a bit. I'm on shift at three,' he said, looking at his watch.

Thank God, Marie thought. She hesitated for a moment, then leaned against his arm and closed her eyes, the sounds of bustling nurses wheeling trolleys and all the other noises of a busy hospital ward receding into the background. She could hear him breathing beside her, his chest rising and falling, then she felt his arm reach around her and rub her shoulder and she settled in against him. She felt safe.

★

She must have fallen asleep, because she woke up when David cleared his throat and shifted in his seat. A small man was standing in front of the two of them, in a creased and crumpled white coat. He had tomato stains on his jumper underneath, and Marie found herself concentrating on them as Mr Moriarty started talking. 'Perhaps this might be something for your mother ...' He looked at them both.

314

'Oh, we're not related,' Marie said, eyeing David. 'And my mother's … ehm … deceased, so I'm his next of kin.'

'Ah.' The doctor looked stricken for a moment, clearly wondering if he should be telling Marie anything, before saying, 'Well, we think that Cormac has been having a series of mini-strokes, which has affected his memory,' he said in a soft Donegal accent that reminded her of Mrs D's. 'He certainly concussed himself when he hit the sink, but I'm not of the opinion that that's the problem.' He ran a hand through his tuft of grey hair. 'We'd like to keep him in for a day or two. We'll do a few tests and see how he gets on.'

Stroke? Marie found that she couldn't take her eyes off the tomato stains on Mr Moriarty's jumper, while the doctor talked on about prognoses and rehabilitation, because her own brain simply didn't want to take it in, that Dada, big, strong Dada, might not be his old self again, even if that old self wasn't much to get excited about. Would he sit at the breakfast table, glasses on his nose, and read the paper, or come back from his morning swim and declare it bracing, or intervene in one of her rows with Grainne? Not that there were any rows any more, and Marie missed them.

She'd always thought that one day Dada might come out of his study and declare that his period of mourning Mum was over. That he'd decided to be much more cheerful and to start to live again. Now, she wondered if that would never happen, or if he'd spend the next months and years reciting the Hail Mary instead.

The thought made her suddenly feel panicky, as if she needed to break into a run. 'I'm sorry, I need to go,' she said, interrupting the doctor in mid flow, jumping up from her seat so abruptly that her handbag tilted off and crashed to the floor, emptying keys, bus tickets, cigarettes and Lucy's toy mouse onto the tiles, along with the leaflet from the clinic. LOOKING AFTER YOUR IUD it proclaimed in block capitals.

'Let me help,' David said.

'It's fine,' Marie snapped, shoving all of the stuff into her handbag, cheeks aflame. She knew that she was being rude, but she just had to get out of this room.

'Marie,' the doctor began, but she interrupted him. 'I'm sorry, Mr Moriarty, I need some air. I'll come and talk to you later.' She didn't even look at David as she sped out the door, even though she felt a flicker of guilt. After everything he'd done for her, she was still being mean to him. Why was that?

She walked down a long series of corridors, all lined with statues of Holy Mary, the Sacred Heart and the Child of Prague. She wasn't sure where she was going, but she just felt she needed to keep walking. Then she found a phone box in the corridor. She rang Con's number, telling him blankly that she wouldn't be able to come over later because Dada had been taken ill.

She wasn't sure what she'd been expecting, but there was a pause at the other end of the line, as if Con was trying to think of the right thing to say. Eventually, he settled on, 'Oh, I hope it's not serious?'

'He fell in the bathroom and hit his head.'

'Oh, well old people do that a lot,' he said confidently.

'They think he's had a stroke.' She didn't mean to sound so blunt, but even as she said them, she wondered if she'd chosen the words to make him sit up and pay attention.

'Oh, God, Marie, that's terrible.' He must have turned away from the phone then, because she could hear his muffled voice talking to someone else. Then it was clear again.

'Is there someone there?'

'Just one of the guys. We have a big case coming up. How are you holding up?' His voice was soft now, sympathetic.

'I'm a bit shaken. I found him when I came home this morning,' she said significantly, but he didn't seem to be taking it in.

'Listen, will you let me know how he is?'

'What?' Marie blinked, not sure if she'd heard him correctly.

'I said, let me know how he is. Give me a call later.'

'OK ...' She didn't mean to sound whiny, she really didn't, but she couldn't help it. She felt tearful and lost and she really wanted him to say that he'd be right over. She didn't want to have to ask him: she wanted him to offer.

'Marie, you know I'd do anything to be there right now, but I just can't get away. Raymond and I have a lot to get through or we'll be out of jobs.'

'OK,' Marie said sadly. Who was Raymond? Was he one of the tweed-jacket wearers she'd seen at the rugby match? It seemed that he'd swapped Seamus and the PLO-scarf wearers he'd hung around with in college, with all their chat about socialism and dialectics, for this new group of respectable young men. Was that what happened when you grew up, that you just ditched one group and made a whole new set of friends? It hadn't happened to her. She still had Claire and Grainne, even though she wasn't with her, and David Crowley. Maybe she wasn't able to move on like Con. Debs and Margaret didn't exactly count as 'moving on'. They were allies in the grim world of St John's, but they weren't exactly friends.

'I'm really sorry, Marie – you do understand?'

'Sure, of course I do,' Marie said. 'I'll call you later.' And she put the phone down softly in its cradle.

David was waiting for her at the doors to the canteen when she wandered down the stairs in a daze. She didn't know how he'd known where she'd be – maybe she'd need to add psychic to the long list of his powers. He was probably Superman in his spare time, she thought, as he handed her a polystyrene cup of water. 'I thought you might need this.'

'Thanks,' she said gratefully, tipping the cup up and drinking until it was empty. 'I must have been thirsty,' she said unnecessarily.

'It's warm in here.'

'Yes, it is.' Why were they talking like this, all of a sudden? Like characters in a Jane Austen novel. Next she'd be asking him if he'd noticed the infelicitous weather recently.

'I came to find you, because your dad's awake.'

'Oh. That's good, isn't it?'

He looked uncertain. 'He's been asking for you.'

'He has?'

'C'mon, we'll go and find him.'

David steered her gently through the corridor, which was lined with rows of orange plastic chairs, on which sat or lay people with various injuries: a child with a huge bandage wrapped around his head; an old man, snoring, his foot, in plaster of Paris, propped up on the chair opposite him so everyone had to step over his leg; a lady with a bright red eye. Foreign body, Marie thought absently as she passed her. Sister Dolores loved foreign bodies; she'd once had to remove a whole candle from a child's ear, one of those little white ones that you paid 10p to light on the side altar of the church. It was a story she loved retelling, and she was always asking Marie to check for them whenever a likely looking patient came in. If the answer was 'no' she'd look faintly disappointed.

Dada was at the end of the corridor, in a tiny cubicle by himself, lying on a trolley underneath a statue of the Sacred Heart. He won't like that, Marie thought. When he was well, he'd spent a lot of time lecturing Marie and Grainne about Catholic idolatry. Now, he looked like a small child, his eyes scanning the room nervously, his arms tightly folded across his chest. As Marie came towards him, he started to cry, a thin wail coming from his mouth, tears rolling down his cheeks.

'It's OK, Dada,' Marie said, sitting on the edge of the trolley and patting his head, stroking the black hair flat. 'You've just had a nasty bang to the head. It'll be all right, I promise.' But still, Dada wailed, a lost, desolate cry. Marie reached out to touch his arm, hoping to loosen his grip a bit, and then he lifted the thing he'd been pressing to his chest and showed it to her. It was the photo of Mum and Frank. 'I miss her so, Marie. I want to be with her. Please just let me go. Please.'

'Dada, shush,' Marie soothed. 'It'll be all right, but you need to stay calm,' she said, trying to tug the picture gently out of his hand.

'Leave it alone!' he yelled, pulling it back onto his chest, where he clutched it, like a small child would a cuddly toy. Marie felt totally helpless, unable to make Dada feel any better, unable to do a single useful thing.

There was a small clearing of the throat behind her. 'Mr Stephenson, I know you're distressed, but …' Oh, God, Marie thought, will you just go away? She turned sharply around. 'David, I'll talk to him. I know what to say, please just … just leave, will you?' She knew that it was horrible of her, after everything David had done, but she knew that she had to be alone with Dada, to see if she could stop the crying, and because she didn't want David to see him like this.

David looked as if she'd kicked him, then said, 'Of course.' And then he walked out, and Marie breathed a sigh of relief, then took Dada's hand and tried to soothe him.

Chapter 13

Marie didn't know where she was for a few moments. She could hear the shush-shush of the sea and the gentle tweeting of the birds, so it wasn't the hospital. She opened her eyes carefully, taking in the pattern of the rug under her chin, the faded mahogany of the bedstead in front of her, the shape underneath it, now snoring gently away, a series of little whistles coming from his nose. She was in Dada's bedroom, on the hard little sofa at the end of his bed, where she'd been for the past week, since he'd been brought home from the hospital.

Mr Moriarty had said that it was 'possible' Dada might have a 'significant episode', but that hospital seemed to be causing him more stress than not, and so, Marie had found herself sitting in the ambulance with him as it took him home, swaying and wobbling around corners and speeding down roads, Dada sitting beside her, wearing the same clothes in which he'd been admitted to hospital, his jumper now stained and dirty, the collar of his shirt a grubby grey. He was wearing odd socks, too – that was the saddest thing. What Mum would have thought if she'd seen him. She'd used to joke that if she weren't there, Dada would dress like a tramp – she'd been right.

His amnesia seemed to have become a vacant depression now, and whilst he knew who she was, he didn't seem to have any interest in her or anyone else. He'd refused to let go of the photo as well, shaking his head vigorously every time one of the nurses had suggested he just put it to one side to eat his dinner or change the drip in his arm. He'd damaged the photo, too, Marie noticed having somehow managed to get it out of the little frame, scrunching it up so that a series of white cracks had appeared in the photographic paper. She felt a surge of anger then. That's my photo, she'd thought, not yours.

The public health nurse, a tall woman with hands the size of small hams, had promised to visit every day, and Mrs O'Farrell had been persuaded, with the offer of a lot of cash, to come in for an extra hour in the mornings, but Marie still found herself collapsing onto the sofa at the end of each day, so exhausted she could barely move. It wasn't that Dada was completely helpless – he wasn't – he was able to get up and go to the bathroom, Marie following at a safe distance to make sure he didn't pass out and hit his head again, and to sit up in bed while Mrs O'Farrell pushed a tray of some revolting-looking stew under his nose, which he'd shove gently away when she'd left the room – it was that he seemed to have given up. The bang on the head seemed to have pushed him over some line, and he'd decided not to cross back again. Marie felt exhausted, not from looking after Dada, but from worrying about him and about his lonely journey into a place where no one could reach him. He seemed to just be waiting now, to join Mum. Sometimes, when she was bringing another tray up to his room or boiling the kettle for his hot water bottle, she wondered what it might be like to love someone so much that you just wanted to die to be close to them again. Did she love Con that much? she wondered.

She sighed heavily now and closed her eyes again, hoping to get a few moments more sleep. That was all she wanted to do, she thought: sleep, preferably forever.

She fell back into a broken sleep, full of strange dreams, where she was following Lucy around the house, the cat's tail aloft as she went from room to room, looking for something. David Crowley was in one of the rooms, reading the *Irish Times* and eating from a brown paper bag of chips, and behind another door was Mum. Marie knew it, because she could hear her calling her name. 'Marie. Mar? Wake up.' She could feel her mother's warm arms around her, pulling her into a tight hug. It was lovely, and Marie wanted to settle into the embrace, to feel herself protected, to feel that there was someone looking after her. The voice called again, 'Mar?'

Her eyelids fluttered open, and she found herself locked in the tight embrace of a pair of solid arms, a pale slant of freckled skin in her eye line. 'Mum?' she said hopefully.

'It's me, Mar. It's Grainne.'

I'm not awake yet, Marie thought, shaking her head and blinking rapidly, trying to nudge herself awake. But the view was still the same, and when she lifted her head, her sister's face smiled down at her. She looked different – her mane of red frizzy hair had been tamed into a sleek ponytail, and her face looked thinner, the carefully applied make-up giving her a grown-up look.

'Gra? Is it really you?'

The person who said she was her sister gave a small smile and pulled Marie into another hug. 'Yes, of course it's me, Mar. Have I changed that much?'

Marie shook her head rapidly, trying to wake up. She wanted to feel her sister's arms around her, but still, she flailed around as if she were drowning, trying to break free. She got to her feet, dizzy, and looked over at Dada in the bed. He'd need to be woken shortly for his tablets, and then she could put a wash on and find something in the fridge that he might eat …

'Marie?' Grainne was sitting on the couch now, in the space that Marie had vacated. She looked a bit lost and hurt.

'I'm sorry. I was fast asleep,' Marie began. 'I was having this funny dream and then … ' She didn't want to tell her sister about Mum. 'And then you were there.'

'Yes.' Grainne smiled. 'I'm here, Mar. David came to get me.'

'David?' Marie repeated.

'Yes, David. And we came home on a plane, not on the boat!' Grainne said, suddenly animated. 'I've never been on a plane before. It was a bit bumpy, but we had a lovely lunch with proper cutlery and cups and saucers and little squares of food, like postage stamps,' she said. 'David's lovely, Marie. He's quite handsome now that he's had his hair cut,'

Oh, God. David Crowley, I will kill you, Marie thought miserably. What am I going to do with Grainne, on top of everything else? It was unfair of her, she knew that, but she couldn't cope with another responsibility right now, she just couldn't.

'Mar, aren't you pleased to see me?' Grainne said sadly. 'Have I done the wrong thing again?'

'Oh, no, Grainne.' Marie tried to sound reassuring. 'Of course you haven't. I'm thrilled to see you, really,' and she bent down and pulled her sister into a hug, a big, tight squeeze, inhaling a scent of shampoo and perfume. Her sister smelled different – sophisticated, grown-up. She didn't smell of Hubba Bubba bubblegum any more. She felt tears spring to her eyes, but she vowed not to cry. Instead, she blinked away the tears and released her sister, looking at her newly slim figure, the fashionable crop top and pink trousers she was wearing, the pink court shoes on her feet. She looked pretty and sophisticated, as if she'd been beamed in from another planet. 'I've really missed you, Gra.'

'You have?' Grainne looked hopeful.

'I have,' Marie said, holding her at arm's length. 'You look so different.'

'Miss Selfridge,' Grainne proclaimed. 'It's really cheap, but the clothes are fantastic, you'd love it, Mar. They've got everything, even jewellery and make-up. It makes Arnotts look like some old shop down the country.' And she fingered the sleeve of her pretty top.

'I'm sure it does,' Marie said, feeling a flicker of resentment that her choices were confined to Dunnes Stores or Arnotts. What was wrong with Arnotts anyway? It had done Grainne perfectly fine before now.

Grainne crept over to the sleeping figure in the bed, his chest rising and falling as he breathed. She didn't say a word, just hovered over him, a curious look on her face. 'He doesn't look very sick,' she said.

'He is sick, Grainne,' Marie said sharply. 'He's had a few mini-strokes and the doctor says that he could have a major one any time. And he's been very depressed.' But what would you know? The words hung in the air.

'Oh.' Grainne stood back. 'Will he die, Marie?'

Marie shook her head sadly. 'I don't know, Grainne. I hope not.' And, as she said the words, she realised that they were true. Dada hadn't been a part of their lives for as long as she could remember, not properly anyway, and yet she didn't know what she'd do without him.

Grainne's face fell, as she sat on the chaise longue, hands on her knees, but then she brightened. 'Well, at least I'm back now.'

'Yes. At least you're back,' Marie echoed faintly.

'And I can help,' Grainne said more animatedly. Seeing the look on Marie's face, she added, 'I know that you think I can't, Mar, but I can. I really can. I learned such a lot at St Mary's, and I'm really capable now, just you wait and see.'

'That's good,' Marie said carefully. There seemed to be an awful lot else to say, too, but Marie found herself unable to speak. Eventually, she blurted, 'Do you want lunch?'

Grainne looked at her as if she were terribly disappointed in her, that she really couldn't think of anything better to say to the sister she hadn't seen in nearly a year. 'Oh, no thank you,' she said politely. She opened her mouth to say something, but then there was a loud snort from the bed, followed by that wail again.

Marie rushed to the bed. 'Dada, what is it?' She could feel Grainne beside her, hovering, and she suppressed the urge to tell her sister to leave her to deal with it. She'd been dealing with it up to now, so Grainne needn't think—

'Nooooooo!' Dada gave a cry, and pointed a long, bony finger over Marie's shoulder. 'No, no, no. Bad girl.'

'Dada, it's Grainne,' Marie said softly. 'She's come back to visit.'

'No, no, no,' Dada kept repeating. 'No. Let he who is without sin cast the first stone …'

Marie turned to see her sister's face, chalk white, tears filling her blue eyes. 'He doesn't mean it, Gra. He's been a bit Bible-obsessed since the accident,' Marie explained, as Dada's wails grew louder. But her sister had turned and fled, the bedroom door closing behind her with a solid 'thud'. That's torn it, Marie thought, patting Dada's head, because she found that that soothed him. 'There, there, Dada, it'll be OK,' she said, wondering why Grainne had had to set him off like that.

Marie spent the rest of the morning cleaning the bathroom, collecting the tin of scouring powder from the cabinet under the sink and sprinkling it liberally over the bath and sink and the loo, then putting on a pair of red rubber gloves and scrubbing furiously. The bathroom didn't really need to be cleaned, and cleaning reminded her of St John's, but she found that she could take her anger out on the porcelain and no one need be any the wiser. Damn David-bloody-interfering-Crowley, with his endless do-gooding, damn Grainne, who hadn't stayed away, damn Dada, who just didn't want to go on living and damn Con … She hesitated then, the scouring pad in her hand. She remembered how he'd been on the phone when she'd called him from the hospital, sort of distant, as if she were calling him from thousands of miles away, instead of from a phone down the road. And then she remembered David and herself, in the bathroom when Dada had hit his head, that feeling she'd had about David, that sense that something was being revealed to her.

She shook her head. No, he was far too much of an interfering do-gooder, his cape around his neck, ready to take flight, like Christopher Reeve in the Superman movie. Maybe Con was his arch-enemy General Zod, she thought, with a giggle, before she corrected herself. Of course, Con wasn't General Zod – he wasn't an evil warlord intent on destroying the universe. Where on earth had she got that idea?

'Marie?' Grainne's voice sounded faint, and in the silence that followed, Marie debated whether to answer or whether to keep on scrubbing. She sprinkled a bit more of the powder onto the pad and went to apply it to the underneath bit of the sink, which Mrs O'Farrell always missed, when she heard Grainne's voice again, this time louder. 'Mar? Lunch!'

Marie sighed heavily and put the scouring pad down. She

opened the bathroom door and a rich scent of meat and herbs wafted up the stairs. It smelled fantastic, and Marie's stomach began to rumble. It seemed that while her mind had one idea, her body had another, and she found herself almost running down the stairs to the kitchen, opening the door to find her sister standing in front of the range, the way she always used to do, wooden spoon in her hand, stirring. She'd tied her hair up in a pink hairband and she was lifting the spoon to her lips, tasting the food and making a little face, moving to the cupboard and taking the salt and pepper cellars down, sprinkling a little bit of each into the stew. It was as if she'd never left, and Marie felt her heart squeeze at the thought of how much she'd missed her.

'Oh, there you are,' she said. 'Lunch is just ready. It's coq au vin.'

'Wow! I've trained myself to really like toasted ham and cheese sandwiches,' Marie said, sitting down at the place Grainne had set at the table. She'd laid it properly, with table mats, glasses and the old damask napkins that hadn't been used since about Christmas 1975.

'Do you need a hand?' Marie said, as her sister took a couple of plates out of the warming drawer and ladled something that looked like mashed potato onto a plate, followed by another ladle of the stew.

'No thanks, I can manage,' Grainne said bringing the two plates to the table, her face screwed up as she popped them quickly down. 'Ouch, hot,' she said, waving her hands and blowing on her fingers.

'Asbestos hands,' Marie joked. Mrs D had always used to

scold Grainne about never using a tea towel to handle hot plates and how she must have asbestos hands.

Grainne didn't say anything in reply, just gave a small smile, lifting up her knife and fork.

'I'm sorry. I didn't mean to mention Mrs D,' Marie said. Grainne had only just learned that Mrs D wasn't actually there any more. That all the letters she'd been sending Grainne, talking about the flowers and the sea, had been from Donegal, not Abbotstown, even though Mrs D had continued to pretend she was here. Marie could hardly blame her.

'Oh, don't be silly Mar,' Grainne said quietly. 'We can't just avoid talking about everything, you know.'

'No,' Marie said. The silence that followed was deafening. Marie knew that, once upon a time, the two of them would just have burst into laughter, a sudden fit of the giggles, the way they used to do when they were sitting on the sofa in Granny's while she handed around a tray full of green-tinged hard-boiled eggs, each decorated with a sliver of hairy anchovy – Marie would only have to look at Grainne and the two of them would dissolve. She'd forgotten that, she thought, as she tucked into the puddle of yellow topped with the rich, herby sauce, how they used to be on each other's wavelength like that. She wondered if they could ever be like that again. She thought back to that last summer, when Grainne had come back from the beach and had danced around the bedroom, a towel on her head, hairbrush in hand, singing 'Total Eclipse of the Heart', doing the full, dramatic Bonnie Tyler gestures, while Marie lay on the bed reading *Women in Love*, because, of course, she was vastly more sophisticated than her sister. Now, Grainne looked the sophisticated grown-up, and Marie wondered if her days dancing around in a towel were over. Was that the cost of growing up, she wondered – that you forgot how to dance around in a towel to Bonnie Tyler or Duran Duran? But then, she supposed it was hardly the time to be dancing, was it?

'This looks delicious, Gra.' She tried to make her voice really light and cheerful, to make up for the way she was feeling inside, that mixture of love and anger that she felt when she looked at her sister. She was so pleased to see her and yet she was angry with her too, that she got to leave and come back, just like that, when Marie had had to stay. She got to send letters back from Soho coffee shops and postcards of the Changing of the Guard, messages from her new life, whilst all Marie could to was to try to make St John's hospital and her life back in Dublin look as if it were a tiny bit exciting. She knew that she wasn't being fair; Grainne was hardly on a holiday in London, was she? She'd been banished because of her sin, because she lived in a country that hated women. It wasn't her fault, and yet, she'd still got the blame, and when Marie thought about how much she resented Grainne, she felt herself grow hot with shame.

'I know. I used to cook it for the nuns in St Mary's. It's polenta,' she added, as Marie lifted a forkful into her mouth.

'God, it's fabulous,' Marie said, the taste of the buttery polenta mixed with the herby stew mingling in her mouth. She'd trained herself to eat Mrs O'Farrell's terrible food, so this was heaven. 'What's polenta?'

'You mean "what's polenta when it's at home?"' Grainne said, doing another of Mrs D's stock phrases.

Marie giggled.

'It's Italian,' Grainne said. 'It's a kind of grain and you can buy it in the Italian grocers. You just add water to it and lots of butter. It's brilliant with stews like this, because it soaks up the richness.'

'Mmm,' Marie agreed, taking another mouthful. 'How much wine is in this sauce?'

'A whole bottle,' Grainne said gleefully. 'I took one of the posh ones at the bottom of the wine rack,' and she covered her mouth as she tried not to smile.

'You devil!' Marie said approvingly. 'If Dada only knew you were emptying a whole bottle of his finest into the lunch,' she began, before remembering that Dada was upstairs in bed, looking out the window at the sea, all by himself. 'I'd forgotten what a good cook you are, Grainne.'

Grainne nodded distractedly, pausing for a moment to look out of the window, curling a lock of her newly sleek red hair around her finger. Then she said quietly, 'We changed the subject, Mar.'

That was the idea, Marie thought, fork half-way to her mouth. She didn't say anything, so her sister continued, 'Will we make a list of things that we have to not talk about?'

'What do you mean? What list? There is no list, Gra.'

'Not like that anyway,' Grainne said quietly. 'Not one that you pin on the wall, Marie, like a shopping list. I mean, a list of everything that's happened.'

Marie continued eating, the scraping of her knife and fork breaking the silence in the kitchen. A list, she thought.

Where would I even begin? She suddenly thought of Con O'Sullivan, and those nights in his flat with nothing in it, how unreal it had felt, how she'd been a different person with him, just a week ago now, even though it felt like so much longer. Then Dada, and David ... and now Grainne was back, so Marie would have to think about that too, about what had happened to her sister and be reminded how it was all her fault ... She'd have to think about St John's and how much she hated it. She'd have to think about everything she'd tried so hard to forget. And she'd have to talk to her sister about everything *she'd* tried to forget as well. It was all too much.

'You don't want to talk about it,' Grainne said blankly.

Marie was going to say something, but Grainne shot up from her seat and stomped over to the range, ladling a spoon of polenta and then stew onto a plate. 'I'm going to see if Dada wants this, even if he doesn't want me. What does it matter anyway,' she muttered. 'You don't want me either. Nobody wants me. And I didn't even want to come back!' she finished.

'Gra, come back,' Marie began. 'Please.' But the kitchen door was closed firmly behind Grainne, who proceeded to stamp up the stairs to Dada's room like an elephant. Marie put her head in her hands. She should go up there and stop her sister, she thought, but she didn't have the energy for it, for the inevitable fight. Grainne always did bluster her way into places – she had no clue how to read situations, she really didn't, Marie thought, as there was a thunderous knocking on Dada's bedroom and then a bellowed, 'Hello, Dada', followed by silence.

Marie strained to hear. There was Dada's thin wail again.

She sighed and got up from her seat. She'd better go up there, but then she heard Grainne's voice, loud and firm. 'Dada, that's enough. I know that we had a fight when you came to see me, but I've forgiven you.' Then there was another silence, followed by the heavy creak of Dada's bed – Grainne must have sat down on it, and then there was something Marie couldn't quite hear, even though she was holding her breath. There was a long silence, and then the deep rumble of Dada's voice, and then Grainne's reply. And then Marie could hear her footsteps crossing Dada's bedroom and his door squeaking open. 'Bye, Dada. I'll be back in a bit,' yelled Grainne.

Marie bit her lip. What fight? And when had Dada been to see Grainne? Then Marie remembered that 'trip down the country'; what Dada had tried to say to her that morning in the kitchen. Did he know? She waited for Grainne's steady thunk-thunk back down the stairs, but Marie heard the solid thud of her sister's bedroom door instead. She waited for a few moments, then let out the breath she'd been holding in. She sat back down at the kitchen table and eyed the plate of stew. It was still pretty warm, so she picked up her fork and ate it, every single last, delicious mouthful. And when she was finished, she took her sister's plate and ate all of her dinner, too, enjoying the creamy stodge of the polenta, the richness of the winy sauce. She felt famished, as if she was making up for not eating properly for months, and she supposed she hadn't. She'd just eaten horrible dinners at St John's or beans on toast at home, and now, she felt that she could literally eat up the whole pot of stew.

When Grainne came back into the room a quarter of an

hour later, Marie was wiping the plate with a bit of bread she'd dug out of the breadbin, before leaning back on her seat, hands on her tummy. Grainne went over to the pot and looked in, then looked at the two empty plates in front of Marie. 'Have you eaten all of it?'

Marie gave a small burp. 'Yes. I was really hungry.'

'Jesus, have you not eaten in the last year?'

Marie shook her head sadly. And then she burst into tears, big, hot salty tears that ran down her face, and which she couldn't stem, as she flapped around looking for a tissue.

Grainne's hug was brief and fierce, a tight squeeze that nearly took Marie's breath away. 'I'm sorry, I—' Marie began, but Grainne shook her head. 'No sorrys, Mar. Let's not get into sorry, OK?'

Marie leaned into her sister's warm softness. 'OK,' she said quietly.

'Good, now, up you get.' Grainne pulled Marie off the chair, and led her out of the kitchen.

'Where are we going?'

'We are going to walk the pier,' Grainne said grandly, pulling a very nice red coat off the coat stand in the hall and pulling on a pair of red leather pirate boots to match. With her red hair, she should have looked awful, but instead she looked like a blaze of fire, alive and vivid. Marie felt dowdy as she eyed her old blue anorak and the ancient black pixie boots with the silver studs she'd bought two years before with her pocket money.

'Ah, God, not the pier, Gra, it's freezing.'

'You'll need to walk off that polenta,' her sister said smartly, 'or else it'll stick in your stomach.'

'I like it sticking in my stomach,' Marie mumbled. 'That's what it's there for.'

She mumbled and groaned, but somehow her sister managed to persuade her into her outdoor clothes, wrapping a scarf tightly around her, as if she was a little child, then nodding. 'That's better.'

'If you insist,' Marie grumbled, following her sister out the door into the bitter winter wind and onto Seaview Road. The waves were an angry grey, topped with white, slapping against the walkway at Seaview, and the smell of salt and seaweed filled Marie's nostrils, even while her teeth chattered with the cold. God, it was grim, she thought, eyeing her sister in her red coat, wondering how she was feeling when she looked at the grey sea, the leaden sky, about being home. Marie watched Grainne's strong back as she marched ahead, leading the way in her red coat, ignoring the glances of the little old ladies and mums with prams as she strode briskly along, Marie trotting to keep up. She's making an announcement, Marie thought, as her sister marched on. She's telling them that she's back. She's so much braver than me.

'Wait for me,' she said plaintively as Grainne walked ahead. 'You're going too fast and I'm weighed down by polenta.' Her sister stopped and she ran to catch up with her, and she found herself tucking her arm into Grainne's and letting herself be gently pulled along, past the yacht clubs and down the slipway to the pier. It was deserted because of the weather, the gale a near-roar as they struggled down to the bandstand, the waves crashing against the stonework sending gusts of spray over the walkway.

'I was thinking about Christmas,' were Grainne's first words, the wind whipping them from her mouth as she spoke.

'What?' Marie half-yelled.

'I said, Christmas. It's only ten days away.'

The thought of Christmas had never once entered Marie's head. What on earth was Grainne going on about? 'Gra, I couldn't care less about Christmas,' she began.

'Well, maybe you should,' Grainne said sharply.

Marie had to stop, even though there was a force-ten gale blowing in her face. 'What do you mean, "Maybe you should"? I hardly think I've had time to think about Christmas, with everything else that's been going on.'

Grainne folded her arms, that cross look on her face that she'd always worn when she was a child, her mouth turned down at the corners, a vertical line breaking her forehead just above her nose. 'Oh, "everything else that's been going on". You're trying to make me feel bad.'

'I'm not, Gra,' Marie yelled above the din. 'I know what you've been through—'

'No, you don't!'

'No, I don't,' Marie agreed sheepishly, 'but … you still left.' She didn't add the words, 'You left me all alone,' because she figured that would make her sound like a complete baby, but even as she thought it, she realised that she felt it – she felt the hurt and the pain of having been abandoned in some way, even though she'd never admitted it to herself. She'd been too busy feeling sorry for Grainne, feeling guilty that she'd left her sister when she'd most needed her, never realising that she resented her too.

'I was hardly gone on a little holiday,' Grainne said.

'I know.' Marie gave her sister's arm a little squeeze, but Grainne shook her off. 'Anyway, now I'm back,' Grainne muttered. As if that was enough. As if it were enough to have just appeared in Dada's room, like an angel come down from heaven.

'A lot changed while you were away, Gra.'

Grainne gave a toss of her red hair, but it flipped back in her face, covering her mouth and nose, and she pulled it angrily out of the way. 'It doesn't look like it to me. Dada's sick, I know, but he's still in his room, hiding, and you're still moping around the place.'

'I am not moping!'

'You are. And I have a feeling I know why. But I won't ask you right now. Instead, we will plan our Christmas holiday, like normal people, with a tree and presents and tinsel.'

'Tinsel.'

'Yes.' Grainne's mouth twitched. 'What's wrong with tinsel?'

'I'm allergic to it. It brings me out in a rash.'

'Well, then we'll have holly or paper chains or something, but we *will* have Christmas. And we'll invite Granny over here, so we don't have to get food poisoning again. Who knows, maybe we'll invite David-bloody-interfering-Crowley, as you call him, in for a little drink.'

'I can't imagine anything worse,' Marie said, but she was smiling, just a little bit. She couldn't help it. Even when Grainne was being ridiculous, she was funny.

'He really likes you, you know. He told me.'

Marie shrugged. 'Gra?'

'Yes?'

'Will you be staying long?'

Her sister dug her hands into the pockets of her lovely red coat and looked out over the sea, towards Howth. Marie wondered if she was imagining making her way back to Wales on the ferry and then onto London, and whether London was home now, not here.

'Are you thinking about your friend?'

Grainne turned to her, a sad smile on her face. 'I'm thinking about lots of things, Mar.'

'You don't have to stay, you know. I can manage just fine.'

Grainne gave that little smile again. 'You don't mean that.'

Marie thought about that, about whether she should just lie and insist that she did, but instead, she shook her head. 'No, I don't.'

'Good, well, that's settled then,' Grainne said, pulling the hood of her coat up and walking away from Marie down the pier, towards the lighthouse.

Marie called after her, 'Gra – can we go home? I'm soaking wet and freezing and I'm afraid I'll be washed away.' Her stomach felt queasy as she watched the waves breaking over the pier. She imagined what it would be like to swim in those huge, nasty-looking waves and she gave a shiver, pulling her scarf more tightly around her. Ugh. And she had a swimming lesson on Tuesday, she thought miserably – she'd missed the previous one because of Dada, and she knew that she could just not go back, but there was something about it that made her want to stick it out.

Her sister turned her head and shouted, 'No. We are walking all the way to the lighthouse and back,' marching off towards the lighthouse right at the end of the pier.

Since when did you get so bossy? Marie thought grumpily, as she hesitated for a second then jogged after Grainne.

Chapter 14

Marie decided that she didn't want to tell Grainne about Con – not yet, anyway. She wanted to hug it to herself for a bit longer, even if his phone call that afternoon had been his first since Dada's accident. 'I'm really sorry,' he said. 'That case just ran on and on and—'

'That's OK!' Marie found herself interrupting, not wanting to hear his excuse, because if she did, she might need to decide whether she believed it or not. Better to just be pleased that he was back, even if saying yes made her feel a bit like a used hankie, to be balled up and thrown into the bin when it wasn't needed any more. Don't be silly, she chided herself as she went upstairs to see if she could find something acceptable to wear – he's just been too busy to call, that's all.

David-bloody-interfering-Crowley appeared later that afternoon, of course, and when Marie went to look out of her bedroom window, there he was, tidying the garden, which had got completely out of hand since Creggs left. Marie watched him through the window as he pruned the overgrown shrubs and tethered the rambling rose to its arch, even though the rain had hardly let up all afternoon, gritting his teeth as he tried to uproot some of the bamboo that was threatening to take over the garden. She watched him closely, the way his shoulders moved as he pushed the spade into the earth, the look of concentration on his face as he snipped away at the clematis outside the kitchen window, Lucy-lou wrapping herself around his legs as he worked. She'd taken a shine to him, had Lucy. She would, wouldn't she, Marie thought. Even the cat loved David.

Marie watched him and then she waited for the feeling that she'd had in the bathroom. She looked at her hands, to see if they were shaking, then she put them to her cheeks to feel if they were hot, but they weren't. Instead, she just felt a bit irritated, a bit annoyed with his goodness, with his Christopher-Reeve-as-Superman tendencies. Why could he not just go and save the world, she thought … didn't he have anything better to do? Why was he so nice to her when she clearly didn't deserve it? And why had he had the bright idea to bring her sister home? Maybe he thought it would help Marie, but it wouldn't, she thought – instead, it would make her worry about a whole new set of things, on top of all the things she already worried about.

Still, she thought she'd better make him a cup of coffee, seeing as he was killing himself on a freezing December afternoon, and she'd bring him out one or two of her fig roll stash while she was at it.

He was leaning on the spade when she came out, like an old farmer. 'Breastfeeding the shovel,' Mrs D had used to call it. Marie tried not to laugh as she handed him the mug.

'What's so funny?' he asked, accepting it from her and putting the shovel against the wall.

'Nothing,' she said, pulling the two fig rolls out of her pocket and handing them to him. 'Sorry, they're a bit battered.'

'That's OK,' he said, taking them from her and putting one into his mouth. She felt it again then, as she watched him eat, that sense, that 'oh' feeling. She couldn't put her finger on it, because she hadn't felt it before – she didn't get any 'oh' feelings with Con, but then, she supposed, their relationship was on another level.

'You've done a great job with the garden,' she said, trying to be nice.

He shrugged. 'The Old Dear's always getting me to tidy ours. I have a degree in rose pruning at this stage,' and he gave a brief smile.

'How is your mum?' Marie asked, conscious that she sounded as if she were about eighty, but hoping that she also sounded at least a bit civil.

'She's fine. She keeps saying she'll drop up and see your dad.'

'He'd like that,' Marie said. Dada had always liked Patricia, David's mum, because she was a 'bloody good laugh', and because she'd been the only one to ask him how he was after Mum had died. Not that that had made Dada any more gracious about accepting her offers of help, keeping her firmly at arm's length. He probably wouldn't like a visit at all, Marie thought, but the lie was more polite.

'I hope you're not really pissed off with me,' David said suddenly, not looking at her, but instead jabbing at the soil with the tip of his spade.

'Pissed off about what?' Marie said, knowing exactly what he was talking about.

'About going to London, you know, to get Grainne. I thought it would help. You're all by yourself here and ... at least, you *were* by yourself,' he mumbled.

'How could I be pissed off?' Marie said, picking Lucy-lou up and hugging the cat to her, because she needed something to hide behind. Lucy had never once been picked up and she didn't like it, clawing at Marie and giving an outraged miaow, so that Marie had to put her back down on the ground again.

'The way you usually are pissed off,' David said dryly, taking a sip of the coffee and then a chunk off the other fig roll, nodding appreciatively. 'Hmm, fig rolls are kinda nice. I thought they were only for grannies.'

'I like fig rolls,' Marie said defensively. 'And what do you mean, I'm usually pissed off?'

'I mean, you're usually pissed off. With me.'

'That's not true,' Marie said, absent-mindedly picking the cat up again, then putting her down. 'I'm really grateful that you did that for me – I mean, going to get Grainne. I know it was expensive and I'll pay you back ...' she began.

'I don't think you're grateful, Marie. I think you're really annoyed,' David said quietly.

'Oh, for God's sake, I'm not,' Marie said. 'How could I be annoyed after everything you've done for me? How?'

The answer was in her question, so he said nothing, just picked up the spade and began to dig. 'How's Grainne?'

'What? She's fine. Why?'

'She seems a bit ... over-excited,' he said.

'Oh, she's got this bee in her bonnet about Christmas. She dragged me into Hector Grey the other day to buy industrial quantities of tinsel and that awful spray snow.' Marie wrinkled her nose. 'Not to mention the two plastic robins and the reindeer.'

'I've seen the reindeer.' David smiled, and Marie giggled. The reindeer was the size of a Shetland pony and had had to be carted home on the bus. Marie wondered who exactly her preparations were for – hardly for herself and Dada. Grainne had always loved Christmas, but not *this* much. This had the air of stockpiling for some unexpected natural disaster. Two huge hams in the larder, a turkey the size of an ostrich ordered from Mahon's, a Christmas pudding that she'd spent the whole afternoon making, giving out to Marie because she should have made it over the summer to give it time to mature. There was something frenzied about it, Grainne's cheeks bright red, her eyes ablaze with an expression that Marie didn't recognise. She knew that Christmas was only a week away, but she was trying far too hard, she thought, to get it all right. Marie wondered when it would all come crashing down around them, and what she'd do then.

'Maybe she just wants it to be a nice Christmas for everyone, after everything that's happened,' David offered helpfully.

'Yeah, maybe,' Marie said, taking the cup and turning to bring it back into the kitchen. 'I'd better see if Dada needs lunch.'

'Marie?'

'Yeah?'

He looked as if he was going to ask her something, but instead he just said, 'Oh, nothing. See you around.'

'Yeah. See you around,' Marie said, going back inside. She turned at the door and said, 'Thanks.'

David looked alarmed for a second, then smiled briefly and continued digging. 'You're welcome.'

She boiled an egg for Dada's lunch and put some toast on, cutting it up into postage-stamp-sized bits, then going upstairs with the tray. He'd be hungry by now, she supposed, because Mrs O'Farrell had brought him breakfast at seven o'clock that morning so that she could go to her granddaughter's christening – at least, that was her latest excuse. She really was useless, Marie thought, but then she needed her for when she was out at work, and even Mrs O'Farrell was better than no one.

She was on the landing outside Dada's bedroom door, tray in one hand, about to shove the door open with her hip, when she noticed that it was already half-open. She could hear Grainne's voice drifting out, and she held her breath, listening, waiting for the right time to break it up.

'I'm just going to sit down on the edge of the bed, Dada, if that's OK,' her sister said, and there was a heavy creak, followed by a silence, then, 'Oh, the mattress is really soft. How do you not sink down into the middle? Mum used to like a good, firm mattress, do you not remember?'

Uh-oh. Marie waited for the wail that would surely follow, but instead there was another silence.

'Dada, I've come home to help Marie out for a bit,' she could hear her sister say. 'I can see that she needs it, because she's really worn out, and it must be hard looking after you and doing her job as well.' Grainne paused then, and Marie could hear the clink of teaspoon against cup as she stirred. 'And so I'm going to look after you, too, Dada.'

There was a mumbling and muttering then, and the beginning of a Hail Mary, and then Grainne's interruption. 'Dada, I don't care what you think about me, or about what you think I've done. You can be very quick to judge, you know, but I want you to stop all this giving out to me and praying and just let me help you. You can tell yourself it's for Marie's sake, if you like, but you'll just have to put up with me. OK?'

Marie strained to hear if there was any response from Dada. He must have nodded or something, because Grainne said, 'Lovely. Now, what'll we do. Will we read some poetry?'

What on earth was she doing with poetry? Marie wondered. There was a long silence, and Grainne continued. 'Mum used to love Yeats, didn't she, so will I see if I can find any?' There was a rustling and a shuffling – Grainne must be looking on the bookshelf under the window, Marie thought. 'Now, how about Blake – oh, I don't think I like him. I did him in school and he kept going on and on. Seamus Heaney, no, I can't understand his stuff,' and then there was another pause. 'Oh, I've got it, Yeats. Look, Dada, here's Mum's old copy, do you remember? It's got her name on it. Máire Ní Chiosáin. Imagine that.'

Marie couldn't see Dada's reaction, but as she stood there, rooted to the spot, she could still see Mum reading it, leaning back on her deckchair, which she used to park in the back garden all summer, while Grainne and Marie fought and played around her. Occasionally, she'd break into a verse of the 'Lake Isle of Innisfree' or 'September 1913', and when the girls would moan, 'Aw, Mum, stop!' she'd smile and say that she was just giving them an education.

'Oh, look, "Sailing to Byzantium", I remember this,' Grainne was saying, her voice getting further away, then coming closer again. Marie shrank back, in case her sister saw her, putting the tray gently down on the chest of drawers. '"That is no country for old men,"' she began. '"… An aged man is but a paltry thing, a tattered coat upon a stick". Oh, that's good,' she said, and Marie smiled and listened as Grainne read the poem, the lovely words rising up in the air and wafting out through the door. '"Unless soul clap its hands and sing, and louder sing, for every tatter in its mortal dress … of what is past, or passing, or to come" …' And then there was a long silence, followed quietly by 'We'll have another one tomorrow. What do you think, Dada?'

Marie peered in through the open door then to see Dada lying in bed, his hands on the bedspread, a peaceful look on his face, and Grainne sitting beside him on the bed, the book clasped on her lap. As she stuck her head around the door, Dada's eyes caught hers, but he didn't look away, and in that look she could see everything about his life now, the fear and the pain of it, and yet, the expression seemed to say something else, that he'd heard something he liked and that he might like to hear more. It was a kind of miracle, Marie thought now. And the person who had done all that was Grainne.

*

Marie didn't let on that she'd heard them when Grainne came downstairs after lunch, busying herself with a batch of mince pies that she'd left in a tray beside the range. She let the silence fill the space, and it felt good to have her sister working beside her in the kitchen, the way they'd done when they were children, Marie with her homework on the table in front of her, chewing on her pencil, Grainne making fairy cakes or an apple tart. As soon as Grainne was able to, she'd learned to stand on a little stool, chopping board or baking bowl in front of her, and Marie had used to like Grainne's steady beating and stirring and the clatter of pots and pans as she did algebra or learned about the Civil War. All that was missing now was Mrs D, bustling into the room to tell Grainne that she was making an awful mess and how did she expect her to get a dinner on the table, and to tell Marie that she wouldn't pass a single exam if she didn't know her multiplication tables.

Marie looked at Grainne's back now, at the steady movement of her arms as she stirred, and she wondered if Grainne was thinking the same thing. She opened her mouth to say something to her sister, but decided to let the silence rest.

'Mar?'

'Yeah?'

'Do you think Dada will get better?' Grainne didn't turn around, so Marie found herself addressing her sister's back.

'I don't know, really,' Marie said. 'I think it depends on whether he wants to.'

'Hmm. I don't think he really does, Mar. I think he wants to die, to be with Mum.'

'I think you're right,' Marie replied.

They let the bleakness of this thought settle in on them

both, then Grainne turned, mixing bowl in hand. 'Mar, will you come to Midnight Mass with me?'

Marie tried not to make a face. Midnight Mass? Frankly, she'd rather die. 'I thought that you didn't believe in God any more.' The minute she said the words, she regretted them, because Grainne looked so downcast. Her lip trembled and the mixing bowl shook slightly in her hand. 'I mean, you said you didn't say your prayers much in London …' Her voice trailed away.

'I don't, but, look, it's complicated,' Grainne said. 'Would you come? Please?'

'Well, OK then,' Marie said.

Her sister came over and gave her a floury hug. 'Thanks.'

'Sure,' Marie said doubtfully, thinking that Grainne would probably forget about it anyway.

The rest of the day passed in a blur. Half of St Anthony's had the flu and poor Mrs O'Brien looked as if she wouldn't last the week. Her daughter had even been to see her, a large lady in a too-small anorak, who'd sat beside the bed, looking as if she couldn't wait to leave, while her mother lay there, chest heaving, a film of sweat on her forehead. Poor Mrs O'Brien – she didn't even have the energy to go on about greyhounds any more. Only Mrs Spence was her usual self these days, insisting on her daily dose of romance.

Marie had just changed a dressing on Mrs Spence's leg and was in the kitchen making Mrs O'Brien's 3.30 tea, when Sister Dolores bustled in. 'Nurse Stephenson!' she barked.

Marie jumped, so that the kettle splashed hot water on the counter. 'Yes, Sister?'

Sister Dolores sighed. 'For the love of God, will you just

relax!' She opened the bread bin and took out two slices of brown bread, proceeding to butter them with the butter that she always insisted be left on the counter. She hated butter from the fridge.

'Sorry, Sister.'

'Yes, well,' Sister muttered. 'I wondered how your father was,' she said after a while.

'Oh, he's fine, Sister,' Marie said. 'Improving.' He was improving a bit – Grainne's good food and a daily diet of Yeats seemed to make him feel a bit better.

'Well, that's good,' Sister said, looking up and eyeing Marie sharply. What was it about her, Marie wondered, that she always knew when Marie wasn't telling her everything? Maybe it was a special skill that all nuns had. A kind of radar.

'I'll ask the Archangel Raphael to intervene,' she said, taking a pot of jam out of the fridge and spreading it onto the two slices of buttered bread.

'Thanks, Sister, that would be … helpful,' Marie decided. 'Ehm, I've got to change the sheets on Mrs Derby's bed, so I'll go and do that … ' She pointed to the door, to show that she was just leaving, and made to bolt out of the kitchen, before Sister could ask her anything else, but Sister Dolores's voice called her back. 'Nurse Stephenson?'

Uh-oh. 'Yes, Sister?'

'Tell me something. Are you planning to make nursing your vocation?'

Marie didn't know what to say for a moment, so she just hopped nervously from foot to foot while she tried to think of a suitable answer, but then Sister Dolores glared at her. 'Do you need the bathroom?'

'No, Sister.'

'Well, stop that hopping then. I asked you a question.'

'I don't know, Sister.'

'Well, do you like nursing or don't you?' Sister said, picking up one of the slices of bread and biting into it. Marie had never seen a nun eat before, and she wasn't sure where to look.

She shook her head.

'I'll take that as a no, then,' Sister Dolores said through a mouthful of bread and jam.

Marie nodded.

'Or is that a yes? Will you speak up, please, Nurse Stephenson, and put me out of my misery.'

'No, Sister. I hate it.' That's torn it, Marie thought, as the words left her mouth and she waited to see what Sister would do to her.

Sister Dolores rolled her eyes to heaven. '"Hate", is it?'

Marie looked down at the ground. 'Yes, Sister.'

Sister Dolores took another bite out of the bread and jam. 'Holy Mother of God.' She sighed then, as if Marie were possibly the most stupid person she'd ever met. 'Let me tell you something, Miss Stephenson, or Mizz or whatever it is you young women call yourselves nowadays. I hate it too, did you know that?'

Marie shook her head. 'Well, I do,' Sister Dolores continued, a small smile on her face. 'I do it because it's God's will.'

Oh, that old chestnut, Marie thought, trying to look interested, but Sister Dolores wasn't fooled. 'I know what you're thinking, young lady, but I went into the convent and the Mother Superior asked me if I wanted nursing or teaching, and I said nursing, because I thought I might get to see more of my sister in St Vincent's if I did. That was all the choice I had – to serve others and to serve God.'

'Yes, Sister.' She didn't need the lecture on God's will – God's will had never been any use to her or her sister.

'But you young women have choices these days. It isn't the Dark Ages, is it?'

'No, Sister.'

'So, what are you doing in St John's, if you have a choice in the matter? Reading romantic novels?' The nun wrinkled her nose. 'That's not nursing, I can tell you.'

'No, Sister,' Marie thought, her lip trembling. She felt that she wanted to confide in Sister Dolores, to tell her everything, but she knew that that would be a huge mistake. Best to just stay quiet.

Sister Dolores sighed. 'Go back and empty Mrs O'Brien's bedpan and give her that cup of tea, and do your best.'

'Yes, Sister.' Marie scuttled out of the kitchen as quickly as she could, but Sister Dolores's voice called her back. 'Nurse Stephenson?'

'Yes, Sister?'

'Don't let me see you back here after Christmas. There must surely be other things in life for you to do.'

Marie didn't answer, just blinked and trotted back to the ward, teacup rattling, to change Mrs O'Brien's bedpan.

Chapter 15

Marie's head was spinning when she got home, and the last place on earth she wanted to be was in St Malachy's at twelve o'clock at night. Claire had asked her if she wanted to go to a Christmas Eve party in Trinity, and that sounded infinitely more appealing. After Sister's lecture, Marie needed to get drunk and then sneak around to Con's for the 'late supper' he'd proposed, but she supposed she'd promised Grainne. She'd go and then she'd see if she could cycle to Con's on the old black bike that Mrs D had left behind, even though it would take her a good three-quarters of an hour to get there. The bike hadn't been used since Mrs D's departure, but Marie knew there was a bicycle pump in the pantry, so she could pump up the tyres if they were flat, she supposed. It'd give her something to do, to stop her thinking further about what Sister Dolores had actually said and what that might mean for her. She'd been hanging onto the idea of nursing for so long now, even though she knew she was rubbish at it, that she couldn't see what might lie beyond it, and the future seemed a vast abyss into which she might fall, never to be seen again. She knew this seemed melodramatic, but she also knew that with everything that had happened, she'd kind of forgotten who she was and what her dreams used to be. And, she supposed, she didn't have the courage to follow them any more. Besides, she thought, as she opened the hall door and waited for her sister to follow her into the dark and down the coast road to St Malachy's, it was Grainne who'd be really good at nursing. She had the spirit for it ... or she would have done, once upon a time, she thought. She could imagine her, chatting away to everyone, but also being really good at the practical stuff that Marie was useless at. She'd always been good like that, Grainne.

'All set?' she said, as her sister appeared behind her on the porch, in that vivid red coat and boots, now with the addition of a red beret pulled onto her hair. She'd certainly cut a dash in St Malachy's, Marie thought, wondering if that was the point of the whole thing. The idea made her feel uneasy, thoughts buzzing around in her head, Sister Dolores with the bread and jam, Con, Dada, Grainne ... everything seemed to push and shove inside of her brain until she wanted to yell, 'Stop!'

She was so preoccupied that she didn't really notice that Grainne had been silent all the way to St Malachy's, but as they approached the wrought-iron gates in front of the church, she stopped, then took in a deep breath, letting it out again with a gush.

'Are you OK?'

'I'm fine,' Grainne replied, squaring her shoulders as if she was going into battle, leading them in through the gates, past the large, white-painted statue of Jesus with the heavy cross on his shoulder with Mary looking on anxiously, and in through the front porch. Marie hesitated, hovering in the porch over the Mass leaflets and the brochure for the parochial trip to Lourdes. She wasn't sure about going in by the front porch – they'd always used the side entrance, because they were always late, and Father Griffith would make a point of calling out latecomer's names, so Mrs D would pull them into the side aisles where he couldn't see them.

But Marie had to follow Grainne, who was marching right up the middle of the church, which was now packed, scanning the pews for any sign of an empty space. Heads turned and watched her progress, the heels of her red boots tap-tapping on the tiles, as she looked left and right. When she'd see someone she knew, Grainne would lift a hand in a wave and mouth 'hello'. Marie walked behind her, wondering how quickly she could find somewhere to sit down and disappear. Eventually, two rows from the top, Grainne found a space at the far end of the pew, so that everyone sitting there had to get up to let her in. 'Excuse me,' she said loudly, and then, 'Thank you,' as she passed each person. Marie hesitated at the end of the pew, wondering if she could just sit somewhere else, but the full row was still standing, so she followed her sister, tripping over scarves and handbags, apologising all the way along the pew until she squeezed in beside Grainne, uncomfortably close to an elderly man in a Crombie coat that smelled of mothballs. He smiled at her, two rows of shiny false teeth.

Marie sat back and tried to take in her surroundings without alerting Mr False Teeth, whose head was about four inches from hers. The smell of St Malachy's was still the same – incense mixed with damp coats and candlewax, now with an added top note of Guinness, it being midnight on Christmas Eve. Even though she hadn't dared to look around her on the way to her seat, she was sure she'd seen Mr Devlin, her old geography teacher, and David's parents, Patricia and John; her face grew hot as she wondered if David was there too. She hadn't seen him. He might be on duty, she thought, at the new Casualty department at St Benildus's. Casualty was really busy in the city-centre hospitals, but Marie could imagine him liking it there – it would suit his Superman tendencies, she thought meanly. He'd be able to save the world there and not waste his time on her.

The organ started then, a faint wobble followed by a crescendo of out-of-tune notes, then a thin, wispy voice began to sing 'Away in a Manger' and a few joined in. Marie turned to catch Grainne's eye – they'd always found the wobbly lady singers highly entertaining – but she was looking straight ahead, an expression that Marie couldn't read on her face. She felt her stomach tighten, and she looked to the end of the row to see if there was any easy escape route, but her way was blocked by a row of handbags and by a large golf umbrella. She stole a look at her sister, whose gaze was fixed on her Mass leaflet, and she wondered if Grainne thought about her baby and whether it would be in Limbo now. She slid her arm into her sister's and gave it a little squeeze. Grainne's smile was brief and didn't meet her eyes.

There was a cacophony of coughs and mumbling as Father Griffith appeared on the altar, and the congregation got to its feet. He was flanked by two altar boys in their cassocks, each wearing a pair of bright white trainers on his feet, the same solemn expression on each face, as if doing God's work was the most important thing on their minds. Marie thought of Sister Dolores and she wondered how many people in this congregation actually thought about doing God's work, or even thought about God at all, or whether this was just a ritual for them, like it had been for Mrs D, who just loved having a place to go to – to belong, to feel that she was part of a group of enthusiastic ladies, all moving flowers around the place and arguing pleasantly about ironing altar cloths. Marie had never bothered about belonging; it had never interested her. Instead, she wanted to stick out, to blaze a trail – or, at least, she had done. Now, as the organ wobbled into life and the hymn began, she stood with everyone else and wondered if, instead, this was where she belonged. Maybe it wasn't so bad, she thought, to be jammed in amongst this familiar group of people.

Marie tuned out while Father Griffith went on about the specialness of the whole occasion and the power of the Lord to make everything basically perfect. Her sister moved on the seat beside her, but when Marie stole a glance to see what she was doing, she was still looking straight ahead, as if she was giving the priest her whole attention. Marie stood up and sat down at the appropriate moments, mumbling the responses to the prayers and half-listening to the readings, and then, as the priest took to the lectern to deliver his sermon, there was a repeat of the cacophony of coughs and splutters and then silence.

Father Griffith had always liked being in charge, and he gripped the lectern now, ready for action. 'The Lord has seen fit to return some of his flock to the fold this Christmas Eve, and I'm sure we'll all thank him for that.' He smiled, as many people nodded. 'It is one of the scourges of this time in our country that so many of our young people must leave to seek employment, banished from these green fields to an alien land, far from our own people.'

Then, he took a deep breath and said, 'But what of those among us who are banished from home for their sins? Be it gambling or alcohol or fornication – the Lord does not distinguish between evils, he merely understands them all as the work of the Devil incarnate,' and here, he scanned the congregation, his beady eye alighting on various poor souls. Honestly, they'd probably told him stuff in confession and now he was using it to humiliate them – even though he'd been seen coming out of Sheridan's Bookmakers on more than one occasion. The man was such a hypocrite, Marie thought.

And then he continued, 'What are we to say about those women whom our community casts out because of their sin? "And near that place … sat women … and over against them many children who were born to them out of due time sat crying. And there came forth from them, rays of fire and smote the women in the eyes. And these were the accursed who conceived and caused abortion."' He paused to let the words sink in, then said quietly, '"The Apocalypse of Peter", written in 25AD, and these words are as true today as they were then. A battle has taken place in our country this year, and at the centre of that battle has been the very origins of life itself. The battle has been won by the forces of good in our country, by those who understand the sacredness of human life, but as our Holy Father said, we must not "weaken our witness". We must remain a shining light and an example for other countries.' He paused for another few moments to let his words sink in, a satisfied look on his face. He'd covered all the bases and was clearly feeling mighty pleased with himself.

Marie felt her cheeks grow hot, and it took every ounce of self control for her not to jump up in the pew and yell, 'What about you, Father? Are you without sin?' She made a small movement, but felt the insistent pressure of Grainne's hand on her arm. Her face was chalk white.

Marie was still fuming when the bell rang for Communion, sitting rigidly in her seat while the wobbly singing began again, 'Oh, Holy Night,' filling the church as people got up and walked along the pews to the centre aisle for Communion, like sheep. She turned to her sister. 'I'm going,' she hissed.

'Wait,' Grainne replied. 'I have to get Communion.'

'Are you serious?'

'Of course I am, Marie,' Grainne said, getting up. 'Excuse me,' she said and walked along the pew and out onto the aisle, taking her place in the queue now shuffling to the altar. Marie watched her, in her lovely coat and hat, head bowed, hands crossed, and she prayed that her sister would get Communion from one of the ministers of the Eucharist, not from Father

Griffith, watching the queue move slowly forward, heart in her mouth. But no, Mr Daly moved to the right and there Grainne was, face to face with Father Griffith. She lifted her head and looked him right in the eye, holding her hands out expectantly. Father Griffith seemed to shrink back for a moment, before recovering and putting the host into her hand. 'Body of Christ.'

'Amen!' Grainne said loudly, turning to the left and walking back to her seat, head bowed, kneeling then to pray. Marie realised then that Grainne was the real hero, not her, who just ranted on to herself about the injustice of it all but did nothing. Grainne had the courage to face Father Griffith down, and to stand and take her place in the congregation, while she just sat around and complained that life wasn't quite the way she wanted it to be. She was just making excuses for herself, that was all, while Grainne and Claire and David and everyone else got on with the business of living. Well, enough, she thought as she sat on the hard wooden bench and inhaled the rich smell of incense. That was it; she'd had enough.

She made sure that she took Grainne's arm on the way out, waiting until her sister had finished the sign of the cross, holding her tightly against her as the two of them walked back down the aisle – the middle one: they weren't going to slink out – Grainne smiling and waving to familiar faces, as if she were Princess Diana at St Paul's Cathedral.

Two pews from the end, Grainne stopped dead. Marie looked around her sister's shoulder and saw an older woman in a black lace mantilla, head bent, a set of mother-of-pearl rosary beads in her hands. She must have been saying a decade of the rosary, because she was moving the beads through her fingers, her lips moving as she said each prayer. Marie could see Grainne's eyes boring into the woman, and as if she sensed it, the woman looked up and when she saw Grainne she gave a small, doubtful smile, as if asking herself if she knew this girl.

'Gra?' Marie said, giving Grainne's arm a small tug.

'Hang on, Marie,' Grainne said. She let go of Marie's arm and went towards the pew in which the woman was kneeling, clambering over a walking stick which had been jammed upright into the kneeler and she sat down beside the woman, extending a hand. 'I'm Grainne Stephenson,' she said.

The woman took her hand and shook it reluctantly, her grey eyes full of fear.

'You don't know me, Mrs Daly,' Grainne continued. 'I'm a friend of Anthony's. He's told me all about you.'

'Oh, yes,' the woman said quietly. 'What did you say your name was?'

'I said it was Grainne Stephenson. Please tell him that I was thinking about him. Oh, and that I'm back,' Grainne said, loudly enough for those in the general vicinity to hear. 'Perhaps I'll call in to see him in Mahon's some day. I believe their lamb chops are lovely.'

The woman seemed to shrink back on the pew, her mantilla slipping off her shampoo and set.

'Bye now,' Grainne said, pumping the woman's hand again, before turning back and clambering out of the pew to the aisle.

'Let's get out of here,' she mumbled and strode out of the front door of the church. Marie followed meekly behind.

★

They waited until they were almost home before they screamed out loud, a mixture of hysteria and relief as they yelled into the bitter winter air. 'Grainne, you were just amazing,' Marie shouted. 'The look on Father Griffith's face!'

'Yes, well.' Grainne smiled. 'I didn't do it to show him up, you know. I don't hate God or Holy Mary or anything. I just hate people like Father Griffith. I don't like hypocrites.'

Marie took a deep breath. 'Did you know Mrs Daly was going to be there?'

Grainne's shoulders tensed and she shook her head. 'No,' she whispered. 'I got an awful fright, Mar, but then I thought I'd been able to manage Father Griffith, so I'd manage Mrs Daly. And I did.'

'You did, and you were amazing. I couldn't have done what you did. It's incredibly brave, Gra.'

Grainne looked thoughtful for a few moments, but she didn't say anything and the two of them walked the rest of the way home in silence, Marie wondering if she'd said or done the wrong thing. If she should have stood up in church and yelled at Father Griffith, or walked out, or given Mrs Daly a piece of her mind. Instead, she'd done nothing.

They'd reached the house now, and Marie quietly pulled the key out from her pocket, remembering that time, a little more than a year before, when they'd both sneaked in after the party up the mountains. It seemed like a million years ago and the girl she'd been then seemed like another person. She'd been so excited, she remembered, so alive.

As if reading her mind, Grainne said, 'Do you remember that time we sneaked in and Dada caught us?'

'I do,' Marie said, opening the door and letting the silence settle around her as they both understood that Dada wouldn't be surprising them tonight. 'It seems like a long time ago now.'

'It does, even though it's only a year and a bit. Time's funny like that.' Grainne shrugged. 'Anyway, I'll go and check on him,' Grainne said, walking quietly up the stairs while Marie went into the kitchen and put the kettle onto the range, picking her cigarettes out of her coat pocket. They were both grown-ups now, she thought, as she heard her sister's footsteps on the stairs, with no one to tell them what to do, what to wear or how to behave. No Dada, with his funny ideas, no Mrs D, telling Grainne that she wasn't to be making a holy show of herself. It was strange to be a grown-up when you were only seventeen or eighteen, Marie thought, as she pulled a cigarette out of the packet, to know that other people relied on you and that you couldn't just do whatever you wanted. Maybe that was why she'd agreed to Dada's plan that she study nursing, because that responsibility just came naturally to her. She could have fought harder, she supposed, but maybe she felt that she just didn't have the right to be young and to do silly things, like Claire did, to experiment with being an adult, to try it on for size and to drop it if she just didn't feel like it. She didn't have a choice, and neither did Grainne. She'd always had to be a grown-up, whether she liked it or not, and Grainne had grown up in the hardest way possible.

So, they were both the adults in the house now, and it was lonely and scary, but, Marie realised, it was also kind of … interesting. Or, at least, it could be.

There was so much to think about, though. She'd have to talk to Dada about money for a start. It was okay now, because Dada had shown her the ring binder where he kept a note of all the bills and the envelope where he kept his chequebook and she'd been surprised at how organised he was, but what about if … She shook her head then, because she didn't want to think about 'if'. Not just yet.

When Grainne came back downstairs, she said, 'He's asleep.'

'Great,' Marie replied, taking her cigarettes and lighter to the back door. 'Do you fancy a ciggie?'

Grainne looked taken aback. 'I don't smoke.'

'Don't look so prissy, Gra.' Marie laughed. 'Come on, you can watch me kill myself slowly out in the back garden.'

'Oh, all right then,' Grainne said, putting on her coat and following Marie outside. Marie sat down on the back step and lit her cigarette, and Grainne sat down beside her. They didn't say anything for a while, until the cat appeared from behind a rose bush, eyes bright, black tail bolt upright as it came up to Grainne and rubbed itself against her legs. She shrank back a bit before tentatively stroking it between the ears.

'Where did you get, Lucy?' Grainne asked.

'She found me and adopted me, didn't you, Lucy-lou?' Hearing her name, Lucy's eyes flicked over Marie and then she miaowed.

'I'll get you dinner in a minute,' Marie said, taking another pull on her cigarette.

'Mrs D would have a heart attack if she saw Lucy.' Grainne giggled.

'She sure would.' Marie laughed. 'She says cats are good for nothing but extermination – maybe that's why Lucy turned up after Mrs D went. She knew she'd be safe.'

'I miss Mrs D,' Grainne said softly. 'I think I'll have to go and visit her.'

'You don't know where she is,' Marie said.

Grainne gave her sister a look. 'Where else would she be but back home in Ballyshannon? She always wanted to go back, do you remember? She was always going on about that garda that she met at the dance.'

'God, yeah. That's where she said that dress came from,' Marie said.

'What dress?'

'Oh, my debs dress. It was Mrs D's and I think she'd worn it to that dance. She got a dreamy look in her eye when she took it out of the wardrobe.'

'Poor Mrs D. She must have been in love once.'

'Well, I suppose it happens to everyone.'

'Yeah.' The two of them sat there for a while, and Marie listened to the wind and the sounds of the waves crashing against the sea wall at Seaview. She felt the weight of everything that they weren't saying to each other, the new space that had opened up between them, in spite of what had happened at Mass.

'I keep thinking about Mum and Dad all the time these days, do you?' Marie said suddenly.

'What do you mean? The way they were together?'

'I just remember them when they'd come in after a night out, and Mum would make some joke about Dada misbehaving – when Dada would no more misbehave than fly to the moon – and he'd just laugh and tell her that she'd led him astray, and then he'd kiss the top of her head, and they just seemed made for each other. They were better together.'

'Hmm, I don't know,' Grainne said quietly. 'They used to row, you know.'

'They did? Why don't I remember?'

'Oh, Mar, you always wanted to believe that they were just perfect, but they weren't. Dada would always complain that Mum would talk to the dogs on the street and how she didn't need the world to be her friend, and Mum would say that Dada was just an uptight Protestant in a Catholic body.' They both snorted with laughter at that. 'But I think you have to be yourself when you're with someone else – I think that's the test.'

'Like you are with Liam?'

Grainne blushed. 'Well, yes, I suppose.' And then she added, 'And like you are with David.'

'I am not!'

'You are,' Grainne insisted, elbowing her playfully.

I will ignore that, Marie thought to herself. 'Do you think Dada loved Mum too much? Is that why he fell apart after she died?'

'I guess so. But you know, he's sick, but he hasn't given up and that's a good sign. Maybe Dada's more interested in living than we think.'

'Maybe,' Marie said doubtfully.

'Mar?'

'Yeah?' Marie rolled her eyes to heaven, the way she used to when Grainne would pester her with questions.

'I think I will tell you what happened with Anthony Daly.'

'Are you sure?' Marie said, and when she saw the look

on Grainne's face, she regretted her words immediately. The truth was, she wasn't sure she really wanted to know, because she was just too scared. It was selfish, but it was the truth.

'I'm sorry, Gra. Tell me. I want to know.' Grainne looked doubtful. 'I mean it,' Marie insisted, nudging closer to her sister so that she could feel her warmth beside her, in her lovely red coat. Grainne leaned into her, pressing her full weight against her, as if looking for Marie to support her, to hold her up.

'Okay then.' Grainne sucked in a deep breath and began to talk.

'Well, he was nice at first, or I thought he was, because at that stage, I'd drunk two bottles of Stag,' Grainne said. 'It's disgusting, by the way, Marie.'

'If you'd drunk a whole bottle of whiskey, it wouldn't have been your fault, Gra, you mustn't think that,' Marie interrupted, but Grainne gave her a stern look. 'I'm telling you, Mar, so will you let me, please?'

'Sorry,' Marie said.

Grainne sighed. 'I thought he was like me, because he was doing pass subjects for the Leaving. That made two of us who weren't very clever. I remember he said, "Leave that stuff to the brainboxes and not to the likes of us," and I felt kind of glad that he wasn't brainy either, that he was just ordinary like me. He asked me to go for a walk on the beach and I'd seen you leave and I thought, I can do that, too. I can go off into the night with a boy … I should have known when he asked me about Imelda and I told him that she was my best friend, and he just laughed and said, "What, that

368

knacker?" I don't think anyone should talk about anyone else like that, do you?'

Marie shook her head.

'"That girl would go with anyone," he said, and then he winked at me. I didn't know what he meant by that, but then he said, "So, what about her friend? Is she a little knacker, too?" We were on the beach, Mar, down the far end near the rocks, and I looked around and there was no one there, and then he put an arm around my shoulder and neck. He had me in a kind of arm-lock and he tried to kiss me.' She wrinkled her nose. 'He sucked at my neck like a vampire and he gave me a horrible lovebite. I was trying to wriggle away from him, but he just laughed and he said that Imelda had told him that I was majorly on for it.'

'I said, "I'm not on for anything," and I tried to jab him in the ribs with my elbow, but he was too strong, and I felt him pushing me onto my hands and knees. I remember that the stones were really cold and wet and they dug into me. I was crying like a big baby, I remember, and I was trying to crawl away.' She made a face. 'As if I could. He was just too strong, Mar.'

'He grabbed hold of one of my ankles and told me to shut the fuck up. That's when I knew, Mar, because he used bad words. And he pulled me so hard that I fell down onto my tummy and there was a rock that stuck into my cheek and then he used another bad word and he was trying to pull at my dress. I had a big bow on the back of it and I could feel him pull at it, as if he was going to rip it off.'

'And then I was on my back, and the worst thing is, Mar, that I just didn't move. I just lay there, like a stupid rag doll, while he pulled at me.' She made a jabbing motion at the top of her coat. 'And he pulled at my dress until it ripped and I could see my bra. And do you know what I thought?'

'No,' Marie whispered.

'I thought that it was a good thing that I'd worn my best one, not my usual horrible grey sports one, can you believe it? What kind of a fool thinks that?' she said bitterly.

A fool who has no choice, Marie thought.

'Anyway, I'd been crying and screaming, but I knew that it was no use, and I tried to lift my knee to give him a dig, but he managed to push my legs apart and … well … ' Grainne looked down at the ground now. 'I thought that if I went somewhere else, just kept staring at the stars in the sky, that I could imagine that I wasn't there. That I was up there, floating around in the sky, not on that horrible cold beach.'

She knew then, Grainne said, and the only thing she could do was to go somewhere else in her head until it was over. 'He didn't even help me up after. He just left me there. He wiped … himself with a bit of tissue and threw it onto the sand beside me, as if I was a bag of old rubbish. And he said … he said that Imelda was right. I wasn't much good after all.'

'Oh, Gra,' Marie managed.

'Once I realised that he wasn't coming back, I just wanted to go home, Mar, but I couldn't find my knickers. I started to cry then, because I didn't want to walk all the way home without my knickers. I hadn't a clue, really. The pain was terrible, Mar, and you know what?'

'What?' Marie said faintly.

'I was worried that if I got up and walked, some bit of me would fall out onto the sand. I thought that Anthony Daly had pushed something loose with, you know … so I had to hold myself up inside.'

'Oh, Gra,' Marie said, pulling her sister towards her so that Grainne's head rested on her shoulder. 'I'm so, so sorry.'

'It's not your fault, Mar,' Grainne said sadly. 'You warned me about Imelda, but I wouldn't listen, and I drank the Stag all by myself.'

'For God's sake, Gra, it's not your fault. You must believe that. You did nothing whatsoever to encourage that boy. Nothing you drank or wore made any difference. You could have drunk forty bottles of Stag and it would still be Anthony Daly's fault. He's the one who did that to you.' And I let it happen, because I wasn't looking after you, she added silently.

Grainne lifted her head from Marie's shoulder and sat up straight, shivering. 'Mrs D told me that. She told me that the only person I should be blaming is Anthony Daly. I know she's right. I know that you're right, but I keep replaying the night over and over in my head and thinking that if I'd only done something … if I'd fought back or shouted, or punched him in the face. Why wasn't I stronger, Mar? Why didn't I fight him off?' She shook her head, tears filling her eyes.

'Stop, Gra,' Marie said, reaching out to stroke her sister's hair, shushing and patting until Grainne was calmer. Then she said steadily, quietly, 'You did not make that happen, Gra. Anthony Daly used his power over you, because he's angry and a bully and vile … and the only person who is to blame is him.'

'But I do blame myself for the baby, Mar. I can't forgive

myself for that.' And, when Marie went to open her mouth to say something, Grainne silenced her with a warning finger. 'Don't, Mar. Please.'

Marie turned to face her sister. 'You need to forgive yourself, Gra.'

'I don't think I ever will, Marie, but that'll have to be OK. I'll never get over it, but maybe that's a good thing. I think it's helped me to understand quite a lot about myself. That I'm a bad person and a good person at the same time.'

'Oh, Gra. How can you not think you're a good person? You are the best person I know,' Marie said, her hand shaking as she lit another cigarette. She thought for a while before saying, 'It's not too late.'

'What?'

'To go to the guards. To tell them what happened. They'll arrest him then, before he does it to someone else. He'll go to prison.'

Grainne looked at Marie as if she couldn't believe how naïve she was. 'I don't believe that, Mar, sorry,' Grainne said. 'I think the guards will say that I led him on. Dada said so.'

'But how—' Marie began to protest, but Grainne said, 'Because it happens all the time. And please don't go on at me about it, because I've decided.'

'OK. Sorry.' Marie took a long pull on the cigarette, blowing a cloud of smoke into the air, wondering how and when Dada had given Grainne that advice, and what right he had to give it.

'Do you have one to spare?' Grainne said eventually.

'Sure.' Marie handed her the packet and Grainne lit one up, puffing a cloud of smoke into the night sky.

'I could get used to this.' Grainne laughed. 'They're nice.'

'No way, Gra. They'll give you cancer and all kinds of health problems …' Marie began, before stopping herself.

'No more big sis, Mar. There's no need,' Grainne said quietly.

'I know, but I *am* your big sis,' Marie said. 'That's the way it is. I may not always have done my job, but it's who I am.' She thought for a moment, before adding, 'Will you give me the chance to be your big sis again? Will you forgive me?'

Grainne hesitated. 'I'll think about it. Is that OK, Mar?'

Marie swallowed down the hurt. 'Sure.' But Grainne was right, she reasoned – she had to earn the right to be her big sister again.

'Good.' And then they sat there for another while, looking at the navy sky, which now had a sprinkling of stars in it. Marie's backside was freezing and the tips of her fingers were numb from the cold, but she didn't want to move, in case Grainne moved too and the moment was over.

They didn't say anything else to each other that night. Instead, they both climbed wearily up the stairs. Marie got into bed, shivering as she slipped under the covers, and lay there for a few moments, replaying the events of the night in her head. Then there was a gentle tapping on the bedroom door and Grainne stood there, two hot water bottles in her hand. 'I made one for you,' she said, and she lifted the covers and climbed in beside Marie, snuggling down beside her, the way they had done when they were children.

'Would you like to see Con again?' Grainne said suddenly.

What on earth had made her think of him? Marie thought, as she rubbed her feet against the hot water bottle, her toes stinging with the heat. Grainne always used boiling water for the hot water bottles, no matter how often Marie told her not to. She tried to think of a reply and, in the silence that followed, she turned and saw the look of realisation dawning on Grainne's face. 'You already are.'

Marie nodded. 'Sort of. I bumped into him at a rugby game and then … well, things went on from there.'

'Oh, Mar,' Grainne said sadly.

'I'm sorry, Grainne, I didn't mean for you to find out—' Marie began, but Grainne interrupted her.

'Don't be silly, I don't mind about Con, Marie, it's not that. It's just …' and she shook her head. 'Nothing.'

'You think he's not good for me.'

'I didn't say that.'

You didn't need to, Marie thought.

And then Grainne gave a little smile. 'Did you have sex?'

'Yeah. At least I got that out of the way.' And then, realising what she'd said, Marie's hand flew to her mouth. 'Sorry, Gra, I didn't mean it like that.'

'Ah, for God's sake, Marie, you can't walk on eggshells all the time.' Pause. 'Was it any good?'

I do not want to talk about this with you, Marie thought. 'It was okay.'

'I think if it's okay the first time, you always think it will be okay. And if it's not okay, you think it'll be terrible forever. I don't want to have sex with Liam, even though I really like him.'

'Gra, don't say that. He sounds lovely and he's perfect for you. And when it's right, you'll be alright, too. I promise.'

Grainne gave her a look that said, you have no idea. She

was probably right, Marie thought. She really did have no idea, no idea at all, and even though Grainne had told her everything, she couldn't put herself in her sister's shoes. She wished she could, to spare her the pain, but she wasn't able to take that burden from Grainne.

'Tell me about him.'

'Liam? Well his mum and dad are from County Mayo, and he's a really good swimmer – that's how we met, when I went to the swimming pool for training. And he's a carpenter and he likes Depeche Mode and American movies and nice food. He doesn't even mind Richard Gere too much.' Grainne giggled. But then she added, 'And he wants to live in County Mayo and have six kids.'

'And how do you feel about that?'

'I don't know, Mar. Scared, I suppose. I don't know if I want to have children.'

Marie nodded. 'I know.'

'Maybe one day,' Grainne said sadly.

Marie patted her hand. 'Gra?'

'Yes, Mar?'

Marie smiled at the reversal. 'I really missed you when you were away, you know. It was awful without you.'

'I know, I'm sorry that I left you to look after Dada like that. If I'd have known …'

'Well, maybe it was better that you didn't know,' Marie said.

'Why? So I could persuade you to leave that mouldy old hospital?' Grainne said. 'When are you going to leave, by the way?'

Marie made a face. 'Sister Dolores asked me the same thing. I can't. I need the money, Gra. I don't know what's going to happen with Dada, and this house is too big and expensive and I've no idea how long we can pay for stupid Mrs O'Farrell …'

Grainne looked thoughtful for a moment. 'I'm going to ask Granny to help out,' she said. 'It's the least she can do.'

'Gra, you can't do that! Dada wouldn't approve at all.'

'Well, either way, we need to sort it out. Maybe David's dad can help us. He's an accountant.'

'Ah, no, Gra, David's done enough.' More than enough, she thought to herself.

'Well, whatever,' Grainne said impatiently. 'Either way, Mar, you are going to do what you want to do from now on and I am going to look after Dada.' And when her sister tried to protest, Grainne stopped her. 'I've seen an ad for a waitressing job in a restaurant in town, so I'm going to apply and see if I can get to do any cooking there, and I am going to mind Dada in my spare time and get rid of that stupid Mrs O'Farrell and you are going to journalism college, which is what you should have done all along.'

'But I don't have the points in my Leaving Cert …' Marie said doubtfully.

'So, get them. Sign up for the subjects you need and do your CAO form and by next year, you could be in college.'

'That's not really fair, Gra. You can't give up your life for me,' Marie said, but Grainne interrupted her. 'Listen, you gave up enough of your life for me, Marie. I thought I needed it, because I wasn't able to do anything for myself, but it wasn't fair on you, or on Mrs D. Look at what she had to do – no wonder she ran off to Ballyshannon. But if London taught me anything, it's that I'm able to look after myself.'

'Perfectly well able!' Marie said, laughing.

'Perfectly well able,' Grainne repeated. 'Mrs D was right. I may not be as clever as you, Marie, but I behaved like a baby. And now I have to take responsibility for myself.'

'If only Mum could see us now. She'd be proud of us, I think,' Marie said softly.

'She would,' Grainne agreed. 'Mar?'

'What?'

'David Crowley likes you.'

For fuck's sake, not you too, Marie thought, shuffling in the bed, tugging at the blanket and wishing that Grainne wouldn't hog it all the time. 'I know.'

'Don't you like him, even a bit?'

'Maybe,' Marie said. 'If he wasn't such a do-gooder and so kind and helpful all of the time, you know? It's just insufferable, it really is. What?' she added, as her sister's face creased with laughter.

'Marie, you are so funny. Why can't you see what's right under your nose?'

'I have no idea what you're talking about,' Marie said, turning in the bed so that her back was to her sister.

'Mar …'

'It's not funny, Gra,' Marie said, pulling the blanket under her chin, fuming. She was ashamed of herself, after everything Grainne had told her, but she just couldn't help it. Why did she have to go on about David Crowley like that?

Chapter 16

She was still fuming three days later, in spite of the lovely Christmas they'd had, thanks to Grainne. They'd invited Granny, who had actually come, much to their surprise, stepping gingerly over the threshold, as if the house was diseased, in her moth-eaten fur coat. Normally, Marie would have been cross, but now, she didn't mind, because she knew that Granny was just afraid – the house had always been Mum's territory and Marie knew that Granny had always been secretly afraid of Mum. She'd described Mum once as a 'closet intellectual', and Dada had got very cross with her. Now, though, she just seemed old and frail, sitting at the dining-room table, her son, in a wheelchair, beside her, her head tiny under a tight perm, her rings loose on her fingers as she sliced into the turkey with its apricot stuffing and pronounced it delicious, and how impressed she was that they'd both grown up so much. Grainne and Marie had exchanged a look and gone back to eating their Christmas dinners.

Even Dada had perked up a bit, laughing at the corny jokes in the Christmas crackers and even attempting one of his own, something about Paddy Englishman, Paddy Irishman and Paddy Scotsman and a plane trip – it wasn't entirely clear, but they all laughed heartily at the muddled punchline, grateful that Dada was at least trying.

He seemed to have improved a bit in the last few days, Marie thought, sitting up in bed so that he could see the sea out of the bedroom window, asking for the *Irish Times* with his breakfast egg. His arms and hands shook, and he found it hard to turn the pages of the paper, so they'd developed a system where he'd bang on the floor with a walking stick they'd found under the stairs and one of them would go upstairs and turn the page for him. And, once or twice, Marie had heard him laugh. Grainne would go upstairs after lunch for their poetry session and after a bit of murmuring, Marie would hear a blast of laughter. She couldn't imagine what was so hilarious about Yeats, but if Dada found something to laugh at, well, it was a relief. She still wasn't sure how keen he was on living, but at least he seemed slightly more cheerful, and it was all down to Grainne.

Still, she thought now, as she sat on the top deck of the bus, heading towards Con's, it was ironic that she was going to meet Con, a full year after she'd failed to turn up at the club that first time. She'd completely forgotten, in fact, so distracted was she by everything that had happened to Grainne. Con just hadn't seemed important any more – he'd just receded in her mind until he was a vague shadow, a smudge on her memory. And now … well, she wasn't sure what he was or how she felt about him, really. He was a mystery, and Marie had thought that was infinitely more exciting than dull old David. It was a modern kind of arrangement, she supposed, neither of them hanging out of the other, but was that what she really wanted? She thought about that phone call she'd made to Con from the hospital, where Con had told her he was too busy, but David-bloody-interfering-Crowley had sat there all night, and brought her coffee and had brought her sister home, too. It wasn't Con who had been there for all of the important things, but David.

She pushed the doubts from her head as she got off the bus and made her way along the little street, lined with cottages, and knocked on his door, her stomach bubbling with a mixture of excitement and something else, something that felt like anxiety. She recognised that feeling as one she always had around Con, and for a second, she wondered if she should just go, just sneak away back down the street, but then the door opened and Con was standing there, in a suit and tie.

'Hi!' she said brightly. 'I'm sorry I don't have long, I'm just off shift, but I thought I'd come along anyway, because I haven't seen you in a while …' She knew that she was gabbling, and when he didn't reply, her voice petered out.

'What is it? Aren't you going to ask me in?'

He shifted a bit from foot to foot. 'Ehm, it's not a great time.'

'What do you mean, "It's not a great time"? You asked me to come. Are you going out with the other devils for some Masonic thing?'

'What?'

'Are you going to a work thing?'

'Oh, eh … no, it's just—' he began, but then a voice called out from behind,

'Cornelius? Who is that?'

'Hang on a sec, Mammy,' Con yelled over his shoulder. 'Look, Marie, I'm really sorry …'

As he spoke, a large woman in a pink suit with freshly set hair appeared behind him. Marie wondered if this was Con's alcoholic mother; the woman who hid bottles in her wellies. But it didn't look very likely, she thought – this woman didn't look like the kind of person who hid bottles in her wellies. Rosary beads, maybe, but not vodka. And who was Cornelius?

The woman gave Marie a stern, granite-faced look, and Marie felt her insides melt, but she leaned around Con and stuck out her hand anyway. 'I'm Marie Stephenson, Mrs O'Sullivan, I'm a friend of Con's … ehrm, Cornelius's.'

The woman gave Marie a long, hard look, then turned to Con. 'Have you forgotten your manners?'

'Oh, yes,' Con said nervously. 'Come in, Marie.'

'Thanks,' Marie said, stepping over the threshold and following Con and his mother up the stairs to his flat.

'I'll make the tea,' Con said hastily, ushering them both into the sitting area, and then leaving them, while he busied himself in the kitchen. Marie could hear the clatter of teacups and the hiss of the kettle as she and Con's mother, the vodka-hiding alcoholic, eyed each other across the coffee table.

'The weather's been very nice,' Marie ventured.

Granite Face replied, 'It has. Unseasonably dry.'

'Yes,' Marie agreed faintly.

'So, are you one of Cornelius's law school friends?'

'Oh, no. I know him from Trinity, at least …' Marie's voice faded. It was clear that Con's mother didn't know the first thing about her and she felt a bit disappointed about that. Maybe Con was embarrassed because she was a nurse, and not a trainee barrister, like him. But then, if Con's mother was as … wayward as Con said she was, why would she be bothered? Yet this severe-looking woman didn't look wayward. She looked fearsome.

'I see that you are a nurse,' she barked.

'That's right, in St John's Hospital,' Marie replied politely, looking down at her uniform, nervously fiddling with the buttons on her cardigan. She'd been expecting that Con would be removing it right about now, and instead, she was sitting in his living room, being interrogated by his mother.

'And your parents?'

'I beg your pardon?'

'Your parents,' the woman repeated, as if it were perfectly obvious what she meant by the two words.

'Ehm, well, my dad's a judge,' Marie said, noticing that the woman perked up then, 'and my mum's … my mum's deceased.'

The woman's eyes widened for a moment. 'May the Lord rest her soul.'

'Thank you.'

The woman gave the smallest nod, then sat there opposite Marie, arms folded. God, Marie thought, how long was this going to go on and when could she leave? She wondered if she could just make some excuse about work, but then she thought she'd better wait for Con to appear with the tea, as he'd gone to the trouble.

'Cornelius is very busy with his studies,' Stone Face said into the silence.

'Yes, he is,' Marie agreed.

'He's at a very important point in his life, and he can't afford to be distracted,' Stone Face added, giving her a significant look. 'Cornelius has worked very hard to get where he is, and now is not the time for him to throw it all away.'

Marie stared at the woman, open-mouthed. Oh. 'I can assure you, I am not distracting him—' Marie began, but then the door opened and she breathed a sigh of relief. Thank God, she thought, getting up from her chair to help with the tea. But it wasn't Con. It was an older version of him, a man with tight, curly hair and the same intense eyes, but a softer face. When he saw Marie, he cleared his throat and held out his hand. 'Cornelius O'Sullivan Senior,' he murmured, giving Stone Face a cautious glance, as if to check that it was all right to shake the hand of this stranger.

Marie was so shocked she barely remembered to shake the man's hand. What was Con's father doing here? Had he come back from wherever it was he'd disappeared to – was that why Stone Face was giving him that stare? But he didn't look like the kind of dad who ran away from his family – who stood at bus stops and then disappeared forever. He looked like an ordinary middle-aged man, tired and a bit grey.

'This young lassie is a friend of Cornelius's,' Stone Face explained.

'Oh, very good,' the man began. 'We're always delighted to

meet Con's friends – he doesn't introduce them very often,' and he gave a gentle smile.

'She's a nurse,' Stone Face added, as if Marie wasn't in the room.

'A grand job altogether,' the man said. 'The world will always need nurses.'

'Yes,' Marie agreed politely. 'Are you both in town for Christmas?'

Stone Face glared at her. 'Cornelius has won a competition and we are attending the prize-giving.'

'Oh, I see,' Marie said. She didn't know what competition the woman was talking about – it could have been an ice-skating competition for all Marie knew. 'Well, that's fantastic,' she began, before the door opened and Con appeared, tea tray in hand. As he put it down on the coffee table, he didn't look at her. 'Mammy, will you have a cup?'

'I've had more than enough tea, thank you,' Mammy said, a look of grim satisfaction on her face. Maybe she'd prefer a neat vodka, Marie thought, daring to look up at the woman. It was then that she noticed the pin on the lapel of her suit. She knew that pin, because Mrs D had one too. It was a Pioneer pin. So much for the alcoholic, she thought. She tried to attract Con's attention, but he seemed determined to look the other way. Right then, she thought, anger pushing her to her feet.

'Mr and Mrs O'Sullivan, will you excuse me, I just need the bathroom. Con, maybe you'd show me where it is?'

Con looked as if he'd prefer to do anything but, until Mammy said, 'Well?' and he nodded bleakly.

Marie waited until the door of the living room had closed before saying, 'Con, what is going on?

Con shifted nervously from foot to foot. 'Marie, I can explain …'

'I'm listening.'

'It's not what you think …'

'Well, what is it then? I thought you had an alcoholic mother – but that woman in there does not look like an alcoholic, and that man in there looks very like you.'

'He is.'

'He is what?'

'He is very like me. He's my dad.'

'I can see that, Con. I'm not stupid. But I thought you had no dad.'

'Well, not exactly—' he began, before Marie interrupted. 'Either you have a father or you don't, Con, it's not very complicated.'

He looked scared for a moment, but then the old Con reasserted himself and that proud, angry look flashed across his face. 'Look, Marie, everyone makes things up about themselves,' he said, giving her a pitying look.

'I don't,' Marie replied.

'Are you joking? Do you mean to say that you've never made up a story about having passed an exam that you didn't, or won a prize or made a friend? You've never told a single white lie in your whole life? What about Grainne? Does she know about us? Is that not a lie?' His face was a mask of scorn and Marie felt humiliated by that. By his disdain.

But then, she hadn't lied about who she actually was.

'Inventing a missing father is hardly a white lie, Con,' Marie said sharply.

'Don't you think that the truth is a bit overrated?' he said slyly. 'So what if I took a few liberties with my life story? It certainly made me a hell of a lot more interesting – admit it. Everyone loves a sob story, let's face it.'

Marie was baffled. 'I wouldn't have minded the truth.'

He sneered, 'Yeah, right, and do you think you would have looked at me if I hadn't done the whole tortured soul routine? Poor me, seeing my daddy leave on the bus out the window, writing to my mother in the loony bin on a Sunday. Boo-hoo,' he said bitterly.

'You're being nasty, Con,' Marie said.

'And you're a snob, Marie Stephenson, looking down her nose at the lesser orders,' he sneered. 'With your big house by the sea and your books and your classical music. You have it all and people like me don't. So we have to make things up to get by. The world is a hell of a lot nicer to people who have a bit of a story, who can get sympathy, because they just can't help what's happened to them. They welcomed me with open arms to Trinners, let me tell you, all those fuckin' toffee-nosed West Brits,' he sneered. 'You wouldn't understand, because you've never had to lift a finger in your whole life, everything is just handed to you on a plate.'

Marie couldn't think of anything to say. She stood there, arms by her side, a film of her time with Con replaying in her head. All that time, when he'd said he loved her and had never met anyone like her; all that stuff about the writers he liked and how he loved Shostakovich too … it was all just lies. That was why he had nothing in this flat – because he wasn't interested in any of it – he'd just made it all up. He'd probably got it all from those two big encyclopaedias in the living room. And she'd fallen for it.

'That night at the debs, was that all just for show?'

He hesitated then, some other emotion flickering in his eyes. Something like guilt. He reached out to take her hand, but she snatched it away from him. 'That was all real, Marie. I love you, I really do. You were the first girl I ever met that I thought I could really be myself with – and, before you say it, yes, I get the irony. I thought that if I just loved you, it would be enough, that it wouldn't matter about the … stories.'

'How do I know that you're not lying about that, the way you were lying about everything else?'

'It's the truth, Marie,' he said simply.

'I see.'

'So, are you going to sit in judgement of me, like Daddy?' he said.

Marie shook her head sadly. The truth was, she wasn't going to judge him, because she hadn't exactly been honourable herself, lying to her sister and leaving her all alone at the mercy of Anthony Daly, and then sneaking off to meet Con behind her back.

'I kind of almost believed it was true, even if it wasn't, do you know what I mean?' he said abruptly.

'You're a liar,' she said quietly.

'Everyone's a liar, Marie, in one way or another. You of all people should know that.'

She knew that he was right. She *was* a liar. Lying was part of life, she supposed. The truth wasn't always possible, was it? Lies were told to spare people's feelings, or to hide unpleasant truths, or to hide the truth from oneself. Lying made the world go round.

'Just one more thing.'

He tutted. 'What?'

'Where did you come from?'

'What do you mean?'

'That summer. You just appeared one day on the beach and no one knew who you were.'

He smiled. 'Oh. I was a friend of Maccer's, didn't you know that? He asked me.'

No, he didn't, Marie thought, and you told me you were a friend of John's, but what difference did it make now?

There was nothing left to say except goodbye, but before she could speak, the door to the living room opened and Stone Face appeared, glaring at Marie, as if wondering what she was still doing there. 'Cornelius, it's half-past six. Your brother needs to be collected from Heuston and that will take an hour.'

'Yes, Mammy.'

'Your brother.' At least one bit of his story was true, Marie thought bleakly. 'I was just leaving, Mrs O'Sullivan,' Marie said, pulling herself together and sticking a hand out. 'It was a pleasure to meet you and Mr O'Sullivan.'

Stone Face reluctantly accepted Marie's hand, which Marie made sure to give a good, firm shake. Then she turned to Con. 'Have fun!' she said brightly.

Con mouthed, 'I'll call you,' but Marie didn't respond, just walked out of the door and closed it behind her.

She'd manage to hold the tears in, she told herself, until she got on the bus again, shakily asking the driver for a single to Abbotstown, then collapsing on the seat, ready to bawl her eyes out. But as she sat there, looking out the window at the sea as the bus chugged along, at the grey-green lump of

Howth, and the red hats of the mad swimmers bobbing in the icy water, she realised that she actually didn't want to cry. She didn't want to cry, because something in her told her that it wasn't grief but hurt pride that was the problem. How sorry was she really about Con? So he'd lied to her, made up silly stories about a life he didn't have, to make himself seem more exciting. What did she really want from him? Did she love him? She didn't think so – that churning feeling that she'd had every time she'd met him was just anxiety, she thought, not love. No, she thought, as the sea slid by outside the window and a little dog ran up and down the strand, barking. She didn't love Con O'Sullivan.

And the reason she knew this was because she loved someone else.

*

She spent the next week wondering how she might talk to David. She concocted elaborate scenarios in her head, about standing on the end of the pier like Meryl Streep in *The French Lieutenant's Woman*, sea sweeping over the stones as he clutched her in his arms, before understanding that it was this kind of thinking that had got her into trouble in the first place. Con O'Sullivan wasn't Mr Darcy and she wasn't Lizzie Bennett. David Crowley wasn't lovely Mr Bingley, or Superman, or whatever character she'd invented for him. Instead, they were all just people, trying to make a life for themselves, with varying degrees of success.

In the end, David came to see her. She hadn't wanted it to be that way. She'd wanted to make a grand romantic gesture, but instead she'd found herself at work, with a terrible cold, which had left her with a big red nose and greasy hair, clutching a catheter bag of Mrs O'Brien's wee, because she'd just exchanged it for a nice clean one and was off to her least favourite place, the sluice room, to empty it.

'Marie?'

She didn't answer at first. She just heard her name, and his voice, and it took her a few moments to realise that it was David. She turned, bag aloft.

He was standing there in that awful Aran jumper, which he'd thought to pair with brown cords, to complete the trad-band look. All he was missing was the cap, Marie thought. Do I really want to marry one of The Dubliners? she wondered to herself, before asking herself where the 'marry' had come from.

'What are you doing here?'

'I left an assessment for Sister Dolores to fill out. I'm just collecting it.'

'Oh, I think she's in the kitchen. I'll get her for you,' Marie said. 'I need to get rid of this,' and she nodded at the bag.

'Thanks,' he muttered, looking down at his feet.

She walked towards him, bag in her hand. He was blocking the doorway and she had to move around him. 'Excuse me,' she said. As she passed him, she had a sudden feeling, a sense of his presence, of what he might mean to her in the days and years to come. She had a feeling about what her future might be like with him and she knew that it was right. She knew that it would be good, in her heart, the same way as she'd known that it wouldn't be good with Con. She didn't know how she knew. She just knew.

'Oh, sorry,' he said, stepping aside to let her pass.

She stopped. 'David?'

'Yes?' He turned to look at her, and his expression, which had been his usual kind and thoughtful one, changed. He looked hopeful all of a sudden, and he took a step towards her, until he was just a few inches away from her. His eyes were bright and he had two patches of red on his cheeks.

'I think I owe you an apology.'

'Oh?'

'Yes.'

'What for?'

'For not seeing the obvious.'

There was such a long silence that Marie felt the world stop around her, as she stood there, bag of wee in hand. She didn't dare look at his face, because she was afraid to see the expression. Maybe she'd got it all wrong. She'd misunderstood his kindness for something else. She …

'The obvious.' He gave a small smile.

'Yes, the obvious.'

And then she felt his arms around her, and she let herself lean slightly against his chest, while holding the bag of wee as far away from them as possible.

'I'll forgive you.'

'Thanks.' She dared to look up at him then, and his face was open and full of wonder, and she knew that she didn't have to worry any more. She wondered if she might risk a kiss, but then Sister Dolores could turn up at any minute. Instead, she smiled at him. Properly, warmly, a smile that made her eyes crinkle at the corners. A smile that said everything that she couldn't, with a bag of wee in her hand and an audience of twelve old ladies.

'Oh, it's so romantic,' came Mrs Spence's watery voice

from behind them. 'It's just like *Mistress of Mellyn*, except that Doctor Crowley isn't a murdering psychopath, of course—'

'It is not!' Mrs O'Brien could be heard to interrupt. 'It's more like that train station in that fillum, you know the one with the fellow with the big nose in it, whatshisname?'

'*Brief Encounter*, you silly woman,' came Mrs Derby's voice. 'Honestly, you're as senile as you are deaf,' she muttered. 'Anyway, neither of them are married, so it's not like *Brief Encounter* at all, it's more like *Doctor Zhivago*.'

'I should hope not, otherwise the poor girl is doomed,' Mrs O'Brien barked back.

'Oh, what does it matter,' Mrs Spence said. 'It's *Casablanca* and *Roman Holiday* and all of those lovely films, because it's true love. And that's the important thing.'

There was a moment's silence while they all took this in, which was ruined by the doors opening with a crash. Sister Dolores appeared, an incontinence pad in her hand. She looked at them both suspiciously. 'What's going on here?'

David jumped away from Marie, as if she were contagious. 'Oh, Sister, I was just showing Nurse Stephenson here the correct way to disconnect a catheter bag.'

'Were you indeed?' Sister Dolores gave him a look that said that he wasn't worthy of her disdain. 'Nurse Stephenson, that bag won't empty itself,' she barked. 'Doctor Crowley, you are interrupting the work of St Anthony's. Come out of the way please,' and she bustled over to her office. That's torn it, Marie thought. But as Sister Dolores reached the door, she turned slightly and gave a small smile before saying, 'Well, get a move on then.'

'Yes, Sister.'

'I'll see you downstairs after,' David said.

'But I don't finish for another two hours.'

'I'll find something to do.' And he smiled at her. She smiled back and went to empty the bag.

Epilogue

AUGUST 1984

Marie swallowed nervously as she waited for the whistle. She knew that she just had to focus, to keep swimming until her hands touched the bar at the far end of the pool. Maureen had told them that she'd personally drown anyone who went before the whistle, which they'd all laughed at heartily. They'd got used to laughing at Maureen's menacing threats in the nine months of Nervous Swimmers, because she was actually a brilliant teacher. Somehow or other, she'd managed to bully them into actually swimming, kicking confidently, breathing without inhaling a vast amount of water and getting from one end of the pool to the other without disappearing under the surface. Marie thought that swimming was the one thing that would always elude her and now, here she was, at the end-of-term gala, about to race Sheila and her fellow classmates, and all to win a box of Black Magic chocolates and a medal. She didn't care about either – it was getting to the end that mattered.

Marie desperately wanted to get to the end, because her sister was up in the viewing gallery watching her. She didn't want to let Grainne down by doing her usual – not turning her head enough in the water, so that she took in a great big mouthful of it and had to stop to cough and splutter. She looked up and her sister gave a little wave. Grainne waved back and then put her fingers in her mouth and gave a loud whistle. God, she was mortifying, but Marie couldn't help but smile.

Marie hoped that they'd get a move on, because Grainne had to meet Liam after. They were off to Cong for the weekend, because Liam was really into *The Quiet Man* movie and he had to see the place where John Wayne threw Maureen O'Hara over his shoulder and carried her home. If she didn't know Liam as well as she did now, Marie would have wondered what this said about him, but instead, she knew that he was a lovely guy, a soft-spoken Londoner with a love of simple things, like football, which he called 'footy', and walking, and his carpentry, which he did so beautifully. He was perfect for Grainne; he fit her like a glove. But he could be tough, too. He'd taken Grainne down to the garda station to make her statement about Anthony Daly. He'd listened to all of her arguments about how nothing ever happened in cases like this and he'd nodded and said it would be much easier for him to go and bash Anthony

Daly's face in, but that wouldn't help Grainne or other girls like her. So, Grainne had gone with him to the station and had come back two hours later, face white. 'I've done it,' she said and Marie gave her a tight hug, as she'd sat at the kitchen table with Dada, drinking tea.

Dada had had the *Irish Times* in front of him, and they'd both glanced in his direction, to see what he'd heard. At first, he'd said nothing, just continued to scan the headlines, before lifting his head briefly and saying, 'Well done. I'm proud of you.'

'Thanks, Dada.' Grainne blushed.

'I should have done something,' Dada had said. 'I should have done more,' and he folded the paper carefully on the table and had looked at them both. It was the first time he'd ever mentioned what had happened to Grainne and, at first, neither of them knew what to say in response. Eventually, Grainne had said, 'I had to do it myself, Dada.'

'You're right,' Dada had said then. 'Of course you are.' And then he'd got up and shuffled off in the direction of his study, turning at the door and saying, 'I love you both, you know that.'

'Thanks, Dada.' Marie had exchanged a glance with Grainne. It was kind of embarrassing, Dada talking like this, and she'd felt an intense desire to shut him up, to return things to their normal state. ' I'll bring you coffee in an hour.'

'Thank you,' he said, smiling and closing the kitchen door, behind him. Marie hadn't been sure exactly what he was thanking her for, but he'd clearly decided to get better, and that spring had spent less and less time in bed looking out at the sea and more and more time in the garden, or in the drawing room, which hadn't been used in years. He'd decided to catalogue his old law books and papers there, and Marie thought that that would keep him going for at least another year. He seemed to have found a new hope and purpose in life, after all that time, thanks to Grainne, and thanks to Mrs D, whose 'surprise' visit back in June, when she appeared on the doorstep one morning with a huge suitcase, telling them that she was 'just passing', had turned into six weeks of dusting and muttering and cooking terrible dinners.

For a while, the girls had welcomed the old balance in the household, the return to the way things had used to be – it was like putting on an old, comfy pair of slippers. But then, Grainne had begun to moan about how terrible the food was, and Marie had had to tell Mrs D, for the umpteenth time, that she'd already done the wash, gotten through the pile of ironing and paid the electricity bill.

And so, two weeks ago, she'd stood at the breakfast table and announced briskly that she had 'business to attend to' in Ballyshannon. 'And besides,' she'd muttered, 'I can see I'm not needed here any more.'

'Ah, Mrs D, you are,' Grainne had said, jumping up from the table, daring to give her a hug. 'Please stay.'

'I will not,' Mrs D had barked. 'The two of you can manage very well without me and I can see when I'm not wanted.' The words had been harsh, but Mrs D had been smiling when she'd said them, and when she'd added, 'I am so proud of you two, do ye know that? My girls.'

Marie and Grainne had exchanged a glance over the Weetabix, then gone back to what they'd been doing, Marie the *Irish Times* crossword and Grainne, reading a battered copy of *Cosmopolitan*, which Mrs D had kept trying to tidy away, as it was clearly further evidence that the place had gone to hell in a handcart since her departure.

And so, with promises to visit again, she'd gone back to Ballyshannon without too much of a fuss. Marie and Grainne would once have worried about it, about how lonely she might be, but even though she hadn't said a word, the girls had a feeling that there was a man somewhere up in the wilds of Donegal. Maybe the garda she'd met at the dance all those years before – that would be so romantic! Grainne had proclaimed. Marie was pleased that Mrs D had had a happy ending, after everything she'd done for them.

*

Marie's teeth began to chatter and she hoped to God Maureen would get a move on. The pool was freezing. David had wanted to come as well, but Marie had insisted that he stay home. She loved him, but she wasn't ready for him to see her half-drowning in a pink bathing hat and bright yellow earplugs. She may have seen him in his white Y-fronts and he may have seen her in her mismatched bra and pants, but that was as far as she was prepared to go. She needed to maintain some sense of mystery, she thought, although she supposed there would come a time when there wouldn't be any need for that. She had known David since they were children, but she also knew that, in many ways, she would never fully know him. It wasn't possible, she thought, to know another human being completely. And he would never fully know her, but that was OK, because they trusted each other. She always had trusted him, she realised, even in her earliest memory of him, when they were children, and she was standing outside the supermarket, waiting for Mrs D, and he'd appeared on his bike and had offered her one of the squashed jelly babies he had in the back pocket of his shorts. She'd always trusted him, even though it had taken her years to realise that she loved him too.

She supposed she wasn't very original, Marie thought, as she bobbed in the water, but then, originality of that kind was overrated. Maybe she'd keep the originality for her journalism. Her stomach flipped as she thought of the year ahead, her first in the College of Communications, and she hoped she'd be up to the job. Sister Dolores said that she'd be brilliant. On her last day at St John's, Sister had had a little party for them all and had presented her with the memoir of a war correspondent, which Marie had promised to treasure, and had said that she was a credit to herself, even though she wasn't cut out for nursing, which was an understatement. Mrs Spence had given her a pair of saucy knickers. They were purple nylon with a black lace heart embroidered on them. God knows where she'd got them from, or her peculiar advice, which she'd offered at the top of her voice, not to 'make him wait'. 'Men are like that,' she said. 'You need to give them some kind of an outlet …' She'd mouthed the word 'outlet' and she'd looked at Marie significantly. Marie had tried not to laugh as she'd accepted the gift, and she knew that she'd miss Mrs Spence, and in a strange way, she'd miss St John's, the safety of it, the predictability. The new world seemed dangerous and exciting all at once, but she thought she was ready for it now. When Maureen blew the whistle, Marie pushed herself off the wall and began to swim.

Acknowledgements

To my family: to Colm, as always, for listening and for vast reserves of patience, and to Eoin, Niamh and Cian for always being there and for the bickering which reaches me in my shed in the garden.

Thanks to my agent, Marianne Gunn O'Connor for her steadfast support and to Patrick Lynch. Thanks also to all at Hachette Books Ireland, particularly my editor, Ciara Doorley, for her steady hand and calm guidance, and to Joanna Smyth, Breda Purdue, Jim Binchy, Ciara Considine, Siobhan Tierney, Ruth Shern and Bernard Hoban.

Emma Dunne made some very helpful suggestions just when they were needed and I also thank Liz Clarke for nursing lore.

To Eleanor Kennedy, Nerea Lerchundi and Veronique O'Leary, my thanks for coffees and friendship and to Enda Wyley, for support and laughter during the writing of this novel.

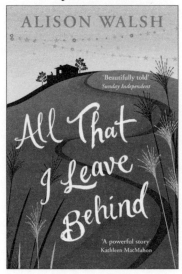

ALL THAT I LEAVE BEHIND

It hadn't been Rosie's idea – a 'quaint' wedding at her childhood home in the Irish countryside. Nevertheless she finds herself back in Monasterard after a decade away, with her American fiancé on her arm and a smile fixed to her face.

As expected, the welcome from her siblings isn't exactly warm. Mary-Pat, the one who practically raised Rosie, is avoiding her. June is preoccupied with maintaining the illusion of her perfect family. And Pius, who still counts the years since their mother left, is hiding from the world. Each of them is struggling with the weight of things unsaid.

In the end, it's their father who, on the day of Rosie's wedding, exposes what has remained hidden for so long. And as the O'Connor siblings piece together the secrets at the heart of their family, they begin to forgive the woman who abandoned them all those years ago.

Also available as an ebook